TAINTED
BLOOD

SAM C. LEONHARD

Dreamspinner Press

Published by
Dreamspinner Press
4760 Preston Road
Suite 244-149
Frisco, TX 75034
http://www.dreamspinnerpress.com/

This is a work of fiction. Names, characters, places and incidents either are the product of the author's imagination or are used fictitiously, and any resemblance to actual persons, living or dead, business establishments, events or locales is entirely coincidental.

Tainted Blood

Cover Art by Anastasia Koldareva   www.creativelly.narod.ru
Cover Design by Mara McKennen

ISBN: 978-1-61581-410-7

Printed in the United States of America
First Edition
May, 2010

eBook edition available
eBook ISBN: 978-1-61581-411-4

ACKNOWLEDGMENTS

I would like to thank the following people for helping, cheerleading, and offering a reassuring pat to the shoulder whenever necessary.

- Many thanks to Mary M. Ardagna, who had the dubious pleasure of reading and correcting the draft version. She must have had many sleepless nights getting through the mess I sent.

- An abundance of thanks and hugs to Nicole, who supported me with much-needed feedback, virtual lemon tea, a shipload of commas and grammar corrections as well as a shoulder to cry on. There would have been a lot of plot holes in the story without you, my dear!

- Special thanks to my very own petulant poetess, Theresa, not only for editing the manuscript and getting it ready for submission, but for creating and maintaining her fabulous website too. Without the site, I would never have gathered enough motivation to write at all, and without her support and friendship, I would have given up pretty soon.

- Lots of hugs to Anastasia Koldareva—better known as Elly in fandom—for creating the cover art and patiently dealing with my out-of-proportion sketches and grumbly e-mails.

- Slightly blushing thanks to Gabi's brother, Oliver, who agreed to read a few chapters and who told me what is actually possible and what is not.

- My sincere thanks to Elizabeth North, Lynn West, and my editors at Dreamspinner Press. Without their thorough, careful, helping hand, this book would not have been completed.

CHAPTER ONE

"DAMN this shit," Gabriel Jordan murmured, trying to get some life back into his frozen feet by stamping them repeatedly on the pavement. "I need to get another job. And better shoes. And while I'm at it, a decent place to sleep. Food would be good too. Oh, and a coat. A warm one."

Grumbling, Gabriel shoved his hands under his armpits and hunched his shoulders. He was tall, too thin for his height, and far too hungry to give up just yet. His leather jacket allowed the wind to blow right down his neck despite the length of his hair, and he swore under his breath because he hadn't even managed to get himself a better sweater. It was December, and the air smelled of snow. Not only did he have to remain here for at least another hour, but he was dressed as though it were a warm summer evening. The only piece of winter clothing he had was a cap, thin and moth-eaten—a most necessary disguise, however, as his hair was flaming red and far too recognizable.

If he weren't so hungry, he'd quit for the day. Images of a huge, steaming cup of tea plagued him, which was a clear sign that his body required some warmth.

His boss, though, heartless bastard that he was, had told him not to come back to the office without at least half a dozen pictures. "Pictures I can see his face in," the boss had clarified. "Wright's face and the face of the bitch he's screwing. His wife's paying good money for proof he's betraying her, so get out there, wait in front of her flat, and don't forget to put a new battery into your fucking camera this time."

Naturally, Gabriel had done as ordered. He needed the money—needed it badly enough to take on even the lousiest jobs. He hadn't eaten in two days. His fingers were white from the cold, and he had a strong feeling he would lose a fingertip or two if he didn't manage to get warm soon. But finding warmth was as unlikely as getting some food. Or a picture of that stupid idiot he was supposed to catch *in flagrante*. Gabriel had been standing at this windy corner since before noon. He had probably seen three people all day, one of them a toddler riding home in its mother's arms. No surprise there—it was Christmas Eve, and Gabriel very much doubted that his target was daft enough to be with his lover on a night like this. The man—a fat bloke with thinning hair and ridiculous eyebrows—was probably at home right now, telling his children stories about Santa Claus.

For a moment, Gabriel wondered if there were stories told about Santa in the hidden worlds too. Surely they had more pressing problems—like keeping the portals closed and guarded so no humans would invade their worlds and attempt to kill them. Ever since the portals had been discovered, humans had tried to ignore that there were races and worlds other than their own. They closed their eyes to the fact that mermaids, vampires, fae, and werewolves actually existed and sometimes even lived amongst them. And if humans couldn't ignore it any longer, they would attack. Somehow, Gabriel doubted that people on the other side of the portals cared about an old man in a red coat.

"And I'm here, turning into an icicle." Shivering, he made sure his camera was ready for the umpteenth time. Stolen from a shabby little shop a few months ago, it was the only thing he owned apart from the clothes on his back and the knapsack at his feet. It also guaranteed a somewhat regular income. His boss, a quite lazy and wealthy private investigator, used him for the more complicated spying jobs—the ones where it was required to actually leave the office—so Gabriel was out on the street day and night, taking pictures of errant men and women cheating on their spouses, employees stealing from their employers, and children buying drugs from teenagers barely older than themselves. It was a most depressing way to earn money, but at least Gabriel was able to buy himself an occasional warm meal.

Right now, he couldn't see being able to afford to anything to eat in the foreseeable future. He'd probably end up going to the mission so he wouldn't starve.

A glum prospect indeed. Even more depressing, his stomach ached at the thought of mission food. It wasn't very picky at this point.

All of a sudden large, wet flakes started drifting down from the graying sky. Soon it would be too dark to see anything at all, never mind take pictures of cheating husbands, and he wasn't keen on getting the lens of his camera wet, either. Getting the face shot his boss wanted was looking rather bleak.

"I should call it a day," Gabriel murmured, wishing he'd stolen a scarf and gloves along with the camera. And some boots—the soles of his sneakers had more holes than Swiss cheese. His socks were wet and his toes frozen into numbness; he'd catch a cold if he didn't get out of the wind soon. Anyway, if he hung around here much longer, someone would finally call the police. He was extremely good at hiding, but a long-haired, poorly dressed young man loitering in the corner of a closed shop would become suspicious eventually, especially on Christmas Eve.

Just when Gabriel was about to give up, he saw movement out of the corner of his eye. Not in the street, but somewhere higher up, somewhere outside one of the apartments. *Probably a pigeon*, he thought, shrugging his shoulders. *Or someone shaking out a blanket. Maybe even a runaway child, clutching a teddy bear in its arms.* The latter part he'd seen too often; as a child, he'd run away from adults who didn't care whether he stayed home or not. Running away from foster parents had been one of his main pastimes, at least until he'd finally managed to run away for good at the age of fifteen.

There. There it was again, that faint, nearly invisible movement. The light was dimmer now as more snow blurred his vision, but something had caught his attention. It was not a bird or a blanket, and there was no ladder in sight; a child would have chosen an easier exit than the plain wall. No, this was something else, and although it was highly unlikely that his suspect would enter his lover's apartment through the window, it was at least possible that he had caught a burglar at work. In that case, he'd try to get a picture. Either his boss would pay him or he could blackmail the burglar. In either case, a warm dinner was looking more and more like a reality.

Gabriel picked up his worn, old knapsack and edged closer to the building where he'd spied the motion, sheltering himself in a doorway where the wind and snow couldn't reach him. The house was old, not in the best condition, and it looked as though it had been neglected somewhat. The windows were mostly dark, and he could hear someone arguing just slightly louder than the faint music in the background. The smell of roasting potatoes in the cold winter air made his stomach grumble. As he looked upward, he noticed that on the top floor, the last window to the right was ajar. It hadn't been earlier, he knew that with certainty, for he had been staring at that particular window for most of the day. In fact, it hadn't just been closed. The curtains had been drawn as well.

Every so often, he could see the beam of a flashlight glance off the walls and darkened windows where the intruder had entered; someone was searching the rooms, and this someone was almost certainly neither the young lady who lived there nor her fat lover.

"Whoever it is, I'll get his picture," Gabriel told the streetlamp as he ducked out of its light.

He didn't have to wait long. Whoever had climbed up there only needed moments to find what he was looking for. One long leg slipped over the windowsill, then a second. For a moment, the burglar sat on the sill, looking out into the city's darkness. Gabriel couldn't see him clearly—he was too far up, the light from the streetlamp didn't reach that far, and the snowflakes insisted on landing right in his eyes whenever he looked upward and strained to focus on the man's face.

However, he had seen enough. The man sat on the windowsill as if it were a lawn chair. In Gabriel's opinion, he radiated arrogance, if only because he wore no coat, no cap, and no mask. Not even gloves. "Not afraid of leaving fingerprints," Gabriel murmured, fishing for his camera. The man was bound to climb down at any moment now—there had to be a rope somewhere—and he didn't want to miss a single shot.

Just when Gabriel was taking the camera out of its case, the man jumped.

Gabriel nearly had a heart attack, and he barely managed to keep hold of his camera. He saw the man fall, tumbling in mid-air; he saw him smash to the pavement, bones crunching as they broke. He saw blood splatter on the ground, tainting the innocent, white snow. He heard the sickening sound of skull hitting stone. He wondered how it was possible that a human being could look so ugly with his insides turned out. And then he realized that none of what he'd just seen had actually happened.

The man had jumped, yes, but hadn't fallen. Instead, he was floating slowly toward the ground like a giant moth. His arms were spread wide, and Gabriel realized that he had been wrong—the man was at least wearing a long scarf, and it was whipping through the air, its color gleaming surprisingly green against the dirty gray of the wall.

"What the hell?" Gabriel murmured, lifting his camera quickly, hitting the record button. A little video of this impossible event would help him believe it, if nothing else.

As slowly as the snowflakes falling around him, the man sailed softly to the ground. Gracefully, his feet touched the pavement not more than ten feet away from where Gabriel stood. He wore dark trousers, a gray shirt, black shoes, and that horrendously green scarf. With a bored gesture, he brushed a single snowflake off the sleeve of his shirt.

Impossible, thought Gabriel. *People don't jump off buildings and float down to earth like feathers. They drop like stones!*

The stranger looked completely normal: slightly taller than average and of a slender build; no more than thirty; short, straight, mouse-brown hair; no mustache, no glasses—there was nothing interesting about him at all, really. All right, maybe his eyes were worth a second look. At first, Gabriel had believed them to be brown, but after a second look, he saw that, even in the dim evening light, they were quite clearly very blue. *Ice-blue*, Gabriel thought, and he shivered.

Then he saw the long, thin scar running down the man's left cheek and frowned. He looked to be upper-class despite the fact that he wasn't wearing a coat. On further inspection, he also looked older than thirty—maybe around thirty-five or even forty—for his black hair was streaked with gray.

But... wasn't his hair brown only a moment ago? Gabriel blinked hard. How could he have missed that, and why had he thought the man's hair was short and straight when in reality it was curly and long enough to touch the collar?

Anyway. The light must have tricked his eyes. The man would have fit perfectly in a posh office, a lawyer's chair, or on a yacht, hairstyle notwithstanding. A scar, though, was definitely unexpected. It gave the strong impression that this man knew how to fight, and hell, was he really staring at the stranger, camera still filming?

Perhaps he had started a little at the realization and drew the man's attention, for the man turned and addressed him. "Good evening," the stranger said. His voice had a lovely mellow timbre, which reminded Gabriel of hot chocolate with just the right amount of whipped cream.

"Hi," he said, dropping the hand that held the camera. Filming the man suddenly seemed unimportant. Seeing him was what counted, talking to him, listening to that wonderful voice.

"I see you've got me on film," the stranger said, stepping a little closer. "How inconvenient. And I suppose you saw me jump from the windowsill as well?"

"Yep." Short answers were the only thing he could manage, Gabriel discovered.

"That is not good," the man said calmly. "First, I nearly get caught by a nosy neighbor, and now I'm talking to someone who shouldn't even be able to see me. I suggest you forget what just happened. If you would hand me your camera, please."

As if in a dream, Gabriel handed the camera—his life's bread—over to a complete stranger, as unconcerned about it as though it were a useless piece of junk. He was a puppet on strings, and was there an edge of coldness in the otherwise warm, friendly voice? Those eyes… they were so blue… so incredibly, icy blue. Unnaturally blue—he'd never seen the like before. Piercing. Demanding. They made it impossible to disobey the owner's orders.

"Look here," Gabriel began, but the thought fled his mind quicker than he could speak it when the man took the camera out of his hand and brushed his warm, slender fingers over Gabriel's cold and clammy skin.

He'll take the camera, Gabriel's mind screamed. *Without it, I'll starve!*

As if his inner scream had been heard, the man said, "I will not steal what is yours. I will merely erase any proof of what happened here. In addition, you will not remember anything after your nap."

What nap? Gabriel had just enough time to think before the man drew a complicated pattern in the air with his fingers. He vaguely remembered seeing something like this before, but he felt suddenly sleepy, and catching that memory was no longer important. Warmth infused his frozen bones, and he had the strange sensation of being in a bed, covered by a fluffy duvet... so different from standing on a windy corner on an icy night.

"No," he whispered, struggling against being sent to sleep against his will, but his eyes dropped closed, and from a great distance, he heard the stranger say, "Here's your camera back," before walking away. The man's steps sounded hollow, surreal, on the snow-covered pavement.

I'm dreaming this. The thought was crystal clear in Gabriel's mind. *I'm dreaming I'm asleep. How strange.*

Slowly, his knees gave way, and he slid to the ground. The wall behind him caught his fall, ripping holes in his already pretty sorry-looking jacket. The pavement was cold; the snow on the ground soaked through the bottom of his jeans. His head sunk toward his breast, and the last thing he was aware of was his camera slipping out of his numb fingers. *It's going to break... the snow... it'll damage it.* His camera would be useless.

No! Wake... wake up!

Confused and groggy, Gabriel managed to open one heavy-lidded eye. He was sitting half on his folded-under calves and half on the wet, cold ground. His camera was just hitting the ground with a nasty little breaking sound. He could feel his mouth was ajar as if he'd spent the day getting pissed.

"'S goin' on 'ere?" he mumbled, reaching out blindly. His fingers found a spout, and he managed to get to his feet, swaying like a sapling in a storm. "I just had... did... I saw.... Hey, you! Wait!"

Was that his voice? Since when did he sound like an old man, all hoarse and weak? Shaking his head, Gabriel leaned heavily against the wall, his foot kicking the camera, sending it slithering into a puddle. It was as if he were watching a tragic accident on the news, and he felt physically sick as he observed his one worthy possession expire along with all hope of a warm meal and bed.

"Shit," he murmured weakly, rubbing one hand across his dirty, tired face. "Not my fucking day. Where the hell is that guy?"

"You are surprisingly awake, my friend," a familiar, warm voice said, and Gabriel's worn-out body jerked in shock. He hadn't heard the man come back, hadn't seen any movement, although he'd been staring after the dark figure before his eyes had closed. He could have sworn the man had left, vanished into thin air, at least ten minutes ago, but here he was, standing only an arm's length away under the steady, golden glow of a streetlight that had not too long ago been flickering weakly.

Warm fingers searched for the pulse in his neck. Gabriel flinched back, or rather, tried; he was unable to move. The warm, happy feeling returned, his eyes became heavy as lead once again, and if he hadn't managed to catch the man around the wrist, he would have ended up on the ground again, most likely asleep for longer than a few seconds.

"Stop it," Gabriel hissed around his heavy tongue. "Whatever you are doing, stop it right now!"

"Hmmm," the stranger said, moving back a step. "You are not entirely human, are you? What else is in your blood? Elf? Vampire? Fae? No, not fae blood. Fae don't produce redheads, not even after several generations. And the riverghosts tend to keep halflings under water. That would leave…?" Questioningly, the man raised an eyebrow, expecting and encouraging an answer.

"Shapeshifter."

One word, just one small word, but Gabriel felt the small hairs on the back of his neck rise. He had never, ever told anyone about his heritage.

"Ah. Wolf, if I am correct. Or lynx, maybe? Your eyes give you away. Wonderful eyes, don't take me wrong, but hunter's eyes nevertheless."

"Wolf," Gabriel confirmed. Until now, no one apart from his mother and grandmother had known what he really was, and he preferred to keep it that way. His various foster parents had taken him in solely because he had looked so very cute, absolutely human, and they had believed he would be easy to raise. It was impossible to detect nonhuman genes in a child. Most people would trust their eyes rather than listen to the small voice whispering that their new family member might be part vampire—after all, very few vampires lived in the human world, and anyway, if a child *looked* human, naturally it must *be* human.

His great-grandfather had been a pure-blood shapeshifter, but Gabriel had always looked absolutely human. He had been beautiful as a little boy, with his dark red locks and sweet smile. Therefore, he never had to stay for longer than a month or two in the orphanage before someone decided that he was just the child they wanted. The people who took him in had all been nice, for a while at least. Until they realized that he was different—too silent, too shy, and far too much in love with his freedom. Very soon, they began to look at him with eyes that spoke clearly of their second thoughts about taking him in. In no time at all, they would begin treating him like a stranger—that is, if they remembered that he was even there at all. Usually, he ran away after a few weeks at the most, and usually, he ended up back in the orphanage after three months tops, the foster parents all too willingly bringing him back themselves most of the time.

With a jolt of guilt, Gabriel realized that he had allowed his thoughts to drift—something that rarely happened, and never around company. However, this man, this stranger, seemed to have unusual powers, as though he was willing Gabriel's thoughts to wander so he could pluck them right out of his head. Right now, the man was staring at him with his head slightly tilted, as if Gabriel were a particularly fascinating insect.

"Shapeshifter, or werewolf, as it's more commonly called, although that's nonsense, given the fact that only about one-third of shapeshifters turn into a wolf. Do you have to transform?" Curiously, the man pulled at a strand of red hair that had escaped from Gabriel's cap and was waving in the winter wind, obviously trying to get a better look at his face.

"Keep your fucking hands off me," Gabriel growled, and he stumbled backward only to find the wall blocking his way. The doorway was too small for both of them; all he wanted was to get away from this man, this someone who acted so strangely, who knew too much, who….

"Hang on. Didn't you just float to the ground?" Gabriel craned his neck to look up at the window he had been staring at for the better part of the day. How could he have forgotten that rather significant piece of information? "You broke into that apartment—I saw you! Even took pictures. And I filmed you when you jumped off the windowsill like a bloody falcon or something. I thought you were falling, but you weren't. You landed right in front of me." With a sudden push, Gabriel shoved the man and made him stagger backward. "You did something to me. You made me sleepy. Hell, you are one lousy bastard!" he finished lamely, unable to think of anything else to say.

Obviously unimpressed by Gabriel's anger, the man reached out his hand in what looked like a friendly gesture. "Tennant. Dr. Tennant," he replied coolly. "You should not be able to remember any of this, you know. You should be fast asleep on the ground, as I used a Forgetting rune *and* a Sleeping rune. Actually, you should not have been able to see me in the first place, neither when I entered the apartment nor when I left. Hmmm. Well, it is quite obvious you are neither oblivious to what has happened nor are you asleep. Both facts pique my interest."

Tennant paused, hand still extended. "Are you able to perform such a basic social behavior as shaking my hand, or would you respond better if I forced you?" Impatiently, he thrust his hand forward a bit, urging Gabriel to take and shake it. "And your name would be?"

Gabriel stared at the hand and then the man who had introduced himself as Tennant, tentatively took the offered hand, and finally said, "Gabriel. Gabe, that is. I mean, my name is Gabriel Jordan. Shit, man, how do you do that—make me feel like a five-year-old?"

"One of my various talents," Tennant answered lightly, then bent down and picked up the shattered camera. "Come along. You look like a scarecrow. How old are you? Eighteen? Twenty, maybe?" Wrapping the green scarf around his neck, he turned and walked away, obviously expecting Gabriel to follow.

Gabriel glanced back at the house he was supposed to be watching but figured there wasn't any sense waiting to get a picture any longer, as it was now completely dark and snowing heavily. Pulling his cap lower to protect his face from the snow, he thought, *Could be worse, getting picked up by an arrogant asshole*, and followed Tennant. "I'm twenty-seven," he clarified belatedly and in a slightly threatening voice. Shouldering his knapsack, he continued, "Just so you know, I work out, and you wouldn't stand a chance against me in a fight, so don't get any funny ideas. Where are we going, anyway?"

"Home," Tennant answered, sounding surprised. "Where else would we go on Christmas Eve?"

"HOME" turned out to be a tall, narrow house in the middle of nowhere, surrounded by warehouses and empty shops. Tennant had driven them there in an old Mercedes, a big, black car that had coughed nastily when the motor started. They had driven through the night for at least an hour, and Gabriel had feared more than once that the wheels would lose contact with the slippery road and they'd end up in a ditch. The entire drive, Tennant hadn't uttered a single word, and it was the perfect opportunity for Gabriel to mourn not only the loss of his camera but his job as well. Without a camera, no pictures. Without pictures, no money. And without money, he had only two options left: go to the mission or starve to death. Neither option was particularly appealing.

He turned the broken camera over in his hands repeatedly, assessing the damage, hoping somewhere in the back of his mind that if he looked at it long enough it might not be as bad as he knew it was. The lens was broken. He had no idea how that could have happened—after all, he had dropped the damn thing before. Facts couldn't be changed, he supposed. Either he stole a new camera or he was in really deep shit. Stealing, on the other hand, was dangerous, despite the fact most people tended to overlook him. If he was caught, he could end up in prison, which would mean steady meals and a roof over his head, but there was always the off chance someone would realize that he was partly nonhuman and consider his death preferable to wasting taxpayers' money.

No use thinking about it now. Tennant had pulled the car into a garage, and the door was slowly closing behind them.

Uneasiness claimed Gabriel. He had never just followed anyone home like that. He wasn't stupid; he knew there were perverted bastards out there, only too eager to slaughter anyone who was daft enough not to choose the company they kept carefully. "The world has moved on," his grandmother used to say. "People hate us for what we are. Your own mother hates you for what you are, Gabe. So you better hide. Hide and stay hidden. Don't trust anyone. Don't believe anyone. Hide well, my love. Hide, or you are dead."

Usually, Gabriel stuck to his grandmother's advice. He lived on the streets and only went to the mission when it got too cold or when he went without food for too long. No one, apart from his grandmother and his mother, knew that he was a bit different. He hadn't told anyone, although sometimes the temptation had been strong. There were only a handful of people he could call friends, and even they didn't know. His various bed partners didn't know, either. He slept under bridges and in empty houses, he managed to earn enough money to keep going, and he hoped for nothing more than to stay hidden so no one would find out who he really was.

So why had he followed this stranger, this Dr. Tennant, into his car and now into his house? He didn't know a thing about the man, just that he could float through the air, knew about runes, and had tried to lull him to sleep. "Do you plan to kill me, Doc?" Gabriel asked, wishing in the same moment he had kept his mouth shut. How stupid was that, asking a possible murderer about his intentions?

Tennant snorted. "I could have killed you in the doorway simply by using a stronger rune and letting you sleep until your blood had frozen," he reasoned. "A nice, clean death, and no one would have thought twice about yet another dead homeless man, too thin and too dirty to care about. Come inside, Mr. Jordan. I have no idea why I was compelled to invite you here, but you may as well have dinner with me and explain why you were able to shake off my Sleeping rune."

Tennant switched on the light, and Gabriel had to squeeze his eyes shut for a moment. Always sensitive to light, they were especially so after a few hours in near darkness. When he opened them, his mouth sagged open. For some reason, he had expected an average living room stuffed with heavy furniture, thick carpets, and ugly paintings. Tennant's house had looked unimpressive from the outside, and walking upstairs from the garage hadn't given an indication of anything else but the home of an average, uppity man with not enough money to buy himself a decent car.

"Holy shit," Gabriel breathed. "It's amazing! It's... wow!"

The room, like the house itself, had an extremely high ceiling, accentuated by long, narrow windows and immaculate white walls. The floor was covered in light-colored wood; no carpet was in sight. Instead of fluffy, plush armchairs, a low, cream-colored leather sofa dominated the room. Several plants, some small, some large, some of them high enough to be called trees, had been placed around the room. Candles stood on the windowsills, table, and some of the shelves. Tennant lit them one by one, bathing the room in warm, golden light. The walls were lined with bookshelves made of the same light-colored wood as the floor. Gabriel ached to rush toward them, touch the volumes they held, peruse the titles, pull out one after another and read them on the spot until sunrise. It had been so long since he had held a book, much less read one.

Tennant watched him in silence. "Glad you like it," he said dryly, "but don't think for a single moment you can as much as lay a finger on anything before you have a shower. You stink, your clothes are filthy, and your hair is greasy, at least the bits I can see from under your cap. The bathroom is waiting; I will prepare dinner in the meantime."

Gabriel narrowed his eyes. Tennant was practically ordering him around, something Gabriel hated very much. His various foster parents had all discovered sooner or later that ordering him around was a very bad idea. It also seemed Tennant, as harmless as he was portraying himself to be, was definitely up to something odd.

"Fuck you," Gabriel hissed. "I don't know what's going on here, but I'm not stupid. I'm leaving, and you better not dare try and stop me."

Tennant, already walking in the direction of what must be the kitchen, just shrugged his shoulders. "As you wish. Leave through the front door, though. I have no desire to go out into the cold again and open the garage door for you. Good evening and good-bye, Mr. Jordan."

Slamming the door shut behind him was only a small satisfaction. "Freak," Gabriel growled under his breath, putting on the gloves and scarf he had just stolen from Tennant. "Damn bastard. I bet he thought I was a hooker. Probably wanted to rape me, then cut me into pieces or something." Taking long strides, he walked down the deserted street. No lights shone in the windows of the buildings around him. Only behind him, in Tennant's house, could he see the warm shimmer of the candles.

"Shouldn't have allowed him to bring me here. Should've stayed in town. I could be at the mission now, eating soup." Stuffing his hands deep into the pockets of his trousers for warmth, Gabriel angrily kicked a brick out of his way. The wind had picked up, and it stuck its icy fingers under his jacket and down his back. He shivered.

No use denying it: tonight would be one of the coldest nights of the year so far, and his chances of surviving out here were small. Tennant had been right about one thing—he was homeless. The streets had been his home since he was fifteen. More often than not, a bridge served for a roof, and he'd sleep wrapped in an old blanket he kept in his knapsack, hidden from others. It was his way of life. He was used to it, and he liked it, but in winter it was hard. Really hard. At least every third day, he was forced to go to the mission. Winter had been early this year and harsher than usual.

Suddenly he realized Tennant hadn't tried to stop him from leaving at all. Although he must have seen him stealing the gloves and the scarf, he hadn't intervened. On the other hand, what had he expected? That the man would slaughter him right there on the spot, in his entrance hall? Get blood all over those clean, white walls?

"Ridiculous," he murmured to himself. "Much more likely that he just didn't want to be alone on Christmas Eve. I was stupid not to take an invitation to dinner when I got one. I bet the food would have been better than what the mission's serving."

"Definitely."

Gabriel nearly jumped out of his skin for the second time that day. No one was able to sneak up on him—his ears were too good and his nose too sharp. Nevertheless, this guy, this Tennant, had managed to do so twice already.

"Tracking rune," Tennant said, stomping his feet. "In the scarf. Look, I have no intention of killing you. I am merely curious how you were able to see me and fight my runes. And you are correct. I dislike eating on my own on Christmas Eve. Now would you come back and have dinner with me? Please?"

Not too many options here, Gabriel thought, staring at the man and assessing the situation. *If I stay out here, I might be lucky enough to freeze before I starve. If I go with him and he poisons me, at least I die with a full stomach.*

"Right," Gabriel said. "Dinner. Nothing else."

"A *shower* and dinner," Tennant countered. "How can you stand the smell of your dirty clothes?"

As they walked side-by-side back toward the house, Gabriel involuntarily pulled his jacket tighter around his rail-thin body. "They're the only clothes I own. If I wanted to wash them, I would be naked for at least an hour, and so far I haven't found a nudist laundry."

Oddly enough, he felt embarrassed. Normally, he had no problems with self-consciousness. However, in the company of Tennant, with his elegant, undoubtedly expensive clothes, faint foreign accent, and profound knowledge of runes, Gabriel felt like an uneducated idiot.

"If you lend me a robe, I'll have a shower," he finally spat out.

Tennant just laughed.

CHAPTER TWO

"I SHOULD shower more often." Gabriel sighed and rolled his shoulders contently under the hot, hard stream of water. His knapsack and clothes—or rather, the rags he called clothes—lay on the floor beside the sink. The door to the bathroom wasn't just locked. He had shoved a chair under the handle as well. Just in case.

The bathroom was fascinating. Where the living room owned a simple elegance, the bathroom resembled a cave more than anything else. There were no tiles, merely a stone floor and large, uneven rocks for walls. Big plants with even bigger leaves stood in the corners, ivy covered the ceiling, and tiny, white flowers seemed to grow directly out of the windowsill. The towels were big and warm and fluffy, and the soap smelled of honey and spices. Gabriel had a strong feeling that he could spend hours in here if he wasn't careful. The last time he had bathed was last summer, in a little brook he had found in one of the parks, but he hadn't enjoyed it, fearing someone might see him and he'd be sent to prison for exhibitionism. Ever since, he had managed to clean his face every now and then, but never more. Water and soap and shampoo in abundance were a luxury for him, and he had no intention of ending this too soon.

Dirty water circled the drain. Gabriel couldn't believe it, as this was the third time he'd scrubbed his skin raw with the sponge. By now, he had also washed his hair, and he had even cut his nails and brushed his teeth under the constant splatter of the water.

Finally, he stepped out of the shower, rubbed his hair dry, and wrapped a towel around his waist. A silver comb lay above the sink on a ledge of rock. He couldn't even remember when he had last used one. He picked up the comb, turned it between his fingers, and frowned.

He'd taken a shower. There were clean towels, and he'd practically used up the soap, shampoo, and toothpaste. Warmth surrounded him, and to top it all off, there was the prospect of food.

"I shouldn't be here," Gabriel said. All of it felt slightly wrong, especially the privacy the bathroom offered and the knowledge that no one would storm in at any moment, demanding that it was now his turn to get clean. One of the reasons he rarely stayed at the mission was that there were too many people and not enough space. Here, in Tennant's house, there was only one other person and more than enough space to feel comfortable.

"Better enjoy it as long as it lasts," he decided, and he began to drag the comb through his hair. For some reason, he couldn't be bothered to cut it; by now, it reached halfway down his back, and Tennant had been right—it had been greasy.

Hesitantly, Gabriel looked at his reflection in the mirror above the sink and brushed wet strands of hair away from his ears. Sometimes, he was sure they were pointy, just a little bit, but not enough to be considered suspicious. Sometimes, he told himself that his eyesight was failing him and his ears looked as normal as any other human being's ears. Maybe they did look normal, although he could never quite convince himself of it.

But it wasn't only the way he looked. No one must ever know that he heard much better than the average man, that his nose could identify a person from a mile a way, or that his fingers, a bit longer than usual, were much stronger than they looked. Even when he occasionally got into a fight, he made sure that his grip stayed loose and he didn't put his strength behind the punches—he could break a bone without effort, and revealing that ability would certainly land him in prison. Humans were incredibly paranoid about the other races, the ones hiding behind the forbidden portals, and they did everything to keep themselves safe and separated.

Critically, Gabriel scanned the freckles on his face, the dark, strangely delicate eyebrows, the high cheekbones and full lips. And his eyes, of course, those strange eyes Tennant had called wonderful. Pale, gray irises, circled by a darker, maybe even black, ring. A wolf's eyes. His grandmother had called them "hunters' eyes." *Eerie*, Gabriel sometimes thought in the darkest hour of the night, when he lay awake, worrying and wondering where to get his next meal from and whether someone would eventually figure out that he was different just by looking at him. Colorless eyes, cold and cruel. Animal eyes.

He was tall and slim, and his bones stood out too prominently due to lack of food. His skin was strangely hairless, considering that one of his ancestors had been covered in fur. He was too pale, which was no surprise for this time of the year, but it was a fact that bothered him nevertheless. It made him look weak, and in combination with the lack of girth, he might even appear sickly to some. He couldn't afford to look weak; he wasn't particularly muscular, so the healthier and thus more dangerous he appeared, the less likely he was to be drawn into a fight.

Strangely enough, his bed partners, male and female alike, seemed to like the way he looked. Gabriel, though, happily avoided mirrors whenever possible. He could see the wolf lingering inside him. He feared that one day it would break loose, that he would lose control, and that he might hurt someone he liked. It was a nightmare, one he preferred to keep at bay by not dwelling on thoughts about his heritage, but one that practically jumped at him now that he was looking into his reflection's eyes.

Tennant, for whatever reason, had seen what he was, just like that. "So what?" Gabriel said to the image in the mirror, ignoring the fear that crept up his spine. "Even if he tells the cops, they won't find me. No one ever finds me."

Determined, he turned away from the mirror and its revelations. When he bent to pick up his clothes, he realized that they were still filthy.

And they stank. Tennant had been right, the smell was horrible. Now that he was clean, the stench of the clothes, unwashed for several months, of sweat and dirt and even blood, was overwhelming. Disgusted, Gabriel paled and pressed his hands across his nose and mouth. "Shit," he exclaimed, shocked. "I can't wear those. They need a spin in the washing machine. Or two. Actually, I need new clothes." A hole in his jeans had grown bigger than his spread hand, and the shirt couldn't even be called a shirt anymore. "Why the hell hasn't anyone said anything?"

Simple. Because no one cared for him that much.

Standing naked on the dark stone floor, Gabriel didn't even want to touch the rags he had worn for at least the past three years. "Well, I can't eat wearing a towel round my waist," he murmured, looking for a dressing gown.

As he scanned the room for something he could put on, there was a sudden bang-bang-bang on the bathroom door. "Mr. Jordan," Tennant called. "I've no intention of insulting you, but your clothes are anything but presentable. I took the liberty of getting you some clothes out of my wardrobe. We are about the same height. They should do until you find the time to buy yourself new garments. I'll place them outside the bathroom door. Dinner will be ready in ten minutes."

Stunned, Gabriel stared at the closed and locked door. "Wouldn't be surprised if he could read thoughts," he murmured to himself. Waiting until he heard Tennant walk away, Gabriel carefully took the chair away, unlocked the door, and finally opened it.

A clean pair of jeans, a T-shirt, shirt, sweater, underpants, and thick, woolen socks awaited him, neatly folded and placed on the floor. Quickly, he took them inside and dressed even more quickly. He disliked being naked. Not wearing clothes made him feel vulnerable.

Surprisingly enough, Tennant had been right: the clothes fit nearly perfectly. The trousers were too loose, but the sweater was deliciously warm. Now he only needed to find a washing machine and a way to clean his leather jacket.

Maybe I should think about that later. His stomach growled, demanding food. His nose, annoyingly sensitive at times, picked up the scent of roast potatoes, turkey, and gravy. "Can't believe it. A proper Christmas dinner." Licking his lips, Gabriel took his knapsack and went to find the dining room.

More candles. Expensive-looking plates. Crystal glasses. Bowls filled with food and arranged around a large platter, which held a turkey. And there was Tennant, already waiting for him.

Gabriel wasn't at a loss for words often, but now, he didn't know what to say. Or do.

"Sit," Tennant said, picking up the knife to begin carving the turkey. "Help yourself. I tend to cook too much when I can be bothered to seek out the kitchen. I assure you I have put poison in neither the food nor the wine."

"Good to know," Gabriel said, and he sat down. What else was there to do?

"And in case you still have doubts, I swear an oath that I have no interest in harming you. I will neither murder you, nor rape you, nor cut you to pieces and bury you in my cellar, nor anything else you might have feared."

"How do you know what I fear?" Gabriel couldn't help asking the question. He knew it wasn't easy to read his face, as every single person he had met in his life had complained how cold and absent he appeared even in the most personal of moments. That Tennant put his finger on his doubts so easily came as quite a shock.

Tennant smiled. "I would fear the same, I guess," he simply said.

A big piece of meat landed on Gabriel's plate. Slowly but surely, believing this was just some sort of strange dream, Gabriel reached for the potatoes. He took too many, overloading his plate, but he didn't care. The last warm meal he had eaten had been several days ago. Even if he wanted to, he simply couldn't be polite and take only one or two spoonfuls. Still, he managed to wait until Tennant had taken the first bite before he dug in, devouring his food, gobbling it down, always fearing—

"No one will take your plate away, Mr. Jordan," Tennant said, sounding friendly as well as amused. "Eat slowly, or you will throw up sooner or later."

"Too good," Gabriel replied, mouth full. A lifetime ago, one of his foster mothers had beat some manners into him—in theory, he knew how to behave, but right now, the painful emptiness of his stomach made him ignore that he was shoving the food down his throat as if he were an animal. "You've no idea how hungry I am." Deliberately, he put down his fork and knife and poured himself some wine. Just half a glass—the last thing he needed was to get drunk.

Thoughtfully, Tennant rolled the stem of his own glass between his slender fingers. There were scratches on the hand that held that glass—Gabriel assumed Tennant had hurt himself when climbing through Lorelei Kinney's window. *What was he doing in that girl's apartment, anyway?* he wondered for the first time.

"I can see that you are hungry. It is very obvious to me that you don't eat on a regular basis. Given the circumstances, you are surprisingly healthy."

"Am I?" Gabriel asked. "How would you know?"

"Runes, Mr. Jordan. Always runes. Handled with knowledge and care, they can tell the one who is able to control them nearly everything about nearly everyone. You, for example, are healthy apart from a small cold. No liver problems like so many who live on the streets—I assume you are not an alcoholic. You don't smoke, as your lungs are as clean as freshly washed linen. No blood diseases, either. Not even fleas or lice. As I said, surprisingly healthy." Casually, he speared a sprout and ate it, clearly satisfied with his observation.

"Anything else you know about me?" Gabriel asked, unable to prevent a sharp undertone from creeping into his voice. Tennant's words were unnerving, no matter if they were true or not.

Tennant must have detected it. Visibly surprised, he lowered his glass. "I know you are homeless. I know you have spent hours watching Miss Kinney's apartment. You told me that you have wolf blood running through your veins. From your very human appearance, I deduce that one of your grandparents was a werewolf. What I don't know is if you need to transform, as you haven't answered my earlier question concerning this matter. I don't know anything about your hopes and dreams, your life, your job, if you have one, or your plans for the future. Why do I make you so nervous, Mr. Jordan?"

"Don't call me that," Gabriel said sharply. "Mr. Jordan was my father. My name is Gabriel." Defiantly, he pushed his plate away. Suddenly, he wasn't that hungry anymore.

Tennant nodded. "Gabriel, then. Now, do you have to transform or not? I ask out of curiosity, nothing else."

Gabriel thought about it for a moment. Very few people had shown any sort of curiosity about him so far. It was a strange change in the way his relationships normally went. Usually, he spent time with people who found curiosity only in a bottle. Finally, he decided if Tennant wanted to know about him, he would tell him whatever he wanted to know. The one and only secret he had was his nonhuman heritage, and Tennant knew about that already.

"I couldn't transform if I wanted to, which I don't. Walking under the full moon is no problem, although I tend to chase rabbits when I'm out on such a night." Slowly, he pulled his plate closer and loaded it with a second helping—his appetite was back with a vengeance. "My grandmother was half werewolf. My father killed himself after the big economic crash shortly before I was born. My mum is a crack junkie. I rarely drink, I don't smoke, and I wouldn't touch drugs if you paid me to. I do live on the streets. When I'm too cold or too hungry, I seek shelter in Father Barley's mission on High Street, but I can't stand being there for long. Too many people." A bite of meat, a swig of wine. "I live on the streets," he repeated quietly, as if surprised by the fact. "All of my possessions are in my knapsack. I own thirty-four cents, a dirty blanket, and a camera. Oh, no, hang on. I don't own a camera anymore. I dropped it because you put a Sleeping rune on me."

At least Tennant had the decency to look slightly embarrassed. Gabriel, though, was suddenly in a talkative mood.

"Living on the streets isn't bad," he said matter-of-factly, as though this kind of conversation was completely normal. As though this evening wasn't the least bit strange. "In summer, it's even good. In winter, it sucks. I was watching that lady's apartment in order to get a picture of her and her lover. My boss is a private investigator and the biggest slave-driver in history. With the money I would have gotten for that picture, I could have bought myself a burger and fries. This is better. You are a damn good cook, Doc. Now I'd like to know something. What were you doing in my target's apartment?"

Silently, the candles flickered golden patterns onto the tablecloth. The bookshelves were covered in shadows, and Gabriel couldn't help but wonder if he would be able to find some information about runes in them. *Would be a worthwhile thing, knowing about runes.*

So far, he hadn't met anyone who knew more than theories about "the ancient art," as his grandmother had called it. "Wonder why I told you about my boss and the pics and my life," Gabriel said, contemplating the possibility that the half glass of wine had already been too much for him. After all, he wasn't used to alcohol.

Tennant got up and carried their plates into the kitchen. It allowed Gabriel to gather his thoughts, and he was grateful for it. This evening had been strange, to say the least. He was warm, he was clean, and he had eaten more than he had thought possible. Dinner had been delicious. The room he was in was marvelous, and his companion was strange. Definitely very, very strange.

"Hey," he called out when Tennant didn't turn up again. "You know more about me than even my closest friends. Not that I have any, that is. No one I'd talk to. No one who knows I'm partly wolf. Only fair if you tell me who you are, Doc!"

For many long minutes, silence was all that answered him. Faintly, Gabriel could hear the clinking of dishes and assumed that Tennant was tidying up. *Nothing here fits*, Gabriel thought, leaning his head back against the chair. *He doesn't look like a burglar, and still he raids an apartment. His car is cheap, but his house tells me he's rich. His clothes are expensive, but the scar on his face tells me he was once in serious trouble. Really, I would like to know more about him.*

All of a sudden, Gabriel was tired. Maybe it was the warmth and the food—*bad combination if trying to stay awake*, he mused, struggling to keep his eyes open. He might have fallen asleep if Tennant hadn't chosen that moment to come back into the dining room.

"Dessert," he said. "Don't doze off before you have tried my apple crumble."

Gabriel couldn't help but laugh. "I'm stuffed, man," he objected, staring disbelievingly at the cake in front of him. "Although… some of that cream might fit inside."

Just when he had his mouth full, Tennant said, "I was looking for love letters," and a bite got stuck in Gabriel's throat. Coughing, he tried to force some air into his lungs. Tennant was next to him in a heartbeat, slapping his back. "What?" Gabriel wheezed after several considerable attempts to clear his throat.

"She's quite beautiful, don't you think?" Tennant asked. "Miss Kinney, that is, the young lady whose apartment I visited earlier on and whom you were trying to catch with your camera. Perfect figure, perfect skin, long, blond hair, a voice that can drive you crazy. You know who I am talking about."

"She's a bitch," Gabriel stated matter-of-factly. "She takes what she wants, and when she's through with you, she throws you away. Anyone who becomes her victim is bankrupt in less than a month. Don't tell me you had an affair with her. I wouldn't believe it—you definitely still have all the money one could wish for."

Tennant sat again, casting him a thin smile. "I didn't say I had an affair with her. I might have wanted one, though. I tried to convince her that I love her. Writing poetry is not one of my talents, be assured, but I tried it nevertheless. When I found out she had chosen someone else, I decided to get my letters back so she wouldn't be able to use them against me. My business is small, but prosperous. She could have blackmailed me with those letters. I couldn't risk it."

"Did you find them?" Gabriel asked, still coughing slightly. "The letters—did you get them back?"

Tennant shook his head. "No. I was just about to search her bedroom when I heard a sound outside the door and decided to leave. I will have to go back eventually, but when you proved to be harder to keep off my track than I had assumed, I thought it a better idea to bring you here and find out how you managed it. So tell me—how did it feel?"

Gabriel swallowed the bite he had just taken. "How did what feel?" he asked. "Seeing you jump off the windowsill?"

"Fighting with my rune," Tennant clarified. "You should have fallen asleep right on the spot. Yet you didn't. Did you create the counter-rune?"

Gabriel grinned, somewhat happy that his host was so obviously confused about what he had done. "What's a counter-rune? I have no knowledge of the things. I became tired, and I remember sliding toward the ground. It was wet and cold, and somehow, I opened my eyes again. Can't have taken more than a few seconds. It wasn't like fighting against something, just like… like waking up after a long night."

"Hmm." Tennant looked at him thoughtfully. "I'd like to try it again. Using the Sleeping rune on you, that is. You are tired; I can see it. It should work better this time. But if I am right, you will be able to shake it off even easier than the first time."

Gabriel couldn't suppress a shudder. From out of nowhere, his earlier fears flared up again. "Forget it," he snapped. "I won't let you use a rune on me. Too dangerous. Actually, I think it's time I go back to my place."

He was halfway out of the dining room when he remembered the dirty clothes on the bathroom floor. "Shit," he murmured, turning. "Look, Doc, I can't pay you right now, but do you think I could keep the clothes you gave me for another day or so? I will have mine washed and return yours as soon as possible." He was pleading, and he knew it. Still, the thought of so much as touching those dirty clothes disgusted him.

"Forget it," Tennant replied lightly. "Keep the clothes. I can spare them, and yours won't keep you warm over the winter anyway. Take one of the coats as well. I swear there is no Tracking rune on them. Unfortunately, I cannot prove it. Oh, and don't forget your camera. The lens was split, but I managed to replace it. Should work fine now. Just don't try to catch me on film again."

Gabriel stood rooted to the spot, staring at the older man in disbelief. Tennant calmly looked back at him. The house was quiet, and from the road, not a single sound could be heard. The candles flickered, the room smelled of dinner and dessert and wine, and damn it, how could Tennant look so harmless?

"If this is an attempt to lure me under your spell, I'll kill you," Gabriel said weakly, knowing well how poor his threat sounded. "I haven't got a clue why you're being nice to me, but I really don't want to go outside right now. I'm tired, and frankly, I don't have anyplace to go. The mission won't let anyone in at this time of night, and I don't know how to get there anyway."

"Stay, then," Tennant said. "Could you at least think about letting me use the rune on you? Please?"

Gabriel shook his head. "I don't want to offend you, but no."

"I see," Tennant said. "How about something harmless, then? A Tickling rune?"

Step by step, Gabriel reentered the room. He didn't know why he did so, only that he wanted to stay. He sort of liked the man, he had to admit. He was gut-wrenchingly friendly, he hadn't done him any harm so far, and he had even repaired the camera. There it was, on the mantelpiece above the fireplace. It looked as good as new, and Gabriel walked over to it, picked it up, switched it on, and took a picture of the dessert. Flash, click—it worked. What a surprise. It seemed as if there was much more to Tennant than first met the eye.

But he had suspected so from the moment he had seen the scar, hadn't he? The thin scar across the man's left cheek, indicating someone had sliced him with a razor blade. Tennant's face was open and unguarded, the ice-blue eyes bore an amused sparkle, and to be honest, Gabriel could see him as neither a murderer nor a rapist.

"Who are you?" Gabriel asked quietly. "Where's your wife, your family, your kids? Why do you invite a stranger into your house on Christmas Eve, a stinking, homeless, half-starved stranger, when you are so obviously rich, and educated, and all?"

"Unmarried, no children, no family," Tennant responded casually. "I am just a man who failed to get some silly love letters back from a woman unwilling to notice him. I am moderately wealthy. My firm produces umbrellas, as ridiculous as that might sound. Nothing special. My hobby, though, is runes, and yes, I know it is forbidden knowledge. I don't care. You managed to shake off one of the stronger ones like a dog shakes off water, no offense intended. Despite the fact that you are a good-looking young man underneath all the dirt, you spent all day outside, nearly freezing to death, in order to get a single picture for a boss who clearly doesn't pay you enough for such a job. I am a curious man, Gabriel, and you are interesting. Let me try the Tickling rune. Please." Pulling the chair back, Tennant invited Gabriel to sit down again. "I promise to make some espresso afterwards," he said with a grin.

Gabriel just let himself slump down. "I'm going to regret this," he stated to no one in particular. "I know I'm going to regret this big time!"

WRIGGLING in his chair as if he were sitting on charcoal, Gabriel couldn't help a scream emerging from his lips. He had tried to keep it inside, to no avail.

"Stop it!" he shouted, and immediately, the sensation of hundreds of tickling fingers all over his body vanished. The feeling had been quite close to pain, he had to admit, wiping tears out of his eyes and a bead of sweat off his brow. However, a huge grin spread on his lips, and with a laugh, he reached for a glass of water on the nearby table.

"Hellfire," he wheezed. "That was bad. Didn't believe a tickle could make you scream. Thanks for stopping it." With a sigh, he looked at the book that lay open on the table. He could see the runes written on the thin parchment, and he was strangely fascinated by the thought of reading the book himself.

Tennant closed the volume with a thump. "I didn't. You fought the rune. Eventually, that is. After one minute, thirty-seven seconds, you managed to shake it off. Which should be impossible without using the counter-rune. Amazing. Truly amazing." There was definitely an approving look in his cool eyes, accompanied by suspicion. "I cannot believe that there is only a bit of werewolf mixed into your genes, Gabriel," he said, tilting his head thoughtfully. "Shapeshifters are very responsive to runes; I checked that a couple of years ago. You should be rolling across the floor by now, howling with laughter. We need to do some more tests."

Gabriel threw a leg over an armrest. It was past midnight, another inch of snow had fallen outside, and he longed for a bed or at least a part of the floor where he could find some sleep. Nevertheless, he felt extremely well. *This is fun*, he thought contently.

Aloud, he said, "Look, can we call it a day, Doc? I'm exhausted. Maybe we can continue this tomorrow?" There, he had said it. Tomorrow. Indicating that he'd be willing to stay the night, or have breakfast with him in the morning.

For at least an hour, Gabriel had been contemplating whether he should say something along those lines, but then Tennant had made it clear that he didn't want his guest to leave, so he figured it was possibly all right.

Without comment, Tennant switched on the light. "There's a guest room at the end of the hall. It can be locked, in case you were wondering, and no, I don't have an extra key. Put a chair under the handle if you like." There it was again, that slightly mocking voice. Gabriel guessed that Tennant was inwardly laughing his head off at his fears, but at the moment he didn't care.

Yawning hugely, he just said, "Thanks. And hey—I really appreciate your hospitality."

"I'll still need a blood sample tomorrow," Tennant replied dryly.

SLEEP didn't come easily, and when Gabriel finally managed to find his way into dreamland, he tossed and turned restlessly. Faceless monsters chased him; unnamed fears made him shiver. It had been three years since he had slept in a bed, and although he eventually moved to the hard but much more familiar floor, he didn't sleep any better.

Around three in the morning, he gave up. Splashing cold water on his face, he looked out of the window into the winter night. It had ceased snowing; a few stars sparkled. The world looked peaceful, and for some reason, the sight made Gabriel sad. "Guess I need something to read to make me sleepy again," he said to the dark room, for some reason wishing he weren't alone.

Silently, he opened the bedroom door. The hall was dark, but from the living room came a faint light. Pretty sure that Tennant was fast asleep, Gabriel sneaked onward to the big bookshelves that had caught his eye so many hours ago. Maybe he could find a proper horror story or at least some crime novels. He rarely read due to lack of opportunity, but he enjoyed books whenever he found one in the bin.

Maybe he could take a look at one of the rune books too.

The living room was as empty as it should have been at that time of night. Gabriel went to the shelf near the fireplace and let his index finger slowly wander over the backs of the books. All were old, all bound in leather, and not a single one looked as if it offered harmless entertainment. The one light in the room—a small alabaster lamp standing on a sideboard—just allowed him to read the titles. Or it would have, if he had been able to read them.

Not one title was written in Latin letters.

That one there, the thin one on the top shelf, looked promising, though. It didn't even have a title—the back was too small to bear any words. Somehow, it called out to him, so Gabriel stretched and pulled it out. Flicking through the pages, he saw that he could read it.

Runes. Runes on every page, but what was more, what was ideal, was that next to each rune was an explanation of what it stood for. "A dictionary," Gabriel murmured, raking his hand through his hair. "Right. While I'm here, I can at least see if I can find that Sleeping rune the doc used on me. And the Forgetting rune. Would come in handy." Absent-mindedly, he pulled a chair close, pulling his bare feet up. He only wore jeans and a T-shirt, but luckily, the room was warm despite the late hour.

For the next ninety minutes, he worked his way through the pages. Not that it was easy—even with the explanations, he understood little more than a short phrase here and there. More than once, he doubted that the explanations were really written in English, as they talked about the otherworld, the afterworld, the never-to-be wishes, about threat stones and blood bindings. Maybe he would've given up if he hadn't found a rune for which the explanation simply said "Protection."

Gabriel reached for his knapsack, which he never let out of his sight and where he had stored the repaired camera. "What if I could prevent you from ever breaking again by painting this stupid little pattern on you?" Turning the camera between his fingers and eyeing the rune, he tentatively drew a line on the metal with his fingertip.

There was a flash of blinding light, and the invisible line he had just drawn flared up in bright gold. Gabriel nearly dropped the camera out of shock. He hadn't expected anything to happen, really. He had thought it a game more than anything else. Now there was that golden light, and hell, he should finish this, or something bad might happen. A half-finished rune couldn't be good, he supposed. He tightened his grip and drew another line, and another, until the rune was completed. No more flashes appeared, but with every touch, the metal was covered in more golden lines. The rune glowed in the darkness of the room, brighter than the lamp on the table.

"Now what?" Gabriel murmured. "Am I supposed to say something? You can't stay like that, rune. You look nice, but people would get suspicious if they saw you. Using runes is forbidden, you know? So hush, vanish. Go to rune land or wherever you live once you have been used."

The rune sparkled a bit but didn't vanish. The metal, though, began to feel slightly warm. Maybe it was because his hands were sweaty; maybe it was the magic he had used without really knowing what he was doing.

"Shit," Gabriel said aloud, and then the metal got hot, really hot, and he heard soft steps on the planks and felt his heart sinking.

Tennant. What a surprise. Thinking the man was asleep while offering shelter to a stranger had been a stupid assumption in the first place. "Look, man, I'm sorry," Gabriel began, half turning in his chair to look at his host. "I thought I could prevent the camera from breaking again. Didn't mean to mess things up."

Tennant just raised one questioning eyebrow. Taking the camera out of Gabriel's hand, he turned it in order to see the still brightly glowing rune. "A Protection rune? You used a Protection rune for such a small and unimportant purpose?" He sounded genuinely surprised. He definitely didn't sound annoyed or angry.

He made a small movement, and the rune lost its brightness. A moment later, it was gone. One of Tennant's naked feet tapped an irregular rhythm on the planks; he was nervous, Gabriel realized. Nervous and maybe even a bit—

"This scares the life out of me, Gabriel," Tennant admitted. "You shouldn't have been able to read the book. You definitely shouldn't have been able to draw the rune. Well, drawing it isn't the problem, of course. A child can draw a rune. However, being able to feed it with power, to make it glow, to make it work, is an entirely different matter. How did you do it? Who trained you? Who told you about runes? And most importantly—who are you really?" The curiosity in his voice was very prominent now, and furthermore, he seemed to be much colder and more suspicious than when they had dined together.

As usual when falsely accused, Gabriel lashed out with tightly controlled anger. "I have told you my name, Doc," he snarled, getting up. He was maybe half an inch taller than Tennant, but he knew that he could make himself look bigger and more threatening if needed—a gift from his werewolf ancestors. "I am a nobody. A penniless sod you picked up from the streets, and you know what? You shouldn't have been able to see me, either. Even the ones who know me tend to overlook me—I'm practically invisible. But you saw me and brought me here and even cooked and offered me a bed for the night. No one told me about runes. I've heard about them, like everybody. I know they are prohibited. I have never seen one in my life or known anyone who has, apart from you, and I haven't got a clue what the problem is. I couldn't sleep, I was bored, and so I went to find something to read. Sorry if I touched something precious. And I'll go now, if you don't mind." Very slightly, Gabriel bared his teeth. It always worked. It was a scary sight, and he knew it.

Tennant reached out and placed a hand on his shoulder. "You won't go anywhere," he ordered. "Not now, and not tomorrow." He pushed Gabriel back into the chair as easily as if he were a child and not a full-grown man. "You will stay here, in my house, until I have found out everything there is to be found out about you. Is that understood?"

When in danger, Gabriel always fought his way out. He couldn't change into a wolf, and he looked like a relatively harmless human man, but inside, as all his foster parents had found out eventually, he was much wilder than he looked. It would be easy to break Tennant's neck and get out of the house; it would cost him no more than—

Casually, Tennant drew a rune into the air, and Gabriel lost all will to fight. All strength seeped out of him, and as he was so very tired due to lack of sleep, he couldn't fight the rune, and so he slipped out of the chair and crashed to the floor, unconscious.

CHAPTER THREE

GABRIEL didn't wake up in the usual way: asleep one moment, wide awake and alert the next. He woke up screaming, gripped by pain and panic, and he wanted to jump up, to flee, without even knowing why he was so scared. Moving, though, was impossible. From his throat, no sound emerged, and only a single bead of sweat ran down his temple.

White ceiling, curtains in front of a big window. A bed and a mattress.

Bedroom. He was very clearly in a bedroom and not outside on the street, covered by his dirty old blanket.

"Where am I?" Gabriel croaked, struggling against his bindings. "Where the fuck am I, and what happened?" There the panic was again; it squeezed his heart and his brain and made thinking and remembering impossible.

At least the pain was subsiding. A moment ago, his head had been about to explode; now, nothing more than a slight pounding was left, although he couldn't have been awake for more than a few minutes.

Light pierced his eyes—sunlight. It streamed in through the window, accompanied by a mild breeze. Why did he think that outside it should be dark and cold, cloudy, the pavement covered with snow?

With all the effort he could muster, Gabriel stopped trying to free his hands. They were bound by his sides, and it was impossible to lift them very much at all. He shivered, and suddenly, a name dropped right into his mind.

Tennant. Dr. Tennant. Tall, with graying hair, a wonderfully warm voice, and blue eyes. Ice-blue eyes. Cold, curious eyes, and suddenly Gabriel remembered the dinner, the Tickling rune, and that he'd gotten up early to find something to read.

"Oh, shit. Damn. Shit. *Fuck!*" More panic. He had just remembered that Tennant had knocked him out, that he must have been the one who had bound him to the bed, and actually, it was probably a miracle that he was still alive.

"I've got to get out of here," he croaked. "He's going to kill me. He's a fucking murderer after all. Why was I so stupid not to walk away when I had the chance? Wait, I did leave, but then I just had to come back here with him!"

Gabriel became louder with each word until, at the end, he was shouting out his fear and fury at the white curtains, the white walls, and the closed door. He had been scared before—when his grandmother had gone mad, dooming him to a life at the orphanage and with various foster parents; when one of his foster fathers had beaten the shit out of him for running away again; and the first time he had slept outside on the streets. But never in his life had he felt so helpless, so vulnerable, and never, ever had he been so sure that he was going to die within the hour.

"Help," he rasped. "Anyone here willing to help me?"

The door opened, and Tennant stepped inside, carrying a tray. Gabriel had to clench his teeth, or he might have screamed. Only cowards screamed, and as he wasn't one, he managed to say "Hi, Doc," through gritted teeth. "Any chance you might release me and let me walk out of here unharmed?" Lacing his words with sarcasm had never been a problem for Gabriel, and he was really glad that he was able to keep control over his voice.

Silently, Tennant put the tray down next to the bed. Gabriel didn't want to look, didn't want to see what torture instruments lay upon it, but his head sort of moved on its own.

A cup, a pot, and a plate of sandwiches. Strange. No knives, no hooks, nothing one could do harm with.

"Do you plan to stuff the sandwiches down my throat until I suffocate?" he asked. "Maybe burn me to death with the tea? Come on, you can do better than that. I bet there's a rune that causes incredible pain or maybe drives me mad or something."

Tennant shook his head in sympathy. "You talk a lot of nonsense, Gabriel. How about keeping your mouth shut before I decide I can't stand your constant chatter and kill you despite my initial plan to unbind you?" A butterfly knife appeared in his hand with the flick of his wrist, its blade sparkling in the sunlight.

Gabriel opened his mouth and closed it again. Sometimes, his brain won out against his mouth. Not often, but if there ever was a perfect time for this unlikely event, it was definitely now.

Tennant pulled the thin blanket back, and Gabriel was most relieved to see he was still wearing the jeans and T-shirt he'd put on the night before.

Obviously, the doc didn't seem to be a perverted bastard who liked to rape unconscious victims. On the other hand, Tennant might have dressed him again afterwards.

A quick cut, and Gabriel's right hand was free. He might have been able to catch Tennant's wrist, but the man stepped out of reach before Gabriel could as much as think about trying to grab the knife. "Eat a sandwich, Gabriel," Tennant said in a nearly friendly voice. "You've slept for two days. You must have been exhausted, or I wouldn't have been able to knock you out so easily."

"You knocked me out because you are an evil bastard, and once I am free, I will tear you to pieces," Gabriel growled. He couldn't help it. The wolf inside him despised being bound, being at the mercy of an ordinary human who had used unfair tricks to capture him.

Tennant just laughed, pulled a chair close, and sat down next to the bed. Pouring himself a cup of tea and taking a bite from one of the sandwiches, he proved with these simple gestures that neither the food nor the drink was poisoned.

Taking out a piece of paper, he began to read aloud. "Gabriel Jordan," he said. "Age twenty-seven, born on September 7th. Father Tobias Jordan, deceased. Mother Tessa Rose Jordan, née Parker, known crack-addict and working as a prostitute on Elisabeth Street." Leisurely, Tennant stretched out his long legs. Gabriel, dumbstruck by the sudden change of subject, tried to free his left hand and failed, then sat up a bit, reached out, and took a sandwich, devouring it in two bites. He nearly choked on it, but he was ravenous.

"Your father's mother, Bellatrice Jordan, born in Sussex, England, moved to the States at the age of thirty-four. She was a shapeshifter," Tennant continued, pouring a cup of tea for Gabriel. "Your mother dumped you in a bin right after you were born. You lived in an orphanage for a year; then your grandmother took you in until you were six. Unfortunately, she decided to become a full-time wolf, and when your mother refused to take on the responsibility, you went back to the orphanage. Seven foster parents were paid to raise you; you didn't stay with any of them. At the age of fifteen, you vanished, presumably to live on the streets. Occasionally, you work for Luis Mallfrick, getting the trickier pictures for him. You have never been in prison nor in hospital. Have I forgotten anything?"

It took Gabriel several attempts before he could answer. In the end, he straightened up a bit further and took a sip of tea to soothe his rough throat. "The names of my wife and ten children, and my favorite food," he finally managed. "How the fuck did you find out all of that? Are you with the government or something? And why did you bother in the first place?" Belatedly, he thought that maybe he could try unfastening the binding on his other hand, only to discover that his wrist was fixed to the bed frame with a strong, flexible band that was impossible to rip apart even with the strongest fingers.

Tennant just cut that one open too. "Don't misunderstand," he warned. "I won't let you go yet. I still have too many questions, Gabriel. But I don't want you to think I mean you harm. I don't. Once I have figured out what you are, you will be free to leave, and you have nothing to fear from me in the meantime. Not too much, anyway. I will ask you for a blood sample. I might ask you to work with runes. That should be it. I think."

Gabriel swung his feet out of the bed and got up on wobbly legs. One sandwich wasn't enough to assuage his hunger, and one sip of tea was far from being enough for his dry mouth. "I will be missed," he said wearily, knowing only too well that it was a lie. Mallfrick didn't give a damn about his employees, and he hadn't seen his mother in more than ten years. "My friends will be looking for me already."

Sighing, Tennant got up and opened the door. "You don't have friends, Gabriel. Maybe someone will miss you, but not enough to go to the police. You are not married. No offspring, either. I could let you rot here, and no one would notice. Besides, despite the nice, sunny day, it is still freezing outside. What do you have to lose? Stay for a few days, or maybe even a couple of weeks. I can offer you regular meals and a warm bed. I'll even pay you, if you insist. How does that sound?"

Gabriel's eyes widened. He'd expected murder only half an hour ago, and now he was being offered a bed, food, and payment? "What d'you need a blood sample for?" he asked, crossing his arms over his chest. He knew it was a stupid question compared with all the others he had already asked, which Tennant hadn't bothered to answer so far. Talking kept his mind off his shaking hands, which he hid under his arms.

"How about a proper lunch instead of another sandwich?" Tennant offered, still holding the door open. "I'll answer your questions, all of them, but at present, I am hungry. Though if you prefer, you may stay in here."

Gabriel looked around the room and saw his knapsack on the floor next to the bed and a pile of clothes too—his clothes, the old ones, freshly washed and neatly put together. A quick check of the knapsack revealed that the blanket was inside and that it had been washed as well. No stench anymore.

"You even left me my money," he said dryly. "All thirty-four cents." Then he began to laugh, silently at first, but with growing intensity. When tears began running down his face, Gabriel sat down hard on the bed, his whole body shaking, his long hair clinging to his wet cheeks. *Who am I trying to fool?* he thought. *I'm like dough in his hands. I can very well eat before he cuts me into pieces.* Although he didn't really believe the cutting-into-pieces part. Tennant had something bigger in mind, it seemed, but he was not regretting his earlier decision to come back to this house anymore. "Lunch it shall be, then," he said, and he walked past Tennant toward the kitchen.

GABRIEL stayed with Tennant, not once setting a foot out the door and not missing it, either, as the temperature remained below freezing point. He ate, he slept a lot and more deeply than he had since he was a little boy, and he read.

There were so many books in Tennant's flat that Gabriel wondered whether the man had read them all. Most of them were old and written in a language Gabriel couldn't yet decipher, though he was learning fast. But some were different, like the little one he had skimmed through the night Tennant had knocked him out. Naturally, he held on to those, and he found it surprisingly easy to get a grip on the principle of using runes. It was not that complicated once one thought about it properly.

"It's like using a computer," Gabriel said to his host one evening after dinner. "I haven't got a clue how to switch the damn things on simply because I never learned how to do it. But I could learn it. Same with runes. You just need to teach me, and I will be able to use them just like you."

Tennant grinned. "Honestly, Gabriel," he mocked, "you shouldn't threaten me. Never a good thing, threatening me. You are good with runes, and you can read books you shouldn't be able to read. You are, after all, mostly human, despite your heritage, and humans hardly ever learn how to read runes, how to use them, just as they are commonly unable to open portals. Even if you were fully shapeshifter, you ought to need years to attain the level you have reached in a ridiculously short time."

Gabriel grinned back at the man. Once he had accepted that Tennant wasn't as dangerous as he came across every now and then, he had seen that the doctor had a friendly nature, possessed a surprisingly ironic humor, and was an extremely good cook as long as the recipe didn't involve pasta. He obviously enjoyed having a guest, and more often than not, he offered his help when Gabriel had a problem understanding a sentence or an explanation. Tennant even encouraged him to actually use the runes, even on him, on occasion. Three times, Gabriel had made Tennant sleepy, once causing him to forget the past few minutes. The Protection rune, though, was taboo.

"That one is a powerful rune," Tennant had explained. "Used to keep harm from loved ones. It only works temporarily when drawn into the air. It cannot be used on artificial things, and please do not try drawing it on your camera again."

Other runes, though, were perfect for training. The first one Gabriel had managed to use properly was a Finding rune: an item marked with this rune couldn't get lost, at least not for long. It had taken Gabriel half a day to draw it correctly; it made his knapsack impossible to lose ever again.

"Comes in handy, that one," he had said, glowing with joy up to his hairline. "I always manage to forget the damn thing in a corner of the mission or under a bridge, and I've had more than one fight over it to get it back."

Tennant had just handed him another book and told him to master the Light rune.

APART from rune-schooling, Tennant tried to find out why Gabriel was able to read the books and feed the runes with power in the first place, but he was unable to come to a conclusion. He took a blood sample; he scanned it, put it under the microscope, mixed it with whatever he thought useful, and bit out a string of colorful expletives when it became apparent that he wouldn't be able to solve the riddle anytime soon.

"You don't fit any pattern, boy," he grumbled after a particularly long day in his study. "I know that there is more to you than a drop of shapeshifter blood, but I don't know what it is. That it is not fae blood is the only thing I'm certain of. And vampire is unlikely. Not impossible, but unlikely, given your obvious lack of cravings for virgins. Now would you stop pacing like a wild panther, or are you trying to drive me crazy?"

Gabriel smashed a flat hand against the wall. "I'm the one who's going crazy, Doc. I need some fresh air. All this time inside is far too much for me. I miss the street under my feet, so if you don't mind, I'll go for a walk."

Tennant frowned and shook his head, his concentration on the sample again. When the silence stretched uncomfortably, he looked up, confused. "You are still here? I thought you wanted to go for a walk. On the other hand, a simple walk might be a bit tedious, don't you agree? How about something more adventurous?"

"Like what?"

"Like trespassing?" he suggested. He got up from the chair he'd been sitting on and turned his back to the microscope he had used to examine the drop of Gabriel's blood. "I have to go back to Miss Kinney's flat. Having someone watching my back wouldn't be a bad idea." A mischievous smile curved his lips, as if he knew how much his guest needed a bit of distraction. "I'll even allow you to draw the Floating rune on your coat once we're done. I clearly recall your stunned gaze when you saw me coming down last time."

Gabriel didn't hear him; he was already putting on his boots.

BREAKING into an apartment was less exciting than Gabriel had expected, especially since the house seemed to be completely deserted. On most windows, the shutters were down, there were no sounds of voices, televisions, or arguments, and as usual, the janitor was nowhere to be seen.

"It was harder the first time I tried it," Tennant said as he pried open the front door. "I had decided to use the door, and there were people everywhere. Once, I even bumped into a kissing couple. Who would have expected people to be kissing in the storage room? So I went up the wall instead. Ah, finally." Gently, he pushed the door open, and they slipped quietly inside and up the stairs.

It was equally easy to break into Lorelei Kinney's apartment. Inside, the light was dim—here as well as everywhere else, the shutters blocked out most of the light. The air was stale, as if no one had been there for days, discarded clothes lay on the rugs, and in the kitchen stood a single cup with cold tea.

"Seems she had to leave in a hurry," Gabriel commented dryly. "Either her lover was waiting outside, or she was late for an appointment. Theater, presumably. Or opera. She loves both."

Tennant's eyes narrowed when he saw the mess in the living room: every inch of the floor was covered with records, books, and more clothes. Glasses surrounded the lamp on the small side table, and the one plant was close to dying from lack of water.

Without comment, Gabriel went into the bathroom. "Wow," he exclaimed when he saw the huge bathtub. "That's closer to a swimming pool. What did she need that for—training for the Olympics?"

Tennant had come to stand behind him. Gabriel could feel the warmth his body radiated and smell the faint fragrance of sandalwood soap. For some reason, the combination made the small hairs on his neck stand up, and he quickly stepped away from Tennant.

Just as Gabriel drew a glass of water for the plant, Tennant said, "She's a mermaid," and picked up a hairbrush. A few long golden hairs were caught in the bristles.

Gabriel watched him pluck one out. Then his brain caught up, and he asked, "What?" thinking he'd misheard.

"A mermaid. You know, human torso, fish tail, able to breathe under water, likes sailors, especially when they've drowned. That sort of mermaid. Never heard of them?"

Picking up a huge, fluffy, slightly moldy-smelling towel, Gabriel replied, "Didn't notice her having a tail last time I saw her. She was wearing a skirt short enough to reveal half her bottom, and her legs were endless. I wouldn't push her out of my bed, I must admit, although I prefer guys. You must be wrong about the mermaid part. Or nuts. Yeah, nuts would be a good explanation for nearly everything that has happened these past few weeks." Disgusted—his nose was more sensitive to the stench in the room now that he showered regularly—he threw the towel into the corner.

Tennant grinned. "Merpeople can choose between tail and legs, Gabriel. Naturally, she had legs, living in a world like this. Still, she needs salt water on a regular basis. Thus the size of the tub."

"All right, I get it." Gabriel picked up a second towel. It harbored a family of spiders. "Who would believe that such a beautiful woman could be such a pig behind closed doors?"

Tennant, having found the bedroom, pulled up the blinds, and opened the curtains. Outside, the sky was dark with low-hanging clouds. It would be snowing again soon.

It wasn't the dim light or the fact that Lorelei Kinney had a few interesting little secrets. Something else made Gabriel frown. "What's that smell?" he asked, stepping into the living room with flaring nostrils and quickly walking toward the bedroom. "It was there before, but now it's stronger. Since you've opened the bedroom door. It smells bad. Don't you—"

"Over here," Tennant said with a flat voice. He stood close to the big window, the same one he had used to get in and out of the flat. "Stains. Hidden by the curtain. I don't want to switch on the light. I've got a suspicion, though." Kneeling down, he dipped one fingertip into a brown patch on the carpet.

Involuntarily, Gabriel turned his head away. Suddenly, the stench grew stronger, as if Tennant had freed some molecules that were now directly hitting his nose.

"Blood," he said through clenched teeth. "That's definitely blood." He forced himself to take another step. "More next to the bed, Doc."

"Ah, yes. Much more. It seems as if something nasty has happened in here since my last visit. Most of the blood is splashed against the window. When I entered this apartment on Christmas Eve, nothing was out of the ordinary: no mess, no clothes lying around, and definitely no blood on the floor."

"No wonder I didn't smell the blood earlier," Gabriel said. "The window had been covered by the curtain. The blood is on the window—the murderer must have done it." Suddenly, he whirled around. "Someone's at the door," he hissed. Grabbing Tennant's arm, Gabriel pushed the doctor into a niche next to the wardrobe. Luckily, Tennant was slim, or he wouldn't have fit.

The door was kicked in, and it crashed down with considerable noise. A roar similar to that of an angry bull pierced the silence of the apartment, and Gabriel earnestly considered hiding under the bed when a man, big, bulky, red-faced, and looking extremely furious, stormed into the bedroom.

"Murderer!" he shouted. "You killed my Lulu, and now I'll kill you!" From out of nowhere, the man produced a knife bigger than his forearm, swinging it like a scythe and nearly beheading Gabriel.

"Hey! Stop it!" Gabriel shouted, jumping onto the bed and out of reach of the madman. "I've killed no one. Lorelei wasn't here when we came in—I mean, when I came in, and I haven't got a clue where she is. Stop trying to kill me, man!"

Sweat was pouring down the big man's face. He was breathing like an old air pump, and he'd stopped swinging the knife. He looked lost and confused more than anything else. With a clumsy jump, the man landed on the bed as well, balancing awkwardly, as if the mattress were a surfboard.

"You killed her, you bastard," he said heatedly. "She's been gone for weeks now! The apartment *never* looks like this. She never leaves clothes lying around! If she isn't dead, where is she? What have you done with her?"

The knife swung in a wide arc, and Gabriel jumped, tripped, and landed hard on his ass. Those eyebrows... they were huge and bushy, resembling small, hairy caterpillars more than anything else. "You are that guy," Gabriel stammered, moving backward through at least ten pairs of high heels. "That guy, what's his name, the one I was supposed to catch on film. Come on, I know your name!"

"Die, or tell me about Lulu right now!"

"Wright! Steve Wright, and Lorelei is your lover, and you know what? Until you stormed in here all berserk, I thought you had killed her!"

Wright lost his balance and dropped his knife to stabilize himself. Then, with an animal-like cry, he grabbed a statue off the windowsill, swung it, and hit Gabriel right over the head.

HEADACHE. Again. Shit.

"I hate fucking headaches." Although that had come out a bit more whiny than he'd intended, Gabriel still wondered why he felt as if he'd been out all night drinking.

Sitting up was not an option, obviously, as even thinking hurt. "What did you hit me with? A truck?" Gabriel croaked, trying to concentrate on the face that swam in and out of focus. Not a big, red face, though. A face with blue eyes.

Wright had brown eyes.

"Doc?" Gabriel asked. He tried to sit up in earnest, mainly with the intention of getting to his feet again so he'd be ready to run away. If that madman was still somewhere in the flat, things were going to get worse.

Tennant put a cool hand on Gabriel's forehead and held him down on the mattress. "Lie still," he ordered. "You were hit by a massive bronze statue. Artemis, I'd say. The statue, that is. Not the one who hit you. That was Mr. Wright looking for Miss Kinney. He believed you had killed her until I told him we had nothing to do with her disappearance but are here to investigate the reason for her disappearance. Are we not, Detective Jordan?"

"Huh?" Calling Gabriel's state of mind "confused" would have been an understatement. Rolling his head to the other side, he managed to make out Wright's massive figure cramped into a chair three sizes too small for him. His hands, surprisingly pale and nearly feminine in their fragility, covered his face. He was sobbing heartbreakingly.

"Damn," Gabriel murmured, finally finding his way into an upright position. "Detective?"

"Yes?" Tennant said, his eyes slightly widening as if warning him not to say anything that would give them away.

Rubbing the growing bruise on the side of his head, Gabriel eyed the bloodstains on the carpet. It was a sickening sight, knowing—or at least guessing—that the blood had once been inside Lorelei Kinney's body. After all, he had followed the woman for more than a week, tracking her like a hunter tracks his prey, in order to get a picture of her and Wright kissing or, ideally, screwing each other senseless. He knew her daily routine, he knew where she liked to eat, he knew when she left for work and when she came back home. She owned a little shop, selling fancy clothes to ridiculously young girls.

And she had a taste for filthy rich men.

"Sir?" Tennant's inquisitive tone interrupted his thoughts. "Mr. Wright, I can understand that you are distressed and worried about Miss Kinney's absence, but if you could tell us when you last saw her, it would be extremely helpful." Handing the big man a handkerchief, he patiently waited while Wright blew his nose.

"The day before Christmas Eve," Wright managed to say after another blow. "We went shopping. Well, she bought the stuff; I paid for it. Expensive day, that was. I even sent the wife to her parents and put on the kinky underwear Lorelei had given me for my birthday, even though they itch like hell. Couldn't see her on Christmas, obviously. The wife would have slaughtered me. New Year's Eve she—Lorelei, that is—didn't answer the phone. I thought she was still angry with me because I hadn't bought her that necklace she wanted. We were supposed to go to the theater. She didn't turn up, and she didn't answer her phone. Her mobile's been switched off. She told me never to come over without her, but I just had to." With shining eyes, he looked at both Gabriel and Tennant. "Where is she? Did someone kill her? Is that her blood on the ground? Please, officers, I beg you, you must find her!"

Just as Tennant opened his mouth to reply, a small voice from the door said, "She's been gone since January 6th."

Surprised, Gabriel turned his still-aching head and saw a woman, about four feet tall and wrinkled like an old apple, standing in the doorway. With both hands, she nervously kneaded the hem of her sweater. Her skirt revealed twig-thin legs, and one eye twitched constantly. Gabriel nearly twitched as well, out of sympathy.

Tennant just raised an eyebrow as the woman said, "Sorry, sir. The door was open. I'm the cleaning lady. Sally. Miss Kinney was indeed angry with Mr. Wright and was ignoring his phone calls. On January 6th, she came home around five o'clock. I was waiting in front of the door—I don't have a key—but when she looked into the apartment, she told me to leave. I haven't seen her since. Whenever I knock, no one is there. But I swear that she has never, ever left her clothes lying around. Sir."

"Told you so," Wright chimed in.

Tennant held up a silencing hand. "Enough," he said, and Gabriel could barely suppress a grin. *The doc even sounds like a police officer,* he thought. *Didn't know he was that good an actor.*

"I want you both to go to the nearest police station and make a report," Tennant ordered. "And Sally, please leave your contact details in case I have some questions later."

Obediently, Wright stood up, nodding eagerly. Sally toyed with the hem of her sweater, then scribbled a few words on a piece of paper and handed it to Tennant.

Gabriel considered it a good time to add, "We'll continue investigating, won't we, Officer?"

"Precisely," Tennant replied, shoving both Wright and the cleaning lady out the door and closing it safely behind them. "That was close," he stated with a sigh. "Let's get out of here. Nothing more to find."

"What about the blood?"

"Not hers. She's a mermaid, remember? Green blood. I don't know what has happened here, but I am certain that we won't find any further clues. Besides, I'm hungry. Let's grab something to eat."

"About time you said that," Gabriel answered.

"SOMETHING to eat" wasn't, as Gabriel had expected, a quick meal in one of the various little restaurants along the way. Not even Indian or Chinese seemed good enough. Instead, Tennant chose a restaurant that looked so very posh that Gabriel felt his stomach cramp simply at the sight of the huge entrance. *La Laterna Magica* was written in suspiciously small, even humble, letters above the door.

"I'm not going in there," Gabriel stated categorically. "They'd throw me out the moment I stepped inside. I can do without that, Doc."

Surprised, Tennant stopped and turned to look at Gabriel. Tonight, he wore a long, dark cashmere coat, matching scarf and gloves, black trousers, gray shirt, and a waistcoat. Gabriel wore jeans, leather boots, a black sweater, and a woolen coat. His hair was bound back in a braid, but it was still very, very red and very, very long. Too red and far too long and clearly belonging to someone who was considered undesirable in that sort of restaurant.

Just when Gabriel was about to take a step back into the shadows, a waiter opened the door, ever so slightly bending his head to greet the new guest. When he saw the second, younger man, his nose wrinkled.

"Igor," Tennant said. Just that one word, but he put a threat into it. Then he said coolly, "Gabriel, are you coming? I reserved the table this morning; we are expected."

"Welcome to La Laterna Magica," Igor sneered.

Shit, Gabriel thought. It was obvious that he had no choice but to go inside, and he followed Tennant into the restaurant.

AFTER their coats had been taken away—Gabriel had refused to hand over his knapsack, though—they were seated at a small table near one of the windows. It was clearly the best table in the restaurant; carefully, Gabriel put the knapsack onto the ground and pushed it under the chair with his feet. Igor watched him doing it with a disapproving sneer, then lit a candle and wordlessly handed each of them a wine list before vanishing in the direction of the kitchen. Tennant, clearly feeling comfortable, quickly scanned through the available wines. "A Cabernet would be nice. Or maybe a young Chardonnay?"

"You're crazy, bringing me here," Gabriel hissed. He felt out of place, and he hated it. "I wish you hadn't done it. I wish you would at least have had the decency to warn me!" Bowing his head, he wished he could hide behind the menu; he was blushing, something else he deeply disliked.

"Warn you that we'd go for dinner?" Handing the wine list to a passing waiter and ordering the Chardonnay, Tennant took a piece of bread, broke it, and ate it.

Gabriel could smell the yeast, the corn, and the sunflower seeds the bread was sprinkled with. Warmth was wafting his way—the bread had come straight from the oven. His mouth watered; he was hungrier than he'd known. And he wanted to talk about what had happened in the apartment, about Lorelei and why she had vanished, about the blood, and about how disappointed he was that they had skipped the floating-out-of-the-window bit. Instead, he was here, and people were staring at him as if he were a rare animal, wild and possibly dangerous. Slowly, he leaned closer to the doc. "Don't you know what they're all thinking?" he asked quietly. "Doesn't it bother you? Because it bothers me."

With a sigh, Tennant dropped the bread onto his plate. "I didn't know you could read thoughts," he said. "I don't know what anyone in here is thinking about. I assume most guests are looking forward to a delicious dinner. I know about half the guests; some of them are my customers. But I do not know what they are thinking." A small nod brought Igor back to their table, and Tennant placed their order. When they were alone once more, he said, "I do hope you like fish. The salmon is simply to die for."

Gabriel very nearly jumped up and left. "You don't get it, do you? Let me explain, then. See that woman at the bar? The one with the black hair and the red top? She is thinking, 'Why has he chosen this little prick? Why not me?' The woman sitting at the table near the big plant is devouring you with her eyes, a bit worried that you might be richer than her husband, and is wondering why you've brought a dirty tramp into this restaurant. I bet she's considering whether she should ask her husband to have me thrown out. It's so damn obvious. Why can't you see it?"

"Now look—" Tennant began, but Gabriel ignored him.

"The guy over there, the one with the young lady, is wrinkling his nose just like good old Igor did, and the two men who are having dessert are discussing if they should offer you a price for me. They see my clothes, my hair, they look at my shoes and compare your age with mine, and every one of them thinks I'm a pro. Or to phrase it so even you understand: they think I'm your fucktoy. Why else would you bring someone like me to a place like this, with me so damn obviously nowhere even near your league?" His voice had become louder. Not embarrassingly loud, but loud enough to turn a few more heads.

Shit.

Tennant stared at him in silence. Then he scanned the people Gabriel had pointed out to him. Naturally, everyone was looking in another direction by then, but Tennant frowned nevertheless.

"I didn't consider that," he finally said. "I've dined here for at least ten years, sometimes three or four times a month. Until today, I have never brought a guest. I didn't think it could cause that much attention, but it seems as if you are right about your assumptions."

"Let's go, then," Gabriel urged.

Tennant shook his head in amusement. "If we leave now, everyone will think I couldn't wait until after dinner before devouring you," he pointed out. "Besides, the salmon is delicious. Which brings this down to one question: are you?"

Their argument hadn't lasted more than a few minutes, but by then, Gabriel was more angry than embarrassed and in a fighting rather than a running-away mood. Impatiently, he pushed a loose strand of hair out of his face.

"Am I what?" he snapped, and then Igor appeared, carrying two plates.

"Are you my fucktoy?" Tennant asked as if they were alone. Igor just stood there like a statue with the plates in his hands.

Gabriel couldn't help the grin spreading over his face—he hadn't believed it possible, but suddenly he was enjoying this little chat, especially because now things were clearer between them. Tennant was good-looking, in his way, and Gabriel wouldn't have minded a night in his bed, but this was better. Friendship was a rare thing, and Gabriel had no intention of risking it, not for a few hours of pleasure and not because of a few stupid people making wrong assumptions.

Therefore, he answered, "No, I'm not. Not yours; not anyone's. And you're after Lorelei Kinney, anyway."

"Correct," Tennant said, now grinning too.

"You still should have warned me, though."

"My apologies," Tennant replied dryly, and Igor was finally allowed to serve dinner.

THEY had an espresso afterwards, and neither Gabriel nor Tennant wasted one more thought on the other guests. "What will you do about Lorelei, Doc?" Gabriel asked, for the first time feeling comfortable in a posh location. "Did you find your letters?"

Tennant nodded, pulling out a thin bundle of papers from the inner pocket of his jacket. "I'll burn them as soon as we're home. Hopefully, I'll remember not to behave so stupidly the next time I fall in love."

Grinning, Gabriel emptied his cup. "For some reason, I can't see you behaving stupidly at all, Doc. You give the impression of having everything under control—all the time. Declaring us to be police detectives was a brilliant idea. This way, we escaped unharmed, Lorelei will be reported missing, and you have your letters. As I said, brilliant."

Shit. That had come out more admiringly than he had planned.

"Look, Doc," he added quickly, feeling his ears burn. "I need to go and see my boss. Have to earn some cash, and then there are my friends and all...."

At a loss for words, he didn't know how to continue. The time he had spent in Tennant's house had been great, but it was obvious it couldn't continue this way. He had always earned his own income, sparse as it was; he had never lived on anyone's generosity, and he liked Tennant too much to press him into offering him permanent shelter. The doc might do it, which was even worse. Gabriel had the strong impression that Tennant was, in general, a solitary man. His house was designed to be his home and no one else's. Taking in a man with dubious heritage and a major lack of manners was probably not what Tennant wanted to be doing.

"I've got my knapsack and will pop into Father Barley's mission. Guess this is good-bye, then," Gabriel said.

"It appears so," Tennant said, and Gabriel felt an odd, piercing pain stab his heart. He had hoped Tennant would at least try to persuade him to stay.

"You know my address," Tennant continued, obviously oblivious to Gabriel's divided feelings. "I expect you to come back once you've sorted things out." Then he looked up, saw Gabriel's stunned face, and continued, "What? You didn't think I'd let you walk away just like that, did you? I like you, Gabriel. I haven't solved the riddle of your heritage yet, either. Besides, I cannot imagine you'd rather sleep on the streets than in a bed. I'll give you until the weekend; then I'll come and look for you, dragging you back if I have to. Is that understood?"

Tennant's words were laced with amusement. Had anyone else dared to speak to Gabriel like that, he would have punched him right in the face.

"Sure, Doc," he said. "And once I'm back, I'll show you how to properly cook spaghetti."

"I didn't know it lacked flavor," Tennant objected indignantly—he was mocking the younger man, and Gabriel realized that he really liked the easy way they had developed a friendship out of nowhere.

"Your spaghetti, Doc, is nowhere near being *al dente*," he said. "There's a trick my gran showed me when I was five, and maybe, if you behave yourself, I might be persuaded to share it with you."

Taking his knapsack, Gabriel walked away into the night, knowing that he would return to Tennant's house and the man himself much sooner than Tennant might expect.

Chapter Four

WALKING through the quiet streets was calming as well as strange. The streets were rarely this deserted, but the cold had come back in January, and obviously, people had decided to stay inside rather than getting frostbite. Most of the streetlights were out as well—destroyed, by the looks of it—and the stars sparkled in a very dark night sky. Gabriel pulled his coat tighter around his body and shoved his hands deep into the pockets. Freed from the ribbon, his long hair whipped all around him, a crisp wind playing with the strands. Eventually, he pulled it back again so he was at least able to see where he was going.

The night was beautiful in its strangeness. Only the occasional car disturbed the silence. He enjoyed the freshness of the air and the cold that chilled his face.

As usual, Gabriel found the thought of sleeping in the mission tonight revolting. It would be loud there and a bit too warm. It would smell of stale food and unwashed bodies.

He stopped and looked up at the sky, searching for Orion's Belt. Of course he couldn't find it—too many houses in the way. Then he thought, *Why does he want me to come back?* only to realize that this wasn't the main question. *Why do I want to go back? Why do I consider him a friend, even though I just met him a few weeks ago?*

Sighing, Gabriel went on, heading for the mission for lack of a better option. At least the people there would surely distract him from a riddle he couldn't solve.

"GABE! Oi, look, Gabe's back!" The small, bald woman screamed with joy and threw herself right into his arms. Fine, Marita had needed a few moments to recognize him—the shower must have changed his appearance profoundly, he guessed, and the new, clean clothes too— but what the hell. He was strangely moved that she had remembered his face at all—enough to ignore the dirt on her hands and the smell of an unwashed body emerging from her. Most people couldn't remember his name even if he told them half a dozen times.

Marita was about half his size, didn't weigh more than a sparrow, and wore at least ten skirts one over another. She hugged him as tightly as she could; Gabriel just managed not to screw up his nose. Hopefully, he'd get used to the place in another few moments, or he wouldn't be able to stay for long. "We thought you were dead, or kidnapped, or maybe that you'd found a better job."

"Or a rich lover," Billy chimed in, not moving an inch away from his bowl of chili con carne, which smelled acceptable, though it didn't contain any meat at all. "Where've you been, man? Not that we've been worried, you know, just curious."

He shoved a spoonful of chili into his mouth. His sweater showed clear signs of the other meals he'd both cooked and eaten in the past few days: cornflakes, toast with butter and honey, and enough coffee to leave an abundance of stains, making the original color of the sweater unrecognizable.

The room was packed with people; behind the counter, Father Barley handed out dinner. For the most part, however, people ignored each other. Suddenly, Gabriel wished neither Billy nor Marita had seen him come in. He would've sneaked out unnoticed otherwise, because frankly, he was feeling really uncomfortable in here. *Just like in the restaurant*, Gabriel thought desperately. *I didn't belong there, but I don't belong here, either. Not anymore.*

Damn. How perfectly great, choosing this moment to doubt himself, his life, and everything else.

"Marita," he forced himself to say, and he even managed to put some fondness into his voice. "I'm not dead, and no one kidnapped me. In fact, my plan for tomorrow is to go to Mallfrick and beg him not to kill me. How're you, then, sweetie?" Gently, he brushed his thumb across her dirty cheek, pretending not to notice that her eyes were suspiciously wet. He definitely hadn't expected her to react so strongly to his disappearance.

"Fine," she sniveled. "Great. One less mouth to feed when you're not here."

Billy finally finished his dinner and joined them. He, as well as Marita, usually recognized Gabriel even when they met on the streets. They found a table in the corner where Billy looked Gabriel up and down as if he were a sickly horse.

"Fancy clothes," he stated coldly. "If it's not from the money you made from Mallfrick, I guess you've found someone who pays for a fuck. Pays a lot, by the looks of it. That's one fine coat you've got there. Warm and without holes and all. Not even a bit dirty. You tell me you've slept on the streets these past weeks, and I will call you a lousy liar. How could I have been so stupid to believe you wouldn't sink that low, Gabe?" Disgusted, Billy slammed his hand on the table, making Marita jump.

Gabriel hugged her tightly. He knew why Billy was so aggressive: he had earned his money on the streets for several years until a punter had beaten him up so badly he ended up in the hospital. Billy had once been a handsome man, but now, at the age of twenty-nine, he looked sixty. He didn't have more than five or six teeth left in his mouth, owned a nose no one recognized as such anymore, and sported only one-and-a-half ears. His face was uneven—his jawbone had been broken in several places—and his short, blond hair stood up in spikes and was as dirty and uneven as the rest of him. All in all, he was a very unapproachable, if not dangerous-looking, man.

"Easy, Billy," Gabriel soothed. "No one paid me anything, and definitely not for a fuck. I stole the clothes, and I slept in an empty house. On Christmas Eve, I was so damn cold I couldn't stand the thought of spending one more minute outside, so I found myself a nice place and vanished for a few days. Sorry, man. Should've let you know." Calmly, he reached out a hand, palm up. *How easy it is to lie*, he thought, mildly surprised. He rarely lied, not to the few people he considered as friends, anyway.

Billy looked at him through narrowed, bloodshot eyes. After a few heartbeats, he finally slapped Gabriel's hand and sat down. "Shit, man, sorry about that," he grumbled. "Seen it too often. None of these assholes ever believe me when I tell them that in the end, the street breaks you. They try it anyway. Idiots."

Marita edged a bit closer to Gabriel. "You smell nice," she said, tucking into his side and wrapping a thin arm around his waist. "Like sunflowers. And your hair is clean. You had a shower!"

"More than one, sweetie. It was a nice place, some sort of abandoned office building, and they hadn't switched off the water and electricity. I'll take you there, if you like." Deep inside, he cringed; he hated to lie to someone he liked.

Marita just shuddered. "Water's bad," she declared. "Makes the skin thin, and then you get ill."

From a distance, Father Barley waved his hello; Gabriel just nodded in acknowledgement. It was too warm in here; the smell of beans, farts, and unwashed human bodies was overwhelming, and he wished he were elsewhere. *Elsewhere, like in Tennant's house.*

Even Conchita was there, slinking over at that very moment. "*Hola,*" she cooed. "Want someone to warm up your bed tonight, honey?"

He wondered how to answer her. In the past—as recently as a month ago, in fact—he would have taken her up on her offer. Every now and then, they had shared a bed; Conchita was generous with the charms of her large-breasted, big-hipped body. Although he preferred men for his pleasure, she was good fun, and so far, he'd never turned her down when she was in the mood for love.

Only tonight, the thought of her flesh under his fingertips was as revolting as the smell of the beans. Flashing in front of his inner eye, he saw ice-blue eyes, gray-streaked hair, and a thin, amused smile.

"Get out of my head, Doc," Gabriel murmured to himself, then remembered that Conchita was still waiting for his answer. "I'd love to, babe," he began, not having a clue how to continue.

Something must have shown in his face—annoyance, maybe, or even the disgust he felt—because Billy said, "Remember, man, you wanted to check on Pepino," as if they'd just been talking about the young drug addict. "He's off the smack again, he's out of his mind, and he'll calm down when you go and talk to him. You promised. Sorry, Conchita," he said. Then to Gabriel, he added, "He's in the back room. Go and see him before he chews up his nails." Hands wrapped around a mug of steaming hot tea Father Barley had put in front of him, Billy winked at Conchita. "In case you wanna warm up my bed, love, I'm available."

"In your dreams," she said, and she stalked off.

"Thanks, man." Gabriel sighed with relief. "I'm not in the mood for her company tonight. So Pepino's trying to get clean again?"

Billy nodded. "Yep, and he won't make it, as usual. Tell him a bedtime story or something. Now that I've made up the tale, you can't stay out here where the lovely Conchita can see you."

Marita tugged at his hand. "I'll take you to him," she said, and Gabriel followed more than willingly. The back room was quiet; hopefully, he could spend an undisturbed night there, even if it meant spending it with Pepino.

"I'M COLD," Pepino whispered for the umpteenth time. Gabriel considered the possibility of killing him just to get a little sleep; instead, he finally got up and sat next to the boy on the thin, threadbare mattress. Pepino was pitifully scrawny and shaking like a stalk of grass in a storm. "Cold, cold, cold," he murmured.

Helplessly, Gabriel put his hand on Pepino's shoulder. He couldn't remember how often the boy had tried to give up heroin nor how many times he had sat next to him, trying to calm him down. "Come on, man, just sleep a bit," Gabriel said. It was way past midnight; from experience, he knew that neither of them would close an eye tonight.

"If only I could," Pepino rasped. "See, if only I could sleep, I could see this through. I know I could. I just need to close my eyes and rest. Can't you help me? Please?"

For some reason, the pleading voice pierced right through Gabriel's defenses, something that had never happened before. He wasn't usually concerned about anyone else's well-being. He mainly tried to survive as best he could without hurting others. Tonight was different, however.

Gabriel hesitated only a moment. "I want you to lie still, hear me? I'm going to tell you something I haven't told Billy and Marita, so you better listen, and you better not say a word about it tomorrow." Well, Pepino most likely wouldn't be able to remember his own name in the morning, so Gabriel hoped his secrets were safe with the boy.

"Sure, man," Pepino said, and he obediently stretched out.

"I met someone," Gabriel began, knowing it sounded wrong. "Not what you think, not someone to fuck. He's different; don't ask me how. On Christmas Eve, when I was supposed to catch this woman and her lover for Mallfrick, he jumped out of a third-floor window, floated gently to the ground, and told me it was because of a rune."

No comment from Pepino. He just listened, kneading his hands as if they were dough, and didn't say a word.

Gabriel smiled. Pepino was only seventeen, and in some ways, he was even younger than that. Obviously, he loved a good story enough to calm down a bit.

"I went home with him. Tennant, his name is. A doctor, don't ask me what kind. He can cook, and he gave me clothes and a bed to sleep in. And he told me about runes."

Slowly, Pepino folded his hands over his chest. Was it Gabriel's imagination, or did the boy's breathing deepen?

Gabriel leaned back, rested his head against the wall, and closed his eyes. "Runes," he whispered. "They are amazing. Powerful. Before I left the restaurant—I was dining at La Laterna Magica earlier on, can you believe it?—he drew a rune on my camera with a permanent marker, and now it cannot be stolen, lost, or destroyed. I tried it. Well, he forced me to try it. Told me to smash it to the ground, and when I refused, he did it. It fell, and I saw it shatter into a thousand pieces, only it didn't. And then he stepped on it, jumped on it, and still nothing happened. He even threw it away, right out into the night, but when I looked, it was safely in my knapsack. See? Here it is, the one thing that belongs to me, the one thing that earns me honest money."

With big, half-mad eyes, Pepino stared at him. Gabriel hardly noticed, though. "I can draw runes," he mused, not in the shabby little room anymore, but elsewhere, somewhere clean and safe. "Tried it the first night, and it worked. Used the wrong rune, of course. The Protection rune is strong, far too strong for me. But I used it, at least for a fleeting moment. After that, I drew Tickling runes, Tracking runes, once a Forgetting rune. Even a Floating rune, but I didn't try it out to see if it worked. That would have happened today, but we ended up leaving the apartment through the door rather than the window. Pity."

Suddenly, a thought struck him. "Pepino," Gabriel whispered. "Do you want to sleep?"

Pepino just nodded, a pathetically small, hopeful nod.

"So sleep then," Gabriel said, taking the boy's hand and carefully unbending the cramped fingers. Pepino's palm was sweaty and dirty, but it didn't matter. With the tip of his finger, Gabriel drew a pattern about half an inch above the skin, a pattern not overly complicated and well practiced in the past weeks.

In the darkness of the room, the slight glow was impossible to overlook; a pale, silvery glow, like moonlight, rose above Pepino's palm, growing stronger with each line Gabriel added.

"Cool," Pepino said hoarsely, and then his head dropped to the side. A moment later, he began to snore.

"And it works," Gabriel added.

He didn't sleep at all that night.

THE next morning before anyone else was awake, Gabriel left the mission, stepping over sleeping bodies and feeling as though someone had used him as a punching bag. It wasn't just the night without sleep; somehow, the drawing of the rune must have weakened him. However, he needed to see Mallfrick before his boss decided someone else would serve him better.

As expected, Mallfrick was in a lousy mood. When he saw Gabriel's face, he grabbed his mug and threw it at the young man, shouting, "Where have you been, you useless idiot? I've been waiting for those pictures! Where are they? You better have them!"

He looks like a fat cockroach, Gabriel thought, smirking. "Hi, Luis," he said. "Nah, I don't have any pictures. They went shopping the day before Christmas Eve, but nothing worth putting on film. Not even a peck on her cheek. I nearly froze my feet off waiting in front of her apartment, but I didn't see her, and I didn't see him."

"Fuck off, then," Mallfrick roared, this time throwing a folder in Gabriel's direction. "I don't pay you for nothing. No pictures, no cash."

Had he really once been afraid of this man? Gabriel couldn't believe it, seeing him sitting in his oversized chair, out of breath simply from swearing. "Lorelei Kinney's gone missing," he said, for the first time unimpressed by his boss's shouting. "There won't be any pictures of her anytime soon, I'd say." Casually, he dropped into the spare chair, stretching his legs. "So. How about another job?"

Just seeing Mallfrick's jaw drop open was worth a fortune.

"Since when have you got balls, boy?" the fat man finally said. "Another job, after you messed up that one? You think I'm nuts?"

Briefly, Gabriel thought of putting his boots up on Mallfrick's desk, but that would have been too much. He didn't have a clue where his attitude came from, he just knew that after last night, after having used the rune, something had changed. He wasn't a coward, but he had never thought it worth the trouble to stand up for his rights—too much effort, too much hassle. Seeing Pepino still sound asleep this morning must have triggered it.

Gabriel picked up his knapsack and walked toward the door. "Another job, or I walk out of here for good," he challenged, realizing that he meant it. Working for Mallfrick was horrible at best, often boring, sometimes dangerous. In addition, the cash was forgettable. Leaving was one of the best ideas he'd had in a long time.

Some of his thoughts must have shown in his face, as Mallfrick shoved his body out of the chair, reached for a high shelf, and pulled out a thick folder. "Caramel," he snapped. "The singer—the band, the one playing those noisy songs?"

Doorknob already in his hand, Gabriel turned around. "What about him? He's famous, he's not married, he's a known cocaine user. No more secrets left, I'd say. Who wants a picture of him doing what?"

Mallfrick giggled, a sound that made Gabriel cringe. "Caramel is on the way to the top, boy," he explained. "His competitor, Conga Joe, is jealous and wants something that will break the man. You know how that Caramel fellow's always singing about all the girls he's had and how hot he is for pussy? Well, Conga Joe says Caramel is gay. So go and get me a picture of him snogging a man. Or a boy. Or a goat, for that matter. Anyone, any*thing*, as long as it's male. *Comprende?*"

"Sure," Gabriel said. "Whatever, as long as you pay me in advance. You owe me anyway, Mallfrick."

"Go and tell Monique I said to pay you," the fat man hissed. "Just get out of here now. Can't stand the sight of you any longer."

CARAMEL, rising star on the pop music scene, was easy to find but impossible to get close to. He was surrounded by friends, his manager, groupies, and who knew who else. Living as he did in one of the most expensive hotels in the city, it was impossible to catch him doing anything private—like snogging whomever, no matter if they were male or not.

At least, getting close enough would have been impossible for any ordinary person. Gabriel, on the other hand....

Gabriel walked into the lobby and straight toward the staircase without anyone noticing him. Not that the lobby was empty—it was quite the opposite. But for some reason, no one so much as looked in the young man's direction, despite the fact that he was clearly neither a guest nor a groupie. He'd left his knapsack back at the shelter, knowing that Billy was there to watch and protect it; he'd taken only his camera, as it was the only tool he would need today.

His grandmother had once called him a predator. Gabriel could only guess that as a predator, it was second nature to make himself undetectable when necessary. No one could see him if he didn't want them to, and even then, most people forgot a moment later that he'd been there.

Watching the people lounging in the lobby, Gabriel chose the very moment they were looking in another direction, distracted, or when he could get along unnoticed by curious eyes. It was easy, really, if one knew how to do it. Whenever he was out taking photographic evidence of people cheating on their loved ones, he used his inherited skill, not thinking about it twice.

He hid in a small room stuffed with brooms, vacuum cleaners, buckets, and rags on the third floor. It smelled heavily of cleaning supplies, but the good thing was that the door to Caramel's apartment was right around the corner. He only needed to wait.

CARAMEL, a tall, milk chocolate-colored young man with a goatee and Rasta locks, sneaked out of his suite shortly before lunchtime without anyone following him for once. He went upstairs, and Gabriel followed him, absolutely sure he wouldn't be detected. Caramel was in a hurry, and although he looked over his shoulder once or twice, he didn't pay his surroundings much attention. When he reached a door at the end of the corridor, he knocked, the door opened, and there it was, the required kiss. Just like that.

Gabriel grabbed his camera harder than necessary and forced his arms to bring it to eye level. The couple was clearly visible. Caramel's hand rested on the other man's bottom, and they kissed as if there were no tomorrow. The corridor lamps provided enough light to get a decent picture, and now Caramel's lover—about the same age, but taller and of a heavier build—moved, pushed the singer backward until he was against the wall, and trailed kisses from mouth to throat. The singer's eyes were closed; both men were oblivious to the world and to the fact that another door could open at any moment and their secret would be revealed.

Maybe they want to get caught so the lies can stop, Gabriel thought, and he made a decision. He lowered his camera and took a step out of his hiding place. Determined, he walked over to the man who was so seriously snogging Caramel and tapped him on the shoulder. "Hey, you," he said, and the man jumped, his eyes wide with shock.

Showing his empty hands, Gabriel smiled in a most harmless way. "You two should get inside," he suggested. "I was sent to take pictures—there are rumors that you're gay, Caramel, and your rival wants to see you broken to pieces for singing all those songs about girls with big tits while in reality you like to sleep with men. Even if you want to come out of the closet—don't let it happen like this, man. Just a warning." With that, he turned and left, not looking back, feeling the weight of his camera reassuringly heavy in his pocket.

Outside, Gabriel had to take a few deep breaths to calm down. He hadn't planned to do that; all he had wanted was taking the sodding pictures, deliver them, and go back to the mission. For once, he'd made the right decision. Now the only question was how he was going to break the news to Mallfrick.

And then? Stay at the mission? Continue working for Mallfrick?

Forget Tennant?

"No way," Gabriel said aloud to a lamppost. "Mallfrick can get his damn pictures elsewhere. I want to learn more about runes, I don't want to sleep on the street ever again, and if I have to beg Tennant to take me in, I will. Shit. I hate begging. Although—he won't make me beg. I don't think."

The dubious look he got from a passer-by was enough to shut him up. All that was left to do was pick up his blanket and knapsack from the shelter. He would say goodbye to Marita and Billy and even Pepino, if the boy wasn't back on the drugs already.

BILLY looked at him strangely. "You're going to quit? You're leaving Mallfrick?" he asked, raking his hands through his blond spikes. "Man, are you out of your mind?" Dumbstruck, Billy sat down.

The mission was half empty; it was only because of the lingering cold that Billy was in at all. Usually, he left early, wandering the streets, begging for some cash, and picking up anyone who needed shelter.

Marita didn't say anything at all.

"I can't work for Mallfrick any longer," Gabriel tried to explain. "The job he gave me today was really, really bad. I was there; I could have taken the pictures. I decided I don't want to have anything to do with his dirty work any longer. I'll find something else, or at least—"

"You were the only one of us who actually had a job," Billy said weakly, something that made Gabriel very uneasy. Billy never sounded weak. Never, ever.

To get rid of the uncomfortable, stretching silence, Gabriel pulled out the money he had got from Mallfrick's secretary a few short hours ago. "Here," he said, his voice harder than he'd intended. "Marita, get yourself another skirt. A warm one—I've got a feeling this winter is far from over. Billy, go and celebrate with a nice, big burger and fries and everything else you like. I'll be gone for a while. Wanted to tell you last night, but Pepino sort of got in the way. Don't worry if you don't see me for a couple of months."

Getting up, he grabbed his knapsack and was about to leave when Billy snatched his wrist, holding him back. "Has this got anything to do with Pepino feeling better today?" he asked, nodding toward a table at the back of the room. "He said he slept like a newborn baby and that someone told him a bedtime story. Couldn't remember who it was, mind, but he's eaten, Gabe! Have you ever seen Pepino eat anything here?"

Hesitantly, Gabriel took a step toward the lone boy sitting at the corner table. True, he *was* eating—porridge, by the looks of it. That couldn't be Pepino. After years on the streets, using drugs, and being abused by anyone who was willing to pay—and sometimes even by someone who wasn't—Pepino's body was destroyed, his stomach included.

"He just fell asleep," Gabriel said helplessly. "Like a child. I told him some nonsense about fae and werewolves and runes and such. This is impossible!"

Silently, Billy stepped up behind him and said, "Yeah. Impossible. So I wonder what you did to him besides telling him stories. And I wonder what will happen to him once you and your... *skills* are gone."

For a heartbeat, Gabriel considered staying. Not going back to Tennant, not quitting his job with Mallfrick—staying here at the mission, using the Sleeping rune on Pepino, and trying to forget that there was more out there, much more, to learn and to see.

And trying to forget Tennant.

Impossible.

Without a word, Gabriel walked out of the mission.

THERE was only one more thing to do, and that was to go to Mallfrick and tell him in person that he wouldn't do his dirty work anymore. Presumably, the cockroach would demand his money back, but even if Gabriel hadn't handed it to Billy and Marita, he wouldn't have given it back. He'd earned that money with previous jobs, and Mallfrick was richer than most people thought anyway.

Deep in thought, Gabriel wandered through the streets toward the private investigator's office. It was past lunchtime, and he hoped he wouldn't have to wait too long for Mallfrick—the man loved to go for long lunch breaks, and Gabriel had no intention of bothering him while he was eating. He'd done that once—a very bad idea, as Mallfrick had the waiters throw him out of the restaurant the moment he walked in. He wouldn't do that again. No, he'd just go to the office and wait.

And what was that smell, anyway?

Concerned, Gabriel stopped on the way up to Mallfrick's office. The stench in the air was unusual for the building, although it was located next to a Chinese fast food restaurant. This wasn't the fragrance of garlic or coriander, nor did it smell of alcohol or fish sauce. It was a stronger smell, not entirely unpleasant, but unusual nevertheless.

Hadn't he smelled something similar not too long ago? But this was different. This here hit him right in the gut, and Gabriel wanted to growl and hunt as much as he wanted to flee.

Unable to keep an alarmed frown off his face, Gabriel went upstairs to the second floor. The first door belonged to a lawyer; the rooms to the left were empty. Mallfrick's office was the one to the right, hidden behind a solid wood door.

A door that stood slightly ajar, intensifying Gabriel's worries. Mallfrick was paranoid when it came to his door—it was always kept closed, it was always locked when no one was inside, even if the secretary went down the hall to the restroom, and the entire time Gabriel had worked for the man, he had never, ever seen it ajar without someone holding down the handle, either entering or leaving the office. Doors and shutters closed was Mallfrick's credo. Seeing it ignored was worrisome at best.

Maybe, as Mallfrick was out for lunch, Monique had been a bit lazy and left the office without closing it and locking up?

Unlikely. She was nearly as bad as her boss, a harpy in human form, and she was proud to always act according to her boss's wishes. She wouldn't have gone anywhere without locking up.

Hesitantly, Gabriel pushed the door open with the tip of his finger. Immediately, the smell became stronger—coppery, sweet, and slightly moldy as well. Involuntarily, Gabriel turned his head and clenched his teeth, barely able to keep his stomach under control. He even had to press a hand to his mouth and nose. Yup, he made up his mind—the smell was rotten, horrible, and not the least bit pleasant. For some reason, it reminded him of graveyards and tombstones.

"Mallfrick? Hey, Luis, are you in? Monique? Anyone here?"

The light was strange too. Mallfrick liked his office to be bright as long as the brightness wasn't cast by the sun, and the lamps were on continuously, casting their clear, white glow onto the carpets and the furniture.

Today, though, the drapes were open, and the light wasn't white, it was orange.

"What the hell is going on here?" Gabriel muttered, taking a step into the office's anteroom, domicile of Monique the harpy. As anticipated, it was empty, the chair neatly pushed close to the table. The computer was switched off—clearly, the secretary was out for lunch.

The lamps, as well as all the windows, were smeared with a sticky, orange liquid. Every so often, thick blotches trailed tracks toward the windowsill, pooled up, and hit the carpet. Gabriel had just enough time to think, *This liquid is causing the stench,* and *That's some strange sort of blood,* when something—someone—brushed his shoulder.

Freaked out, he jumped, bumped against the table, cursed nastily, and then finally turned around to see who was there or what had scared the life out of him. After all, the anteroom wasn't that big, so it was unlikely that someone had hidden behind the door. Gradually, Gabriel's eyes grew bigger, wandering upward to the ceiling, where a fan silently rotated in slow motion. It was an old-fashioned thing, beautiful in its simplicity. Often, Gabriel had welcomed the cool breeze—in the summertime, that was. But it was winter now, and he knew that Mallfrick hated the cold. The ceiling fan wasn't used in wintertime.

It usually wasn't used to hang people from its blades, either. Bits of people. An arm here, some flesh there, clothes and a shoe hanging from its laces. And a head—a big, ugly head that had once belonged to a fat cockroach named Luis Mallfrick.

It really is blood, then, Gabriel thought, staggering backward. *The stuff on the windows is blood, and Mallfrick is dead, and that surely was not suicide—and I thought it smelled interesting? Fucking werewolf genes!*

His stomach protested, although it was empty; he would have thrown up in the middle of dead Mallfrick's office if not for a hand grabbing his wrist, pulling him from the soiled, horrific room out into the corridor.

"Tell me you didn't kill him, Gabriel," a familiar voice said, pulling him farther away, toward the stairs. "Tell me you aren't a murderer."

CHAPTER FIVE

SHAKING and feeling sick to his bones, Gabriel just stared at Tennant, unable to comprehend where the man had come from and at a loss as to why he was even here in the first place. It was taking quite a bit of effort not to throw up, so he didn't fight when the doctor took his wrist in a hard grip and painted a rune on his palm. A stinging sensation shot through him from his hand up to his shoulder. Gabriel gasped as the rune flared up in a pale orange. "A Truth rune," he stated, not really surprised. "Go ahead then, Doc. Ask what you need to ask."

Tennant looked at him, surprise clearly written on his face for the briefest moment. Not letting go of Gabriel's wrist, he urged, "Did you kill the man in there? Did you have anything to do with his death, either directly or indirectly?"

Gabriel stared at the rune, then into Tennant's eyes. "No," he whispered. "I didn't kill him. I don't know who did. I wanted—"

At that moment, the rune flared up, turned an angry red, and vanished with a small *pop*. Gabriel flinched, expecting pain, but there wasn't any, and there was no mark on his skin, either.

Tennant let go of him. "Glad to have that out of the way," he said. "Useful thing, the Truth rune. I didn't think you'd done it, but I needed to be sure." He checked the corridor. It was deserted, which was good, as being seen standing only a few feet away from a murdered man would have caused all sorts of problems with the police.

The door to Mallfrick's office still stood ajar. With weak knees, Gabriel took a step toward it—and hesitated. "What would have happened if I had lied?" he asked, simply because anything was easier to face than what lay behind that door.

Tennant was right beside him. "The rune would have burned itself into your skin, marking you a liar," he explained curtly. "Can I have your camera for a moment? I need to take a few pictures. Of course it is necessary for us to leave this place as soon as possible, but I think the pictures will help in solving this case. Eventually, that is. The camera, Gabriel? It's the wrong time for daydreaming, you know." Without waiting for a response, he rummaged through Gabriel's knapsack until he found the camera and resolutely went back into Mallfrick's office.

"Goodness," Gabriel heard him mutter. "What a mess. Should have worn my old boots. Should have stayed at home, come to think of it."

Gabriel listened, leaning against the wall outside the office and scanning the corridor, the staircase, and the elevator in case someone approached. Before his inner eye, though, he could see an arm... a foot... and Mallfrick's face, or what was left of it.

"What are you doing here, Doc?" he called out to take his mind off of the horrible memories, more than a little glad that Tennant hadn't asked for his assistance.

"Got a call," Tennant called back. Gabriel heard the small clicking sounds of the camera. "Someone gave me this address, said I needed to get here immediately"—click—"and as I just can't resist a riddle, I jumped into the car and came here. Arrived a few minutes before you did. Didn't see who did it, though. When I heard steps, I hid in the empty office over there. Luckily it was just you, not the murderer." Slightly pale, he closed the door behind him, handing the camera back to Gabriel. "Shall I take you back to the mission?"

Gabriel shook his head. "I wanted to tell Mallfrick that I quit. Haven't decided yet what I'm going to do, but I think the mission is the last place I want to be right now."

Like thieves, they tiptoed down the stairs, out of the building, and across the street before Gabriel began to shake violently. That smell—that horrible smell—was in his nose again, swamping his brain, and paralyzing his tongue. He felt the blood drain from his face, and his legs suddenly seemed to belong to someone else. There were no more colors; sound was muffled and flat. From far away, he heard a voice speaking words, but they didn't make sense, nor did he know whose voice it was.

Arms around his shoulders, around his waist. Warmth in his face. Then, from out of nowhere, a sharp, unpleasant smell under his nose.

He blinked, and the colors came back.

"Gabriel?"

That was Tennant, saying his name. And there was that smell again, only this time it was accompanied by a taste—equally sharp, equally unpleasant, burning on his lips. Gabriel coughed, swallowed, and felt heat explode in his stomach. Whisky. He hated whisky.

"What?" he finally managed.

"That was your first time seeing a murder victim, wasn't it?" Tennant asked, putting the half-empty glass on the table of what Gabriel figured was the Chinese restaurant. "We were barely out of the building when you began to stagger. I just managed to get you in here and force some alcohol inside you, or you would have fainted."

"Shit," Gabriel replied weakly. "Double shit. I never faint."

Still, his hands were shaking, and his legs—well, he was glad he didn't have to stand on them right now. Leaning back, he said, "I can still smell the blood. I can still see his head hanging from—" Then he jumped up, rushed toward the small restroom in the back, and finally threw up.

IN THE end, they stayed in the small restaurant, watching the building across the street as the police cars rushed in and the officers stormed upstairs. They observed the arrival of the ambulance and eventually, the coroner's truck, and sometime in between, Tennant ordered a bowl of plain rice and some tea for Gabriel.

"Eat," he said. "That was a nasty shock, and I can see that you haven't eaten this morning. You're too pale; you need sustenance. Drink the tea first—it's sweetened, and the sugar will help erase the dizziness. Hopefully, that is. I was right, wasn't I?"

Gabriel took a sip of the tea, then nodded. "I've seen a lot since I began living on the streets. Enough blood and dirt for a lifetime. A few deaths too. Someone I knew was killed in a car crash, someone else overdosed. Many of the girls come to the mission bleeding, beaten up by their pimps or by someone who didn't like their face. A murder victim is different."

The spoonful of rice somehow didn't want to go into his mouth, but he forced the food down anyway. Strangely enough, he felt better after he'd eaten a bit.

"There's blood on your shoes, Doc," he pointed out when he was finished. "On the soles. I can smell it."

Tennant raised an eyebrow, an already familiar gesture and one Gabriel considered reassuringly predictable. "Is there? Good, because I didn't have time to take a sample. I want to put it under the microscope once we're home. You are coming home with me, aren't you?"

Was that hope in the doctor's voice? Gabriel smiled. "Definitely. Told everyone I wouldn't be back for a while. They knew—everyone knew—how much I disliked Mallfrick, and today, I sort of blackmailed him into paying his debts for old jobs. The cops will be after me. I mean, if you'd rather not have me in your house, I'd totally understand," he said, hearing hope once more—but in his own voice.

"May I see your ID, please?" a cop asked suddenly, rudely interrupting their conversation. "There was a murder in the building across the street, and we're checking the surrounding shops and restaurants in case someone saw anything. Your driver's license or something similar, sir."

Gabriel paled again, but for different reasons. Since the portals had been discovered, everyone was required to have an ID and carry it too. To obtain an ID, one needed to give a blood sample—proof that there was no centaur or anything similar amongst one's ancestors. Gabriel, who had never lived anywhere long enough to get an ID and was hiding from the government for obvious reasons, didn't own as much as a library card with his name. Unfortunately, being unable to provide identification on demand was about as suspicious nowadays as walking around with hooves and a tail. He would end up in prison within the hour, especially if the cops discovered his working relationship with the murder victim.

While those thoughts were shooting through Gabriel's head, Tennant placed his driver's license on the table, or at least something that for a split second looked like a driver's license. In reality, Gabriel realized, it was just another business card.

"I'm Kevin Glicks," Tennant said smoothly, "and this is my business partner, James Ivory." Flashing Gabriel a warning glare, he continued, "James, hand the man your ID. I'm sure he has more important things to do than chat with curious citizens."

Gabriel shook his head once, hoping the cop hadn't seen it. With all his might, he tried to signal Tennant that he didn't have a damn passport, but the doctor didn't seem to understand. "James. In your jacket, for Christ's sake. Honestly, occasionally I wonder why I put up with you."

The officer turned to Gabriel, Tennant's so-called driver's license in his left hand and his right resting on the gun in his holster.

Gabriel shuddered. Having no other choice but to go along with the show, he reached inside his coat, the one Tennant had given him. Inside was nothing. Of course not.

"The inner pocket," Tennant said impatiently, and there was something—a thin card, easy to overlook. Not an ID. It seemed to be—

Gabriel pulled it out and handed it to the cop. He saw that it was a paper menu from La Laterna Magica. Tennant must have put it in his pocket during one of his previous visits. Gabriel clenched his teeth in desperation. He very nearly snatched the menu back, but it was too late.

The cop took it and examined it closely. A moment later, the officer handed back the menu and Tennant's so-called driver's license too.

"Thank you, sirs," he said. "Have a nice day." Without another word, the police officer turned and left the restaurant. Apparently, he didn't consider it strange at all that Gabriel had handed him a piece of paper with the opening hours and main dishes of a posh restaurant.

Gabriel shook his head. "Runes again?" he asked quietly.

"Runes again," Tennant confirmed. "He believes what I have told him. He thinks he just checked our ID, but it will only last for a short time. In about twenty minutes, he will begin to wonder about my driver's license and your passport, and he will remember that something was odd. We should leave."

"Fine with me," Gabriel said wholeheartedly. "Anything, as long as we get some distance between us and that building. Besides, the smell of blood on your shoes is disturbing. Let's go home."

Tennant cast him one of his rare smiles. "Home. Good decision."

HOME, Gabriel thought as he stepped inside the quiet house just ahead of Tennant. *I shouldn't think of this house as home. It isn't, and it never will be.*

Still, it was good to be back. The living room was cool, and while Gabriel stood, slightly lost, in the middle of it, Tennant took off his coat, knelt down, and lit the logs in the fireplace.

Hesitantly, Gabriel picked up the book that lay on the small table next to the big chair he'd sat in the first night. Surprise, surprise—a book about runes. One he hadn't read yet but wanted to lose himself in very much.

He'd been gone for two short days and he missed reading? How stupid was that? Missing the bed, the food, the warmth, or even the man would have made sense, but not missing the books. Books only brought trouble. They made people wish for things they couldn't have, hope for false truths, long for hidden worlds that they would never be able to visit, given the fact that opening a portal to any hidden world was illegal.

In his case, the books made him believe he could one day master the runes just like Tennant had, although it was obvious that it would take years, if not decades, to learn and understand them. He didn't have decades; he didn't even have months, and he knew it. Soon enough, Tennant would tire of sharing his house with him. That always happened as soon as Gabriel took a liking to someone. After all, Gabriel was not entirely human, and thus he was worth less than the dirt on the street. That was how his mother had seen it. Tennant wouldn't be any different.

"Tainted blood," Gabriel murmured, and he put the book back onto the table. "Don't forget it."

"Forget what?" Tennant asked from his position on the floor, where he was blowing life into tiny flames in the fireplace. He looked at the book Gabriel had just put down. "Not what you've learned so far, I hope. I am positively flabbergasted at how far you've come and how much you've learned in such a short time. You knew I was using a Truth rune on you; do you know how hard it is to recognize a rune someone else is drawing? Let me tell you, it is nearly impossible, especially when the drawer knows what he's doing and draws the rune quickly, like I did. It seems that the skill runs in your blood, Gabriel. It will not take long before you can read the big volumes."

Getting up, he wiped his hands clean on his trousers; he'd taken off his shoes outside, and for the first time since Gabriel had stormed out of Mallfrick's office, there was no trace of that sickening, sweet, strange blood-smell. Something about that smell had definitely been odd.

"Didn't smell like blood," Gabriel mused, thinking more clearly now that he was safe. "Didn't look like blood, either. It was orange. It didn't smell like human blood. Would have recognized it."

Tennant looked at him expectantly. "What is your conclusion, then?"

Gabriel frowned. "I think Mallfrick was from a hidden world. I think he was less human than I am."

BENT over a microscope, Tennant observed the blood he'd scraped off his shoes. "Come and take a look," he finally said.

Gabriel, having waited patiently, stepped up to the table and had no clue what to do. In theory, he should have learned about biology, blood types, and the differences between the races in school, but he hadn't attended school on a regular basis. At age six, he'd gone to foster parents for the first time. Claire and Elroy had sent him to school, they had fed and clothed him, and then they had locked him up after he'd run away for the first time. Claire had tried to teach him at home, but to no avail. He had just tried to run away again. There had been no more school after that—they had sent him back to the orphanage.

The pattern had remained the same throughout the rest of his childhood. Orphanage, foster parents, several attempts to run away, and back to the orphanage. School, learning, and education in general had never been that important. He supposed he should be glad he had at least learned how to read and write. Pepino, for example, couldn't even scribble his own name.

A microscope, though, was something he'd only seen on TV. He had seen Tennant using it before without really understanding what it did and why. To him, it looked dangerous.

Apparently, his feelings showed clearly on his face, as the doctor pushed him down on the stool and said, "Just take a look. A microscope enlarges things, in this case the victim's blood. Instead of a drop of blood, you will be able to see what the blood is made of—the cells—and if you are right, the cells will look different from human cells. Here, let me change the sample. Right. That's human blood. Tell me—what do you see?"

With a few moves, he had changed the tiny piece of glass that held Mallfrick's blood for the other, and Gabriel finally dared to look through the eyepiece. Irritated, he blinked once, and then he grinned.

"They look like sour drops—you know, those candies?—only with a dent in the middle," he said. "There are lots of them, hundreds. How much blood did you take?"

"A prick with the needle into one's finger and you get what you see," Tennant said. "Now look at this sample—that's your blood."

Again, Gabriel looked, but this time, there weren't drops, and the color wasn't the bright red he had just seen moments ago. Instead, his blood seemed to be paler in general, and the cells were elliptical, not round. In the middle, there was no dent, and the edges appeared frayed. Each cell was neatly divided in half by a faint, dark line.

"It's the line that confuses me," Tennant said as if he had read Gabriel's thoughts. "The form and color is vaguely *Homo Canis lupus*, and at first I thought the line was an error in the sample. It isn't— there's another race mixed into your blood besides shapeshifter. I just haven't figured out which one. Anyway"—he changed the sample once more—"that's Mallfrick's blood. What do you think?"

"I think he wasn't human, and I'm speaking out of experience," Gabriel grumbled, but he bent to look once more. These cells were different from both samples he'd checked so far. "He's neither human, nor wolf, nor whatever it is that makes my blood strange."

"Correct." Gabriel could hear the smile in Tennant's voice and was ridiculously proud. "Now how do the cells look?"

"They are white, they are flat, and they look dead," Gabriel shortly summed up what he saw. "That, in combination with what I know of Mallfrick—he never left the building during daylight, he was fat as a pig, but I never saw him eat, and he always had the drapes closed—leaves one conclusion: he was a vampire." Satisfied, he leaned back and nearly fell off the stool—it didn't have a backrest.

Tennant reacted fast by catching him, putting one hand on his shoulder, the other at the small of his back. An unimportant gesture, friendly and meaningless. Quickly, Gabriel stood and moved away, ostensibly to make way for the doctor, who sat back down on the stool. Tennant looked through the eyepiece.

"Vampire indeed," Tennant said. "You are good. Really good. Took me an hour to figure that one out!"

"Well, you didn't know the man, or you would've guessed immediately," Gabriel said absently.

Suddenly, he found himself struggling with a flood of emotions he hadn't expected washing through him. There was longing—that was the most prominent—accompanied by the desire to touch the narrow strip of skin showing just above the doctor's collar. A few unruly black locks were in the way, but that bit of neck looked so soft—and warm too.

How would it taste? Gabriel wondered. *How would it feel to press my lips against Tennant's skin, taste his unique fragrance, feel his pulse beneath my fingertips?*

Gabriel blushed at his thoughts but couldn't help dwelling on the image a little longer. What would it be like to take off Tennant's shirt, reveal his chest and abdomen, see his muscles, hear his heartbeat?

Maybe he could even go lower, open the belt, take off those expensive trousers that hid Tennant's legs and ass, and—

Shocked, Gabriel shook his head, even dug his nails deep into his arm to clear his mind. *Where did that come from?* he wondered, staring at Tennant's hands holding a vial. *I don't desire him. I cannot desire him—he's a friend!*

Gabriel quickly dismissed the lustful rush that had just shot through him as the result of the fact that he hadn't had a decent lay for more months than he could remember. It was an easy explanation. Harmless. He didn't desire the man, not at all!

In his experience, desire, true desire, only caused problems. A quick fuck here and there didn't do any harm, but what he had felt just a moment ago had been more. True desire was dangerous, as it led people to make poor decisions and rash commitments. Sometimes— more often than not, actually—desire even turned people into liars. Or worse, into stammering idiots. Gabriel had never desired anyone enough to forget his own interests or his own safety, and he was proud of it.

Until now, and the object of his desire was not only a man he had known for just a few short weeks, it was someone he liked too.

Slowly, Gabriel loosened his grip on his arm and, swallowing hard, made a decision born out of desperation: he wouldn't think of Tennant in this way ever again. He wouldn't dwell on thoughts about what the other man might taste like or what it would be like to have that fair skin beneath his fingertips or those lips beneath his own. If he didn't put these thoughts out of his mind, it would most likely cost him the doctor's friendship as well as shelter and being able to eat on a regular basis. He wouldn't risk it.

"So... a vampire, then?" Gabriel asked, glad that his voice sounded completely normal. "Should have known, the way he sucked money out of people. Question is, why was he killed, and how?"

Tennant turned toward him. "What do you mean, how? The usual way, I should say: with something large and sharp."

Glad that the topic was making his stomach roil again, thus taking his mind off his cock, Gabriel shook his head. "That wasn't what I meant. How did the murderer get into the office? There weren't any tracks on the ground, and besides, you need an appointment for that door to be opened. A vouched-for appointment, that is. He wouldn't let in anyone he didn't know or who hadn't been recommended by someone he knew."

"I have taken enough pictures to check this out," Tennant interrupted him. "Give me the card, we'll have a look."

How odd it was to be part of a "we," Gabriel noted, watching Tennant open his laptop and put the card into the slot. Immediately, the hot knot in Gabriel's stomach returned, and he gulped, trying to brace himself for the sight of blood and pieces and—

Windows. The first picture was of a window in Mallfrick's office. Splattered with blood, true, but at least there were no severed body parts to be seen.

"Thank goodness," Gabriel sighed, pulling a chair close and sitting down.

"Don't want you to faint again," Tennant remarked matter-of-factly. "Now then. What do we have here?" He leaned closer until his nose nearly touched the screen. "Is that... yes. Definitely. See it? I know how the killer got in and out. You too?" Steepling his fingers on the table, he waited patiently until Gabriel examined the picture more closely.

The window, the blood, the door, and part of Monique's desk could be seen—and wasn't that a shadow on the floor? A shadow. But what was casting it? It looked odd, misshapen... ah. Damn. That was Mallfrick's shadow, or what was left of it anyway. Obviously, the ceiling fan was just outside the picture frame. Shouldn't there be tracks?

"There aren't any tracks on the ground. Whoever slaughtered Mallfrick would have stepped in the blood," Gabriel said slowly, not entirely sure where he was heading with this. "No tracks means... hmmm. The murderer must have been covered in blood. Mallfrick hadn't been dead long when I came in—ten minutes at the most. His blood hadn't even dried yet. There should be tracks, but there aren't, which means the murderer neither entered nor left through the door."

Tennant smiled. "So you think he—or she—used—" He didn't finish the sentence.

Something in Gabriel's head clicked. "A portal! The murderer used a portal, and that means—"

"It means that whoever killed Mallfrick most likely wasn't human, either," Tennant said. "Very few humans know enough about runes, let alone have the ability to feed them with power, so only a select few can use portals. It might have been another vampire. Maybe it was a family feud, or maybe Mallfrick drank from the wrong person?"

"Could be," Gabriel said doubtfully. "But then, have you considered how Lorelei fits into the picture? I mean, what if the two cases are related? She was a mermaid, Mallfrick a vampire; she's gone missing, he's dead. There was blood in her apartment and blood in his office. Sounds suspicious to me."

Instead of further discussing the topic, Tennant slipped off the stool, went into the kitchen, and began to chop garlic and onions with a knife sharp enough to chop fingers too. "I hope you are hungry," he added when Gabriel followed him. "Cooking clears my mind. I'm afraid this will be a three-course problem at least."

Gabriel stepped to the counter, took a tomato, an egg, and a bottle of vinegar, and began juggling. "Three courses are fine for me. Father Barley's mission feeds you, but the food is—well, let's just say it's edible at best. I could do with a meal or two, especially since my stomach is quite empty."

The tomato nearly crashed into the egg. Unimpressed, Gabriel added a pear into the mix, well aware that Tennant was watching him. He didn't show off often. Impressing the doctor, even with such a small and useless trick, brought a smile to his face.

Tennant flicked his knife and held it out to Gabriel. "Can you do that with something sharp too?" he asked casually.

Unable to resist a challenge, Gabriel set his toys on the counter and took the knife, weighing it carefully. "Nicely balanced," he said, then sent it high up into the air and caught the handle neatly with his other hand. "Don't know about juggling with it, though."

Tentatively, he let the knife perform a loop, caught it safely again, and picked up the pear. He'd never tried this trick with something that could easily cut off his fingers, but he had to admit, trying it was exhilarating. "Tell you what, Doc—you cook, and I will master juggling with the knife before dinner is served." The knife passed the pear in the air. Gabriel couldn't help feeling a certain pride that it hadn't even touched the fruit.

"Marvelous," Tennant said. "I think you should train at throwing knives as well. It's a good thing to be able to defend yourself and the ones you are fond of."

The knife clattered to the floor, and the pear landed right next to it, smashing into a mushy mess. Blushing fiercely, Gabriel quickly cleaned up the mess, glad he had a reason to hide his burning face. Tennant's words had been far too close to the truth, something he didn't want to reveal to the other man.

I am fond of you, Gabriel thought bitterly. *And you are in love with Lorelei. Great. Totally fucking great.*

IT WAS past nine when Gabriel thought of a way to find out what happened to Lorelei, and only because his headache had come back with a vengeance. "Wright must've hit me harder than I thought," he groaned, running his fingers over his scalp in order to find the bruise the man's attack had left. Or rather the crack in his skull—at least it felt like a crack, given the piercing pain he was experiencing. "I should've gone to the police, too, and let them know he tried to kill me."

The chair made a slight scraping noise on the wood floor when Tennant pushed it back. A few steps, and he stood behind Gabriel, who had buried his head in his hands.

"Lean back," Tennant ordered, placing his fingertips on Gabriel's temples, adding gentle pressure, obviously unaware of the fact that Gabriel had stiffened under his touch. "Relax. You'll feel better in a minute or two. Easing pain is not that hard with a bit of acupressure."

"One of your innumerable skills?" Gabriel asked, clenching his hands around the armrests one moment and moaning with relief the next when the pulsating pain ebbed away just like that.

"Better?"

Gabriel didn't bother to answer right away. Something Tennant had said, or maybe something he himself had said, hopped around annoyingly in the back of his mind. Something about Wright, his headache, and the apartment.

There it was.

"We should go to the police," Gabriel said slowly. "Tomorrow, not now. All I want to do right now is go to bed and sleep for at least twelve hours. Tomorrow, though, we should try and find out about your... hmmm, let's call Lorelei your fiancée for the occasion, shall we? Maybe she's in a hospital, or maybe they've already found her."

At the last second, he remembered to avoid the word "corpse"— after all, Tennant was in love with the woman, or at least cared enough to write her letters. And maybe he should try not to think about his bed while Tennant was still massaging his temples. The words "bed" and "massage" gave him bad ideas. Very, very bad ideas.

"It's a lot better now, thanks," he bit out, not wanting Tennant to stop touching him but knowing that if he didn't—if the other man continued to press his cool fingers on his temples—Tennant would find his head in Gabriel's strong, passionate grip as he kissed him senseless.

Shit. Shit, shit—double, *triple* shit! Quickly, Gabriel stood and stepped out of Tennant's reach, deliberately ignoring the surprised look on the man's face.

"What you think, Doc?" he asked. "About the police? You're a good liar; you could easily play Lorelei's fiancé, and with a rune, you could even make them believe it, at least for a while. The cops might have information about her whereabouts, and if so, it would be stupid not to use that source."

Suddenly, Tennant looked tired. He rubbed his hands over his face. Gabriel couldn't help noticing the slight stubble on Tennant's cheeks and wondering how it would be to brush them with his lips.

"Let's go to bed," Tennant said.

Heat flushed Gabriel's cheeks, and he turned away as quickly as possible, muttered a "'Night, Doc," and slammed the door to his room shut.

"WHO are you looking for? Lorelei Kinney? You're not the first one to come looking for her, dear. Take a ticket!" Chuckling, the police officer winked at Tennant, who looked hurt and worried in just the right mixture.

"Miss Kinney happens to be my future wife," Tennant said brusquely. "I would be grateful if you could point me in the direction of the officer in charge, ma'am."

"Greig!" the officer called out. "One more for you. The Kinney case. This one is the fiancé, so you might want to treat him nicely."

Tennant cast Gabriel a thin smile, then went to Officer Greig's desk and sat down. In Gabriel's pocket sat a stone with a Hiding rune: Tennant had insisted on him bringing along to the police station and had provided him with the rune-stone so Gabriel would feel safe there. He hated the police; it was always possible that someone might get suspicious and lock him up just because they didn't like the color of his hair or the way he crossed his legs. At least that was what Gabriel believed. With the rune, he felt better.

Tennant was exquisitely dressed today, subtly emphasizing his power, money, and general superiority. Tucking up his trousers before crossing his legs, he placed a photograph in front of Officer Greig. "This is Lorelei. She is the love of my life, she's gone missing, and I want her back. Do you happen to have any information about her whereabouts?" Icily, he tapped his fingers, making it clear he wasn't used to waiting.

Officer Greig wasn't impressed. "Her *lover* was here before you," he said, a cruel undertone to his voice. "The lady was well-liked, it seems. Your name?"

Tennant pulled out one of his many business cards and handed it over. "I am quite aware that my fiancée was having an affair. The fact doesn't change my interest in her. Do you know where she is?"

Greig took the card. "Percy Archibald Grimsby the Third," he read. "Well, Mr. Grimsby, a body was found two nights ago at around two-fifteen at the docks. It was lying face down in the water. A fishermen stumbled over the victim on his way home. The body's currently in the morgue. Since you're practically family, we would be grateful if you could identify the body. Sir."

Methodically, the officer pulled out a sheet of paper, signed it, and handed it to Tennant. "Give this to the coroner. He'll show you the body." Then the officer nodded in Gabriel's direction. "The guy over there—he's with you? If he is and if he knew the lady, it would be better if he could identify her. She isn't a pleasant sight." Suspiciously, Greig looked Gabriel up and down, clearly noticing the long hair, the jeans-and-sweater outfit, and the uneasy look on the young man's face. Apparently, the rune-stone didn't make one invisible.

Tennant turned too. "He's my nephew, officer. He will indeed accompany me to the morgue. Be assured, though, that I am capable of identifying my fiancée myself. If it's her. Good day."

SIDE by side, they walked back to Tennant's car. Gabriel had pushed his hands deep into the pockets of his coat. He was more than glad to be out of the police station.

Tennant was silent, keys jangling in his hand. "Hope you didn't mind being my nephew," he said absently. "I always carry a shipload of business cards with me. Each one carries the same rune, making the one who touches it believe I am the man I claim to be. Comes in handy; remind me to show you the rune when we are back home so you can create your own ID when necessary."

Opening the passenger side door, he waited until Gabriel was seated, then walked around the car and got in himself. Instead of driving off, though, he just leaned back in his seat, staring out of the window. "I shouldn't drag you into this," he murmured, more to himself than to Gabriel. "Might become dangerous. Don't want you to get hurt."

Involuntarily touched by Tennant's grave tone, Gabriel put a hand on his shoulder, knowing full well that physical contact wasn't something he should seek but unable to resist. "Do you *plan* on hurting me?" he asked as lightly as possible, remembering his initial fear that the doctor might be a mad serial killer. "I'm safer with you than out on the streets, Doc, believe me. I would have frozen to death without you already, so don't worry about getting me into trouble. Who knows, in your care I might even put on some weight. Let's get to the morgue. I know this is not easy for you, but I think we should find out if it's Lorelei after all."

For a moment, Gabriel thought Tennant would shake off his hand, offended at the touch. Then he saw the man frown slightly as if he didn't understand what Gabriel was talking about.

Tennant looked at him blankly, at the hand on his shoulder, then finally nodded. "The morgue. Lorelei. Of course." Starting the car, he sped off, leaving Gabriel at a loss as to whether the doctor had been offended or merely surprised by the gesture.

"The cop's right, you know," Gabriel said after a lengthy silence. "I should identify her. Spare you the sight and all...." Admittedly, he didn't sound convinced he could do it, not after yesterday's performance.

Apparently, Tennant felt the same way. "We'll go in together, and you can catch me should I faint at the sight," he said with only a small hint of sarcasm. "I will look at the body. I want you to look through her personal possessions. You might see or smell something I wouldn't. Hopefully, we will get some hint of who killed her."

Strange, Gabriel thought. *He's convinced it's her, he believes she's been killed, and he's acting as if we're talking about a stranger, not someone he was in love with not too long ago.*

LORELEI KINNEY had been a beautiful woman in life. Tall and slim with long, blonde hair and blue-green eyes, she'd broken many a man's heart by simply walking past. Her waist was wasp-small, her legs long and slender. Around her right ankle, she wore a thin, silver chain. Charms dangled off it: a tiny shrimp, a dolphin, and an octopus.

Mermaid, Gabriel thought with a sad smile. *Fond of fish, if nothing else.*

It was Lorelei, of course—he would have recognized her anywhere, even in death, and even after she'd been fished out of the river a few days ago.

She would have been considerably more beautiful, even in death, if not for the cut throat and the ugly bruises around her wrists and ankles. Obviously, her murderer had tied her up before killing her.

"Interesting," Tennant said, pulling out a pair of glasses and putting them on. They gave him a very distinctive look—serious, trustworthy—subtly supporting his right to be there. The coroner, a small man with huge hands and feet, gave him a crooked grin, clearly impressed that, for once, a relative wasn't reduced to a sobbing heap at the sight of the victim. Folding his hands behind his back like a professor about to give a lecture, the coroner drew himself up to his full height, which wasn't very much at all.

"'Interesting' is the right word," he said. "What puzzles you more—the cut throat and the marks around her joints or the fact that she was a… a mermaid?"

"Both," Tennant answered absently. "She was about twice as strong as the average human man. I very much doubt she would have allowed anyone to bind her, and she would have fought an attacker like a lion. Yet there are no signs of a struggle: no scratches, no bruises, no broken bones, nothing. I wonder—" Leaning in, he brought his face close to hers, apparently unaffected by the gaping cut that had nearly severed her head from her body. "No alcohol. Was there any in her blood?"

The coroner shook his head. "No alcohol, no drugs. Her last meal contained rice and fruits. You know she was found at the docks? No fingerprints, no evidence at all. She was naked. No personal possessions, no jewelry apart from the ankle chain." Almost fondly, he placed his hand on the corpse's stomach, right underneath the Y-cut on her chest. "She's a right beauty. No scars, no tattoos, no piercings, and her organs were in perfect condition. Death occurred on Wednesday night between eleven p.m. and two a.m. Say—didn't it bother you that she was nonhuman? Or didn't you know?"

When Tennant didn't react, Gabriel answered for him. "She's his fiancée—of course he knew she was a mermaid—and no, it didn't bother him," he snapped.

Tennant flinched, looking slightly guilty. "Erm, yes. Fiancée. Lorelei Kinney. Mermaid. We were engaged; I loved her. Didn't care about the tail. Sorry. Should have mentioned it." He harrumphed and, ignoring the coroner, said to Gabriel, "I cannot think of a reason why she would have allowed anyone to tie her up without a fight. She was too strong. Obviously the murderer was in her apartment too."

"The blood on the floor!" Snapping his fingers in recognition, Gabriel said, "Yep, that would make sense. You said it wasn't her blood. Maybe she wounded her murderer."

Tennant let a strand of Lorelei's hair run through his fingers. "I doubt it. He would have killed her then and there, I suspect. But she was found at the docks—why would he have brought her all the way there and thrown her in the river if he could have just left her corpse in her apartment? And why was there such a mess? The cleaning woman—what was her name?"

"Sally."

"Sally. She said Miss Kinney never left clothes lying around. So the question is, was the murderer looking for something, or was he waiting for her?"

Thoughtfully, Gabriel stepped closer to the table. The wound didn't bother him as much as he had expected, but then, there was hardly any blood, and the smell wasn't too bad. Mainly, she smelled of seawater, seaweed, and dirt, although these smells were obscured somewhat by the chemicals typical of a morgue.

Her skin was not merely white, but bereft of color, as if the tone of her skin had seeped out of her with her blood. Her cut throat mocked him with its wide, horrible grin, and suddenly, Gabriel wanted to find her murderer very badly.

"Call her," he said over his shoulder. "Sally. Ask her if someone else had a key to her apartment—she liked you, and I bet she'd answer if you ask her politely. If it's neither Lorelei's blood nor the blood of her murderer, someone else must've been in there, and as there were no signs of a forced entrance, this someone must've had a key. A friend maybe, or another lover." He added the last bit deliberately and wasn't really surprised to see no reaction from Tennant at all. If the man really had been in love with Lorelei, he hid it well.

The coroner looked at Gabriel, then at Tennant, and finally back to the corpse. With care, he pulled the sheet that had been covering her up to her waist a bit higher.

Tennant was already dialing a number. "Sally? Yes, this is Detective Talway speaking. We met at Miss Kinney's apartment. Yes. No, I have no information about her whereabouts. Could you tell me if anyone else had a key to her apartment? Yes? The name, please. Jordan, write down that a Miss June Meyers had a key. Thank you, Sally. Yes. Good-bye."

Gabriel stared at him. "She gave you the name just like that?"

"Of course. I asked her nicely, as advised. According to Sally, June Meyers was a close friend of hers, had a key, and often stayed overnight. I say we try and find the lady."

"Erm," the coroner put in, slightly nervous now. "I might have some useful information concerning June Meyers."

THE couch in Tennant's living room was big and cozy, the cushions soft, and there would have been more than enough space for the both of them—if the thought didn't put rather detailed images in Gabriel's mind. Too detailed for his taste, and far too tempting to consider sitting on it... snuggling on it... kissing on it....

Naturally, he took a chair.

Shit, he thought, trying to concentrate on more pressing matters. *This will get out of hand if I'm not careful.* "What did you just say?" he asked, watching Tennant pace up and down the room restlessly, tirelessly.

The doctor stopped in the middle of the room, hands dug deeply into the pockets of his dressing gown. They had each taken a shower as soon as they had arrived home—separately, to Gabriel's chagrin—to get rid of the morgue's smell. Their hair was still wet, but where Gabriel had gotten dressed again, Tennant had put on nothing more than loose, soft pajama trousers and a dressing gown. Which was precisely the problem, as Gabriel was able to catch a glimpse of naked skin every now and then: a collarbone, the pulse in his throat, part of his chest, and a thin, silver necklace that sparkled seductively. Gabriel couldn't even take his eyes off the man's bare feet.

"I said I think I know what happened," Tennant interrupted his thoughts. "I believe that someone kidnapped Miss Kinney's friend, June Meyers, injuring her in the process. The killer leaves a note for Miss Kinney saying where to find her, messes up the apartment in order to make it clear something had happened, and takes her. Miss Kinney comes home, sees the mess, doesn't find her friend but the note instead, and goes to the docks to find June. Where she meets her murderer." He picked up the pacing again. "But why didn't she fight him?" he wondered.

Gabriel laughed bitterly. "Isn't it obvious? The murderer had her friend. She didn't want to risk June's life. The murderer orders Lorelei to bind her own ankles, then binds her wrists himself and cuts her throat. Maybe he promises to let June go if she obeys his orders. Which would mean June meant a lot to Lorelei."

"And that the murderer is a liar," Tennant added, finally dropping onto the couch. "First he kills the mermaid, then her friend. The coroner confirmed that Miss Meyers died after Miss Kinney. Bled to death. Luckily, she had her ID in the pocket of her jeans, or we would still be wondering how he lured Miss Kinney into his trap."

"Lorelei," Gabriel corrected him quietly.

"What?"

"It's Lorelei, not Miss Kinney, to you, isn't it? I mean, you were in love with her. You wrote her tons of letters, compromising enough to need to steal them back. You would call her by her given name. You would grieve. As someone who was in love with her, you wouldn't have been able to look at her body as if it was just a piece of meat. But you did. Conclusion: you didn't love her, you didn't write letters, and you were in her apartment for a completely different reason. I wonder what else you lied about, Doc."

Coolly, Gabriel placed the mug of tea he'd been holding, but not drinking from, onto the table. A strand of his hair brushed the surface; absent-mindedly, he pushed it behind his ear. When he looked up, he was surprised to find Tennant watching him closely.

The doctor opened his mouth and closed it again. He looked puzzled, annoyed, and embarrassed all at the same time, a fact Gabriel found strangely satisfying. Obviously, his accusation had been spot on.

"It's not that simple," Tennant began, clearly trying to find a way to get out of the situation without revealing anything he didn't want to share. "Miss Kinney—Lorelei, that is—was not just a mermaid. She—"

A loud crash made both jump: a window had broken. Simultaneously, they heard a fist slamming repeatedly against the front door. "Open up!" a voice yelled. "Open up now, or I will come and get you!"

CHAPTER SIX

SWIFT as a cat, Tennant got up and switched off the light. "Not a sound," he hissed, but Gabriel had already dropped to the floor—he was on the way to the kitchen to find himself a knife as the doctor slipped silently into the hall and toward the front door.

"Who is it?" Gabriel heard him ask just before he found the drawer with the knives. He took one out, checked its sharpness, and was just about to get a second one when the light was switched on again. Not much more than ninety seconds had passed. Apparently, it had been enough time for Tennant to get to the front door and open it, allowing the stranger to enter his house.

A thin, haggard man stepped hesitantly into the living room. His hair was wild, a brown mass decorated with leaves and twigs. Around his wrists and ankles were tree bark bracelets. From shoulders to thighs, the man was covered by a short tunic made of something that looked suspiciously like grass. A few beetles were crawling over the tunic, and on the man's shoulder sat a raven.

The stranger—at least a head shorter than Tennant—stayed close to the windows, as if the fading light gave him strength and reassurance. He left dirty footprints on the floor and looked as if he were a creature from a different world. With a sudden pang of understanding, Gabriel realized that it was just that: the man was from a hidden world and had entered this one through a portal. He was not human, not at all.

The knife in his hand seemed very much out of place, and Gabriel hurried to put it back in the kitchen, well aware that each of his steps was watched closely by the stranger. With empty hands, he returned to the living room, glad that he could no longer be accused of being impolite. The stranger gave a strong impression of being harmless, looking lost and vulnerable in the harsh light of the living room lamp, as if he wasn't used to artificial light.

"We need your help," the man said to Tennant, raising his hands in a pleading gesture.

Thick, crimson drops fell to the floor, one after the other, leaving a pattern of pain and death on the light planks.

"Are you injured?" Tennant asked. "How can we help?"

The man shook his head slowly, dreamlike. "Not I. My sister. I am Wild Oak. My sister is Sweet Rain, and she is bleeding. Dying. She wants to see you. She sent me to get you. Will you come?"

Tennant's eyes widened ever so slightly. "Sweet Rain," he said. "I met her some years back. How does she know—" He interrupted himself mid-sentence. "I will go with you, but I will not come alone. Allow me to bring a friend, Wild Oak. This young man is dear to me; I do not wish to leave him behind."

Slowly, Wild Oak turned. To Gabriel, he looked like a tree moving in the wind. A leaf dropped from his hair. A tiny butterfly fluttered from his shoulder to his elbow, its bright, blue and yellow wings beautiful in their fragility.

"You said you didn't want to drag me into this," Gabriel said, not knowing where the thought came from. "I thought you were talking about taking me to the morgue and about Lorelei being dead and all. I guess you meant something else. You feared I could get hurt. Really hurt, I mean. So if I come with you, will I be in danger?"

Hearing the coldness in his own voice made him cringe; nevertheless, he couldn't help but ask. That Tennant had lied to him, that there was obviously a lot more to Lorelei's and maybe even Mallfrick's death made him suspicious. In fact, he was feeling betrayed by Tennant, and that hurt a lot more than he would have anticipated had he thought about it before.

"Please," said Wild Oak, his sister's blood still dripping steadily on the ground.

Tennant frowned as if in pain himself but stayed focused on Gabriel. "You might get hurt," he said slowly. "It is possible, but unlikely. On the other hand, you could get killed by a speeding car the moment you step out of my door, die of malnourishment, an attack, or an illness. I cannot change either fate. To be honest, despite the fact that I am concerned about your safety, I would feel better if you came with me. The hidden worlds are beautiful but dangerous. Going there alone is not a good idea, not even for me." Without waiting for an answer, he dropped to one knee and began to paint a complicated rune, large enough that three people could step into it.

Anger welled up inside Gabriel. "'Not even for you' is supposed to mean what, Doc?" he asked, well aware that Wild Oak was taken aback by his outburst. "Who the hell are you, why do you know his sister, and why have you been lying?"

The rune on the floor began to glow, much like the Protection rune Gabriel had tried to use the first evening he'd been in Tennant's house. Now, with an expert doing the job, the glow was much stronger and much more powerful, surrounding all three of them. "I will answer your questions. Later. Right now, there are more pressing things to attend to. Are you coming?" He held out a hand. "You need to keep physical contact with me if you want to step through the portal, else the power would rip you apart."

Tennant looked straight into Gabriel's eyes and right into his soul. At least, that was how Gabriel felt about it—Tennant knew damn well he wouldn't stay behind, he knew about his desire and his poor attempts to keep it under control, and he knew Gabriel had no other choice but to follow him.

"All right," Gabriel said, "I'll go."

Tennant grabbed his arm just above the elbow and pulled him onward, into, and then through the rune.

STEPPING through a portal was like falling through a dream—unearthly, surreal, and scary without leaving him enough strength to scream. Gabriel couldn't feel his body, nor did he know how long it took him to get from here to there. Only Tennant's hand on his arm kept him from diving headlong into a panic; he had the strange feeling that without the man's protective grip, the portal would have ripped him into pieces.

Snow under his feet, crunching and cold. Snow on the surrounding trees, inches and inches of snow. This was not his hometown anymore. It was a forest, and they had landed right in the middle of it. The huge surrounding trees, still and silent and ancient, cast dark, tall shadows—and made him shiver.

Wild Oak had stepped through the portal first, and he didn't wait for his companions to get used to the differences between their worlds. He just ran on with long strides, leaving them behind and obviously assuming they would follow. Dark clouds hung low in the sky, and quiet, tiny snowflakes sailed to the ground, the wind smelling of ice and a coming storm.

Tennant, who hadn't even bothered to put on shoes or swap his dressing gown for a jacket, was just about to follow the running man when Gabriel held him back. "I want answers," he said. "The truth. Who is this man? *What* is he?"

"He's a tree nymph," Tennant said, pulling Gabriel along. "I met his sister some years back, and she knows I travel between worlds. Which could be the reason she sent her brother to get me."

Wild Oak had left footprints in the snow, so it was easy to follow them. "His sister is dying," Gabriel said, thinking aloud. "Mallfrick is dead. Lorelei is dead. Sweet Rain is injured badly enough that her brother's hands are covered in blood. You think all three cases are related. Correct?"

"Others have died before Mallfrick," Tennant replied, hurrying along as he spoke. "One shapeshifter, one riverghost, two elves. One fae. I am looking into their deaths. I fear that Sweet Rain is but another victim of the same murderer. Hopefully, she will be able to tell us who injured her."

He was out of breath now, running fast through the quiet wood without so much as seeing a glimpse of the tree nymph ahead. The doctor's feet sank deep into the snow with every step, wetting the trousers of his pajamas and the hem of his dressing gown; surely, the cold must have numbed his naked feet by now. Even Gabriel, who wore boots, shivered. Tennant, who was anything but properly dressed, didn't seem to care.

"Wild Oak!" he called out. "You're going too fast!"

Suddenly, a clearing opened before them, small and nearly perfectly round. Firs and birches protected the quiet place, and in the middle stood two trees: a tall, slender weeping willow and a huge, old oak.

From out of nowhere, the tree nymph appeared, standing just a few feet away. "We're here," he whispered. "Be quiet; my sister is in pain."

The wind brushed along his naked legs and bare arms, played with his wild hair, which looked much more like moss now than it had in the bright light of the house. Actually, he looked as if he were more tree than man in this strange, pale light.

Tennant took one step and then another toward the weeping willow. The branches of the tree were heavy with snow and hung low, touching the frozen ground like bony fingers. The bark was dark, nearly black, and there were deep, ugly-looking cuts in the slender trunk.

Tenderly, Tennant stroked the branches—a very personal, even intimate gesture. Gabriel, who was right behind him, couldn't help a pang of jealousy from rattling inside. *This is a tree*, he thought, angry with himself. *I'm jealous of a damn tree—better get a grip, boy.*

The branches parted like a curtain opening for a long-awaited friend, and Tennant knelt down in the snow. Where there had been nothing but frozen ground a moment ago, the snow began to melt, revealing wet leaves and muddy earth. A heartbeat later, grass began to grow, fresh, green grass and daisies and violets. The willow's branches shook off the cold, became alive, and there was the butterfly again, leaving Wild Oak's arm and landing on the tree's new leaves.

At the base of the trunk, half covered by branches, lay a young woman, looking as though she were not even twenty years old. She was as slender as the willow's trunk. Her eyes were closed, her face as white as the snow that had surrounded her tree. Her hair, thick and straight, was long enough to reach her ankles and covered her naked body like a blanket. Red hair. It took Gabriel a moment to realize that this wasn't its natural color but was a result of the blood that welled out of her slashed wrists and her pierced shoulders. Fragile and heartbreakingly small she was, beautiful and so very different from humans that it hurt to look at her. Someone like her shouldn't have been bleeding, shouldn't have been lying on the ground surrounded by snow. Someone like her shouldn't be dying. Tennant touched her cheek, and she opened her big, green eyes, tears streaming down her cheeks.

"Hello, beloved," the doctor whispered. "What do you think you're doing, dear, taking a nap in the snow? You'll catch a cold." Gently, he brushed a strand of hair out of her face, revealing sunken cheeks and more blood seeping out of several deep gashes in her chest.

"You," she whispered, her fingers weakly grabbing hold of Tennant's sleeve. "Your eyes. Just... just like him."

"What about my eyes?" the doctor prodded.

Tennant bent lower, but her breathing deepened as if she were falling asleep. Slowly, her head sank to one side, and her hand went limp and dropped onto the ground.

The small butterfly hovered above her head, and Gabriel's throat suddenly tightened with grief when he saw several small, green leaves drop off one of the branches and land on Sweet Rain's now still chest.

"No," Gabriel cried, feeling sick and lost and outraged all at the same time. "She's so young! She can't be dead!" Dropping next to her, he touched her cheek with his fingertips.

Tennant closed his hand over his. "She isn't," he said. "Her body is—it will fall apart under her tree, will turn to earth and feed her roots—the tree is her, too, didn't you know that? This is how tree nymphs live: partly in their trunk, partly in a human body. If she hadn't found her way back here in time, she would have been gone forever. As it is, she will return to her tree-form and sleep for a decade or two."

"What?"

"She isn't dead," Tennant repeated patiently, and he pulled Gabriel up. "Just asleep."

Another few leaves landed on the girl's body, covering her face. A branch brushed through her hair, caressing her as a mother might caress a sleeping child. More branches rustled, shushing them away, and there was Wild Oak, stepping between Gabriel and Tennant and the silent form of his sister.

"Go now," he said. "You have heard her words. There is nothing more to say." Turning, he vanished into the darkness of the woods.

One last look, and Tennant turned as well, away from the dead body of the girl and the slender tree that contained her essence. "We have to walk a bit until we are far enough away to open a portal again. Wild Oak is right—there is nothing left to do here. We should go home."

Dumbstruck, Gabriel stared after him. He was nearly out of sight already; the old trees that surrounded the clearing blocked the sparse light of the just-rising moon. He couldn't believe that Tennant had walked away as if nothing had just happened. It was even more unbelievable given the fact that the girl's last words had been about his eyes, indicating that he had something to do with her death.

"Doc!" he called out, wrapping his arms around his body. Suddenly, he was freezing. Suddenly this, all of it, had become too much. "I won't go anywhere before... well... shit!"

An amused chuckle told him that Tennant was not as far away as he had thought. "We need to let her rest, Gabriel."

The doctor's voice was closer now, and a faint shadow between the trees told the younger man where to go. With long strides, he left the clearing behind, ridiculously glad to do so.

"Don't think I don't grieve," Tennant said once Gabriel had caught up. Leaning against a fir, he absently rubbed one foot up and down his other leg. The belt to his dressing gown had opened; barely visible, the necklace moved with every breath. "I knew her well—that is, as well as you can know one of their kind—and I liked her."

"She didn't look much older than a teenager," Gabriel pointed out. "Was she really that young?"

Tennant's lips quirked. "She is a tree nymph and around fifty years old, very young for her race, true, but older than I am nevertheless. It will take some time for her to regain enough power to create another human body. Until then, I will miss her."

With a vengeance, the jealousy came back. Somehow, Tennant must have seen it in his face, because his eyes widened slightly.

"You think we were lovers?" he asked. "Goodness, Gabriel, tree nymphs are hard to love. Sweet Rain was a friend, nothing more. Now, will you come along or not? You could stay here, you know. Nice and cold. Though I vaguely remember you dislike the cold?"

Gabriel didn't move an inch. It took Tennant a few moments before he realized that he had no intention of coming along.

"You have questions," Tennant stated. "Ask, then, and I will answer. But only if we try to find a good place to open a portal while we talk. A portal takes energy from the one who opens it as well as from the surrounding area. If I open one too close to Sweet Rain's tree, it will kill her for good."

"One question answered, several hundreds to go," Gabriel grumbled, but he finally walked alongside Tennant. "Any idea what she was talking about? Your eyes—what was that supposed to mean?"

"No idea." The answer came fast. "We can muse about that riddle once we are home, and frankly spoken, I would like to leave this world sooner rather than later."

More than just a little bit glad that the subject of Sweet Rain and his sudden flash of jealousy hadn't turned into a topic, Gabriel found himself admiring the swift, easy way Tennant moved—his light step, the nearly dance-like sway of his narrow hips—and he blushed deeply. Luckily, it was dark, or else Tennant might have seen it and asked more detailed questions about his emotional state. After all, the doc wasn't blind—he was bound to find out sometime that Gabriel had feelings for him. Very clear, specific feelings.

"I must admit, there was a time when Sweet Rain seemed to be interested in me," Tennant said lightly, making Gabriel's teeth clench, "but eventually, she figured out that it was a lot better if we remained friends. She was quite insistent for a while, though."

Another one of those dry chuckles and a short shake of the head made it evident that Tennant couldn't believe anyone would be stupid enough to want him for a kiss and more. Gabriel wondered whether he wasn't used to admiration—he was pretty close to drooling whenever the man opened his mouth—or if he was mocking him.

The wind had picked up, and the temperature was well below the freezing point. Nevertheless, Tennant walked barefoot through the ankle-deep snow, oblivious to the cold and the fact that there were tiny icicles frozen to the ends of his hair. Gabriel, on the other hand, could barely keep his chattering teeth under control.

"How come you aren't cold, Doc?" he asked, and that made Tennant stop and turn toward him, visibly surprised.

Tennant frowned and looked down at his chest, only partly covered by the dressing gown, his bare feet, and his hands, which didn't look half as pale and cold as Gabriel's hands. "I can deal with this weather," he said slowly, clearly at a loss for how to explain that someone could get used to such harsh temperatures.

Gabriel stared at the doctor, for a moment not caring that they might still have a little farther to walk until they were far enough away to open a portal. He took in the other man's slightly embarrassed look, saw how the wind blew the dressing gown apart, noticed how Tennant didn't even shiver at that, and then something else struck him.

"Your eyes really are quite strange," Gabriel said, and he boldly put a hand under Tennant's chin, making him look up. "When I first saw you, I thought they were sort of average, but soon I discovered that they were anything but ordinary. And now... you walk through an ice-cold winter night as if we were at a sunny beach. You know how to open a portal. You know more about runes than anyone I've ever met, and you walk through this world as if it belonged to you. You even knew what I was from the first moment you met me, although no one else ever suspected a thing. You aren't human either, are you?"

Too quickly for Tennant to react, he took the pendant that dangled off the doctor's necklace between his thumb and index finger. The shape was unmistakable. "Definitely a rune," Gabriel stated, satisfied, and then bent a bit lower, examining it. "Complicated, but I think I can see a Transformation rune. How do you really look, Doc? What sort of blood runs through *your* veins?"

For the first time since he had met Tennant, Gabriel observed something like shock in the man's face. Clearly, his words had hit home. "You cannot know that," Tennant said hoarsely. "I've met hundreds, thousands of people, and no one has ever suspected me of not being what I wanted them to see!"

"It's easy to see through the walls—or the runes, in your case—of someone I like," Gabriel said quietly. "So I guess I must like you a lot." He stepped back, the warmth of Tennant's skin under his fingertips haunting him. "I want answers," he repeated. "But first, I want to get home. Can you tell me how long we have to walk before we can open a portal? Honestly, unlike you, I'm freezing to death here."

Above the trees, the thin, silver blade of the moon could be seen. Branches swayed in the wind, whispering of a long, harsh winter. The silence seemed to deepen; it was peaceful in the dark woods, and really, there shouldn't have been a reason for feeling scared. However, Gabriel couldn't suppress a sudden rush of panic. He wanted to run, to flee, anything to get away from these trees that were surrounding them. For no reason whatsoever, he felt like prey about to be caught, like danger was closing in on him. Goosebumps appeared on his arm and ran down his spine, and they had nothing to do with the cold.

"Doc," he whispered. "Something's wrong. Someone's watching us."

Tennant looked at him sharply but obviously had no intention of dismissing the younger man's worries lightheartedly. "Are you sure?" he asked, scanning the woods although it was too dark to catch a glimpse of one's own feet.

"Absolutely. I can smell something." With flaring nostrils, Gabriel turned on his own axis in order to figure out where the scent was coming from. It was faint, strange, and appealing. "Hay and fire and smoke," he finally said. "Apples. Blood. Warm. Spicy. Dangerous."

"Not good," Tennant answered, and he spread his arms, palms up. "Maybe I followed the wrong track. If this is the case, we are in trouble. Show them your hands, Gabriel, show them you are—"

A faint sound could be heard above the whispering wind. It sang like a guitar string tapped by skilled, angry fingers. It was not a pleasant sound.

Tennant groaned and staggered. Gabriel whipped around and saw his friend sway and feared he would fall, but the doctor managed to stay on his feet despite the small arrow that was now sticking out of his right shoulder. Blood blossomed on the fabric of his dressing gown; a few drops hit the snow, not red, but black in the night. Instinctively, Gabriel took a step toward the other man, ready to catch him should he fall and listening to the darkness for more arrows or maybe gunshots to follow. Instead, the sound of hooves could be heard above the wind, and dozens of flickering torches appeared, casting eerie shadows on the ground and the trees.

"Stay away from me and don't talk unless someone asks you a question," Tennant rasped, clutching his upper arm with his left hand and putting some distance between himself and Gabriel. The doctor's face had gone pale, and a bead of sweat ran down his temple. He trembled from what Gabriel guessed was pain.

More blood dropped onto the snow, but neither noticed, as their eyes were fixed on the flickering torches, held high in large, strong hands. Bare chests and bearded faces came into view, with long, tangled strands of hair floating down slender backs. The centaurs—about six in all—formed a circle around them. Some held bows, some crossbows. Tails whipped angrily, and flanks heaved.

"Human," one of them spat, clearly disgusted at the sight. "Pity I wasn't allowed to kill you straight away."

Another centaur stepped forward. He was unarmed, his hair tamed into a braid, his beard short. His eyes narrowed when he looked at Tennant, taking in his clenched teeth and the shaft that emerged from his shoulder.

"Human," he said. "You are not allowed to walk in our woods, just as we are not allowed to walk in your world. Give me a reason why I should not kill you and this foal of yours like your people do to us."

Tennant looked at Gabriel for a long moment. "Don't harm him," he said. "He is here because I brought him. He is dear to me, and he is young."

"He is *human*," the centaur argued. Clearly, in his opinion, humans were ideal targets for bow practice. His voice was deep and harsh, and although he was unarmed, he seemed more dangerous than the rest of them put together. "Humans come here to hunt us whenever they manage to open a portal. They consider it a sport. They think we are prey."

"There's shapeshifter blood in him!" Tennant pronounced the words emphatically, shocking Gabriel with the emotion behind them. "Wild Oak asked us to listen to the last words of his sister. Apparently, we got lost in the woods, but we have no intention of causing harm. We just want to go back home." Slowly, he straightened up to be at eye level with the centaur. "And besides—since when is it the habit of your race to be impolite?" Just a tad of arrogance laced his words, just enough to make the centaur's mouth twitch in amusement and surprise.

"In what way am I being impolite?" the centaur asked. "Agreed, you are bleeding because of my order to shoot. But apart from that?"

Carefully, Tennant held out his left hand, dripping with blood. "And your name would be?" he asked. "Sorry for offering the wrong hand. My right is currently out of order."

The centaur stared at the hand, at the man's pale face, and laughed. "I am Kyril," he said, brushing his palm briefly across Tennant's. "These are my woods. If Wild Oak sent you this way, he should have told me about you."

Taking a step toward Gabriel, Kyril stared at him suspiciously, then let his fingers run through the long strands of his hair as if checking whether they were real. Eventually, he touched the young man's cheek, looking deep into his eyes.

"I see it. Your heritage is well hidden, but you are a hunter's child. You are safe in our woods. Tell me, cub—did you come here to hunt us?" His hand suddenly fastened around Gabriel's throat.

"I've never killed anyone in my life," Gabriel croaked as calmly as possible despite the cold dread welling up in him. "Wild Oak didn't send us this way. We must have taken the wrong path. We just witnessed a young girl die, my friend is bleeding, and it was you who attacked us, not the other way around." Impatiently, he wiped the centaur's hand away like an annoying fly. "I mean, look at us—I'm unarmed, and the doc isn't even wearing shoes, never mind any weapons. Do we look as if we were out hunting centaurs? Use your brain, man!"

Tennant was shaking badly by now—it seemed that he was badly injured, and the cold now held him close in its icy grip. His left hand clutched his right elbow, supporting his injured shoulder. "I rarely go hunting wearing nothing but pajama trousers and a dressing gown," Tennant bit out. "Let us go, Kyril."

"You haven't told me your name yet, human," the centaur objected mildly. For some reason, Gabriel was reminded of a cat playing with a wounded mouse.

For a long moment, Tennant was quiet. His labored breathing could be heard clearly in the cold winter air. Drop by drop, his blood soiled the snow, and his face got paler by the minute. "I am not human," he finally said, almost too quietly to be heard.

Gabriel's eyes widened. True, he had suspected Tennant to be of mixed blood, like himself, the rune-necklace hiding his true look, but that he wasn't human at all came as a shock.

Kyril circled the bleeding man, touched him, and even sniffed him. "You *look* human," he stated. Slowly, he unsheathed his knife, not an overly large one, but sharp and deadly looking nonetheless. Even more slowly, he raised it, keeping an eye on Gabriel all the time.

"Don't do anything stupid, cub," he warned, and two other centaurs aimed their bows at him.

Kyril cut the fabric of Tennant's dressing gown from shoulder to ribcage, exposing the wound. From what Gabriel could tell, the arrow was about fifteen inches long, and two-thirds of it was buried in Tennant's flesh.

The knife vanished. Carefully, Kyril dipped a fingertip into the blood running down his victim's chest. Thoughtfully, the centaur rubbed the liquid between his fingers, then finally licked it. "Not a trace of nonhuman blood," he said, without any doubt. "Are you stupid, or are you a liar?"

"I am neither," Tennant rasped. Looking at Gabriel, he said, "Believe me, I would have preferred to tell you this under different circumstances," before turning back to Kyril and continuing. "My name is Aleksei. You have heard of me. I wandered between the worlds for a long time before settling in the world of the humans. I still run errands every now and then. For my own safety, I wear a rune that covers my heritage. Now would you *please* let us go home, Kyril, before I bleed to death?" He brought his left hand to his throat and ripped off the chain around his neck, throwing it to Gabriel, who just managed to catch it before it fell to the snow and was lost.

As soon as the necklace with the rune-shaped pendant was gone, Tennant changed in a subtle, intense way. The color of his skin, gray from cold and blood loss a heartbeat ago, began to glow with a faint, silvery shimmer. His eyes brightened, the blue intensifying to such an extent that it became nearly impossible to look at them. Dark lines appeared on his chest, abdomen, and temples and twined around his wrists like ivy, spreading as if alive, reaching his shoulders and creeping toward his back. They formed complicated patterns, beautiful as well as strangely appealing. Gabriel couldn't help but wonder if they were to be found everywhere on Tennant's body and how it might feel to touch them.

Even Kyril seemed impressed. "You're fae," he stated, and he waved a hand at his men. Bows vanished and crossbows lowered. The centaurs broke the circle and backed off, no longer imprisoning Tennant and Gabriel.

"Aleksei, I have indeed heard of you, and I apologize. You are the one who's allowed to walk through all the hidden worlds, to go where he sees fit. You are free to leave. Though I ask that one day we could meet you again. I have never come across anyone who controls runes like you do."

"Let me survive this encounter first before talking about the next," Tennant managed to say. He swayed, reaching out to maintain his balance, and found Gabriel, who chose to ignore his earlier order not to move and stepped close to wrap a steadying arm around his waist.

One torchlight after the other vanished into the darkness, and the centaurs left quietly, like ghosts. Soon, nothing remained to prove the centaurs had ever been there save for a few tracks in the snow, the smell of burned wood, and the drops of blood from Tennant's heavily bleeding wound.

CHAPTER SEVEN

HAD anyone told Gabriel a few weeks ago that he would be trapped in a wooded area belonging to centaurs with a half-conscious man by his side who wasn't even human, he would have laughed. Everyone knew that the hidden worlds couldn't be visited just like that, and even if they could, it was forbidden. Besides, everyone knew those worlds to be dangerous and deadly, and the rumors alone were reason enough not to mess with portals.

Snow soaked Gabriel's boots, turning his feet into ice cubes. Snowflakes drifted from the clouds above, covering his hair with a thin, white veil. It had gotten colder in the past half hour, and the wind had picked up too. Now that the centaurs were gone, it was pitch black once more. The ancient trees seemed to edge in closer, the air bit his face and fingers, and he guessed they had maybe another half an hour to get somewhere safe and warm before Tennant bled to death and he himself died of exposure.

Suddenly, Tennant's legs gave way and he slipped out of Gabriel's grip and sank to his knees.

The snow crunched as Gabriel knelt down next to him. "Doc," he urged. "You need to open a portal, or I can't get you back home. The Portal rune is still too complicated for me to draw, and you know that. Doc!" Alarmed, he saw the doctor's head loll forward. The hand that held the injured arm was covered with blood, and his breath was now coming in harsh gasps.

"Can't," Tennant whispered. "Too weak. Draw a Light rune. Get that arrow out!"

"Are you crazy? I'll take you to a hospital, that's what I'll do. But you have to open a portal first, do you hear?" He very nearly shook the man in order to force some sense into him.

A thin layer of ice began to cover their clothes, and the blood that had seeped into Tennant's dressing gown was already freezing. Still, a Light rune was easy, and it would allow him to see the damage the centaur's arrow had caused more clearly. Luckily, the Light rune had been one of the first he had learned. Only a few finger-waggles later, a pale, unearthly light shone on both of them, causing Tennant's skin to glow even more prominently.

It looked simply beautiful, or would have, if not for the blood spoiling the picture.

"Mountain ash. The arrow—it's made of mountain ash." Tennant shook heavily now from cold and pain and sank against Gabriel, who could do nothing else but hold him close without causing him further pain. It wasn't a simple thing, either—with each breath the doctor took, his shoulders moved, and with each movement, there came a groan.

"Poisonous. Mountain ash... poisons me. Get it out. Please!" Eyes wide with the visible effort to stay conscious, Tennant looked imploringly at him. His lips were white. His skin, despite the silvery shimmer, was sallow from shock and blood loss. "Please," he repeated before his body went limp.

Gabriel had no other choice but to let him stretch out on the cold, snow-covered ground. Hands numb, fingers and nails faintly blue, he wiped away the snow as best he could, cutting his fingers on sharp ice-crystals as he did so. "Don't you dare die, Doc," he hissed, trying to blow some warmth into his half-frozen hands. "I'll break your useless neck if you die on me!"

Not knowing what else to do, Gabriel moved over to the man's right side and looked at the arrow. It wasn't thick, but it was nasty-looking nevertheless, with a plain shaft and short peacock feathers to balance its flight. If only there were a way to find out about the arrowhead. Somehow, Gabriel couldn't imagine the head would be without barbed hooks, making its removal more difficult.

Tennant's lips moved, and Gabriel bent low to understand him, but to no avail. Tennant was just mumbling and groaning. He was obviously in pain, and Gabriel clearly needed to hurry in order to stop the mountain ash shaft from poisoning his friend any further. Even he knew that the wood made a fae weak, causing pain and taking away their ability to think straight. Not that Tennant would have been able to do much thinking at the moment. Still, he didn't need any more pain and weakness than he suffered from already. Clenching his teeth, Gabriel put his fingers around the arrow's shaft. The wind blew his hair out of his face, which came in handy, as the small light wasn't overly bright.

"Now what?" he asked, hoping that someone would provide him with an answer other than "just pull it out." Of course, there was nothing but silence.

"Shit," he hissed. He pressed his left hand against Tennant's shoulder, ignored the strangled yell, and pulled. As he did so, he turned his wrist, hoping to minimize the damage if indeed the tip of the arrow had hooks.

Luckily, the arrow came out easily—there were no hooks, only a plain wooden head. Tennant screamed nevertheless, his eyes ripping open, and he tried to escape the pain. Gabriel had to press him down hard, using his knee to keep him still. Disgusted, he threw the arrow over his shoulder, where it vanished in a snowdrift. In no time at all, he had shed his jacket and ripped the shirt off his body. It was unimportant; the shirt was needed to stop the bleeding.

Minutes, seconds, or maybe hours passed. Gabriel lost track of time as he tried to stop the bleeding with nothing but a thin bit of fabric. He held on to the hope that he could figure out a way to get them both back to their own world. Well, *his* own world, anyway. Tennant was fae. And his name wasn't even Tennant.

"Just a few more lies," Gabriel murmured, renewing the Light rune and watching his friend's still, ghostly pale face. "Fucking great. No wonder I'm drawn to you, Doc. Fae are well known to mess with people's hearts. Shit, man, I should let you die here for all the lies you've told me."

Desperately, Gabriel shook those thoughts out of his head. He didn't mean it, anyway. The bleeding hadn't really stopped, and what if the wound didn't close and Tennant just laid there until there wasn't a drop left in his body?

"What if I used a rune?"

Not thinking properly about his idea, Gabriel removed the blood-soaked shirt from the wound. It was bleeding profusely for such a small hole. It should be easy to draw the Light rune right onto the skin, shouldn't it?

He tried it—just a few lines. A golden glow accompanied the silver shimmer of the skin for a few moments because there was direct contact with the skin. And there was warmth. Gabriel could feel it; he could feel his fingertips again for the first time in what seemed ages. Then the warmth turned into heat. A Light rune was only supposed to be used in the air, like most runes. The golden glow turned into a fierce red and seemed to sink into his friend's skin.

Tennant howled with pain, kicking his feet and trying to get free from Gabriel's grip with a vengeance. Gabriel had to use all of his strength to hold him down. Blood bubbled, and steam wafted into the air until the rune finally faded away.

The wound had been burned closed. No more bleeding. Tennant, with surprising strength, closed a hand around Gabriel's wrist and removed it so he could turn over and roll up into a fetal position. Leaves, mushy and smelly, stuck to his back and hair.

Helpless, Gabriel touched him, trying to soothe him. "Sorry, Doc," he murmured. "I thought…. I didn't want to cause you even more pain, but I didn't know what else to do."

Tennant needed many minutes to get his breath and harsh sobbing under control. Finally, he coughed and was able to turn slowly onto his back again. Snowflakes landed on his face and hair, but they didn't seem to bother him.

"No," he said, licking his dry lips. "You did well. Can you help me up?"

Gabriel slipped an arm under Tennant's back, helping the doctor into a sitting position. "You should rest. Actually, you belong in a nice, warm hospital bed."

"No hospital," Tennant objected, pulling the loose sides of his dressing gown tighter around his shaking body. "As a nonhuman, I'd end up in prison or—more likely—I'd be dead before you'd left the room. You know that."

Gabriel put his jacket around Tennant's shoulders, a pathetic attempt to keep him warm. The temperature was way beyond freezing, but Gabriel didn't even feel the cold. All that mattered right now was finding a way to get back home.

"Put your necklace back on," he said, fishing for the thin chain in his trouser pocket.

Tennant just shook his head. "No use," he whispered. "I'm too weak to feed it with power. They would see I'm fae. Can't risk it. You have to take me to my house." Exhausted, he lowered his head to his drawn-up knees.

"Whatever." Gabriel was determined to leave this world as quickly as possible, and if he had to promise Tennant the stars from the sky, he would do it—after all, a promise was easily broken. "Just open the portal and we're out of here."

Then realization hit him: Tennant was too weak to use his own necklace, so he wouldn't be able to open a portal, either. The man was sitting, all right, and he wasn't bleeding anymore, but that was about it. He was currently as useful as a log when it came to using runes—much like himself, actually, when the rune in question was dangerous or complicated.

Shit.

That meant someone else had to open the portal. "I'll take you to Wild Oak," he decided. "He can open the portal; I'll carry you. And then... well. We can talk about that once we're back home." Gently, he brushed his hands over Tennant's dark, wet hair, desperately hoping that the gesture remained unnoticed. "Come on, Doc. Just a short walk and—"

"Impossible." Tennant was barely able to keep his eyes open. "Wouldn't make it there and back again. The portal has to be opened away from the clearing, remember? Go. Get him. And hurry!"

"I cannot just leave you here!" Gabriel spat the words. More than ever, he wanted to pull Tennant up, shake him, and maybe even hit him if it would knock some sense into his fae head. "The centaurs could come back, finishing you for good. Wolves, maybe, or vultures, or whatever!"

Tennant managed a weak grin and sank against him, radiating unhealthy warmth while shivering all over. "Vultures only eat cadavers," he whispered, "and they don't fly at night. There aren't any wolves in this world. Too many centaurs." He coughed. "I cannot even stand, let alone walk." The fingers of his right hand sought a hold in the young man's long hair. "I'm dead if you don't hurry. Please. *Please*, Gabriel!"

It was hard to let go of him, to let Tennant's body slip back to the icy ground. Nevertheless, Gabriel got up after he'd wrapped his jacket more tightly around his friend, protecting him against the still-falling snowflakes. "I'll be back in no time," he promised, "even if I have to drag Wild Oak all the way by his feet."

RUNNING through the dark wood was a scary thing to do, Gabriel discovered during the next minutes. No use even trying to use the Light rune—he was busy running and couldn't waste his concentration on anything else but getting back to the clearing as fast as possible. Occasionally, he fell, and at one point he nearly twisted his ankle, but he was determined to make it, so he got back to his feet and went on. Their tracks were easy enough to follow even without light.

When he reached the clearing, the slender weeping willow was covered by snow again, and the body that had lain at its base was gone, maybe decayed to earth already or maybe just covered by leaves.

No one was to be seen.

"Wild Oak!" he shouted, the call loud in the stillness of the woods, loud in his own ears, but still pathetically small. It didn't carry far; it didn't penetrate the depths of the forest, even though he put all his strength into it. He was out of breath, and sweat was running down his back, where it froze.

"Weather's shit. I'm going to get fucking pneumonia," Gabriel wheezed, both hands on his knees, panting heavily. Hastily, he drew a Light rune so he could at least see. "Wild Oak! I promise I'll rip out your sister's tree with my bare hands if you don't come out!"

Nothing but silence answered him.

He approached the willow, not knowing what else to do. He couldn't run any further, and even if he'd found the strength to do so, he wouldn't have known where to go. Either he would find Wild Oak and took him back to his friend to open the portal, or....

There was no "or." If he allowed an "or" in his thoughts, Tennant was dead.

The wind blew ice crystals from the willow's branches. They crossed Gabriel's light, shimmering like tiny diamonds, before moving on into the darkness. Nearly, very nearly, Gabriel believed the tree was breathing. It looked alive, welcoming, even caring.

Hesitantly, he raised a hand to touch the branches. He had seen the girl die; he had witnessed how her essence had left her body, seeping into the tree's bark. He didn't really believe that the willow understood what he wanted, why he was here. Still, he whispered, "I need help," his fingertips an inch away from a frost-covered leaf. "Please, I know you like Tennant, and I need to find your brother!"

A hand landed hard on his shoulder, jerking him around and away from the tree, and Gabriel nearly screamed in shock. Staggering backward, he would have landed hard on the ground if Wild Oak hadn't dug his wood-like fingers into his naked shoulder. The man looked furious and very, very tired at the same time. "What do you want?" he asked. "You were not supposed to come back. You threatened my sister. I will kill you if you have done her harm!" One hard push, and Gabriel landed in the snow a few feet away from both man and tree.

Wild Oak knelt down in the snow, his hands whispering soothingly along his sister's tree. "Has he hurt you?" he asked gently. "Has he—" He didn't finish his sentence. Several of the long, thin branches entwined his wrist and stroked along his cheek. He seemed to be listening; for several far too long moments, nothing could be heard but the wind in the branches.

When Wild Oak got up, he wasn't furious anymore. Silently, he held out a hand and helped Gabriel stumble to his feet, which he couldn't feel anymore. "Sweet Rain says you need help. She sensed fear and desperation. Tell me why you are still here. Tell me where Tennant is."

"As if you didn't know that his real name is Aleksei," Gabriel snapped. He was beyond fatigue, beyond cold, beyond even fear. All that mattered was getting back to his friend and into the warmth, preferably with Tennant alive so he could rip off the man's head once he was able to stand up straight. "I know he's fae. We had a nice little interlude with those horse-men, centaurs, or whatever you call the bastards who shot him. He's back there somewhere," he waved vaguely in the direction he'd come from, "and if you don't open a portal so I can get him back home, he'll die. Sorry for the threat, but come on, look at me—I couldn't crush a grape right now, never mind rip out trees."

A thin smile curved Wild Oak's lips.

Annoyed with the damn wind that insisted on playing with his hair, Gabriel rummaged through his trouser pockets, found a string of leather, and finally bound it back, not at all surprised that it cracked suspiciously under his fingers. Frozen—even his damn hair was frozen! He turned and walked away in the direction where he feared Tennant had already died. After all, he must have been gone for hours by now, not mere minutes. It was impossible that hair could freeze in a few minutes.

The crunching of snow confirmed that Wild Oak was following him. "That's not the way to the centaurs' part of the wood," the tree nymph said. "We need to head north if we are to find your friend."

"Never said he's my friend," he said through chattering teeth.

"You didn't need to," Wild Oak replied, and he took his arm to steady him. "It is very obvious you care for him, or you would not have left him your shirt and jacket."

MAYBE Wild Oak knew a shortcut, or maybe because Gabriel wanted to get back so very desperately they practically flew through the dark wood, and soon they could make out a heap in the snow.

Tennant.

Gabriel was by his side in no time, brushing away the snow that had settled on the still body. Dread even colder than the icy wind pierced his heart. What if the doc was dead? What if he had just stopped breathing while Gabriel was trying to find the damn tree nymph?

"Don't be dead," he whispered, searching for the pulse in Tennant's throat.

A thin, ghostlike smile spread over the wounded man's lips. "Or you'll come after me and break my neck," he whispered, opening his eyes. "Horrible threat indeed." Tennant coughed, a thin line of blood running down his chin. Gabriel hoped it was just because his lips were cracked and not because the arrow had pierced his lungs. "I would… would really like to leave now."

Gabriel didn't care anymore if he might cause further harm. He shoved his arms under Tennant, lifting him as if the man were nothing but a child. He ignored the gasps of pain and turned toward Wild Oak, who had opened a portal already. Blue and gold glinted on the edges of the hole between the worlds.

The tree nymph stepped aside and bowed his head. "The powers of the portal won't harm you as long as you carry Aleksei," Wild Oak said. "I wish you luck."

"Thanks," Gabriel said, stepping through, his burden safely clutched against his chest. His own world called for him, pulled him forward, urged him to leave behind the cold, dark, snowy world where a girl had died and his friend had been almost fatally wounded. He never even gave a thought to Tennant's earlier warning that portals could rip him to pieces, so eager was he to get home. His world was warm and bright—at least, that was how Gabriel saw it. There were people there, and cars, and hospitals where lives could be saved, even if the life in question was already slipping though his hands like a wet eel.

Dizzy and blinded by the sudden absence of wind, Gabriel staggered when the portal closed behind him. The man he carried was heavy, his arms and legs limp, his breathing far too loud in the quiet street they had stepped onto. In the distance, he could hear the noise of cars—they had arrived just around the corner from Tennant's house. It wouldn't be easy to get a taxi, but then, Gabriel had no problem with jumping right in front of a car, hijacking it, and taking the doctor to the nearest emergency room himself.

He was already halfway down the street when he remembered Tennant saying that he wouldn't survive hospital treatment. He was fae. Nonhuman.

They'll think he's dangerous, despite the fact he can't even wiggle his fingers, Gabriel thought, looking at the pale face that rested on his shoulder. Tennant's strange-looking eyes were closed, but his skin still spoke clearly of the fact that he was a stranger in this world. *Even if they just put him into prison, he wouldn't survive the night, and I bet they wouldn't hurry to get a doctor for him, either.*

Much easier to take him back home. Much safer too. Tennant groaned, and Gabriel made a decision. No hospital.

In less than five minutes, they were home.

SWEARING under his breath, Gabriel carried the unconscious man into the bedroom and lowered him onto the mattress. Snow melted, and ice, too, leaving stains on the pillow and blanket, and for some reason, the air seemed to be too warm and somewhat stale in here. Gabriel had an urge to pry open the windows to let in the fresh air and wind but stopped himself just in time. He had always had a certain liking for the outside world, which was the reason why he had preferred to sleep under bridges rather than in the always-crowded mission or even empty buildings, but right now, he had more urgent things to do. Like getting Tennant warm and dry, for example, and making sure he survived his encounter with the centaurs.

First the wet clothes needed to go, and when only pajama trousers were left, Gabriel undid the string and pulled them down Tennant's legs.

The unconscious man shivered constantly. His head sank to the side, and behind closed lids, his eyes moved as though he were having a horrible nightmare. The inhuman silvery tone of his skin was overlaid by a faint blue, indicating that the cold had got to him badly. It was more than clear that he needed to get warm. The question was—how?

Water dripped from Gabriel's hair onto the floor. His leather boots squeaked with every movement, and because he could no longer feel his toes, he finally sat on the bed and took off his boots along with his trousers and socks.

"A hot shower and some tea," he said. "Come on, Doc. We'll get you warm in no time." Carefully, he lifted the unconscious man once more and carried him into the bathroom, hardly believing that there wasn't any snow crunching under his numb bare feet.

Luckily, the shower was big enough for both of them. Gabriel knelt down, supporting Tennant with one arm while switching on the water with his free hand. The first splash was cold—why the hell did water always have to be cold at first?—but luckily, it heated quickly.

When the warm drops hit his skin, they hurt. Like tiny balls of fire, they shot heat into him. It was probably not a bad thing that Tennant wasn't conscious enough to feel it.

When his feet began to tingle, Gabriel had to clench his teeth to silence the pained moans. Life streamed back into his limbs, and he suspected he had been close to losing a toe or two.

Water laced with blood, earth, and the occasional leaf vanished down the drain. Still using only one hand—the other was holding Tennant tight against his chest—Gabriel found the soap and squeezed it in his palm, awkwardly washing first his face, then Tennant's, before continuing with the rest of their bodies.

Silently, the soap slipped over their skin. Gabriel made sure the older man was safe in his arms, unable to slip or hurt himself any further, placing Tennant between his legs and resting his head against his shoulder.

Finally in the shower with him, and he's unconscious, Gabriel mused with an inward growl and watched the blood and dirt as it ran down the drain. *Damn this injustice, and damn the centaurs!* Gabriel would have been the first to admit that he'd never considered it likely that he could share a shower with a naked man without being the least bit aroused. Right now, though, all he could think of was his friend surviving the night.

It took him nearly twenty minutes before he finished washing himself as well as Tennant, all the while avoiding touching the wound or even getting too close to it. Tennant didn't move, he only breathed, but at least he was doing that more easily now. Apparently, the hot shower had been a good idea.

A few minutes later, Gabriel tucked the doctor into his bed, covering him from toes to chin with the biggest, warmest blanket he could find. Where the arrow had been, there was now a blackened, ugly-looking wound, and as Gabriel didn't know what else to do, he just put a bit of gauze on it to keep it free from dust and dirt. Ideally, Tennant would wake up soon so he could drink some tea and even eat a bit of toast. And give some advice, of course. Otherwise… well, he wouldn't think about an otherwise unless Tennant remained unconscious.

Lighting a few of the candles that were placed all around the bedroom, Gabriel looked at the man he had grown so idiotically fond of. Between the sheets, his head propped up on a pillow, he appeared less tall, less strong, and definitely less superior. The sight triggered an urge to protect him—a ridiculous idea, given the fact that there was a lot more to Tennant than could be seen at first sight. Compared to fae, humans seemed to be but flies on the wall. Compared to Tennant, Gabriel was well aware that he knew nothing and would never be able to learn enough to even come close to the fae's knowledge.

"Self-pity. Just what you need right now," Gabriel said. Then he went to make himself a cup of tea and a sandwich. He'd read a bit, check out some runes—Portal runes and Healing runes too—while the doctor recovered. Yes. Good idea.

ABOUT two o'clock in the morning—Gabriel had fallen asleep in his favorite armchair, book lying open across his legs—Tennant attempted to run away. Or at least that was how it sounded: a man desperately trying to get away from his enemy, on all fours, if necessary, and without considering minor obstacles such as tangled bedcovers, or a wardrobe, or the hole in his shoulder and the severe blood loss he had suffered.

Gabriel woke with a start when he heard the noise. The book he had been reading slipped to the floor along with the paper and pen he had been using to scribble down some notes.

"What the hell?" he mumbled. He switched on the light, at first thinking that maybe someone was trying to break into the house before figuring out that the noise was coming from the bedroom.

"Doc?" he called, getting out of the chair. "You awake?

Tennant was far from being awake. When Gabriel entered the bedroom, he was stretched out on the floor, felled by a chair that had blocked his way. His lids were only half-closed, eyeballs rolled upward, and when Tennant picked him up to get him back to bed, his body radiated heat like an open fire.

At least the wound wasn't bleeding again.

Had he really thought saving his friend's life would be that easy? Tennant tossed and turned on the bed, pushing at the blanket and some unseen enemies. Gabriel could only watch in horror, not knowing what to do other than tie the man to the bed so he wouldn't hurt himself or rip his wound open again.

There were no ropes in Tennant's bedroom, but Gabriel found scarves long enough and strong enough to serve as primitive ties. If only he hadn't had such strong objections against tying someone without permission to do so. If only at the age of eleven he hadn't spent an entire weekend bound in his room as a punishment for stealing food.

Binding Tennant was not an option. That meant he had to find another way to make sure the doc wouldn't try to get out of bed again.

Frowning, Gabriel sat on the bed and wondered if it had been the right decision not to take Tennant to the hospital. On the other hand, he could easily call an ambulance right now. They would be here in less than ten minutes, taking care of the doctor a lot better than he could. After all, what use was there in being free when it meant being dead as well?

Gently, Gabriel stroked the unconscious man's hair out of his pale, sweaty face. He was just about to get the phone when Tennant reached out blindly and caught hold of his wrist. The grip was weak; it would have been easy to get free. It hadn't even been an aimed gesture.

It was evident from the man's closed eyes that Tennant was only searching for something, someone to hold onto. And apparently, Tennant didn't want to let go of him again. Instead, he pulled Gabriel's hand under his cheek.

The unconscious man sighed deeply. Simultaneously, the tossing and turning stopped. Gabriel could easily hear the doctor's heartbeat. A moment ago, it had been wild and slightly erratic. Now, with his hand touching Tennant's face, it calmed.

"Hmmm." Gabriel took his hand away and waited.

He didn't need to wait long: Tennant threw his head to one side, kicked the blanket to the floor, and let out a helpless cry. It was so very obvious that he didn't want to be alone, that he needed physical contact, that Gabriel placed both hands on Tennant's naked, glowing chest, hoping to calm him and to let him know that he wasn't alone.

Again it worked, soothing the fighting man. Tennant took a deep, shuddering breath and lay very still for a moment. He relaxed a bit as well.

Thoughtfully, Gabriel took a closer look at the man. He felt the fast, unsteady beat of the heart under his palm, he felt the heat the fever was causing, he saw Tennant's eyes moving under the closed lids, and he knew he wouldn't call an ambulance simply because he knew that Tennant wouldn't survive even the most professional treatment under the circumstances. After all, who would be willing to keep close physical contact with a fae?

Keeping Tennant's body still by holding him down with brute force was not what Gabriel wanted to do, though. It was uncomfortable at best for himself and would leave bruises on the doctor's chest in the long run. As gently as possible, he pulled Tennant's torso up, ignored the pained gasp, and slipped behind the injured man. One leg on each side of the body, Gabriel wrapped his fingers around each of Tennant's wrists, crossed his arms over his chest, and held him in a grip that allowed the doctor to move his head, hips, and legs but kept his upper body and especially his shoulders still.

Perfect.

Well… nearly.

Gabriel could smell the shampoo he had used to wash the doctor's hair and the soap that he had cleaned his strange, beautifully shimmering skin with. Underneath lingered the fragrance of the man himself—barely there, but very perceptible at the same time. Tennant smelled of summer wind and hay fire, of molten chocolate and the sunset—emotions rather than smells, but hell, now Gabriel couldn't help but feel aroused.

Uncomfortable, Gabriel shifted his position in order to regain control over his traitorous body, but to no avail. No matter how he shifted, his body was in close contact with Tennant's, and unfortunately, that was exactly what he had been dreaming about for a while now. Obviously, he would have preferred this to happen with both of them awake and healthy, but he was enjoying it nevertheless.

Hesitantly, Gabriel touched Tennant's naked shoulder, again worried about the heat radiating from the man's body. His fingertips, however, were unconcerned about such worries and moved on curiously. They found the pulse in Tennant's throat, beating slowly now and reassuringly strong. Earlier on, Gabriel had dared to draw a Healing rune; it seemed to be working.

His fingertips traveled on to the jaw, up to the cheek, cheekbone, and a bit higher, where finally they brushed over the soft, barely perceptible eyelashes. Tennant was still unconscious and wouldn't wake up in the foreseeable future. Therefore, Gabriel knew the doctor couldn't feel his back pressing against Gabriel's chest, Gabriel's breath on his neck, or the arms that held him so very close and safe. There was no way Tennant would ever know how deeply the younger man inhaled his scent or how close he was to kissing that neck, only lightly, just once, quickly enough to declare it his imagination. Gabriel had nearly convinced himself to act, but Tennant chose that precise moment to emit a deep, relieved sigh.

Gabriel's muscles tightened when he realized what he had been about to do. A kiss, even just brushing his lips across Tennant's slightly damp hair, was forbidden. It would have meant an unwanted intrusion, and it didn't matter that the doctor wouldn't have been aware of it.

Forcing himself to relax, Gabriel leaned his head against the headboard and closed his eyes. For the moment, things didn't look too bad, despite the fever. For the moment, it was most important that Tennant found some sleep, found his way from unconsciousness to dreamland. If he had to hold his body still until morning dawned, so be it.

THE next few days were filled with ups and downs. One hour, Tennant burned with fever; the next, his skin was cool, and he shivered as if he were still lying on the icy ground of the hidden world. At least the wound, surrounded by Healing runes now, didn't begin bleeding again apart from a few drops whenever Gabriel changed the dressing. All in all, things were much improved. If only Tennant would wake up sometime soon so he could kick him hard for getting injured in the first place and for causing him to go nearly mad with worry.

Whenever Tennant seemed calm, Gabriel sneaked into the living room for a few hours, enjoying the deep silence in the house. He read mostly, sometimes accompanied by a sandwich and a glass of water, sometimes by something he'd cooked. Food was not his first priority. Instead, he rushed through the books, learning as much as he could about Portal runes and the hidden worlds. He forced his fingers to draw the patterns, making sure he didn't feed the lines with power. Sometimes, Gabriel even dreamed about the runes, his fingers twitching in his sleep. He was always glad to wake up in front of the fireplace and not somewhere else, always somewhat concerned he might fall through a portal while dreaming.

And then—who knew what would happen once Tennant was awake again? There was still a murderer on the loose, there were other worlds to be explored, and there was so much to learn. Sometimes, when he was very tired, Gabriel even mused about the possibility that their adventure with Kyril would convince Tennant to leave him at home next time he went on a mission, and that thought alone made Gabriel cringe with fear. He didn't want to be left behind, he didn't want to be separated from Tennant ever again, and so he learned how to open a portal, how to heal wounds properly, how to use a Light rune even when running, to prove that he was actually irreplaceable.

In addition, Gabriel pondered the murders. Sweet Rain's face haunted him, and her last words about Tennant's eyes were a riddle he simply couldn't solve. Had she wanted to say that the doctor had killed her? That was nonsense—she'd called for him in the first place and had been clearly relieved to see him. The logical conclusion was that Tennant's eyes had reminded her of someone, and she had thought it necessary to let Tennant know it. The question was, why had she thought so? Did Tennant know the killer?

That was nonsense too. Obviously, the girl's words hadn't meant anything to the doctor. "If only she had lived one more minute," Gabriel said quietly. "Maybe she would have been able to give us a more specific description."

Useless wishes. Tree nymphs were born as trees, grew up, and eventually learned to build a human-looking body for their souls. Still, when the body was injured, it died, and Sweet Rain wouldn't be able to create a new body for several years. Gabriel had found this bit of information inside a book he hadn't been able to read a week ago, which was, in its own way, as scary as the idea of creatures who could die and still not be dead.

Taking a sip of hot cocoa, Gabriel ran his fingertip across the writing on the heavy book cover. It was a rune. He could remember looking at it the first night he'd spent in Tennant's house, as unable to sleep then as he was now. Back then, it was just a book in a foreign language, Russian maybe, or Arabic, but whatever it was, he hadn't been able to figure out its meaning. But in the past weeks, something had changed, and he had gradually become able to read the runes. It was as if he'd been blindfolded and Tennant had taken the blindfold off, and now he could read this book as well as all the others, learning about runes, the hidden worlds, and the portals that led to them. Each world had its own portal; each portal was opened by a different Portal rune.

Seventeen worlds. Seventeen Portal runes, each one unique, each one the only key to the connected world. Some were easy to draw. Some, like the one to the human world, were ridiculously complicated. In any case it required not only determination to learn how to draw the bloody runes, but the ability to feed them with power too.

Not knowing why he was suddenly able to read the book was driving Gabriel crazy. Nothing had changed, had it? What had triggered this sudden change in his eyes or his brain or whatever was responsible for his ability to read runes?

"Could have been him," Gabriel mused, emptying his mug. "He used a rune on me. Maybe it opened a barrier or something."

It was two in the morning, and he should have been in bed for hours. He was tired, no use denying it. He wanted to sleep. The problem was he had to sleep either in Tennant's bed or on the couch in the living room, so he would be there once the doctor began his tossing and turning game again. It was all right to leave him alone for a few hours; eventually, though, he would become restless, and only Gabriel's hands could calm him down.

Unfortunately, Gabriel loved to sleep close to the man. The other day, he had woken with his arms around him, his mouth dangerously near half-parted, gently snoring lips. He feared, truly feared, that very soon Tennant would wake from his fever for good, only to find himself in a tight embrace with an erection pressed against his backside. If that happened, it would be the end of their friendship, Gabriel was certain of it. Tennant had in no way indicated that he was sexually interested in his guest, and usually, when sex was brought into it, a friendship didn't survive. Which was why—although the damn thing wasn't particularly comfortable—Gabriel preferred to sleep on the couch. His own room was too far away from Tennant's bedroom, and he couldn't risk not hearing the doctor calling for him.

Tiredly, Gabriel looked toward the slightly open bedroom door. For the past few days, he had taken care of someone he barely knew, had changed dressings, had wiped off sweat, had trickled water between dry lips, and had cradled the man whenever possible. And he had done something he had never done before: he had worried. Apart from his grandmother, who had been a deeply disturbed woman even before she'd gone totally nuts, Gabriel hadn't cared about anybody. He didn't waste his emotions. He was unable to muster more than a vague affection for the people who surrounded him. He was definitely unable to love, no matter how much people tried to make him love them.

Lousy timing, really, that he had finally found someone he really, really liked and really, really desired on top of it.

Silently, he padded into the bedroom and sat in the chair he had pulled close to the bed. A strand of his hair had escaped the ribbon; he tucked it behind his ear and put a hand on Tennant's forehead. No fever, but then, that had happened before. The man wasn't shivering either, so hopefully, he'd finally wake up soon.

Then, hopefully, Gabriel would be able to sleep in his own bed again.

Putting his feet up on the mattress, Gabriel leaned back and closed his eyes. Colors and flashes danced in the darkness. He had overdone it, had read too long, had stayed up too late. He should get up and brush his teeth, he should fish for the blanket on the floor, he ought to—

And then he was asleep and dreamed of Tennant reaching out, finding his hand, and pulling it under his cheek once more. It was a lovely dream; it didn't even matter it probably wasn't true.

IMAGES of snow-laden trees drifted through his sleeping mind. The wind smelled of cocoa, the night had a slightly orange quality, and he was lying on the ground, looking up at a single star. It twinkled, this star. Where had he seen this twinkling before?

The star turned blue, ice-blue. Warmth flooded his body. He longed for this blue star, wanted to get closer, wanted to touch it, if possible. Something was special about it. The color? The feeling of contentment it provided or the arousal it caused? How could he be aroused by a star, he wondered, and where did the branches suddenly come from, digging into his back muscles? His legs began to cramp; the branches turned into ivy, wrapping around his feet and ankles, pulling him deeper into the ground. Snowflakes landed on his face. He was immobilized, unable to move as much as his head, and although his shoulders hurt from trying to get up, it was a most stimulating position.

"Gabriel," a voice whispered, and he moaned in anticipation, for surely if there was this voice, there was the possibility of a hand touching him, satisfying him, too.

"Gabriel!"

He struggled, tried to get closer to the voice, tried to embrace the blue star that spoke his name. The ivy yielded, crept away, didn't hold him down any longer, but when he tried to get to his feet, he struggled and fell, brought down by the damn branches.

"GABRIEL! Are you going to wake up sometime today?" Tennant's hand, shaking him. Tennant's face, only inches away from his.

Still half asleep, Gabriel tried to get up from the chair he had dozed off in, tripped over the blanket that had slipped to the ground, and landed hard on the floor, hitting his head on the bed frame on the way down.

"Ouch!" he exclaimed, understanding why he had dreamed of branches and ivy. The blanket was wrapped around him, restricting his movement, and he had driven the armrests of the hard chair into his ribcage in his futile attempt to find a comfortable position in the damn thing.

Unexplainable was the bulge in his jeans, though, painfully hard and embarrassingly obvious. Quickly, Gabriel pulled the blanket closer and thanked all existing and non-existing gods that Tennant was unable to read thoughts or participate in someone else's dreams.

Hopefully.

"Are you all right?" Tennant asked, concerned. "You were moaning and groaning as if you were having a nightmare, so I tried to wake you up."

Ah. That was where the voice had come from in his dream. "I'm fine," Gabriel mumbled, trying to hide his embarrassment along with his erection. "Must've fallen asleep. Anyway, what do you mean, am *I* all right? You should be worrying about yourself, Doc!"

Tennant leaned back against the pillows, clearly exhausted already by the little amount of talking he had done so far. His hair was plastered against his skull, matted by fever and nearly a week in bed, his lips were pale, and his joints stood out far too prominently. He hadn't eaten, of course, and had lost quite a bit of weight.

His eyes were beyond blue. Now that the pain and the fever were gone for good—at least, Gabriel hoped so, anyway—and he could see them in decent light, they were of such an unnatural color that it was more than obvious what Tennant was. Or wasn't.

"How am I, then?" the doctor asked lightly. "Last thing I remember is snow in my face and pain everywhere. How did we get back here? And how long have I been unconscious? And then… do you think there is a chance of something to eat?"

Sitting on the floor covering his groin with the blanket, Gabriel grinned widely with sudden relief. "You can have some burned toast," he offered. "Or burned porridge. Whichever you prefer." He got up slowly, making sure the blanket didn't slip.

"Wild Oak opened the portal. That was six days ago. You've been in really bad shape, and I very nearly called an ambulance a couple times, but then things improved and you just slept and, well, healed, I guess. It's Tuesday, by the way, and I'd say you're out of danger. So what shall it be—toast or porridge?"

"Both, if possible," Tennant said, snuggling into his pillow. "And lots of tea. And the newspaper. Please," he added belatedly.

Already at the door, Gabriel remembered something and fished for the chain he had kept in his pocket all week. "I guess you want that back," he said indifferently, placing it on the bedside table.

Tennant picked up the chain, letting the rune pendant dangle in the morning light. "I owe you a few explanations," he said quietly. "After breakfast, if possible, but if you insist, I'll answer all your questions right now."

He didn't put the chain on. Instead, he dropped it back on the table, a gesture that did more for Gabriel's peace of mind than any number of solved riddles could have done. Tennant saw no reason to hide his heritage from him any longer. Maybe there wouldn't be any more lies, either.

"You'll eat first," Gabriel said, growling the words. "Toast, tea, *and* porridge. If you manage to eat up, I'll allow you to take a shower. *Then* you can answer my questions."

Tennant grinned. "Yes, sir," he said. "I'll try my best to please you."

He shouldn't have said that, Gabriel thought as he went into the kitchen, the tightness of his trousers reminding him painfully how much he wanted the man. *He really shouldn't have said that.*

CHAPTER EIGHT

PROPPED up on his pillows, Tennant managed half a piece of toast and about a third of his porridge before he gave up. "Sorry, Gabriel," he murmured. "Seems I'm more tired than I thought." He leaned back, breathing deeply and evenly.

Watching him for a moment, Gabriel finally forced himself to take the bowl out of Tennant's hands. Silently, he got up. He was just about to walk out of the room when the man on the bed said, "Thank you."

Gabriel turned. "What for?" he asked. "I could hardly leave you there, could I?"

Tennant chuckled, then grimaced. "Ouch. Laughing still hurts." His eyes were shining, more so than they had been a few minutes ago. Apparently, the little food he had eaten had done him some good. "Thank you for not taking me to a hospital. Thank you for staying with me while I was ill. Thank you for taking care of me, and thank you for not freaking out."

Stunned, Gabriel walked back to the bed. Tennant had dark shadows under his eyes, which were even more prominent when compared to his luminescent skin. All in all, he still looked quite ill, and yet it was nearly impossible for Gabriel to keep from reaching out and touching his cheek, from running his thumb across those lips, from bending down and breathing in the fragrance of his skin. "Why on earth should I have freaked out?"

Having pushed himself up a bit, Tennant was now covered only from feet to hips, his belly, chest, and shoulders bare apart from the bandage that covered the wound. "Look at me," he said tightly. "I am not human. I let you believe I was, and I apologize for that, but my regret at not having told you before we went to Wild Oak's world doesn't change the fact that I am not a human man. In my experience, the people of your world are scared of us—of everyone who is not like them—and I expected you to be scared of me too. I was wrong, and I am grateful for it. I don't want you to be scared of me."

Gabriel sat down. The bowl kept his hands busy and gave him time to think of a reply. "Even when I was tied to the guest bed, I wasn't scared," he admitted, "although I should've been. From the first moment I saw you, from the second you jumped off that windowsill, I was lost. I like you—a lot, actually—and I think you know that already. Your friendship means more to me than I can say. That you consider it worthwhile to teach me runes and take me with you to a hidden world flatters me. I guess there's nothing that could freak me out where you are involved."

Slightly embarrassed that he had admitted that much, Gabriel wiped his wrist over his mouth and tried to find something he could look at, preferably not a part of Tennant's body. Clearing his throat, he added, "By the way, besides being ill and all, you look damn good. Don't you ever dare accuse me of being scared of you or the way you look." The chair fell backward as he fled the room and Tennant's eyes, which threatened to burn a hole right into his soul.

Gabriel went into the kitchen and began doing the washing up, a task he disliked but one that kept his thoughts focused. "Shouldn't have said that," he murmured to himself. "Now he knows I'm putty in his hands. Bad. Very bad, that is."

He had never done anything like this—admit his feelings, let someone else see into his heart and mind. Moreover, he had never felt anything like this. His thoughts were on Tennant day and night. He even dreamed of the man, goddammit! Emotions were usually nothing Gabriel was concerned with. He simply didn't have emotions apart from the basic ones like sympathy, fear, pain, or sadness. He didn't have close friends; he had never cared for any of his foster parents. He had never experienced more than raw lust for any of his male or female lovers. In a way, he liked to live on the streets: it was safe not to be bound to a house, to a partner, to a normal life. True, he had liked his grandmother. When she had left, he had been sad for a few days, but not heartbroken. At the orphanage, he had done well because he had never harbored any hope to be adopted—he hadn't wished for a family and had always been deeply confused when foster parents chose him and expected his gratitude and love in return.

And now this. He had lost his heart, just like that. Not just desire, not just lust or the need for a warm body in his bed. This was more, and yes, this was the part that scared the living daylights out of him. The way he looked at it, love broke people, reduced them to stuttering idiots, left them bereft of their own will, coherent thought, and the walls one needed to survive this life.

"I'm too old for this shit." The words sounded too loud in his own ears, and he glanced over his shoulder, praying that Tennant was still in bed and not standing in the doorway, listening to his rant.

His fingers fumbled. Trembling and careless, he dropped a cup, shattering it into a couple dozen pieces, some landing in faraway corners, some near the door. Gabriel had to get on all fours to pick them up. He was under the kitchen table and cracked his head hard when Tennant came in wearing nothing but the bedcover around his shoulders.

Taking a seat, Tennant casually asked, "Do you need help?" a bit hoarsely.

"I thought you were asleep!" Gabriel cursed as his hand landed on one of the shards, nearly cutting off half an index finger.

"I've been in bed long enough. Besides, I am hungry. I am even willing to eat some more burned toast." One foot, fragile in its nakedness, was but an inch away from Gabriel's hand. There was a tattoo of a vine around his ankle.

Too much temptation. Gabriel reached out and traced the vine with his fingertip, following the leaves up to calf and knee. The skin was warm, but not hot. The fever finally seemed to be gone for good. The vine—the tattoo of the vine, he had to remind himself, as it looked very, very real—was only slightly cooler, just enough for him to feel the difference.

"That wasn't there when I washed the blood off your body," he said. "There was some sort of tendril. Not this here. How do you do it?" Eventually, Gabriel managed to order his hand back, although he would very much have liked to go on exploring beyond the knee and way beyond what was commonly seen as decent behavior.

Slowly, Tennant bent over to look under the table. "There is another chair here you might like to use," he said, his voice gently mocking. "Although, if you wish to examine me further, I have no objection."

Gabriel blushed furiously. Obviously, Tennant hadn't meant for that to come out the way it had. Surely, he had offered nothing more than for Gabriel to satisfy his curiosity concerning the tattoos and not given him permission to take him right there on the kitchen floor!

He was careful not to get up too quickly, giving himself a chance of getting his facial expression under control. He picked up a few shards and dumped them in the trash. His head still hurt from whacking it on the table, and his legs trembled in the worst way from the effort not to wobble. Luckily, he was so embarrassed about the whole situation that his cock didn't dare stir.

"Now, how do you do this trick with your tattoos?" he asked after he'd composed himself somewhat. "I'm absolutely certain the one around your ankle looked different the last time I saw it." Harder than necessary, he placed a cup and a fresh piece of toast, buttered and topped with a generous amount of honey, in front of Tennant.

The doctor took a bite, swallowed, took a second bite, and put the toast back onto the plate exhaustedly. "Those aren't tattoos," he finally replied. "The patterns are part of the fae physiognomy. They often take on the form of plants, and they grow and wither throughout our lives. They're built by the pigments in our skin, and changes depend on age, gender, health issues, personal preferences, and state of mind."

Gabriel took the other chair. "Meaning?" he asked. "The latter part, that is. State of mind and all." It was good to just sit here and listen to Tennant's voice—it kept him from having more intimate thoughts and distracted his mind from the feeling of Tennant's skin under his fingertips.

"Meaning that the form of the tattoos, as you call them, varies in relation to my happiness. If I am sad, they perish; if I feel joy, they blossom. A truly unhappy fae or one with profound mental problems would have next to no pigmented patterns. Simple, really." He took a sip of his tea and sighed.

Gabriel looked at him closely. "When you were ill, the lines on your face and chest were barely visible, but whenever I put a cold cloth on your forehead, I could see them more clearly." At the time, he hadn't thought much of it, being too busy doing everything in his power to break the fever. "Was that because of the cold easing the fever?"

"Because you were near me," Tennant clarified. "Physical contact is very important when we fall ill or get injured." Without another word, he used his fingers to comb the hair out of his face. The blue of his eyes was the most dominant thing one noticed when looking at him, closely followed by the shimmer of his skin. Still, there were very distinctive patterns along his temples and the lower part of his jaw. Unlike the vines circling his ankles, these patterns looked less like plants and more like ornaments, giving his face the look of an ancient drawing.

"Not many humans have seen me like this," Tennant said, a distinct uneasiness audible in his usually serene voice. "The few who have were terrified. Humans consider us dangerous—wild, like animals, simply because of the way we look."

Gabriel's mouth acted before his brain could censor the words. "You are the most beautiful looking man I have seen in my life."

Shit.

Immediately, he apologized. "I shouldn't have said that. I mean, it came out the wrong way. It's not that I *like* you or anything." He was close to stuttering, and he knew it, but it didn't change the fact that he had become a stammering idiot.

Tennant's lip twitched, and he smoothly changed the subject, not commenting on the blatant lie Gabriel had just told. "Did you know that right after the first portals were opened, many fae died due to illnesses we caught from the human race? Only a few survived. We still have not recovered from that loss, and children are born too seldom for our liking. To protect ourselves, we restricted contact. Maybe if we had continued to visit your world and allowed you to visit ours, a friendship might have grown between our peoples. As it is, our refusal to share the knowledge of the runes and the portals with your people was considered an act of hostility, and humans began to truly fear us, some even considering us a threat. Ever since, fae who land in your world are hunted down mercilessly. And not only fae. All peoples from the hidden worlds suffer the same fate unless they manage to blend in. Like Lorelei, for example."

"No wonder you wear the rune," Gabriel mused. "I would if I were you. I'm glad now that I didn't take you to the hospital—I would have gone berserk if they had tried to take you away."

Pulling the duvet a bit tighter around his shoulders, Tennant nodded toward the bedroom. "Put it on, if you like. See how it works for you. I assume the change will be remarkable."

Gabriel snorted. "Yeah, sure. There is nothing in me that needs to be covered up. I am an ordinary-looking guy. How would the rune make me look more human than I do already?"

Tennant raised an eyebrow. He had pulled his legs up, his feet resting on the chair, the duvet covering him up to his chin. He looked more like a little boy than a grown man. Not even the dark shadows under his eyes changed that.

"Do you not realize that you appear unique in your own way?" he asked, the steam from his tea obscuring his eyes as he lifted it to drink. "The red of your hair is much deeper, richer, than I have ever seen in a human—it is what gave me the first hint that you weren't entirely human the moment we met. You have the eyes of a wolf—very interesting, fascinating even. One could drown in your eyes...."

Gabriel coughed, hiding his blushing face behind his hands.

"The way you move gives your heritage away too," Tennant continued thoughtfully. "You don't walk; you slink through the world like a hunter, silently and precisely. I also assume that you are stronger than a human man. Believe me, there is a lot the rune can cover up." Smugly, he stretched his back, trying to find a more comfortable position on the chair. "Go and put the necklace on. Let's see how you look."

What else could he do but what had been asked of him? There was no real reason to argue, although Gabriel thought to himself that Tennant was spouting a load of nonsense. If his looks were that remarkable, why was it no one had ever made a comment? Sure, he could move unnoticed in even the largest crowd, he could walk into a hotel and right through the lobby without the concierge so much as glancing at him, and in the past, more often than not, he had had the impression that his various lovers didn't quite recognize him the next morning. Yet his red hair and strange, wolfish eyes notwithstanding, he was ordinary.

There the necklace was, lying innocently on the bedside table: a thin, silver chain, the catch nearly too small to be worked by male fingers, and a pendant that seemed to contain several runes, not just one. It tingled when it touched Gabriel's palm, something he had neither expected nor experienced before, but then, he was about to use it—it was possible the runes were reacting to the power he was about to use.

Shrugging his shoulders, Gabriel opened the catch and slid the chain around his neck. The silver was cold on his skin, and the tingling became more prominent. Suddenly, warmth flooded his chest as if a bucket of heated water had been poured over him. It was irritating, and he couldn't help glancing down to see if he had left a wet patch on the floor. Luckily, the sensation vanished after a few heartbeats, and the chain felt like a chain and nothing more.

"See?" he said to Tennant as he walked back into the kitchen. "No difference. For a moment I thought something was happening, but then it was gone. You were wrong, Doc. Nothing special in me, nothing a rune might think worth covering up."

When Tennant didn't reply and stared at him with furrowed brows, Gabriel turned to see whether there was something behind him that had caught the other man's attention, but there was only the gently dripping faucet in the kitchen sink.

"What?" he asked. "Do I have drool on my chin?"

"You might like to take a look in the mirror," Tennant answered faintly. "The change is indeed remarkable. I must admit, I didn't expect you to look quite so different."

Getting up slowly, clutching the duvet tightly around his body, the doctor went into the hall, holding onto Gabriel's shoulder for support. "Look," he ordered, nodding at the full-length mirror.

Gabriel did—and paled in shock.

The most obvious change was his hair. It wasn't red anymore, not even a single strand. It had turned mousy brown and shortened until the ends brushed his neck. His freckles were gone, and his jaw line looked odd.

Looking into his reflected eyes, he realized they were brown now too. Gabriel never knew how fond he was of his eyes until he saw how they'd changed. These weren't his eyes anymore, and he didn't like it. But he did have to admit that brown eyes were definitely less interesting than his wolf's eyes.

He also seemed to be shorter and stockier. There was even a hint of a belly, and when he ran his hands across his ribcage, he could feel the fat he knew wasn't there. "Wow," he croaked. "Got to lay off the chocolate."

Tennant laughed. "That is only the runes doing a very thorough job. Three of them, actually. Algiz, Othala, and Eoh, woven together, strengthening each other, and thus protecting the one who wears the necklace. And just to make my point—I told you that you look remarkable. You turn heads, Gabriel. You—"

"No, I don't!" Confused and annoyed, Gabriel took off the offending necklace and dropped it into a bowl next to the mirror. Dumbstruck, he watched in the mirror as his hair grew and changed to its familiar color, his stomach flattened, and his legs stretched. Not really such dramatic changes, but important nevertheless. At least to him.

"No one ever knows I'm around unless I let them know," he said flatly and stepped away from the mirror. "People sometimes call out for me even though I'm sitting right in front of them. Sometimes I spend the night with someone and they don't recognize me the next morning. Believe me, man, occasionally I have the feeling I'm invisible. Good for my job, I'll grant you that. That rock star I stalked a while back—I was able to follow him right into his lover's arms without him noticing. There was a time when it bothered me, but I got used to it eventually, being able to blend in wherever I am. But take my word for it, no one thinks I'm remarkable!"

"I do," Tennant stated, visibly confused. Then: "Excuse me. I need to verify something."

Without waiting for Gabriel to answer or even understand what was going on, Tennant removed his hand from Gabriel's shoulder and ran it through his very real red hair, brushing the long strands away from his face.

"Hey!" Gabriel exclaimed. The urge to jerk his head back was strong; he hadn't expected to be touched intimately. Wasn't used to it. Tennant's fingers were warm and gentle, which posed a problem: Gabriel craved his touch and thus needed to get away from it lest he do something unforgivable.

"Hold still," Tennant ordered. "I just want to see the back of your head. I have a suspicion. I won't hurt you, I promise."

Fingertips whispered over his skin, leaving goose bumps in their wake. Gabriel had to steady himself by placing a hand on the wall, his muscles tightening under Tennant's touch, especially since it was so very tender, nearly imperceptible.

Keep going! his heart urged. *Stop it!* his mind cried. Torn between the pleasure Tennant's fingers were causing and the fear that he'd lose control and turn around and kiss the man, Gabriel stood rooted to the spot like a deer caught in the headlights of a car.

"Ah!" Triumphantly, Tennant ran a thumb over an especially sensitive area high at the base of Gabriel's neck. "Thought so. Now let's see what this is."

Tennant took another step, now standing so close to him that the duvet was squeezed in between them. Gabriel could feel the warmth radiating from Tennant, could smell the tea and toast on his breath, could feel the man's hair tickling his cheek. He had to turn his head away and squeeze his eyes shut, anything to be able to keep control over his betraying, longing body, and his jeans once again became uncomfortably tight. That just being near the doctor aroused him this much worried him as much as it excited him—he had never experienced such a strong reaction before, and he hoped Tennant was too busy with whatever he had found to realize that his guest was very close to tackling him and taking him right there on the floor, with or without his compliance.

Tennant didn't know it—no one knew it—but Gabriel was, on occasion, more wolf than he cared to admit even to himself. His instincts were strong, and he listened to them whenever possible. His urge to hunt was equally well developed, and in the past, he had satisfied this urge by chasing suspects for Mallfrick and going after bed-partners who had sworn they would not end up in bed with him. It was the hunt as well as the triumph of convincing a straight guy to sleep with him or a girl to cheat on her boyfriend that gave him the kick he needed, not the sexual act itself.

With Tennant standing close enough to be able to hear his heartbeat, the wolf came to the surface and tried to convince Gabriel that mating right now would be a damn good idea. A growl built up in his throat, his fingers twitched in anticipation of brushing over Tennant's fragile skin, and his cock ached badly enough to make his teeth grind.

The fragrance of Tennant's skin made him feel so dizzy, he was just about to turn his head to claim a kiss when the doctor said, "Did you know that there's a rune tattooed on your neck? A variation of the Algiz rune, by the looks of it. Come into my workroom; I would like to examine it a bit more closely."

The duvet whirled up small specks of dust when Tennant walked away, unaware of how close he had come to experiencing Gabriel's full attention—unwanted attention that would herald the end of any friendship that had developed between them so far.

Gabriel swayed, although his hand was still pressed against the cold wall. Swallowing dryly, he shook his head, trying to figure out what had just happened. "What the hell is wrong with me?" he asked the empty hallway. "I don't have problems controlling myself. I don't jump people just because they smell nice or touch me in a completely nonsexual way. He's touched me before; I've seen him naked. No reason to go crazy because of his fingertips on my neck. That's just not like me!" Desperately, he dug his hands into his hair and pulled, hoping that a bit of pain would bring him back to his senses.

However, his erection, tightly pressed against the fabric of his jeans, continued to demand relief. His muscles urged him to run after Tennant, hug him, hold him, taste him, and take him. His brain teased him with pictures of the two of them rolling naked across the floor, and his lips burned with need for a kiss.

Fucking hell. It had gotten out of control, and he didn't have a clue why.

Well, that was a lie. Of course he knew why. He was suffering the pangs of love. Big time. Since he'd never been in love before, it was even worse: he had no idea how to cope with it, what to do to make it go away, how to treat it so he would feel better. Love seemed to be quite a nasty illness, if it had him thinking about raping a man he truly and deeply liked.

Loved.

Fuck.

"Gabriel?" Tennant called from his workroom a bit impatiently.

"Just a sec." Wearily, Gabriel wiped the sweat from his brow. He didn't know, given his condition, if he could go in there, as that meant being in the same room with the doctor.

Maybe if he took care of his cock first, if he got the immediate need out of his system, it would be easier.

"Be with you in a minute," he called, and he headed for the bathroom.

THE door closed behind him. Plants were everywhere, some emitting a sweet scent, and sunlight shone in through the window while outside a single bird sang a lonely song.

He placed a towel on the cool tiles and slipped his jeans over his hips. He grabbed his cock too tightly, even painfully. He wanted this to be over with as soon as possible. Jerking off was a necessity, not a pleasure, and he would do it only so he could behave like himself again instead of lusting after Tennant like a lovesick teenager.

Moving his fist up and down his shaft didn't do for him what it was supposed to do: he couldn't finish. It only hurt in a tense, anticipatory sort of way. His cock remained rock hard despite his efforts, and he thought of Tennant waiting in his workroom....

A moan, deep and hoarse. Now where had that come from? He was almost always silent in bed unless someone chose to hurt him, which resulted in getting out of the situation as quickly as possible. He certainly didn't moan. Never.

So where had he been? Ah, yes. Tennant. Waiting for him.

Another moan, louder this time. Instead of mercilessly fisting himself, Gabriel slowed down a bit, stroking his cock more than strangling it. It felt good.

The wall behind him was hard against his back. The towel underneath him tickled his thighs. A plant dropped a leaf, and Gabriel thought of ice-blue eyes and snowflakes on silvery skin. Slower. His fingers were wrapped loosely around his length now, sliding the foreskin back, pre-cum wetting his knuckles.

Tennant, resting in his arms, his throat only an inch away from his lips. The two of them together in the shower, soapy water making their skin slippery. Back then, it hadn't been sexual; here, now, it turned Gabriel on beyond belief.

Parted lips, ragged breathing—he was close to climaxing, but unlike a few minutes previously, he didn't want to come. Not yet. He wanted to prolong this a bit, wanted to enjoy it for just another few moments, thinking of the fae he had fallen in love with.

Almost carefully, he thrust into his fist, both feet pressed securely against the floor. Eyes half closed, he licked his lips, dry and slightly swollen from biting them with hungry teeth. If only he weren't alone in here. If only it weren't his hand around his cock, but Tennant's.

"Gabriel?"

The voice sounded muffled through the closed door, but it didn't matter. His name, spoken by the object of his desire, threw him over the edge, and he spilled his seed over his fist and his legs and onto the towel. A low cry emerged from his lungs, not loud enough to be heard outside, but shockingly longing in his own ears.

"How could this happen?" he whispered, his cock finally going limp. "How could I allow myself to fall in love?"

As if you could have done anything to prevent it, his mind replied, but he didn't listen. Satisfied for the moment but disgusted with himself nevertheless, Gabriel got up and washed off the signs of his lack of self-control. His jeans were spotless; he had only soiled the towel, so he soaked it in water, wrung it out, and hung it up to dry.

Pulling up his trousers, he looked around. No traces left. Good.

"Gabriel? Are you all right?" Tennant sounded concerned now.

"I'm fine," Gabriel murmured. "Splendid. Just don't look at me, don't talk to me, and most importantly, don't touch me ever again, or I can guarantee nothing, Doc."

While he had been busy in the bathroom, Tennant had gotten dressed and was now wearing black trousers and a soft shirt. A makeshift sling held his right arm—Gabriel assumed the wound still hurt, although his friend hadn't complained so far.

Sitting at his workbench, Tennant smiled when he saw Gabriel. "You didn't catch a cold or something?" he asked. "You look a bit pale."

Gabriel frowned. "You look pale too. I think you should go back to bed and rest, Doc." Something was different in the way the doctor looked, but he couldn't put his finger on it. As the top buttons of Tennant's shirt were open, Gabriel could see his chest and the thin lines on his skin, showing tendrils of ivy. Hair covered the man's temples; his wrists were obscured by the sleeves. Gabriel took a closer look. "Somehow, you look a bit less bright, if that makes sense at all. What have you done?"

Slowly, Tennant stretched, looking at him oddly. "What color are my eyes?" he asked, a fairly ridiculous question in Gabriel's opinion.

"Blue," he snapped. He was slightly nervous that things might get out of hand again. Ideally, he would have been in his own room right now, keeping his distance from Tennant and calming down a bit.

Instead, he had to deal with the man's presence, which was a bad idea. "They've always been blue, in case you didn't notice the last time you looked into the mirror. Ice-blue. Your hair is black with a bit of gray, you're nearly as tall as I am, and you are neither too fat nor too thin."

Rubbing his hands over his upper arms, he realized that he was cold. Time for a break. A long, leisurely break with a pot of tea, something to eat, a boring book, and no company at all.

"And what pattern can you see on my arm?" Pushing the sleeve back from his wrist, Tennant turned his arm so Gabriel could see the tiny flowers decorating it.

Briefly, he stretched his neck. "Don't know. Some plants. Small, a bit like violets. Why?" A strand of his hair brushed Tennant's skin, a clear indication that he was too close again. A step back was due. Or five.

"Fascinating." Tennant sounded impressed. "I should look different to you. At least a head shorter, with a hint of a beer belly, thinning, short hair, and of course you shouldn't be able to see any patterns on my skin. Say, do you love me, Gabriel? Or at least desire me?" It was a friendly question, asked without the smallest hint of sarcasm. The doctor could have been asking about Gabriel's favorite color or if he preferred red or white wine.

Gabriel blanched. "Neither," he bit out. "Why do you ask? In the mood for sex? I'll think about it once you are able to stand without support." Another step back, and he stood in the doorway, several feet away from the workbench. Hopefully, his body wouldn't betray him by showing clear signs of his real feelings. Hopefully, Tennant wouldn't come any closer or ask any more far too direct questions.

The doctor just raised an eyebrow as if he didn't entirely believe him. "My eye color is indeed blue, and my—black—hair is a bit grayer than I would like it to be. The flowers on my arm are called stardrops. And you shouldn't be able to see any of it, as I am wearing my necklace again." He hooked a finger under the chain, and the pendant gleamed in the light.

Gabriel frowned. The first time he had seen the doctor... hadn't he thought his hair to be short and straight instead of slightly curly, and hadn't he wondered how he could have overlooked those ice-blue eyes at first?

When he said so, Tennant's eyes sparkled with excitement. "You saw through my disguise from the very first time? One possible explanation would be a strong emotional connection or desire, but I admit that it is unlikely that you fell in love with me at first sight. Damn." He seemed really disappointed. "Could you see the patterns on my skin back then?"

Gabriel shook his head. "Not until you'd taken the necklace off."

"Let's assume there is a different reason for why you could see through my disguise at first," Tennant mused. "It is still most likely that you've developed certain feelings for me and are now able to—"

"I have not!" Gabriel shouted. "No feelings, none whatsoever, do you hear me!"

Damn! He couldn't believe that Tennant had put his finger right on the problem without even realizing it!

Again the doctor looked surprised. "Well, if you say so," he commented with a dubious undertone to his voice. "In that case, I am at a loss as to why I don't look as I usually do to you."

Weak with relief that Tennant had let go of the subject, Gabriel forced a grin onto his lips. "Whatever the reason, to me you've always looked like you do now, blue eyes and black hair and all. True, I didn't see the patterns on your skin when we first met. But I clearly remember your eye-color. Ice-blue. Always has been. It's just a little bit dampened now that you're wearing the necklace again. Maybe it's broken?"

Slowly, Tennant shook his head. "No. It works perfectly. So there must be another explanation for your ability to see me as I really am. Actually, it might have to do with your secret heritage, which I still haven't figured out." Visibly concerned, he slammed his hand onto the chipped surface of the workbench. "I need to work harder, find out about your heritage and that rune combination on your neck," he murmured. Opening a drawer and rummaging through its contents, he took out a set of slides and arranged them, obviously planning to examine some more of Gabriel's strange blood immediately.

Without a second thought, Gabriel stepped back into the room. "You'll go back to bed now, Doc. No discussion. I can see your shoulder aches, I can see that you are tired, and honestly, it doesn't matter why I can see your real self. You need to find a murderer, remember?" One arm went around the doctor's waist; easily, he pulled him up and led him out of the workroom.

Suddenly, Tennant leaned heavily on him. "I might have exaggerated," he murmured. "Still. Would have been a perfect explanation if you had desired me. A mixture of heritage and love, maybe. After all, you couldn't see the patterns on my skin at first." He sighed. "Love. Even I know that love always messes things up."

Luckily, the bedroom was close by, and luckily, Tennant couldn't see Gabriel gulp. *It would be the perfect explanation*, he thought. *I did fall in love with him, and now I can see him even more clearly than before. Let's hope he's too dizzy right now to remember what he said in the morning.*

Tennant swayed, then staggered. Gabriel could barely believe only a minute ago, the doctor had looked nearly as healthy as before he'd been shot. Half carrying his friend, he was glad to be able to lower him onto the bed quickly. "You don't want me to love you, Doc," he grumbled, hoping very much the doctor could hear him. The fae's eyes were closed, and he breathed deeply, as if asleep. "I agree with you. Love's awful. Although, if you are ever in the mood for a quick fuck, I might be persuaded."

Covered up to his chin, Tennant opened his eyes. "I doubt it," he whispered. "I have managed all my life without intercourse. I see no reason to change for something that seems to be mostly meaningless to you." Sighing heavily, he sank deeper into his pillows. A moment later, he was asleep.

"What?" Gabriel said, not sure if he had understood correctly. "What? You've never been laid? You've never... meaning... you're still a virgin?"

"WHAT exactly did you mean when you said you've done fine so far without physical love? You're how old? Around forty? And you tell me you've never had... well. You've never made love?" Glad he'd phrased it less rudely but still not quite believing what Tennant had said the previous day, Gabriel looked accusingly over the breakfast table, waving a bread knife while doing so.

A drop of honey hit the table.

Calmly, Tennant continued buttering his toast. He looked much better this morning—no surprise there, as he had slept through the better part of twenty-four hours. As soon as he got up, he'd dragged Gabriel into his workroom again, thoroughly examining the rune on his neck, and only when Gabriel had threatened to bind him to a chair and feed him had he agreed to tea and toast. Right now, though, the subject wasn't as harmless as strange runes.

"Why do people have sex, in your opinion?" Tennant asked. "An honest answer, please."

Gabriel cringed. He wasn't used to talking about personal things. "Because it feels good and because for a little while, you aren't lonely."

"Does it work?" Tennant asked. "The not-feeling-lonely-part, that is. Does it really work that way? Because, Gabriel, I don't believe it does. Not for you, anyway, or you wouldn't waste your time with me, someone you barely know. You would be with the one you love. Instead, you care for me even though we only met a short while ago, even though I lied to you and endangered you."

A few bites, and his toast was gone; apparently, the doctor was finally hungry enough to eat more than just crumbs. "And it wouldn't work for me, either. I require emotions if I am to allow someone to touch me. Deep emotions. Positive emotions. Which is the reason why I did not sleep with Sweet Rain when I had the chance. I have decided not to experience physical love. Logical reasoning, I would say."

"What's love got to do with sex?" Gabriel asked, suddenly feeling cold.

Breakfast had lost its appeal. Funny, really, what a few well-placed questions could do. Tennant's words had made him uneasy simply because they were true. To him, sex was just something that ended the hunt. It wasn't as exciting as the hunt, it wasn't as good as chasing the target, and it usually felt flat and lifeless compared with the excitement of making someone fall for him. In his sexual exploits, there was neither emotion nor real pleasure.

Visibly surprised, Tennant contradicted, "What has love not to do with *making* love? Isn't one required for the other?" He waited for a good answer with tilted head.

The smell of food was now becoming positively repulsive to Gabriel. Pushing back his plate of scrambled eggs, he got up and paced the room. "I just can't believe you weren't curious at least once in the past, let's say, twenty years," he challenged, if only to avoid answering Tennant's question. "Weren't you ever attracted to someone? Didn't you ever want to find out how it feels to fuck?" Deliberately using the rudest word for what Tennant had called "making love," Gabriel went to the living room, briefly stared out of the window, and finally settled on the couch, putting his hands on his knees to keep them from betraying his uneasiness.

"I *am* curious," Tennant replied, following Gabriel into the room. "I have been attracted a few times in my life too. Neither was reason enough to become intimate. I am thirty-nine years old, Gabriel, and of course I wish for someone who loves me and whom I could love in return, but frankly, I consider that an unlikely event, given that I live in your world and not in mine. I cannot show my true self here, which I would want to do if I were in love with someone. Conclusion: I will remain alone."

Gabriel stared at the fae and couldn't believe what he'd just heard. *I am with the one I care for!* he thought, wishing he had the guts to say it aloud. *I am with the one I desire. This someone is* you. *Why the hell can't you see that?* But Gabriel remained silent for several long moments before he finally snapped, "I guess you don't own an umbrella firm, either, do you?"

Tennant chuckled, obviously not surprised by the sudden change of subject. "No, I do not. And runes are not just a hobby for me. They are the source of my income, as few people know as much about them as I do. My help comes at a price, whether someone wants a portal to be opened or needs a necklace similar to mine or requires information about lost relatives. The umbrella firm is just a convenient thing to say if I need a harmless, slightly boring job."

"Any other lies you've told me?" Gabriel asked, deadpan.

Tennant smiled. "A few, I suppose, but those I can't talk about. On a different note, Gabriel, do you not want to know about the rune tattooed on your neck?"

Gabriel felt the same icy dread running down his spine as yesterday. "The Algiz rune, you called it," he said, surprised that he had control over his voice. "Which means... protection?"

"Precisely. Protection and freedom, in a way, but what's on your neck is a variation of Algiz. As far as I could see, there is a Healing rune woven into it. Have you ever had problems with wounds, injuries, or illnesses?"

Slowly, Gabriel shook his head. "Once, I broke my arm, or at least, my gran thought I did. When she found a doctor she could afford, though, he told her that it was nothing but a bruise."

"You heal exceptionally fast, then. Thought so. And you can walk freely amongst others without being seen unless you put yourself in broad display, like when we were in La Laterna Magica or the police station. It's the reason people don't spare you a second glance; it's the reason you—falsely—assumed you were mostly average-looking."

Gabriel had to dwell on that for a while. "I guess it's stronger because it's part of me," he finally said. "I mean, is it common to tattoo such a thing on one's skin?" Hesitantly, Gabriel ran his fingertips over the spot where the rune was. He couldn't feel it, not really, but he knew it was there. The spot had always been a bit more sensitive to touch, and the few times he'd been in danger of getting arrested by the police, it had actually stung. "How does it work?"

"Protection, freedom, and health," Tennant repeated. "The tattoo is tiny, barely visible unless one looks for it. When you said that no one notices you, I knew it had to be there. It doesn't change your features; it makes people look in another direction, makes them forget you the same moment they have seen you. You said you have experienced this many times in your life. Someone must have been very concerned about your safety to do this to you, knowing that tattooing it onto your skin would make it impossible for you to get rid of it."

From out of nowhere, old wounds ripped open, wounds inflicted in the orphanage by children Gabriel had liked but who always thought him to be the new kid even though he wasn't, by adults who simply overlooked him, by teachers who didn't even know he was in their class.

"I thought it was because of me," he said tightly. "That they ignored me because I wasn't interesting enough to take a second look at or to remember my name. Because I'm unimportant, insignificant, and beneath notice." Damn. Was it necessary for the tears to sting behind his eyelids?

"You aren't," Tennant objected gently.

Gabriel didn't hear him. "That's why I hunt, Doc. I hunt men and women alike, lure them into my bed so they have to look me in the eyes, at least for a short time, seeing me while I fuck them. You are right. It doesn't work. Never did—I'm always lonely because no one ever *sees* me. And now you tell me it's because of a bit of ink that even the foster parents I lived with had to think twice about my name, even after two months under their roof?"

Angrily, he wiped a tear out of the corner of his eye, shaking his head to clear his thoughts and get himself under control. It was not an easy thing to do with sympathy clearly visible in Tennant's eyes—and definitely not with the knowledge pounding at the back of his head that the doctor was the one man who *could* see him.

Lowering his head, Gabriel stared at the floor, hands folded at the back of his neck, letting his hair cover his face.

He didn't hear Tennant move until he sat down next to him, placing a hand on his shoulder. It was a small gesture, but soothing nevertheless. "I do not know who tattooed the rune onto your skin." Quiet words, meant to calm him. "I assume it was your grandmother or someone she took you to. She knew about the secret part of your heritage and how dangerous it was for a child with mixed heritage to grow up in this world. Taking this information into account, it would have been the right thing to keep you as safe as possible. Without the rune, looking as remarkable as you do, you would not have lived in an orphanage or with foster parents, but in a ghetto all your life. It is very possible you would not even have reached puberty. A very drastic interference, I must admit, but a useful one and proof that you were loved deeply by whomever did this."

"Tainted blood," Gabriel said with a bitter laugh. "That's what my mom used to call it. Unclean, dirty, soiled. She couldn't look at me, couldn't touch me—she was barely able to talk to me the few times she came to see my gran. That's why she dumped me in the gutter right after my birth: because of my tainted blood. She was shocked when she saw me for the first time as a newborn—she hadn't known my dad had been part shapeshifter. Guess he must have hidden it, like you. Horrible, my mom called me, and an abomination."

More tears. Great. Just fucking great. One by one, they dropped to the floor, leaving tiny stains.

When had he last cried? He couldn't remember. As a child, possibly, when his mother, who he had hoped would one day love him as much as he loved her, turned her back and staggered out of his grandmother's house, searching for her next drug-induced kick.

Tennant's hand was warm on his shoulder, infusing him with reassurance. "You are not horrible, nor is your blood tainted. You were never invisible to me. When I was sitting on the windowsill of Miss Kinney's apartment, the color of your hair drew my attention. It looked like a flame in the twilight, and I realized you were watching me, although you shouldn't have been able to see me. I do not know why the rune allows me to see you, just as I may never know why you are not affected as you should be by my necklace. But I assure you, I will never forget your name, and I will never have to think twice about who you are and that you are a very close friend."

"Good to know," Gabriel mumbled. The fact that Tennant had just called him a friend—a very close friend—meant much more to him than he cared to admit right now.

"The rune on your neck might prevent you from being recognized by people who don't really care about you. But it cannot hinder friendship, and it cannot suppress love. You might like to keep that in mind, Gabriel."

"Once I've stopped crying, I will," he said, rubbing his eyes.

Gabriel finally regained some control, mostly because of the doctor's words. He wasn't a child anymore, and there were in fact a few people who had recognized him even before he'd met Tennant.

Billy and Marita, for example, and didn't Conchita always come over when she was in the mission?

A thin smile curved his lips. Hugging a cushion to his chest, he said, "Now, what were you really doing in Lorelei's apartment? What was she, apart from a mermaid? There are still many unanswered questions, and as you are not going anywhere anytime soon, you might as well answer them."

Smiling, Tennant leaned back into the cushions as well. "I am investigating deaths, if asked to," he began, carefully choosing his words. "Recently—over the last six months, that is—several people from the hidden worlds have been killed. Some have died in accidents; some, like Mallfrick, have been murdered in a very obvious, brutal way. All of them lived in this world, many concealed by runes I had made. At first, I thought it was just because of that: them living here and not in their own worlds. Lorelei Kinney was a client. She asked me to find out who was stalking her, and when she didn't turn up for a meeting, I became concerned. At the time, I thought it a necessary move to break into her apartment. As we know now, she was just busy with Wright, and only days later did she disappear."

"You never did write her any letters, did you?"

Tennant looked a tad embarrassed. "Another lie, I suppose. And no, I didn't. The letters were just a poor explanation for my intrusion. I thought I could keep you from harm if I didn't explain too much. Didn't work, taking into consideration that I ended up dragging you into a centaurs' trap."

Gabriel managed a shaky grin. "She might have been referring to me—Lorelei—talking about a stalker," he pointed out. "I followed her for nearly a week, trying to get a picture of her and Wright."

Tennant shook his head. "No, she came to me before that, and she wouldn't have noticed you anyway. It was someone else."

"The murderer killed Sweet Rain. Did she live here too?"

Absentmindedly, Tennant rubbed his arm, making the patterns on his hand become more visible. "Every now and then, she would visit this world, but she didn't live here. Therefore, my theory must be wrong."

Gradually, Gabriel got his trembling limbs under control. It was surprising what hugging a cushion could do for a grown man. "So now what?" he asked. "What are you going to do once you are fully recovered?"

"Honestly? I don't know. I had hoped to find information in Miss Kinney's apartment, some sign of the one who had been stalking her, abducted her friend, and killed them. No clues, though, nor in Mallfrick's office. All I have is a cryptic line of a dying young woman, referring to my eyes."

Gabriel looked at him. "The blue ones or the brown ones?"

Tennant started to answer, but after thinking properly about the question, he reconsidered. "She knew how I really look," he mused. "I visited her world when I first left home. Spent a summer there. I made the pendant on my chain many years later."

"So she knew your eyes are blue. And she was looking into your eyes—the brown ones—when she died. Perfect." Gabriel snorted. "If she wanted to say the murderer had eyes like you, we don't even know which color she meant."

"I cannot believe it's that easy—her referring to the color and nothing else. She must have been trying to give me a more specific hint, something she thought I would understand." Rarely had Tennant sounded so confused and sad. "She might not have known what she was saying anymore. She was in pain, she was scared—"

"She sent her brother to get you because what she had to say was important. I say we just ask Wild Oak. Go back to her world, avoid contact with any centaurs, and maybe he will tell us that he's seen the murderer, too, and just forgot to tell us about it."

At that, Tennant smiled and briefly brushed his open palm over Gabriel's cheek. It was a tender and very intimate gesture, one Gabriel hadn't expected at all. Obviously, it couldn't have meant what he hoped it meant. Could it?

"I am glad I found you," the doctor said before Gabriel could make a flippant remark. "I am glad you are here. You saved my life, Gabriel, risking yours while doing so. You mean too much to me already. I will not make you go back there, nor will I return in the foreseeable future. My shoulder will need some time to heal. Using a portal while injured would not be safe."

Swiftly, without thinking about it twice, Gabriel leaned over and brushed his lips over a spot on his friend's forehead, hugging Tennant briefly. "In that case, we need to solve this mystery from your bed," he said. "Without me, you are not going anywhere, as you are clearly incapable of taking care of yourself."

Tennant grinned.

A thought suddenly hit Gabriel. "Back in Wild Oak's world, you said you might have followed the wrong track, remember? Leading us to the centaurs' realm? Question is, what if the wrong track was left deliberately? Sweet Rain could have been chosen as a victim just to set up a trap for you. Have you considered that ending up in the wrong area of the woods might have been planned?"

Gabriel stood. It was probably a good idea to replace the cushion on the couch and get out of there, or else he wouldn't be able to leave Tennant with a single peck. "You say each victim so far was from a hidden world. You are fae. You getting shot might have been a first try to kill you—you might be next on the murderer's list, and if that is the case, I will go to hell and back to keep you from further harm."

For a change, it was Tennant who needed to clear the emotion from his throat. Watching Gabriel put on boots and a jacket, he asked, "You do not plan to go to hell right now, do you?"

"I'm going shopping. Might take a few hours. I'll pop into the mission, check on Billy and Marita on the way back home. Don't do anything stupid in the meantime, okay?"

"I'll try not to," Tennant replied. Gabriel had a strange feeling that he might have liked to say something else too.

CHAPTER NINE

OUTSIDE, the sun was shining, a welcome change from the artificial light in the apartment as well as from the clouds that had been plaguing the sky the past few weeks. There was no snow in sight, and although it was still quite chilly, it wasn't freezing anymore.

Thoughts in serious turmoil, Gabriel decided to walk to the bus station instead of taking Tennant's car to run his errands. A little fresh air would do him some good. Getting his emotions under control before he entered the shopping center was essential.

Sneaking up to his neck, his fingertips parted the hair and searched for the tattoo. He couldn't really feel it, but he knew where it was. Always had, in a way. Until now, he hadn't known its significance, but now that Tennant had brought up the subject, he could clearly remember the pain caused by the needle. He could remember crying. And very vaguely, he could remember a soothing hand on his head, holding him down, immobilizing him while someone etched the tattoo onto his skin.

Not his gran. He couldn't imagine the old woman knowing that much about runes, so it hadn't been her who'd created the rune. Maybe she had taken him to someone who had the knowledge, but as the old woman had vanished when he'd been a child and was probably dead for twenty years, there was no way to find out.

It didn't matter, anyway. Only two things were of importance: someone had, by way of protecting him, doomed him to a life where finding a new family or close friends had been awfully hard, if not impossible, and somehow, his ability to become sort of invisible didn't affect the doctor.

Whom, coincidentally, he had fallen in love with.

His heart skipped a beat as he thought of Tennant, and he wondered why he was so reticent to let the doctor know how he felt. He had resolutely denied any emotional entanglement, had denied desire as well as love, because he was too damn scared of something that might become more than a mere one-night stand. In theory, it would have been easy to say, "Yes, I desire you. Let's go to bed." That way, Tennant would be aware of his feelings, but Gabriel hadn't been able to force the words out of his mouth. He was beginning to think a quiet ten minutes in the bathroom would become a repeat occurrence.

Bathroom. *Shit.* How embarrassing! Sitting on a cold floor, pulling himself off while thinking of someone who was a fucking virgin!

"Can't believe it." Gabriel stopped walking. "I should just keep going and never go back."

He was about half a block away from the bus station. He had his knapsack and enough money in his pocket to survive for a month, if he ate sparingly. He stood there, seriously contemplating just vanishing, running from the doctor and those skilled hands that were so good at soothing headaches, aching muscles, or catching him when he fell off a chair.

"I can't go back there, really," he murmured, trying to convince himself. "Impossible. I can't let him know that I want him so badly that I'd drag him to bed whether he likes it or not. He'd hate me for so much as considering it, and it's obvious he doesn't love me enough to go to bed with me willingly, and… and…." Helplessly, he shook his head, trying to get Tennant out of his mind. Naturally, it didn't work. Furthermore, he couldn't leave, not with Tennant being weak as a kitten and the vague possibility that the doctor might be a potential victim on a mad murderer's list.

A bus drove past, and Gabriel began to run. In the distance, he could see others waiting to be picked up, and he made it at the last second. Worrying about the fare was unnecessary—he was absolutely certain neither the bus driver nor any of the passengers would remember him once he was out of their line of sight.

IT WAS extremely strange to walk into a supermarket without the intention of stealing anything. Actually, it was strange to go into a supermarket during the daytime—usually, he sneaked in after dark, hid in a quiet corner, took what he needed, and rushed out again in less than five minutes. Not doing so—being just a normal customer—made him cringe, expecting someone would accuse him of shoplifting any second.

No one even noticed as he walked in. No one thought it strange that he bought lettuce, milk, and pasta. People made way to avoid bumping into him, but apart from that, no one spared him a second look.

It felt strange. Somehow, he had expected the magic that made him sort of invisible to fail now that he knew it was there, but that was not the case. His leather jacket didn't fit in here, nor did his jeans or boots or the fact that his hair was anything but graying and thinning. The mainly elderly patrons, shuffling slowly among the high shelves, didn't consider it odd that he was doing his shopping alongside them. Walking past the dairy section, Gabriel looked up and saw himself in a mirror that covered the wall behind the counter.

Had his hair always been that red? It seemed to burn, and when he moved his head, he could nearly see sparks flaming up. His eyes, the freckles that covered his nose and cheeks, and his lips, ready to part in a growl—why did no one so much as comment on it? Those old guys should take a step or two back; they should be scared of him or eying him suspiciously, if nothing else.

Come to think of it, he should have known that he looked anything but common all this time. Well, better late than never.

Slowly, Gabriel brought his fingertips up to his neck and brushed his thumb over the rune. It worked well enough that he had to say, "Can I pay?" to the lady at the checkout because she had overlooked him, even though he had made enough noise placing his groceries in front of her. When he left the store, no one ran after him, screaming, "Thief!" Of course, he hadn't stolen anything this time, but still, it felt wrong, albeit in a good way.

WHEN he walked into the mission, only Father Barley was there, sweeping the floor. "Good day, my friend," he said with a tired smile. "I can't remember your face, son—have you been here before? You are welcome, but if you want lunch, it will take a little while."

Why am I not surprised? Gabriel thought. "Hello, Father," he said, putting his knapsack with the shopping onto one of the old but clean tables. "I come here every now and then, when it's too cold to sleep under a bridge."

"Huh, really? I have a good eye for faces, but you don't look familiar. Sorry, son." Father Barley leaned the broom in a corner, wiped his hands clean on his cassock, and shook Gabriel's hand enthusiastically. "I promise, next time you walk in here, I will know who you are. What's your name?"

"I'm Gabriel. Say, is Billy in? I'd like to have a word with him." Sitting down on one of the benches felt odd, as if he'd been away for years, not just a few short weeks. The wood had been worn smooth by countless bottoms, the tables looked as if they would break down at any moment, and honestly, Gabriel didn't have a clue how Father Barley managed to provide for the next meal.

"Billy? He's in the kitchen, preparing lunch. I can get him if you like. Would you mind sweeping for me?" With an encouraging grin, the father pushed the broom into Gabriel's hands. "I like the floor free of the most obvious dirt, if you know what I mean."

The floor underneath his feet was sticky; it needed more than a broom to be clean, but Gabriel said, "Sure I'll sweep, Father," nevertheless. Step by step, he brushed apple cores, dirt, paper, crumbs, and the occasional syringe into a corner, picking up a glove and a rotten cap on the way and placing them on a table.

"This place needs to be torn down and rebuilt," he said aloud after making sure Father Barley wasn't around to hear. "Sooner or later, the roof's going to cave in. Much sooner, I'd say, especially if it starts snowing again."

And why did this bother him? He had visited the mission only when there hadn't been any other choice, if it was too cold for too long or if he was too hungry. The mission had never been a place he'd been fond of; the people it harbored were not his friends.

Well, apart from Billy and Marita, perhaps. And Pepino, strange as it sounded, the scrawny hooker who was surely back on heroin by now. None of them would survive the next winter if the mission crumbled into pieces because of the age of the building or the lack of funds.

The broom found some broken glass shards, which scraped across the floor when Gabriel stepped on them. The sound distracted him from his task but triggered an idea nevertheless.

Hadn't he come across a rune just the other night, when Tennant had been fast asleep, a rune that would be helpful here? Not the Protection rune—Gabriel still hadn't discovered what exactly that one was for, and he was mighty respectful where it was concerned. No, a Stabilization rune, whose basic job it was to keep something even as rotten as this building upright for another twenty years.

"Give it a try," Gabriel muttered, setting the broom back in the corner. "Just three or four of them. One right here. One in the kitchen. Two more on the outer walls. Yeah. That should do it."

Without wasting another second, Gabriel knelt down right where he was. Some glass shards cut into his knee, but it didn't bother him. All that mattered was that he managed to finish before Father Barley returned with Billy.

Carefully, he brushed away crumbs and unidentifiable sticky things until finally he had a small patch of floor cleared. Father Barley always swept the dirt into this corner; it was always covered with something, and therefore, it was the best place to hide a rune.

The first line was the hardest—his fingers seemed to hesitate, not sure if they really should be doing this. Gabriel had never asked Tennant if he was actually allowed to use the runes, but then, the doctor didn't exactly own them. On the other hand, Gabriel was nothing but a novice. It was possible that because of his interference, the building would collapse a lot sooner than it would have otherwise.

What the hell—no risk, no fun, and besides, he had made Pepino sleep, and that had been a more complicated rune than the one he intended to use now. The first line began to glow; quickly, Gabriel added the rest of the rune, painting the pattern right onto the dirty tiles. When completed, the rune sparkled in the dark corner, reduced to a shadow, and then vanished.

Gabriel didn't know if it had even worked, and he had no way of testing it. Nevertheless, he decided to believe he hadn't made a mistake, got up, and drew another rune on the outer wall right underneath a big window.

The third one would go near the entrance. Gabriel worked fast, as if he'd been doing this all his life. Just as he was thinking how ridiculously easy this was, one line away from finishing the third rune, a sudden bolt of pain shot through his arm up to his shoulder, forcing out a muffled cry. He gasped but managed to finish the rune before a rush of nausea claimed him, and he staggered back and sank onto a bench. The rune vanished just like the other two, but his fingertip—his drawing finger, so to speak—began to burn. Then it went numb. A moment later, the skin ripped open as if he'd cut himself with a razor blade, and a drop of blood hit the floor. Gabriel cursed, shaking his hand to get the feeling back in his fingers. When that didn't work, he put his finger in his mouth, squeezing his eyes shut with pain.

"Shit," he gasped. "What the hell happened?"

Taking his finger out of his mouth, he stared at it disbelievingly. It was bright red up to the second knuckle, the numbness was spreading, and he watched as blood ran down toward his palm. The pain pierced his elbow as well as all the way up to his shoulder. It seemed as if his body was objecting to the use of runes—or maybe to their repeated use.

"Wish Tennant had mentioned this part," he said, standing and putting his finger back into his mouth. The pain slowly subsided, but he still considered it best to leave it at three runes, not four as initially planned. Besides, if he went into the kitchen now, Billy would start asking questions, and he'd have to explain why he'd painted invisible lines on one of the walls. He didn't need that sort of curiosity.

"Gabe!"

Billy's voice interrupted his thoughts. Quickly, Gabriel pushed his still-bleeding hand into the pocket of his jacket, hoping he'd find the remains of a tissue in there.

"Hey, Billy," he called back, trying to sound less alarmed than he was. A moment earlier, and Billy would have seen something Gabriel would prefer him not to. "I thought I'd come by and see if you're still alive."

Casually, he moved away from the third rune, just in case. A quick glance—no, the other two runes were not visible, either. Good. "You know, with you eating all the shit you cook, you might die of a heart attack soon." Grinning, he took in Billy's haggard form, the kitchen apron he wore, and a piece of onion he was carrying as if he'd feel lost without it.

"Idiot," Billy replied, throwing the onion. It landed near the pile of dirt Gabriel had swept together earlier on. "Thought you'd be gone for a while, buddy. What's the matter—miss me?" Billy came over and gave Gabriel a quick hug, a rare sign of affection given the fact that Billy was as scared of physical contact as he was scared of a blazing fire.

"Missed you terribly," Gabriel answered with a lopsided grin. "You and Marita and Pepino and the food and the smell and all. Couldn't stand staying away any longer. Please let me sleep on the floor tonight so I don't have to go back to the nice, warm flat I found through sheer luck."

Billy took a step back and looked him up and down, eyes narrowing like the last time they'd met. "Sit," he ordered, "and tell me everything. Want something to drink?"

"Tea would be good," Gabriel replied, rummaging in his knapsack. "Chocolate cookies?"

Billy's eyes widened, and he licked his lips. He practically sprinted to the kitchen and was back only moments later, balancing one cup of tea, one cup of coffee, sugar, and milk on a tray. Billy looked like a cutthroat and knew every detail there was to know about the street, but he tried his best to help those who needed help. He didn't touch alcohol or drugs, and he cried bitter tears whenever one of the boys who earned money on the streets was found frozen or starved or beaten to death.

"Chocolate cookies." Billy nearly sang the words. "I'm addicted to them, and you know it, Gabe. Still, I wanna know where you have been. No lies this time, right?"

"No lies." Surprised, Gabriel realized that he didn't want to lie to Billy. Not this time. He ripped open the box and shoved it toward his....

Was Billy a friend? He had never really thought about it, but then, Billy had remembered his name, even when he had been gone for the summer and returned only for the frosty winter nights several months later.

"You're a friend." Gabriel was surprised at the fact as well as at finding himself saying it aloud. "I don't lie to friends if I can help it. I met someone on Christmas Eve. He's damn good-looking, even though he doesn't know if he's gay or not, and I've fallen for him big time and would commit murder if I could touch him just once." He grabbed hold of his cup and downed his tea in one gulp. It was sweetened, it was cold, it tasted horrible—Gabriel wasn't even aware of it. Nervously, he ran his hands through his hair and tortured an innocent cookie by crumbling it to pieces.

Billy looked at him, then smiled. The smile widened into a grin that claimed his entire face. It was rare that Billy showed any emotion; he always said that smiling was for idiots who didn't know how cruel life was.

"You're in love!" he exclaimed, suppressing a laugh. "Fuck, Gabe, you're in love with that guy, do you know that?"

Fearing someone would hear the cheerful words, Gabriel shushed him. "Not so loud, man. Father Barley will scold me if he finds out—he'll warn me and tell me to choose the right path, not the one that leads toward hell. You know he's got a problem with nearly everything that doesn't end up in marriage."

"Gabe's in love," Billy repeated, shaking his head in disbelief. "You, of all people, have lost your heart. Wouldn't have thought it possible, man, with you never giving a damn about the people you screw." Billy leaned in closer. "He's not a pimp, is he? Your guy? He's not selling you or something?" The look of concern on his beaten face was nearly comical. "Seen it too often. Happened to me a few times too. Always fell in love with the wrong ones."

Not knowing what else to do, Gabriel offered him another cookie. "Tennant isn't a pimp. He's nice, he allows me to stay in his house, and he has made no attempt to touch me. Nor will he. He's a teacher, sort of. Don't ask me why I've fallen for him, but I'm damn sure nothing will come of it. He believes in emotions and shit. Unless he falls in love with me, too, there won't even be any fooling around in the foreseeable future. And him falling in love with me is practically impossible."

Billy munched on a cookie. "Sorry to hear that. It's nearly impossible to find someone who loves you back at the same time you love them."

"Wise words," Gabriel grumbled, feeling ridiculously happy that he had shared his secret with someone else.

With a friend, no less.

"How's Pepino?" he asked after a moment, fishing for a second box of cookies from his knapsack. "Back on heroin?"

"You don't want to talk about this Tennant guy, do you?"

Gabriel snorted dismissively. "What's there to talk about? I followed someone I didn't know into his apartment, I didn't run when I had the opportunity, and now I'm not tough enough to leave even though I know he's not interested. Being in his company is not just dangerous, it will break my heart eventually. Tell me about Pepino, Billy, please."

"Pepino's fine." Billy took the last cookie out of the box and held it up to the light as if checking it for moth holes. "He claims you did something to him. Helped him sleep. I know, I know"—he put up both hands in a calming way—"you just told him fairy tales. He says because of you, he can sleep, and because he can sleep, he can eat, and because he can eat, he can stay off the heroin. It's that simple. You should see him. He's put on some weight, his clothes are clean, and he turns more tricks in one day than he got last year in two months. Cash's good for him right now. Shares it with Marita sometimes. If you stay for lunch, you'll see him."

Gabriel opened his mouth to reply but closed it again without having managed to say a word. *The Sleeping rune.* The thought rang through his mind like a bell, making it impossible to think about anything else.

The Sleeping rune. He had drawn it right above the boy's palm, hoping desperately that it would work and that he hadn't messed it up. Pepino had fallen asleep instantly and had eaten the next morning too.

"He's fine?" Gabriel croaked. "Just... fine? I mean, just like that?"

"Not just like that." Billy got up, putting the cups back on the tray. Another hour and the place would be packed with people hungry enough to eat dead rats, never mind a more or less edible lunch. It was close to a miracle that no one had come stumbling in thus far. "He's finally found a reason to stay off the drugs. Hasn't told me what it is. Big secret, he says, but whatever the secret is, it's important to him. Guess you saved his life, Gabe, with you telling him kiddy stories. Not a bad thing for a cold-hearted bastard like you, showing some sympathy for a boy who cannot even remember your name, although he can remember the stories you told him about—how did he put it?— werewolves and runes."

Gabriel stayed for another ten minutes after Billy had returned to the kitchen to prepare lunch for hordes of homeless people with hungry mouths. He checked on the runes he'd drawn, confirming that no one would find them, and considered drawing the fourth one, but he skipped the idea when he saw that his finger was still bleeding. He left the mission quietly, not wanting to be caught in the crowd.

The truth was, he wanted to get back home. Tennant was still weak, and although Gabriel guessed he'd spent the morning asleep on the couch, it was time to check on him. After all, it was always possible that the fever would come back, or he'd get hungry, or someone would come knocking on the door, or maybe the murderer....

No. That was the wrong way to think. Following that line of thinking would drive him crazy. If he were to assume that right now, at this very moment, a madman was breaking into Tennant's house, sneaking up on him, and breaking his neck… Gabriel shuddered.

"He's safe," he assured himself, walking along the street and looking out for Pepino. "Tennant's safe. No need to worry about him."

TWO hours later, Gabriel was about to give up his attempt to find the boy he'd helped to sleep. Most likely, Pepino was busy with a customer, or maybe he had headed toward the mission for lunch. For some reason, Gabriel really wanted to find him. He wanted to see for himself that the rune he had painted hadn't harmed the boy, that he hadn't made a big mistake by pretending he'd known what he was doing.

It had turned into a mild day despite the chilly start, and a soft breeze blew through the streets, bringing with it the first signs of spring. The air smelled promisingly of tiny green leaves. A few birds were singing, and a hesitant sun shone through thin clouds. It wouldn't be long before the first flowers bloomed, or at least that was how it felt at the moment.

A few people were around, most of them male, which was no surprise, since the mission was centered in one of the city's best known red light districts. The streets around the mission were dominated by male prostitutes; every now and then, Gabriel saw a car stop and a boy get in after a short negotiation about the price. He hated this place, always had and always would.

Gabriel felt as if he had been walking for miles. The mission was somewhere south of him. There were not that many pros here, but the few cars that turned up were often quite expensive, as were the few motels that offered rooms by the hour. Suddenly, Gabriel saw a thin line of smoke trailing into the air out of the corner of his eye, and he turned to get a better look. Near the entrance of a motel, he could see the glow of a cigarette, or maybe it was a joint. Yes, definitely grass— the smell was faint but distinct. Someone was taking a break, hidden in a niche around the corner from the entrance.

Gabriel wouldn't have been able to explain why, but he walked over to the tiny glowing point, not able to see more than a shadow of the person who held the joint, somehow knowing it was Pepino. He felt the boy's eyes following him as he crossed the street, and he hoped Pepino wouldn't run away, because he was hard to catch.

"Hi," he called out when he was but a few feet away from the shadow in the niche. The smell of grass was strong here—good grass, not the crap that was sold for a few bucks.

"I'm on a break," Pepino said, his voice friendly but cool. "If you wanna fuck, you need to come back later." He took a toke, inhaled deeply, and closed his eyes with joy.

Gabriel grinned disbelievingly. Until recently, Pepino would have agreed to fuck a goat for a warm meal, and now he could afford to send away someone who might be a well-paying customer? "I don't want to screw, Pepino," he replied. "I was looking for you. Wanted to say hello. I'm Gabriel. From the mission. Remember, we talked a few weeks ago?"

Damn. Occasionally it was really annoying not to be recognized.

Pepino moved. Light fell onto his face, and Gabriel's eyes widened with surprise. The boy looked different. He looked good.

Better than good. He looked gorgeous!

"What the hell?" Gabriel couldn't believe what he saw. He had known Pepino for three years, ever since he had staggered into the mission one night, frozen and crying after he'd been raped and robbed by a customer. Back then, he'd been fourteen and scrawny as a scarecrow, thin and pale and dirty. His eyes had been an indifferent, watery blue, his lips thin, his face far too haunted to be called attractive. Dirty blond hair, dirty hands, and restless manners, Pepino had always resembled a nervous rat more than anything else.

Not anymore.

The boy's hair was still blond, but it had been cut, and it was clean. Without all the dirt, it was curly, and Gabriel unexpectedly wished to touch it, to let his hands run through it. The blue eyes were not watery anymore—now that Pepino was off the heroin, they had an intense quality and promised exquisite pleasure to the one who managed to chat him up. Of course, he was still thin and not very tall—

he was about a head shorter than Gabriel—but the sickly color in his face was gone, as well as the little ticks that had plagued him, like the involuntary shrugging of his shoulders or constantly licking his lips.

Pepino, obviously well aware of his looks, cast him an ironic smile, leaned back against the wall, and drew up one leg, placing the sole of his shoe against the wall. "Gabriel," he said, fake warmth in his voice. "Sorry. Should have recognized you. It's been a while." Slowly, he moved his hip, just enough to draw Gabriel's attention. Narrow hips. Slender legs. Interesting bulge in the thin latex trousers.

Shit.

Gabriel cleared his throat and forced his eyes back up to the boy's face. "Not many people recognize me at first sight," he said. "Must be something I've eaten. I seem to be sort of invisible most of the time."

"You're not invisible to me." Pepino's voice was liquid honey. "Now tell me, what can I do for you?"

He hadn't moved an inch, but Gabriel felt as if Pepino had reached out and cupped his cock with his hands, massaging it to life. Not good. Not good at all. He wasn't here to fuck, and anyway, it wasn't Pepino he wanted. "I just wondered—" he began.

"Wondered about what?"

"If you were all right. Last time I saw you, you were just off the heroin, you know."

Pepino gasped and pushed himself off the wall, narrowing the distance between them in the alleyway. "You! It was you who helped me get some sleep!" Staring at his open palm, he traced invisible lines. "A pattern," he continued. "You drew something on my skin, and I could sleep. Gabriel. *Now* I recognize you—I mean, really, I'm not just saying it! Man, did I say thanks for what you did?"

Gabriel couldn't help but laugh. He had feared the boy would freak out, begin screaming or do something really stupid like call the police—and now all he did was express his gratitude? "Never mind. I just tried to help. Looks as if it worked."

Pepino laughed too. "Helped is an understatement. I slept like a baby that night, and in the morning, I was ravenous. Ever since, it's been no problem at all to stay off the drugs. I mean, look at me!" Spreading his arms wide, he turned around like a dancer, showing himself off, visibly proud of what he could offer. "I have to turn tricks down, or I wouldn't get out of bed all day and night. Still, they come back and beg me for a fuck, *and* they pay me what I ask for."

"That's because you are off the drugs and because you look damn good," Gabriel said hoarsely.

Somehow, the boy radiated a sexual tension that went straight to his groin, and he definitely couldn't deny his interest. A thought struck him: maybe this was the solution to his problem! If he screwed Pepino, he would surely be able to stop thinking about Tennant for at least an hour. It would ease the desire to go back home and screw the doctor instead.

"Bullshit." Pepino came another step closer. Only their clothes separated them now. "It's because you did something to me. I've been off the heroin before, once for as long as a month. I was vomiting all the time, I looked like death, and I felt like a piece of shit. This time, you sort of magicked me to sleep, and when I woke up, I was fine. Just like that"—he snapped his fingers—"I can attract who I want when I want. And you tell me it's because I quit the drugs?" Gently, he slipped an arm around Gabriel's waist, pulling him closer. "Let me thank you," he whispered. "Won't charge you, promise. I owe you big time, Gabe. And you're hot. Most of my customers are old guys with fat bellies and no hair. I could do with a hot guy for a change."

Pepino's hand was on his bottom, squeezing. The other hand, high up on his leg, moved higher until it touched his cock through the fabric of his jeans, stroking along his length. A wonderful feeling, much needed and badly missed. How long had it been since he had last had sex? Weeks? Months? No, sometime last year, in late autumn. A big girl, married to an even bigger guy. Gabriel couldn't remember her name right now, but she had been a good hunt, and even the sex hadn't been too disappointing.

Pepino's lips were at the side of his neck, his breath hot, and then a small, demanding tongue licked his skin. Gabriel surrendered to the boy's hands and his mouth, the teeth nibbling his throat, thinking of Tennant as he slung his arms around the boy, pressing him against the wall and pushing his own hand down those salaciously tight latex trousers.

The small, muscular ass, skin soft as a ripe peach, promised to be tight and welcoming. Longingly, Gabriel searched for the small, puckered hole, found it, and circled it. Stroking Pepino's entrance made him completely hard, and for a moment, Gabriel was tempted to kiss the boy. He wanted to kiss, but then, it wasn't Pepino's mouth he longed for, so he just groaned when the boy opened the buttons of his trousers. Gabriel appreciated Pepino's efforts to free him of his jeans so they could get to fucking as soon as possible. Pressing his full weight against the smaller boy, he—

Aleksei.

The thought flared up in his mind and distracted him momentarily, then only heated his desire. *Imagine it's him you're touching*, his mind told him. *Imagine it's him you'll take in a minute, you'll make scream in a minute.*

Gabriel doubled his efforts to peel the boy's clothes off and to free his own cock simultaneously. He wanted him, wanted Tennant, so very badly it hurt, and if it meant he would have to take a pro instead to ease his pain, if it meant he would have to take Pepino pressed against a dirty alley wall, so be it. Anything, if only he could get the thought of how Tennant's patterned skin might feel under his fingers out of his mind, if he could stop wondering how it would be to run his fingers through his unruly black hair, taste his mouth, breathe in the same air he breathed.

Skin under his fingertips, warm, soft, and completely without patterns. Hair, baby fine and blond, devoid of any gray.

Aleksei.

Pepino moaned into his mouth. Gabriel's jeans slipped over his bottom, and the boy took his cock into his hands with practiced fingers, stroking him with experience and skill while kissing him deeply.

Tennant wasn't skilled in touching a man. He was inexperienced in lovemaking. He wouldn't know how to arouse without even looking, and he wouldn't press his own erection against Gabriel's thigh, slowly rubbing against him to create even more pleasure like Pepino was doing right now.

The fingers around his cock squeezed rhythmically. It was good, far too good to be stopped. But Gabriel's thoughts drifted away. He saw ice-blue eyes and ivy leaves painted upon silvery skin. He felt broad shoulders pressed against his chest, shivering with fever. He smelled soap and shampoo, and he saw blood running down the drain. An eyebrow rose, mocking him, as, from far away, Tennant asked him whether a meaningless fuck had ever managed to make him feel good.

Gabriel groaned and opened his eyes. Blond hair blurred his vision.

He pushed Pepino away. A second later, he stopped kneading the boy's ass. "Stop. Please stop," he managed. "It's not... I don't... please, Pepino. I can't do it."

Instantly, the boy backed off. He was neither angry nor ashamed. He looked at Gabriel knowingly, then said, "It's not me you want, is it?"

Gabriel lowered his head. "No. Sorry."

Pepino turned around while Gabriel pulled his trousers up, a small but much appreciated gesture. "No need to apologize," he said lightly. "I told you, I've had enough tricks for today. Wouldn't have minded another one, but I don't want anyone fucking me who doesn't really want to. So who is it?"

Gabriel put some distance between them—he could still smell their arousal, and it did nothing to cool down his needs. His cock was still hard, his heart still beating fast, and he wished with all his might that there was a chance of kissing Tennant the way he had just kissed Pepino.

"Who's who?" he asked flippantly. Not that he didn't know who Pepino was asking about, but he needed another few moments to catch his breath.

The boy relit the joint, which he had left sitting on the windowsill. "The one you really want. The one who's on your mind and made you hard. Wasn't me, I'd bet on it."

Brushing his hair out of his face, Gabriel managed to look Pepino in the eyes, although he was still quite embarrassed. He had nearly lost control, and he didn't like that at all.

"A friend," he answered. "One I can't have."

"Why not?" Pepino took a toke, eyes dropping half closed. "Seduce him. Get him drunk, share a joint with him or maybe some Ecstasy, and he'll offer you his ass in no time. Always works."

"The man's a virgin," Gabriel spat the words. "Seducing him when he's drugged wouldn't be the problem. Waking up next to him knowing I had done something he didn't want to happen would be. He wants to be in love before he'd as much as consider a fuck. Damn frustrating, I tell you, as it is highly unlikely that he'll ever fall in love with me."

"Oh." Pepino grinned just like Billy had grinned earlier on. "Love. Now that's a different matter." He half turned and tapped on the window behind him. An elderly woman opened it.

"Can I have two coffees, hon?" Pepino cooed, fishing for some coins in his pocket. "Please?"

With bird-like eyes, the woman glared at the two men who stood outside her kitchen, poured two mugs of coffee, and took the cash. She never said a word, just slammed the window closed again once Pepino had taken the mugs.

"Claire. She makes good coffee, and she knows I pay, or she wouldn't have opened her window." He took a sip. "Can't you use one of those runes to make him fall in love with you?"

Gabriel coughed in shock at the casual question. He hadn't considered that Pepino might know more about runes than the average homeless boy, but apparently he did. The question proved that Pepino had a basic grasp of the matter, if not more.

"Doesn't work like that," he bit out, deliberately not saying that he had already thought of it himself and had even looked for an appropriate rune in Tennant's books. "Even if it did, it wouldn't be right. I don't want to force him into my arms. Look, can we drop the subject?" Wrapping his hands around the warm porcelain mug, he realized he was shivering all over, although it wasn't a cold day. All he could think was, *I want to go home.*

"Wanna know a secret?" Pepino asked, seemingly oblivious to the turmoil roaring in Gabriel's heart.

"Sure." Anything to distract his mind was welcome. Anything to keep him from thinking of Tennant or the fact that what he really needed was a bit of alone time to make his trousers fit more comfortably.

"I've met someone too." Sitting on the windowsill in front of Claire's kitchen, Pepino pulled his legs up and leaned his head against the window frame. A sunbeam had found its way into the alley and warmed his face; he looked very young and very content. "Not someone to fuck. I've met my father." Another sip from the mug. "Last year. Didn't know he was my dad back then. He fell over me when I was lying in the gutter. Didn't feel that well."

He took one last toke from the joint before he tossed it away. "He's so beautiful!" Pepino opened his eyes, clearly not seeing the here and now but the past. "I called after him, telling him he looked wonderful. He was disgusted. Spat at me and walked on as if I were a piece of dirt. Well, I was. In a way I still am, but not for much longer."

Gabriel didn't comment on that, but silently, he doubted very much that the man Pepino had seen was in any way related to him, or that Pepino would ever find out who his real father was. Like most pros, he had been born on the streets and born for the streets by a whore who earned her money on the streets herself.

"He came back a couple weeks later. Talked to me. Told me who he was and that he thought I was filth and wished I'd never been born." The memory made Pepino frown, and even Gabriel couldn't suppress a shudder. What a nasty thing to say to anyone, especially someone as young and lost as Pepino.

"You don't believe he's my dad, do you?" Pepino shot Gabriel a knowing grin. "Don't deny it; I can see the doubt written all over your face. I didn't believe it, either, but he proved it. He showed me a picture of my mom. It's the same picture I have in my wallet. He knew my mom's name, and he knew my name too. My real name. Pepino's just what everyone calls me. My mom named me Justin, and he knew it. That's when I decided to get clean." Cupping Gabriel's cheek, he added, "Wouldn't have made it without you. You helped me. So— thanks."

Gently, Pepino pecked a kiss on Gabriel's cheek, then hopped off the windowsill, leaving his mug behind for Claire to pick up. "Gotta go. Whenever you're in the mood for a bit of company, you know where to find me."

"Pepino!"

"Hmm?"

"What do you mean, not for much longer?" Gabriel had to ask. The boy's words had struck a chord: a prostitute never lasted long on the streets, no matter how well he was liked.

Pepino—Justin—cast him a smile that went straight to his groin. "I quit the drugs. I'll quit selling my ass in a month or two, once I've got enough money put aside. Been talking to Billy a lot lately, and he said it's not easy, but it is possible to get out of here. Do you think I want to end up like him, beaten to pieces, now that I've a reason to behave? My dad is disgusted by me. I want him to be proud—he's so fucking beautiful, and I want him to see that I am not the filth he sees me as. I swear, I'll make it."

Gabriel watched Pepino walk away down the street with a spring in his step. The boy's head was held high, and he whistled a merry little tune with skilled lips.

Impossible or not, Gabriel believed that he'd make it. Something had changed the boy profoundly, and whether it had been triggered by his rune or the belief he'd met his father wasn't really important. Pepino radiated self-confidence as well as raw sexual energy. Not the worst combination when one's primary goal was to earn enough money to finally make a living without selling one's body.

CHAPTER TEN

PEPINO walked down the street as if the town belonged to him, and for some reason, Gabriel decided to follow him. It wasn't something he'd thought through; every so often, he acted on instinct, and if he'd been asked why he felt compelled to follow the boy, he wouldn't have been able to give a good answer. He stayed in the alley a few more minutes, following Pepino with his gaze before he went after him slowly, keeping his distance.

He should go home, though. Tennant might be awake and hungry, and the fridge was empty except for half a jar of olives and some mayonnaise. Going back to the mission and picking up his knapsack from Billy wasn't more than a short walk. He could be home in less than half an hour if he caught the right bus.

So why was he following the boy instead?

Pepino didn't rush. He walked slowly but not aimlessly. He had a destination, Gabriel could have sworn it. He looked as though he was about to meet someone. Quite possibly a customer.

A car slowed down and stopped next to the boy. A window rolled down, and an elderly guy leaned out, his intention obvious, easily seen in his greedy face, his eyes undressing Pepino as they talked. Gabriel was too far away to hear what was being said. But when the man opened his wallet and his expression became angry, it was obvious that Pepino had turned him down. The boy just shook his head repeatedly and finally bent down to whisper something into the man's ear, locking one hand behind his neck.

It seemed to calm the guy down. A moment later, the window went up and the car drove off.

"As he said, he can afford to take time off," Gabriel said, impressed. Pepino had denied the man the fuck he was clearly eager to get, had talked to him in a way that indicated he knew the guy, and then he had walked on as if he was a hundred percent certain that his customer would come back later. Impressive. And an indication that whomever the boy wanted to meet was either a special customer or someone he wanted to see very badly.

Like his dad, for example.

Damn unlikely that a father would suddenly turn up out of nowhere, Gabriel thought. Such things only happened in fairy tales. Pepino had grown up on the streets, had lived in orphanages after his mother had been found dead. Not once had anyone claimed the boy as his.

Anyone could fake a picture and find out a birth name. It was much more likely that whoever it was Pepino was about to meet had something else in mind.

"Like what?" Gabriel mused, keeping an eye on Pepino while staying in the shadows. "Why lead Pepino to believe he's his dad? And why tell him how disgusted he is? Why meet him at all if not to have his way with him? Shit, nothing fits here."

Pepino crossed the street and opened a gate that led into a small park surrounded by trees. The bare branches gave clear proof that despite the warm day it was still winter. The ground was muddy. The gate was rusty and creaked on its hinges.

Pepino didn't check his surroundings once. Obviously, he was looking forward to a private meeting, and equally as obvious, it was not a customer he was about to see—not even the kinky ones wanted to screw on mushy leaves or a dirty, cold park bench. This had to be something different.

Pepino was only a few steps ahead. Gabriel sneaked through the still open gate and strolled from tree to tree, occasionally hiding behind a bush. The sun beat down on Pepino's hair, making it shine golden and bright. The effect was decidedly beautiful.

Pepino had called the man who insisted he was his father beautiful. In Gabriel's opinion, that wasn't a word anyone would use when referring to a relative. For a lover, yes. Not for a father.

On the other hand, Pepino possessed an eerie beauty. Gabriel hadn't seen it until today. Well, no one had—the boy had been in the grip of drugs, and heroin would make even a god look ugly. Now that he was clean, it was apparent that there was more to Pepino than anyone had known.

And the boy had mentioned a Seduction rune as if he'd been born with the knowledge.

Gabriel ducked behind a low hedge and rubbed his hands across his face to keep his thoughts in check. *Pepino is beautiful, so is the man who claims to be his dad,* he thought. *Let's see if there is some family resemblance at least.*

Clutching his arms around his shivering body, for the wind had picked up, Gabriel decided to stay for a few more minutes and see whom Pepino was meeting. Hidden between houses, the little park was barely bigger than one of those large gardens rich people owned, at least according to what he'd seen on the occasional soap opera. Not many people seemed to know about it, as there was no trash lying around, nor broken bottles, syringes, or condoms.

A quiet place. Peaceful, even now with all the green asleep for the winter.

Pepino sat on one of the benches, stretched out his legs, and turned his face toward the sun. His posture was relaxed; he was at ease and neither nervous nor suspicious. Actually, it seemed as if this wasn't his first time in the park, as if this was a common meeting place with the one he waited for.

A crow landed on the path and searched for crumbs. The noise of cars and a few children playing football in the street could be heard in the distance. There was nothing more dangerous in sight than the crow and a squirrel looking for nuts it had buried the previous year.

Gabriel shivered. Something was wrong, and he didn't know what. He wanted to grab the boy and pull him away from the bench, out of this park, and back to the windy corner where he had found him earlier.

Ridiculous. On the streets, it was always possible to bump into someone who had a problem with gay hookers. Kids were killed quicker than they poured in from the countryside, and Gabriel knew that as well as he knew that a quiet moment for a hustler was a rare thing. Sitting outside, enjoying the sun and the silence must be heaven for the boy—at least, he looked as if he was enjoying it tremendously.

So where was this premonition of danger coming from? There was no one else around, and if someone had opened the gate, the rusty screech of the hinges would have warned both of them in time.

Clenching his teeth, Gabriel leaned against the tree behind him, a bush protecting him from being seen. He stood still, knowing it would be nearly impossible for anyone who didn't know he was there to see him.

Another cold breeze cut through the air. Then a light appeared—one that was neither sunlight nor artificial. A small sound, like ripping silk, tore through the park. Suddenly, a man walked down the path, although the path had been empty only a heartbeat ago.

"A portal!" Gabriel breathed.

He hadn't known a portal could be felt as well as seen, but then, the last time he had used one, it had been drawn under much different circumstances, and he had been concentrating on the man in his arms. Now, the portal caused the small hairs at the back of his neck to stand up; it made his teeth ache and his eyes water.

Then the light just disappeared, fading away as if it had never been there at all. The cold breeze was gone, too, and there was only the man walking toward Pepino.

Obviously, the man knew how to use runes, which indicated that he wasn't human. He looked human, though. In fact, he looked quite ordinary. Short, dark-blond hair, average height, average stature. Not tall, not small, not thin, not fat. Just—average.

Hadn't Pepino called him beautiful? Well, this man wasn't. He was just another guy in a park, chatting up a prostitute.

And he knew how to open a portal.

Shit. Despite his earlier hope that Pepino really had found his father, this was not right, and it could not be easily explained. Although

Gabriel longed with all his might to go home, he knew he needed to stay, and so he did stay, hidden behind the bushes, and continued to spy.

"JUSTIN." The man's voice was cool, nearly impolitely so.

The boy, who had been close to dozing off in the sunshine, ripped his eyes open, and Gabriel couldn't help but notice that they flared up with delight and something dangerously close to hope. "Ronai! Hi—I mean, hello. Glad to see you. I got your message. Thought you wouldn't come, though!" Pepino sat up and yawned hugely. Apparently, he'd had a busy night, but then Gabriel had known that already. "Come on, sit down. I've had a shower, and I even turned down a customer to be on time. No reason to think I would infect you with anything." He sounded light-hearted, but his smile flickered ever so slightly.

It was clear to Gabriel that Pepino was scared of this Ronai. The boy licked his lips too often, he blinked his eyes too much, and he couldn't keep his hands still. *He wants to please the man,* Gabriel thought. *He longs for his attention, he longs for his approval, and yet he's scared.*

A lousy combination.

Ronai stood in front of the boy, who looked up at him with big, eager eyes. "You still earn your money by selling your body," he said disdainfully. "I just came to tell you that there is nothing you can ever do to please me. That you were born at all is an abomination, that you are still alive, an insult."

Pepino raised his chin and crossed his thin arms in front of his chest as if to shield himself from the man's cruel words. "You're accusing me of selling my ass when you're someone who's buying ass? You fucking hypocrite!"

Ronai raised an eyebrow ever so slightly. "I have my reasons for lying with men," he hissed. "The first time I saw you, you were dirty. Addicted to your drugs, with filthy hair, filthy body, filthy clothes. I was disgusted by you, and I still am." He turned as if to walk away.

It was enough to make Pepino regret his words. He jumped up from the bench. "Look, Dad, I won't do it for much longer," he pleaded. "Honestly, I didn't know what I was saying. In a month or two, I'll have enough money to quit, and then… then…."

He didn't seem to know how to finish the sentence, so he just let it stand between them, the promise that he wouldn't work as a prostitute forever. There had been a quiver in the boy's voice. Gabriel doubted the man had heard it.

For some reason, Gabriel picked up a small stone, about the size of a quarter. It was flat and a bit dusty. He rubbed it clean on his jeans, then picked up a second stone, this one with a sharp edge. Without really thinking about it, he scratched a rune into the first stone: a Hiding rune, designed to make him even more invisible than he already was. Creating the rune hurt like it had back at the mission, but at the moment, Gabriel didn't give a damn. All that was important was that he wouldn't be detected and that the faint glow couldn't be seen from the place where Ronai and Pepino stood. Luckily, the two of them were staring at each other in a way that clearly told of the abyss that separated them. Between Pepino and the man he believed was his father lay worlds, if not several universes.

"Tainted blood," the man—Ronai—said, and Gabriel shuddered at the words. Disbelieving, he took in Pepino's golden hair, his luminous eyes, the faint shimmer of his skin, and knew that one of his ancestors had been from one of the hidden worlds.

Maybe the man—Ronai—was his father after all.

"Why have I never noticed it before?" Gabriel could barely move his lips. Cold dread ran down his spine at the thought that Ronai could see him, could focus on him, would find him behind the bushes and demand answers about why he was hiding, spying on them.

Ronai's concentration, though, was focused on Pepino. "I can see your mother in you." The words were but a faint whisper. "Her eyes, her nose. You are slender like a birch, as she was. I believed her to be of my kind. I was wrong. Because I was wrong, because she had deceived me, all of this had to happen."

Slowly, Ronai took the boy's face between his hands and gently pulled him closer. They stood close, like lovers, eye to eye, as Ronai was only slightly taller than Pepino. Carefully, the man caressed his son's cheek—if Pepino was in fact his son—and tenderly ran his fingers through his blond locks.

"You've changed since I saw you last. Back then, you were just off the drugs, unhealthy looking, not resembling me in the slightest." Gentle fingertips touched full, young lips. "Without the drugs and the dirt, underneath the pain and the sorrow, you look like one of my kind. You are clean; you shine. You actually look like me, like the son you are but whom I shouldn't have, and it grieves me."

Every muscle in Gabriel's body tightened, and from out of nowhere came a horrifying thought: *What if he's the killer? What if he's the one who murdered all those people? What if it was he who tried to kill Tennant?*

Gabriel very nearly jumped up despite his genuine fear of the unimpressive, average man. Pepino didn't look like Ronai, not at all, which meant the man wore a rune that hid his true looks, just like Tennant did. It meant that underneath the average look of a nobody, he was as beautiful as Pepino.

And he was dangerous, Gabriel was certain of it. Who was this man? *What* was he?

Gabriel closed his fist around the small stone, nails digging into his palm, and he could feel the dripping blood seep into the fabric of his jeans. Drawing the rune had ripped his fingertips open again, had cut like tiny, sharp knives into his skin.

"Don't!" he whispered, not knowing what he meant or to whom he was saying it. "Don't do it!"

He felt like he was paralyzed. His muscles wouldn't obey his desire to come out of hiding, to interrupt whatever was happening near that neat, little old bench in this neat, hidden little park.

Ronai had his palms on Pepino's cheeks, and he was looking deep into the young man's eyes. Pepino brought his hands up and circled both of Ronai's wrists, not to push the man away, but to hold onto him, like a child holding onto a much beloved parent. "I am sorry, Dad! I didn't want to bring shame on you, but I have to eat! I promise I will stop—today! I promise I will never go back to the street. I will find a job, a real job and all, and—"

He never finished his sentence. Ronai freed his hands and let them slip just a bit lower, the tips of his fingers adding gentle pressure to the fragile spine. His thumbs brushed over soft, satin skin, over tender, bird-like bones.

With a quick, brutal jerk of his perfectly manicured hands, Ronai broke the boy's neck, both palms pressed securely against the boy's flushed cheeks and looking straight into those eager, hopeful, big blue eyes.

Gabriel's legs gave way, and his breathing stopped. Bile rose in his throat, and he lowered his head to the ground to get the dizziness under control. *Pepino!* his mind screamed. *He killed Pepino!*

No. Pepino couldn't be dead. He'd just been kissing the boy less than half an hour ago! The sound of the body hitting the ground made him nauseous, and he watched with gritted teeth as Ronai stepped back from the corpse.

Pebbles crunched under expensive shoes. The cry of a crow, calling for its mate, announced there would be a feast today. A chill in the air and the smell of blooming jasmine, and there came that sound again, the sound of silk ripping apart.

Ronai was opening a portal. He had killed a seventeen-year-old boy who had believed him to be his father. He had told his victim how much he was disgusted by him, and now he was about to escape.

Impossible. Unbearable. He couldn't let him get away.

Gabriel scrambled to his feet, not caring that his legs felt like rubber and protested being used so soon, not caring that his stomach had turned into a small, hard stone. He ignored his ice-cold hands and the tears running down his cheeks. The stone with the rune he had carved was a reassuringly heavy weight in his palm.

Ronai rose from his kneeling position where he had drawn a pattern into the gravel to open the portal and brushed the dirt and dust off his trousers. He seemed unconcerned that two steps behind him lay a dead body; he simply straightened his shoulders and stepped through the portal into another world.

There was no time to lose, not a second, not even a heartbeat. No time to think this through or ask someone—like Tennant—for help.

"Gotta go after him," Gabriel told himself, stepping out into the sunlight. Ronai was gone, the portal already fading. If he wanted to follow him—"Damn stupid idea!"—he needed to do it now, or he wouldn't be able to do it at all.

The portal could rip him apart, couldn't it? But the alternative was to let a murderer escape, the man who had just killed one of his friends. With one last look at the horribly still body on the ground, Gabriel ignored what he knew could happen and ran toward the portal. It reached for him as if recognizing that he'd done this before, as if acknowledging that he had the right to visit another world.

A lost world. A hidden world. Gabriel fell through the portal, and he couldn't breathe, and he couldn't scream. It hurt like hell, as he'd expected. The portal didn't kill him, though, which came as a surprise, since Tennant wasn't there to protect him, but hell, who cared as long as the end result was that he was still alive? Gabriel felt like he was being ripped apart, as if his joints were tearing out of their sockets, as if his brain were being crushed by an immense fist. There was no sound, no light, no anything—for an endless, eternal moment, Gabriel believed he would fall forever, lost in this place between worlds, and be trapped here until he died.

When he finally hit solid ground, he nearly broke his wrist by landing on it as he fell. Branches from low bushes whipped in his face and left dark welts. The pain and the fear he had experienced going through the portal were mind-shattering, but his instincts made him still the screams that wanted to break free with a hand over his mouth.

Ronai had stepped through the portal only moments before him. Immediately, Gabriel realized he really would be dead at any moment if Ronai had seen he had a follower and waited for him. The man—whoever he was—would kill him as easily as he'd killed Pepino, as carelessly as a child treading upon an ant.

Yet nothing happened.

Gasping, Gabriel forced air into his lungs, watching tiny stars dance in front of his eyes from lack of oxygen. It took him several minutes to recover from his jump through the portal. His muscles felt like he'd taken a beating, and the wound on his hand from using the runes had ripped open further.

"Shit." Gabriel coughed and spat out some blood. Great, he'd bitten his tongue too. The blood from his tongue mingled with the blood that was dripping from his nose. Running through a portal was dangerous and painful, it seemed, but at least he was still alive.

Whatever the reason for his survival—maybe Tennant had been exaggerating when he warned Gabriel not to go through a portal alone—it was time to get back on his feet and make sure the murderer didn't kill him next. Maybe the man was merely waiting patiently, leaning lazily against one of those big trees with the hard branches, while his newest target caught his breath.

Staggering, Gabriel managed to get up. He swayed, and a piercing pain shot through his head, blinding him and making him wish he hadn't followed Ronai into this world.

The smell of jasmine was more prominent now, but the wind blowing off the ocean below was strong and cool. Apparently, the portal had led him to a seaside cliff made of black rocks and lined by a forest. It seemed to be early summer here. The sun burned down on him, making his head hurt worse. His face and clothes were sprayed with his own blood, and the mossy area beneath the trees was looking invitingly soft.

"I should lie down a bit," Gabriel croaked to a squirrel that had hurried down from the top of an oak to take a better look at the newcomer. "I really don't feel very well."

That was a major understatement. Stepping through the portal hadn't killed him, but it had cost him much more energy than he possessed, and he felt weak as a child.

One step and then another, he moved away from the cliff's edge and the spectacular view of the ocean and toward the forest. He scanned the tree line, hoping that he was alone. That there was no one waiting behind a bush to kill him.

The only sounds were birds chirping and leaves rustling in the wind. It truly appeared as if the man he had followed was gone.

And so was the portal.

It took Gabriel a moment or two to fully comprehend the implications: he'd lost Pepino's killer, and he was trapped in this world.

Fucking shit.

Pressing both fists against his temples, Gabriel managed to get his headache somewhat under control, if only just enough to see straight. The light in this world had a different quality—it was softer, not as harsh as the light in his own world. At least that was good news. Now he could only hope the night didn't pose as much of a threat—if the temperature dropped too low, he would freeze to death.

The only question was, what should he do now? True, he hadn't thought this through properly. He'd followed Ronai on the spur of the moment, an act of instinct, hatred, and determination not to let the bastard get off the hook. Now it became apparent that he probably should have spared a second thought to what he was going to do after he'd stepped through the portal.

On the other hand, had he thought twice about it, the portal would have closed right in front of his eyes, and he would have never found out who the murderer was.

Gabriel still didn't understand why he hadn't bumped into Ronai exiting the portal, but then, the sun seemed to be lower here than it had been at home. Maybe going through a portal took more time than he'd thought, and Ronai had just walked on. Gabriel wasn't even sure how much time had passed since he'd arrived. Five minutes? Ten? Not too long, anyway. After all, his nose was still bleeding, but at least the dizziness was subsiding with every breath he took.

There was a faint smell in the air that wasn't flowery or grassy or earthy. It had been there before, he was sure of it, but until just a second ago, it hadn't struck him as odd. Now, for some reason, it did.

Gabriel lowered his head and closed his eyes, letting the wind play with his hair, a red curtain blowing in the breeze. Leaning against a tree for support, he ignored the gentle tickle the strands caused on his cheek, his hurting wrist, the drops of blood that fell freely from the tips of his fingers to the grass, and the urge to turn and run away.

Instead, he concentrated on the smell. It was faint and not at all unpleasant, but definitely strange. Someone had been here not too long ago. Someone who smelled of cotton and leather—the shoes, Ronai's shoes, Gabriel realized, and he concentrated harder on the fleeting fragrances.

Sweat. Adrenaline.

Obvious. The man had just killed; he was bound to be excited about it. But Gabriel could sense no fear or guilt. No pleasure, either. Ronai hadn't killed because it aroused him. He wasn't driven by sex.

Neither had the murderer killed out of impulse: Gabriel had been there; he had watched Pepino's death. Not for one moment had the killer been nervous, not once had he raised his voice to shout. He had killed in cold precision, which made thinking about it even worse. Gabriel wondered how he could be so sure about that simply because of a few molecules in the air that didn't belong to the trees or the grass or the ocean and beach below, but to the man who had opened the portal. To be sure, his nose was good. Better than good. But this?

Gabriel's head snapped up when he heard a twig break, and like a puppet on strings, he followed the sound into the woods. "Not a good idea," he told himself. "I shouldn't be here. I shouldn't be doing this. I really, really should go home."

Well, maybe not right now. Another few minutes. After all, it was possible that Ronai was still somewhere around, and he would find him, and….

No use thinking about a possible "and." *First find the man, then decide what to do*, he thought.

Gabriel didn't need to walk far—ten minutes at the most, although time seemed to have a different quality in this world. Less stringent, maybe; less demanding.

The trees had opened up a bit, and Gabriel saw that he was standing on top of a hill. Below him was a clearing, large and sunny, with a pond in the middle. Soft splashes were coming from the water. It was a scene from a children's book of fairy tales, missing only a unicorn or maybe a witch's house, a roof covered with gingerbread. Gabriel had to smile despite his still-bleeding nose—damn the thing!— and his headache and the piercing pain in his fingertips. It was lovely here, and peaceful too.

Then he remembered the sound of Pepino's breaking neck and sobered up. Beautiful or not, where was Ronai?

More splashes, and Gabriel saw what was causing them: the killer was walking into the water. That damn, worthless, horrible bastard was about to take a swim in the pond!

Downhill in the clearing, the greenish water of the pond sparkled in the sun. Ronai had dropped his clothes carelessly, as if they meant nothing to him. Trousers, shirt, underwear, shoes—all lay in a crumpled heap on the bank, getting soaked by small waves as the man waded out into the water.

A chain dangled from his neck—a chain with a pendant quite similar to the one Tennant wore. Clearly, Ronai was disguising his true features. Apart from the necklace, however, the murderer was naked. Gabriel saw a rounded belly and pudgy hips, pale, slightly unhealthy-looking skin, and knobby joints. Ronai looked as if he were around fifty. He looked as if he were a completely harmless guy. At the very least, that assumption was definitely very wrong.

Then Ronai jumped and dove headfirst into the pond, surfacing moments later, shaking the water out of his hair and roaring with joy.

"As if he hadn't just killed someone a few minutes ago," Gabriel murmured, wrapping his arms around his body, a sudden cold caused by dread and sadness and the general feeling of being in the wrong place at the wrong time claiming him. He was watching a murderer taking a leisurely swim. How sick was that?

It didn't matter who the man really was. He'd never find out his identity without confronting him, and even then, Ronai would very likely kill him the moment he realized that there had been a witness. Continuing to watch him wasn't an option, either, as it would soon be dark. Gabriel wasn't familiar with this world, and he wasn't that good of a spy. What was more, he had the strong impression there was much more to Ronai than met the eye. He could probably see through a double disguise, more than likely knew he was being watched, and was just waiting until he was out of the water to come after Gabriel.

I'll go back home now, Gabriel decided. He was tired down to his bones and hungry on top of it. Tennant would know what to do. Tennant had been looking into the murders for months now and would be grateful for a name and a description, even if it was a false description and very likely a false name.

Ronai waded through the water and onto the muddy shore. His butt was large, his legs chubby. Not a nice sight. And still—it was like watching a wolf in sheep's clothes. Ronai wore runes to disguise himself, Gabriel was as certain of it as he was certain that Pepino lay dead in that park back home. The murderer had said his son looked like him, which meant that without the disguising runes Ronai must be a damn good-looking man.

Just when Gabriel took a silent step back to hide himself more completely, Ronai looked up and stared straight in his direction. He had just finished putting on his trousers, and slowly—very slowly—he fastened them. Leaving shirt, socks, and shoes behind, he shook the last drops of pond water out of his hair and came closer to the place where Gabriel stood rooted to the spot.

Ronai shouldn't be able to see him. The rune on his neck and the Hiding rune on the stone worked perfectly, Gabriel was sure of it. The killer hadn't seen him back in the park, and there had been fewer bushes and leaves for coverage.

He couldn't see him. No way.

Making a rash decision, Gabriel took another step backward, and a twig broke beneath his foot. Snapped loud enough to wake the dead— at least, that was how it sounded in his ears.

Ronai's head shot up, and his hand went to the pendant around his neck at the same time that Gabriel clutched the small Hiding rune stone in his pocket. He was screwed.

With long strides that proved his real body was neither as untrained nor as fat as it appeared, the killer crossed the distance between pond and hill in a matter of seconds. He would soon discover that he wasn't alone in the woods.

Gabriel turned and ran.

More twigs broke beneath his feet, and birds flew upward, disturbed by the noise. Damn it to hell—he needed to get out of these woods and back to the place where the portal had opened. He would figure out a way out of this mess once he got there. Maybe there were some caves in the cliffs he could hide in, or maybe he could climb down to the ocean below.

And maybe I will grow wings and fly away, Gabriel thought bitterly. If he were honest with himself, he had to admit that it was highly unlikely he was going to escape the killer behind him.

His lungs burned, and the dizziness was back. Running this soon after he'd gone through a portal was obviously not a good idea, but then, he really had no choice. Gabriel swore he could hear bare feet hitting the ground behind him, running, following him. He could almost feel the breath of his pursuer on his neck, and it took a great amount of effort not to look back.

His own harsh breathing sounded very loud in his ears, and when he finally reached the edge of the woods—had he really gone that far in?—he hoped against hope a portal would open for him simply because he wished it to happen.

It didn't happen, of course. A portal only opened if one was there to draw the correct rune, and even if he had the time, Gabriel wasn't sure he would be able to do it.

Waves crashed against the small beach at the foot of the rocky cliff, seagulls cried out their lonely songs, oblivious to his peril, and it still smelled of jasmine, although Gabriel hadn't seen any of the little white blossoms earlier.

Behind him, Ronai emerged from between the trees, red-faced and sweaty but with eyes as alert as a hawk's. His nostrils flared, and without hesitation, he focused on the spot where Gabriel stood.

"I cannot see you," he said. "But I know you are there. Show yourself, or I will force you to."

Step by step, he moved closer. Gabriel clutched the tiny stone as if it were a lifeline, not entirely believing that the man really couldn't see him. Tennant had shown him how to draw the damn thing properly, but hadn't thought to show him its effect. Under the circumstances, he found it hard to believe that he could be invisible if someone could pinpoint where he was.

Ronai's angry face and the fact that he didn't focus on him proved Gabriel wrong. The Hiding rune and the rune on his neck were strong magic, that much was becoming obvious. Just in case, Gabriel took a few more steps back, away from the woods and Ronai and toward the edge of the cliff. Not the safest place to be—the way down to the beach seemed horribly long—but the more distance he could put between him and the murderer, the better.

Briefly, Gabriel considered trying to get back to the woods. It would be easier to hide among the trees; he could wait for it to get dark and then try to open a portal. If only Ronai wasn't blocking his way back to the forest, he might have tried it.

As it was, the murderer stood between Gabriel and the tree line. And directly behind him was the edge of the cliff.

Shit.

Ronai stopped no more than ten feet away. The expression on his ordinary-looking face was one of surprise as well as annoyance. Gabriel guessed he was angry that someone else was here, and he was determined to find out who it was and what this someone had seen. It would be in his best interest to get away from this world before Ronai found a way to capture him and start asking questions. Gabriel suspected it wouldn't be a pleasant experience and would probably involve tools of persuasion if the answers failed to satisfy him. Sharp tools. Nasty tools.

Gabriel shuddered. The edge of the cliff was only a foot away, but he considered this a benefit if it meant keeping his distance from the half-naked man.

Ronai moved his fingers. It was a small gesture, and maybe he was just waving a fly away from his sweaty face, but for some reason Gabriel didn't believe that for a second.

No. He was painting a rune.

Instantly, the stone in Gabriel's hand became warm. Very warm.

Hot.

In fact, too hot to be held. It felt like it would burn a hole in his palm if he didn't drop it. Gabriel fought to hold onto it, trying to convince himself that the stone couldn't be that hot, that it was only an illusion, but he had to give up eventually. With a curse, he dropped the stone and with it the Hiding rune he had carved what now seemed ages ago. Hours, maybe days—he had no idea anymore. The small stone arced as he flung it, landing with a sharp crack on the rocks, and broke in half along with its spell. As if a veil had been swept aside, Ronai whipped around, now able to see his opponent.

"Who are you?" he asked, sounding confused. "I do not know you. How did you get here, and why were you watching me at my pond?"

"*Your* pond?" Gabriel replied, trying to look and sound more stupid than he actually was. Having followed a murderer with no better weapon than a stone and a pocketknife certainly completed the picture. He was honestly hoping Ronai would believe he was just someone who was interested in a piece of ass, not the fact that he was a murderer. "Do you live here? I saw you undressing and thought a quick peek wouldn't hurt, and then you got angry and I ran away. Sorry, man. No offense meant."

Amber eyes narrowed suspiciously, and Ronai took another few steps. A few more, and he would be near enough to touch Gabriel. Or push him off the cliff.

Not good. Not good at all.

A vague memory stirred at the back of Gabriel's mind. He knew those eyes; they seemed very familiar. However, no one he knew had eyes that color, nor eyes so cold and angry.

"You used a rune to hide. As you are nothing but a stupid human, the main question is, who gave it to you?" As he spoke, Ronai swiftly pulled out a knife, simultaneously flicking it open. There were stains on the blade. Dark, ugly stains.

Gabriel swallowed hard and decided to give up the charade. "I saw you kill Pepino, so I know you are a murderer. Question is—and I'm the first to admit that it's a wild guess—did you kill Mallfrick with that knife too? Was it you who stepped through a portal inside Mallfrick's office and cut him into pieces?"

He didn't give a damn that with those words he gave away whatever small chance he might have had to get out of this alive. Ronai's slight frown told Gabriel his guess had been well aimed.

"You're the killer we've been looking for," he accused. "You're hiding behind runes, and you know what? I won't tell you who I am or how I managed to follow you. I won't tell you anything!"

Another step back. Gabriel could feel the empty space at his back and several hundred feet of nothing but air between the rock beneath his feet and the sand below.

"You're bleeding," Ronai stated, tipping his head. "You came through the portal I opened?"

The knife was steady in his hand. It was a hell of a lot scarier than if he had shown off a bit, flicking it, waving it around. As it was, he projected the perfect image of a professional killer.

"Going through a portal without protection is madness, and the wounds prove you don't know how to protect yourself from the portal's power," Ronai said. "You should be dead. At the very least, you should be lying on the ground screaming, unable to talk, to stand, or even to think."

"Sorry to disappoint you. Any objections to me leaving now?" Gabriel rebutted lightly. Sarcasm was probably not the wisest course of action, but at least it reassured him that his brain was still working.

Ronai lunged. With a harsh scream, he attacked, knife held high in the air with the obvious intention of plunging it right into his opponent's chest. Gabriel could nearly feel it piercing his heart, and out of sheer fright, he jumped too. Jumped backward, where there was no ground left for him to land on.

At least no ground nearby.

Tumbling, Gabriel fell, his scream sounding shrill in his own ears. From above, he heard the frustrated, angry yell of Ronai, who was unable to follow him if he didn't want to end up a shattered mess at the bottom of the cliff.

Water, I need to reach the water or I'm dead, Gabriel thought, close to panicking. His hands waved through the air. If he had had wings, he would have managed to become airborne, so enthusiastic were his attempts to avoid hitting the ground.

Without realizing it, his fingers moved. Quickly, deftly, they created lines in the air, and his instincts kicked in, feeding them with power, his body's last-ditch effort to save himself. Had he been able to think about it beforehand, he probably wouldn't have done it, or he would have tried to paint another pattern, one more familiar, one closer to home. As it was, his fingers clearly didn't want to be attached to a dead body and acted without consulting the brain first. They drew the first Portal rune he'd learned from Tennant's books, the easiest one, but unfortunately not the one that led back home.

Golden light exploded in mid-air when the portal opened. Harsh, blinding pain made him retch, his head and his body feeling as though they were being crushed by a giant fist. The beach wasn't visible anymore, nor was the deceptively soft-looking sand. It wasn't so bad not being able to see where he would die in a few seconds.

He didn't even realize he was falling through a portal, as occupied as he was with screaming.

His heart beat in a wild staccato of fear and regret. He was still falling, and he hated it. He could smell as well as hear the ocean and had the oddest moment of surprise when a seagull's wing brushed his cheek. He was screaming and cursing and then screaming louder, screaming loud enough to drown out the noise of those cursed seagulls, loud enough to make him forget he was still falling, close to death, as once more he tumbled from one world into another.

The tips of his fingers ripped open from nail to knuckle. Then the gashes traveled up his arms, over his elbows and to his shoulders. More blood shot out of his nose, and this time out of his mouth, ears, and eyes too. For a brief moment, his heart stopped beating, and he thought, *This is how dying feels.* All panic was gone, but he was drowning in pain, drowning in a different ocean, far away from any beach and, luckily, far away from Ronai too.

GABRIEL would have died if the icy water he had splashed into hadn't jumpstarted his heart back into service. Shocked at the sudden coldness, it began beating frantically, and his lungs tried to draw in some air, filling with water instead. He sank, pulled down by the weight of his boots, and he suppressed the newly flaring panic and fingered the laces with numb hands, fearing he wouldn't make it. The boots came off, and socks as well, then vanished in the darkness of the sea. Gabriel kicked upward, toward the surface, toward light and air, finally reaching both, able to breathe again. And he saw that here, in this new world, there were also seagulls, which laughed at him while swiftly winging through the evening breeze.

Choking and coughing, Gabriel fought for air and light and life, not knowing where he was and expecting Ronai to come after him, to follow him even here in the middle of an ocean, wherever *here* was.

Hang on. Hadn't he been in this situation before, where he didn't know where he'd landed, didn't know where Ronai was, or whether or not he'd be killed?

"Shit! Fucking lousy shit, fucking portals, *fucking* hidden worlds!"

The salty water burned in his open wounds, he was having an awful time keeping his head above the water's surface, and there were too many waves to see if there was any land nearby. The sun was low, just about to vanish on the horizon. Clouds were darkening the sky. With a sudden pang of guilt, Gabriel realized that he should have returned home hours ago. Instead, he'd been stupid enough to get himself into yet another mess, one he very likely wouldn't get out of without help. He wouldn't survive long in this ocean, being tossed about like a toy boat, bleeding and with a mind-splitting headache.

To distract his mind from more pressing matters, such as how long a man could swim, whether there were sharks in this ocean, why using the portals caused him so much pain, and whether Ronai would be able to follow him, he thought of Tennant. Tennant, whom he had left behind in a safer world than this one, injured and weak and waiting for his return.

A wave tumbled him around, and more water washed into his mouth and eyes. Would it be such a bad idea to just let himself drown? At least there would be no more pain. And no more guilt. He hadn't been able to help Pepino, had watched him being killed as if he'd been watching television. He'd let the boy's killer escape too, so what use was he?

Tennant, Gabriel mused as the waves played with him, a toy of the ocean, lost in its endless vastness. Tennant wasn't that ill any longer. He would manage. He'd sleep, he'd phone the supermarket to deliver the groceries, he'd order a pizza and come to the conclusion that his guest had had enough of him and left, returning to the streets.

Ridiculous. As if he'd ever leave Tennant. As if he'd stay away deliberately.

Perhaps dying wasn't such a good idea after all, pain or no pain. If he were dead, he'd never see the doctor again, he'd never learn all there was to learn about runes, and he'd never be able to track down the murderer.

Ronai. The killer's name was Ronai. Not tall, not good-looking, with amber eyes and blond hair and a belly and a rune-pendant, indicating that he hid his true looks. Looks similar to his son, who had been beautiful, even if it was only for a short amount of time.

Coughing up some more water, Gabriel pushed the wet hair out of his face and rubbed his eyes to ease the burning—a useless attempt. Twilight and clouds: a bad combination if one wanted to see very far, but he managed to verify that there was no shore anywhere nearby. Water and nothing but water from left to right and front to back, and there was the horizon, as far away as possible with the sun just touching it. Another couple of minutes, and the light would be gone.

Meaning it would be dark soon.

Now, what was it he'd been thinking earlier about sharks? Great. The panic rolled in again, and Gabriel swam frantically for a few yards, stopped, then swam in the opposite direction instead. No matter that his arms and legs felt like lead and that the constant pounding in his head was driving him half crazy. No matter that there was nowhere he could swim, as the ocean was equally barren on all sides. Swimming seemed the only logical thing to do, unless….

Unless, of course, he opened another portal.

Brilliant idea. Why hadn't he thought of it before?

With a great effort, Gabriel pulled one arm out of the water, exhaustion warring with the need to get home as quickly as possible. The water had washed off the blood, so he wasn't reminded about the dangers of opening yet another portal. It should be easy to manage it— he knew the rune that opened the portal to his own world by heart, for he'd painted the Portal rune for his world dozens of times when Tennant had been unconscious with fever. He was pretty sure he would remember it correctly.

On the other hand, he might not survive going through a portal again so soon, given the pain and the damage the last portal trip had caused. Still, the odds for his survival were better than if he remained on this water world. Too bad the rune to his world was so complicated. His fingers might have remembered it first, and he wouldn't be swimming in this icy ocean right now but at home instead.

Shivering with cold and dread, Gabriel pulled his hand above the waterline once more. With his eyes burning from the salt and his legs becoming heavier by the second, he knew he had to get out of the water soon or he would sink to the bottom like a stone.

He licked his lips only to find them cracked and raw and drew the first line, ignoring the pain that shot up his arm to a point behind his forehead. It was as if he'd been hit by an axe. Tears ran down his cheeks, and he gritted his teeth as he tried to brace himself. He drew the second line, feeding the rune with power. Blood and water dripped from his fingers, making him yell deeply and harshly, the pain threatening to rip him apart. Skin and flesh sliced open. More gashes appeared, slashing his fingertips to his upper arm, as if inflicted by an invisible knife. Not deep enough to cut a vital artery, but deep enough to ignite the fear that he wouldn't be able to finish the rune.

As if he hadn't screamed enough already, as if he weren't in deep enough shit, now he found himself losing consciousness in the middle of an ocean. Forcing his eyes to remain open, he drew the third line. The familiar golden light appeared, competing with the brilliant colors of the sunset. Gabriel kept his mouth closed and his nose above the surface and tried not to swallow any more of the horribly salty water as the depths reached out for him in an eager attempt to embrace him for good and drag him down for an eternal slumber amongst mud, fish, and dead seashells.

"Come on!" he croaked hoarsely, trying to scrape together enough strength and power to finish the damn rune.

The waves wouldn't leave him alone, tumbling him around like a rag doll, making it nearly impossible to stay focused on the faintly glowing lines. Maybe he had already lost too much blood. His head hurt too much to remember the correct look of the rune. His fingers were too numb, and when he tried to move them in the proper form, the light that emerged from the half-finished rune faded even further.

Gabriel cursed nastily, but he wasn't willing to give up yet. He wasn't going to be fodder for sharks or any other creatures that lived in these seas. He wasn't going to drown.

Perhaps he really could have done it, could have opened the portal, if he hadn't been wrong in his assumption that there was no land in sight after all. With one last cruel, joyful move, the waves threw him hard against sharp rocks. There, in the middle of nowhere, was a small island, no larger than ten feet across and three, maybe four feet above the waterline. Headfirst, Gabriel smashed into the rocks, blood pouring from the gash. He lost eye contact with the golden light of his escape route, so the few lines he had already managed to draw paled, then vanished for good.

He truly wished he'd be done with yelling sometime soon. It was becoming tiresome.

Cut, bruised, and bleeding, Gabriel floundered as the rocks tore at his hair, ripping strands out of his head. This place didn't offer shelter so much as a short delay from dying. Blood from the gaping wound on his forehead streamed into his eyes, which didn't matter at all, since the sun had gone down and darkness had fallen over this world.

Gabriel's heart was still beating, and his lungs were still breathing, but that was about it. Keeping his eyes open was no longer an option. Vaguely, he hoped he wouldn't roll off the rock before the darkness claimed him as well. Then he lost consciousness.

CHAPTER ELEVEN

PAIN. What a surprise.

More pain, accompanied by an unbearable thirst. Better not to wake up. Better to stay unconscious.

SUN shining in his eyes. Unfriendly, harsh, hot, piercing beams. Lips as dry as the desert. Mouth burning with the need for a drop of fresh water—just one little drop.

HEADACHE, bad enough to make him wish he were dead.

Was he?

Already?

A groan. No, he wasn't dead. Not yet.

HIS throat was made of sandpaper. A lifetime ago, he'd known what it felt like to have water touch his lips, splash on his tongue—clean, sweet water, not this salty poison that surrounded him.

He couldn't move, he could only breathe, and even that just barely. His arms and legs—were they still there, or had they fallen off into the sea? He couldn't feel them any longer. Was that the sun high in the sky? No, impossible. The sun had set just a few moments ago. Half an hour at the most. It couldn't be shining down on him, burning his skin, burning his eyes, shriveling his brain to the size of a raisin.

He would die here on this rock, on this world that was not his own.

The prospect didn't even bother him.

Rain. Sweet, cool rain on his face and in his mouth. His lips, cracked and dry, parted slightly to allow the water in. Swallowing hurt, and thinking hurt. Actually, absolutely everything just fucking hurt. He should have had enough sense to die hours ago instead of fighting, instead of refusing to give in, instead of clinging to his worthless little life. After all, no one cared if he lived or died.

Aleksei.

A faint whisper, barely audible. Who had said it?

Ah, yes. He had. His mind, his memory, was reminding him of his responsibility to a man who more or less consistently lied to him.

Who was injured. Whom he cared for and longed for.

Useless. No way to get back to him. No way now to find out if the man was open for seduction.

What a stupid time to think about seduction, he had to admit.

Someone laughed—was that him? It sounded terrible, barely human. Well, he wasn't human, was he? He was fish fodder, or would be as soon as the sharks found him. Or the sea monsters. Or maybe even the dragons. Was that a fin over there?

IT MIGHT have been a fin, but that was definitely a seagull sitting on his wrist. Keeping its balance in the wind and rain, it explored something between the fingers of his right hand. It was beautiful. Smaller than the seagulls back home, it had a black beak and black stripes on the outer edges of its wings. And it was curious. It sat on his wrist as if it belonged there, its feet cold and strong, and Gabriel had just begun to wonder what was so interesting when it moved and hacked its beak right into the flesh of his index finger.

Ouch! he thought, not strong enough to say it aloud. It didn't make the seagull fly away either.

A sharp beak on an overeager seagull was a very bad combination when one was barely able to move one's eyelids. Too weak and far too confused to react properly, Gabriel just stared at the bird and its tail and waited for its next move.

He didn't have long to wait. It bit him then, pulling and yanking and trying to separate his finger from his hand. Determined, it ripped with all its might, as if the bloodied finger were a dead fish rather than still-alive flesh. When this effort failed, the bird struck a third blow, drilling its beak into the soft spot between the knuckles.

Finally, Gabriel was forced into action. He croaked hoarsely, pulled his hand away, and tried to hide it under his body so the damn bird couldn't have another go at his fingers.

The seagull took off and looked down at him from the sky. Oddly enough, the damn bird actually look annoyed.

"Fuck off," he whispered. Where had his voice gone? And where was he, anyway?

A surge of water washed over his face—the wind had picked up, and the waves were getting high.

He was wet. Not a dry stitch on his body. Although he didn't seem to be wearing much: a soaked shirt, soaked trousers. His naked feet were miles away, or so it seemed. It was hard to move them. Actually, he wasn't entirely sure he still had feet.

Cold. Freezing. Thirsty. Hungry.

Pain.

Shit.

The bird had come back and landed where his hand had been only a moment ago. Its eyes were black and accusing. *If you were dead,* they said, *I could eat you. If you were dead, you couldn't fight.*

"Dead," Gabriel said to the bird. "I'm not dead. Why should I be?" With immense effort, he raised his head, trying to figure out where he was. The light was scarce—a storm was about to hit, that much was obvious.

A storm would wash him off this little, rotten rock of an island back into the ocean. Where he would undoubtedly drown.

If he drowned, though, the seagull couldn't eat him.

If he drowned... if he drowned.... There was a problem with the concept of him drowning, but at the moment, he couldn't remember what that problem was. Apart from being dead, of course.

Inquiringly, the seagull cried, obviously wanting to know if it could have another go at his fingers.

Gabriel raised his hand and held it close to his eyes. Focusing wasn't easy, but eventually, he saw the cuts and the blood and understood that the bird just considered him a nice alternative to fish. Possibly, it was as hungry as he was, given the lack of land and the wildness of the waves.

"Shouldn't have told me 'bout runes, Doc. Wouldn't be here without the damn things." Exhausted, he rested his head on his arm. A wave washed over him again, rattling him, trying to pull him along.

Not yet. A few more minutes, just a bit longer. No rush. No hurry. He'd follow the waves, eventually following them all across the ocean, a corpse turning into a heap of bleached bones.

Only problem was, he wouldn't see Tennant again.

Gabriel frowned. If he died, he wouldn't be able to tell Tennant the killer's name. *Ronai*. He needed to tell the doctor that a man named Ronai had killed all those people, Mallfrick and Lorelei, he was sure of it, and now Pepino too. The bastard had killed Pepino, and for fuck's sake, what was he still doing here in the middle of this cursed ocean instead of back home where it was warm and dry and where he had been expected for hours at least, if not longer?

Spitting out water and blood, Gabriel forced his unwilling body onto all fours, dragging himself a bit higher up on the rocky patch and a bit farther away from the hungry waves and the bottom of the ocean.

"Need to get out of here. Need to leave. Portal. I need to open a fucking portal. Fucking damn shit!"

Shaking, he grabbed for a rock the size of his fist, knowing if he delayed following his decision through for a single moment, he might pass out again or lose the will out of sheer fright of the portal's power.

His fingers were numb, which was good, but his skull seemed to be filled with wet cotton instead of a working brain, which was bad. His brain was out of service due to blood loss, dehydration, lack of food, and the general catastrophic situation he was in. Thinking in general wasn't easy right now. The bird seemed to be in a better position to do the thinking, but then, the bird most likely didn't know the rune that would open the portal back to his world. So Gabriel forgot about the seagull and drew the first line by dragging the stone in his hand along the stone under his knees.

Great: there was the pain again, that blinding, head-splitting pain clarifying that a bit of a rest hadn't changed the problem that he wasn't supposed to open a portal.

It didn't matter. He *needed* to get back home. Tennant was waiting. Maybe the fever had worsened again and the doc needed help, and here he was, lazily chilling out on a rock.

The second line, then the third. There were only seven lines in this rune. Not too many, if one put it in perspective.

Gabriel bit his lips bloody to keep from screaming but failed. With each breath he took, he groaned, and then he yelled loud enough to convince the seagull he wasn't going to be dying anytime soon. Finally, it flew away.

Stars exploded in front of his eyes, and Gabriel didn't know if he was imagining them, if they were pain-induced, or if the portal was causing them. He drew the last line of the rune, weak and desperate and longing for home so badly that he had to support his right hand with his left so he wouldn't drop the rock.

The portal opened silently and unspectacularly. For a moment, a heartbeat, the blink of an eye, Gabriel thought he was dreaming, fantasizing he had opened it, imagining he had found a way out of this mess. Yet the portal was there, right in front of him, and it didn't disappear when he dropped the stone, which immediately rolled into the water and sank.

Throat dry with fear, Gabriel painfully gathered all his limbs and crawled toward the portal, Tennant's voice sounding clearly in his head, warning him never to pass from one world to another without assistance.

"Done it twice already," Gabriel rasped, his hands leaving bloody imprints on the black rock. "Third time surely won't kill me."

But he wasn't sure. He was scared, but then, the portal wouldn't remain open forever, and so he crept on, slowly, like an overgrown lizard, blood and sweat and seawater dripping from his face. He was thinking of home and Tennant—*Aleksei!*—and warmth and something to drink, and when the portal embraced him, drawing him closer and then inside, all he could do was hope the unbearable pressure on his body wouldn't crush his bones to dust.

Once more he screamed, just once, before he left the ocean and the rock and that damn greedy seagull behind. He tumbled through the portal and briefly wondered what would happen if he hadn't remembered the rune correctly. Would he land in yet another world? He was certain he wouldn't be able to muster the strength to go through this torture again. Then suddenly he was through the portal, landing hard on the other side, collapsing on a floor made of light wooden planks in a house as far away from the hidden worlds as possible.

He was home. Tennant told him later that he landed right at his feet, but Gabriel missed that part; he passed out the moment he finally reached safety.

ARMS around him, rocking him. A tender, warm voice soothing him. Lips near his ear, murmuring reassuring nonsense, telling him all was well, all would be fine, and that he would feel better soon.

Not a bad start.

Hands stripping off his wet clothes, a relief as both his trousers and shirt were soaked with salt water, which burned in every wound on his body. The floor was cool on his skin, or at least Gabriel thought so—there wasn't enough warmth left in him to properly tell.

He blinked his eyes open, trying to focus, trying to see. What he saw was Tennant's concerned, worried face and those wonderful ice-blue eyes.

"Hoped you'd do it," he croaked, trying to smile.

"Do what?" There was concern in Tennant's voice too. "Care for you? Save your life? Try to stop you from losing your mind? What happened, Gabriel? Who attacked you?"

Naked, Gabriel lay on the ground while Tennant painted runes all over his body. Now he was certain this must be a dream. Apparently, he had only imagined that he'd opened a portal. In reality, he was still stuck on that damn rock with that damn seagull happily pecking out his eyeballs. Quite possibly, he was already dead and in heaven.

Well, in that case, he might as well tell the truth. "Hoped you'd undress me eventually. Hoped you'd be naked, too, though."

The smallest smile curved Tennant's pale lips, but he didn't reply, just continued to draw runes on Gabriel's skin.

"I'm allergic to runes," Gabriel stated, trying to brace himself for more pain. Nothing moved except his lips and his fluttering eyelids; other than that, he seemed to be completely paralyzed. "Do I still have legs?" he asked, and damn it to hell, was that a tear trickling out of the corner of his eye? "Can't feel them, you know. My hands, either." He didn't want to cry, not where Tennant could see it, but he couldn't stop the tears from running down his face.

Tennant swallowed. "You are not allergic to runes. You used them excessively, and I believe that is what caused most of your wounds. I assume you were in a fight, too, given the state you're in. I am trying to ease your pain by drawing Protection runes all over you. Your legs are fine, as are your hands and fingers. They're just numb. I will make sure you won't lose so much as a toe."

Gabriel thought about that for a while. This was all so surreal, strange, outside his experience. "Any seagulls nearby?" he had to ask. If there were seagulls in Tennant's house, he would try and crawl away. "Hate them. Horrible things. One tried to eat me. I think."

Briefly, Tennant interrupted the task of covering Gabriel's skin with runes to cup his cheek. It felt marvelous. Gabriel turned his head and pressed his face into Tennant's touch, smelled the soap the doctor must have used sometime today, and ceased to feel embarrassed for his tears.

"Where on earth have you been, Gabriel?" the doctor asked, brushing wet, salty strands of hair out of his face. "I looked for you everywhere. I went to the mission, but they didn't know anything. I searched for you all over, but couldn't find you. I would have gone to get some help today if you hadn't managed to come back to me." Quickly, he wiped his sleeve over his eyes.

Nothing made sense anymore. "Been gone for only a few hours, Doc. A day at the most. Why worry?" There was something else he needed to say, but unfortunately, he'd forgotten what it was.

Runes down his arm, runes across his forehead, runes on his chest. Luckily, they didn't hurt, but they did make him feel even number. A faint feeling of warmth washed through him, and he became tired, so very tired, all of a sudden.

Tennant bent low, then a bit lower. Low enough for a kiss, but he only whispered, "You've been gone for more than a week, Gabriel. I knew you wouldn't just walk out on me. I feared you were dead. I feared I would have to go to the morgue, identify your body, that the murderer had killed you."

Gabriel's eyes widened. That was it! "Ronai," he croaked, but his tongue was so very heavy, like lead, like a millstone. "Seen him. Killed—"

"Shhh." Tennant's hand was warm on his cheek. "You will sleep now. Another few hours, and I wouldn't have been able to save your life, so all you will do now is rest until I say you can get up. Understood?"

"Hmmm," Gabriel managed before he drifted off into dreamland.

SUNLIGHT shone in Gabriel's face, which was a good thing in itself since it was a friendly sunlight, neither harsh nor burning. He was thirsty, but it was bearable, and he was as hungry as a wild wolf after a long, cold winter. His stomach growled loudly.

Slowly, Gabriel opened one eye, then the other. There was the sun, its beams draped across the bed covers. It shone in through the window, and that was really, really good because there usually weren't any windows on rocks in the middle of an ocean.

Hadn't he opened a portal to get away from there?

He stretched, yawned, and was about to scratch his stubbly cheeks when he noticed that his fingers were bandaged, each one individually, as well as both hands and all the way up to his elbows.

At least I still have fingers, he thought, trying to waggle them a bit. It was a beautiful day. He was alive, he was back home, he could even move his fingers a little bit—and his toes, which indicated that his legs were still attached to his body. Great!

So where was Tennant?

Contently, Gabriel snuggled a bit deeper into his pillow only to realize that there was no pillow behind him. No pillow he'd known was so bony. No pillow he'd known had—so far—ever grown arms.

Certainly no pillow snored.

Very carefully, Gabriel turned his head and saw a shoulder, an arm, and part of a shirt-covered chest.

Ah. Tennant was behind him, holding him like Gabriel had held him not too long ago. What had the doctor said? That he'd been gone for over a week? That couldn't be possible. He'd been on the rocky island for a while, maybe even two days, but he could never survive more than that. He must have misheard.

A name dropped into the darkness of Gabriel's half-asleep mind, stirring the quiet surface and making him shudder.

"Ronai!" His voice croaked. It was about time he drank some tea to soothe his throat. But not before he told Tennant about the murderer.

"Doc! Wake up, will you?" Pity he had to end this so soon, lying in Tennant's arms, but what he had to say was much more important than his own pleasure.

"Doc!" Struggling and fighting with the bedcover, Gabriel tried to awaken the sleeping man behind him, already regretting that once the doctor was awake, he would get up and thus move away from him. No way would he have another chance for such close contact, especially not when he was naked.

Taken by surprise by the discovery that he wasn't wearing any clothes, Gabriel checked to see if he at least was wearing underwear by lifting the duvet and pushing a hand underneath.

Stark naked. He wasn't wearing a single stitch. Nothing but black lines covered his skin, but they were just paint, not fabric.

Now how was it possible that, although starving, thirsty, and had only barely escaped death, the first thing that happened when he woke up was that he got hard?

Flushing, he pulled the bedcover up to his chin and thought of seagulls, of icy water, and the murderer's cold eyes.

It didn't really work.

Tennant's arms tightened around his waist, pulling him into an even closer, more intimate embrace. Gabriel could feel the man's heartbeat against his back and his breath on his neck and nearly moaned with delight. Good gods, how he wished Tennant were naked too!

Useless wish. "Doc!" he said as firmly as possible, finally waking up Tennant.

"Whsit?" he mumbled.

"Would you let go of me? Please?" Gabriel asked, not believing that he actually just asked the doctor to let him go.

Tennant chuckled sleepily and opened his arms. "Sure. Although I was really enjoying holding you so close." He yawned, slipped out of the bed, and stretched. "It is surprisingly comfortable to sleep with company. Tea?"

Gabriel couldn't answer, as he was too busy staring. Tennant wore a shirt and trousers, but the shirt was unbuttoned down to his waist, showing enough skin to make a man drool, and the trousers didn't hide a well-shaped, wonderfully large, delicious-looking morning erection.

Tennant followed his glassy gaze and raised an eyebrow. "My apologies," he said smoothly. "The warmth of your body was obviously very arousing. I want you to stay in bed until I have taken care of this… problem. Breakfast in about ten minutes." With that, he headed for the bathroom, leaving a dumbstruck Gabriel behind with the image of

Tennant getting himself off in the shower and a cock hard enough to hammer a nail into a wall.

Double, triple fucking shit!

Gabriel was painfully hard, and he needed to take care of it before Tennant came back. Who knew how quickly the doctor could jerk off? Gabriel leaned over the edge of the bed and snatched a sweater lying on the ground. Kicking the duvet away, he vaguely wondered at how well he felt, then wrapped one hand around his aching length. With the other, he pressed the sweater over his groin.

"Someone should invent a Cleansing rune," he bit out. Then he thought he heard Tennant groan with pleasure and came in a short and bitter spasm without really enjoying it, regretting it almost immediately.

"Should have stayed in that other world. Should have drowned," he said, falling back onto the mattress. No arms were there to catch him, no lips to kiss his neck. Just a cold and empty bed and a soiled garment he needed to put into the washing machine at the first opportunity.

A decision needed to be made, and he made it quickly, without thinking it through. He couldn't stay. The temptation was too great, and his chances of success approached nil. "As soon as I have told him about Ronai, I'll leave."

CHAPTER TWELVE

"THE man's named Ronai. He's killed a friend of mine—well, someone I knew—and I believe he killed the others too."

Head down, face covered by hair, and hands wrapped around a mug of tea, Gabriel sat at the kitchen table, hoping he could say what he had to as quickly as possible so he could pack up and leave, ideally before lunch. He had eaten his breakfast—gobbled it down, he had been so ravenous—and now the basic hunger was gone.

Tennant was watching him closely. "Why do you say that?"

"It's something he said—that Pepino's existence is the reason that he did what had to be done." Briefly, Gabriel glanced at Tennant. "It's just a gut feeling. I can't prove anything. He broke Pepino's neck as if he'd done it before. He tried to kill me. Anyway, it doesn't matter. Ronai is pudgy and blond, and he's totally average apart from the rune he wears around his neck. A rune like yours. He's hiding his true identity, so you'll have to do some research, but then, that's your job. Thought I should let you know. It's the sole reason I made it back here." He took a sip of tea to wet his dry throat, but couldn't get the image of Tennant's bare skin out of his head. It made thinking really hard.

Fascinating, how long one could stare at a plain tablecloth without considering it boring.

"The question of you meeting the man who murdered those victims is of less importance, Gabriel," Tennant said calmly. "Right now, I want to know where you have been, and I want to know who attacked you. Because of your rune, you have healed exceptionally fast, but that doesn't change the fact that you nearly died. Gabriel? Are you going to answer sometime today?" Tennant hadn't touched his breakfast. His tea and toast had both gone cold.

Gabriel shifted his shoulders uncomfortably. He didn't want to be this near to Tennant, but the thought of leaving was equally unpleasant. "I don't know where I've been," he finally managed to say. "In the middle of an ocean, on a tiny rock, accompanied by a seagull. No one attacked me but a hungry seagull. It tried to eat my fingers. Thought they were fish, I guess. I was bleeding and dizzy, and the first time I tried to open a portal, it nearly ripped me apart."

"You opened a portal?"

Surprised, Gabriel looked up. "Of course I opened a damn portal, what did you think? I saw Ronai kill Pepino. I followed the murderer through the portal he'd opened and ended up near a forest at the edge of a cliff. Saw the guy taking a bath—that's how I learned about his rune necklace. He saw me, though, and I ran. In the end, he tried to kill me, and I thought jumping off the cliff would be a smart way out. Somehow, I must have opened a portal in mid-air, because I landed in another world instead of breaking all my bones on the beach below the cliff. Fucking hurt, falling through the portal, though. Even more than the first time."

"No wonder you lost a few days." Tennant's voice sounded strangely flat. "I assume you eventually opened a portal that brought you back home?"

"Took me a while," Gabriel mumbled. "I bumped headfirst into a rock, and going through those portals hurt like hell. I wasn't attacked— I came out the other side looking like I'd been slashed with a razor. And what do you mean, I lost some days?" It was impossible to look at Tennant any longer; like a guilty schoolboy, Gabriel stared at the table and concentrated on sitting still. He knew very well he wasn't supposed to use the more powerful runes, and a Portal rune was certainly very powerful.

"Three portals?" Tennant sounded as if he'd told him he'd beheaded a dragon. "*Three?* Are you crazy? You followed someone through a portal you didn't create yourself, and then you opened two more on your own, and you are still alive? Actually, you are not crazy. You must be mistaken, as that's completely impossible."

"I'm *not* fucking mistaken," Gabriel snapped. "The damn portals nearly ripped me apart, which is the reason it took me so long to get back here." Taking a piece of toast, he took a bite just to have something to do. "When I drew some runes at the mission to prevent it from falling apart, my fingers began to bleed. I didn't think much of it, but then it really hurt when I created a Hiding rune so Ronai wouldn't see me, and then I followed him through the portal and nearly collapsed. The rest is more or less fuzzy, but I know it hurt. Sorry, Doc, for messing with the runes and all."

Tennant shook his head. He looked more troubled than anything else. "You are truly worried about *messing* with them? Gabriel, going through a portal unprotected is suicide. It requires years of training, it requires knowledge as well as skill, and it requires help, at least at the beginning. I simply cannot understand how you managed it. You should have died the moment you followed the killer into another world, never mind been able to open two more portals. But apparently, you only lost time in the process of passing through, which means that, although only a couple days passed on your end, more than a week was gone by here. It is a miracle you were able to follow the murderer. I am completely at a loss as to how you managed to get back to me."

Slowly, Gabriel turned his hands and for the first time looked at the patterns on his skin. Tennant had painted runes on him, he remembered, and they could still be seen easily.

"How long will they last?" Gabriel asked, tracing one of the lines with his fingertips.

Tennant cast him a small smile. "Covering you with the runes was necessary to prevent you from further harm. I didn't know at the time what had happened to you, so I used the strongest runes available. I don't know exactly when, but eventually, they will fade away. The power of the portals went against you. You know, you could have ended up with less brains than a daisy. Covering you with Protection runes will help you heal, but you will always carry the scars."

"If you say so," Gabriel replied, taking the doctor's words as the accusation they weren't meant to be. It would make it easier for him to leave Tennant in another hour. "I promise to die next time I use a portal—less messy. Actually, I swear never to use runes again, if it makes you happy. Just find Ronai, will you? He broke Pepino's neck just like that. The boy thought the killer was his dad, that's why he went to meet him. I don't even know if his body is still in that little park." The thought was horrible. "I need to find out. He wasn't exactly a friend, but I sort of liked him, and…."

Tennant rubbed his hands across his face. If it was true what he'd said earlier on, if he really had searched for Gabriel, it was no surprise that he was tired. "The boy's body was buried yesterday," Tennant said. "When you didn't come back from your shopping tour, I first thought you had spent the night at the mission. The next day, I went looking for you. A bald young girl said you'd gone after Pepino. In the end, I managed to reconstruct the path you had taken. When I came to the park, the police were still there. A man walking his dog had found the body just a few hours earlier."

More crumbled toast. Talking about the killer and Pepino hurt a lot more than Gabriel would have thought.

"Could it be the same man?" he asked. "The one who killed Mallfrick and Lorelei and the others? I remember accusing him of having killed Mallfrick. He didn't deny it, but didn't say he did it, either. Call it a gut feeling, but I really think this Ronai is your man."

Sighing, Tennant pushed his plate away. "My theory was that the murderer kills only the ones who don't belong in your world. All the murders were committed here too. Then he tried to kill Sweet Rain in her own world. Although clearly his handiwork, my theory was wrong because of the circumstances of her death. She isn't even dead, not really." Frustrated, he spooned some sugar into his tea. "Pepino, now, was partly fae—unlike the other victims, part of his blood was human. Because of this fact, he doesn't fit at all in the killer's method of operation. My conclusion is that Ronai killed Pepino and maybe Sweet Rain, but not the others. But that sounds equally unlikely. I tend to trust your feeling that it was the same man. If that is the case, I haven't got a clue how the killer chooses his victims. His style in killing varies tremendously. It might just be that his reasons for choosing his victims vary too."

Wearily, Gabriel rubbed his eyes. "Pepino was half fae? Great. No wonder I was making out with him. Seems I'm attracted to any damn fae who happens to smile at me."

Tennant raised a questioning eyebrow, but at that moment, a memory stirred in Gabriel's head. He frowned.

"What?" Tennant asked.

Gabriel shook his head. "Something Pepino said about his dad. Something… shit, that damn ocean truly fucked up my brain." Frustrated, he pressed his hands flat onto the table, trying to concentrate, trying to remember Pepino's voice. What was it the boy had said?

"He's beautiful!" Finally, Gabriel remembered that small piece of information. "And then Ronai said that Pepino looked very much like him. They were father and son, after all, and if it's true what you said, that Pepino was half fae, then his dad was fae too. A beautiful fae, and he hides it with the rune he's wearing. The killer is one of your kind, Doc. And if he really killed Sweet Rain, and if killing her was really meant as a trap, then it is quite possible that this Ronai guy killed all the victims, not only two!"

Tennant stared at him, taking several moments before he answered. "That would explain a few things," he finally said. "Fae know more about runes and portals than most races. We can be ruthless in our wrath, and if we have a reason to, we kill without regret. However, the thought of a fae killing his own people is terrifying." His voice trembled, and his hands weren't entirely still.

Gabriel decided to ignore it lest he reach out and embrace the man, trying to comfort him. "There's nothing left for me to do. I cannot help you find the killer. I told you everything I know. Just find a way to stop him. After all, Ronai doesn't seem to be a common name."

Shrugging his shoulders, Tennant got up and made fresh tea. "Ronai isn't a name at all," he said. "It means 'storm'. I have no idea how to find him. And what do you mean, nothing else left to do? Do you intend to leave and let me do all the work on my own?"

The genuine surprise in Tennant's voice was too much for Gabriel. He jumped up, letting the chair clatter to the floor. "I can't stay, Doc! Are you blind, or what? I want you. Badly. Earlier when I was drooling at the sight of your hard cock, you should have realized it. I can't get you out of my mind. I dream of you, I fantasize about you, and I would have drowned in that fucking ocean if it hadn't been for you. I cannot even think properly when you are around, so yes, I have to leave, and this time for good. This love nonsense is not for me. I just want sex, a meaningless one-night stand, and as you said, that's not for you. It's a lose-lose situation. "

Exhausted by his outburst, Gabriel picked up the chair, wondering when he had begun to tell his friend such huge lies. After all, the main problem was that he wanted more than sex. "I'll leave you in peace, Doc. Runes are obviously not something I can handle, you are obviously not available, and I can do without my heart getting crushed to pieces."

Wonderful. At the last moment, he had to go and admit that he was emotionally affected. *Perfect*, he thought. *Well done, Gabe. Why don't you tell him you've fallen for him and make the embarrassment complete?*

Kettle forgotten in his hand, Tennant clearly didn't know how to answer. Silently, he watched as Gabriel drained his cold tea and left the kitchen.

GABRIEL went to his room, closed the door behind him, and sat on the bed. His stomach hurt. Wrapping his arms around his waist, he wished he could lie down and fall asleep right on the spot to escape this horrible feeling of loneliness. He'd never felt so empty. He'd never felt so lost, not even when he was stranded on the rock, nearly dead, bleeding and without any idea how to get back home.

Home. What a joke. There was no place he could call home, and that he had called this place home in the past few weeks had been a stupid act of self-delusion. In a few minutes, he'd be gone, back on the streets and sleeping under bridges, as he had done for most of his life.

He'd miss this room, though. He'd miss this house, its warmth, and the fact that someone here cared about him. No doubt Tennant liked him. A lot, even. No doubt Tennant would miss him. Still, he didn't have a choice. If he stayed, it would break him. Seeing Tennant without being able to touch him, talking to him knowing that there wouldn't be more, would eventually prove to be too much.

Seduce him, Pepino's voice whispered in his mind. *Fill him up with wine and dope, make him high, and he'll offer you his ass. Isn't that what you want?*

He'd done it before, hadn't he? When chasing an unwilling victim, when persuading a straight guy to come into his bed, anything was allowed. Rape was out of the question, of course, but unfair methods were not. Often, his bed partners had woken up in his arms unable to run fast enough to get back to their normal lives, disgusted at themselves for what they had done under the influence of alcohol, drugs, and one kiss too many.

He'd never do anything like that to Tennant. A one-night stand wasn't what he wanted, either, not if he was honest with himself. He wanted a lot more. Leaving now would save Tennant from his unwanted attention, and he wouldn't make a total fool out of himself by admitting that he'd fallen in love.

Time to pack up. Not that there was that much to put into his knapsack. Hang on. Hadn't he left it with Billy at the mission when he'd gone looking for Pepino? It had been packed with the shopping he'd done minus some chocolate cookies he'd shared with Billy—so how was it possible that it was here, next to his bed?

"Because Tennant brought it back when he went looking for you, idiot." Gabriel almost slapped his forehead. The doctor had told him he'd gone to the mission, hadn't he? "I bet Billy was a bit confused when he saw you, Doc." Gabriel grinned sadly. "Pity the runes disguise your real looks. If Billy could see you the way I do, he'd understand why I've fallen for you."

Quickly, Gabriel checked to see if everything that belonged to him was still there and found that although Tennant had taken most of the groceries, he had left the sweets he'd bought inside the bag, which was just as well, since he was hungry again. A bar of chocolate wouldn't really satisfy him, but it was better than nothing. Tennant had warned him that it would take a while for him to recover fully.

A rune on his wrist caught his attention: it was glowing faintly, and it didn't cover the freshly healed wounds underneath, angry, red scars, not really deep, but large in number. Across his hands and arms they ran, up to his shoulders and down his back and chest as if he'd been whipped. Then, there were the wounds he had received when the waves had crushed him against the rocks, and the seagull's marks on his fingers. The scars wouldn't make hiding any easier, and they would certainly cause questions from anyone who saw him without a shirt. Questions he would be unwilling and unable to answer, of course.

Right now, though, the scars were the least of his problems. Dozens of runes could be seen too. A quick look in the mirror confirmed that they decorated his face as well—his forehead, temples, cheeks, eyelids, and lips.

Even for him it would be impossible to go out onto the streets looking like this.

He had planned to leave immediately. So why was he grinning like mad now, realizing he'd need to wait for another couple of hours?

AROUND lunchtime, the sweets from his knapsack were gone, and Gabriel was as hungry as a wild wolf once more.

This was just silly, sitting in his room like a stubborn little boy. Besides, maybe Tennant needed help washing up or cutting onions in the kitchen. Although Tennant had said his shoulder was fine and had healed well, Gabriel didn't entirely believe it, so he opened his door in order to find something to eat as well as to offer his help.

He found Tennant in the living room, sitting motionless on the couch.

The doctor was always busying himself with some sort of task except during rune lessons or when they were having a quiet chat. It was unusual to find him just sitting and staring at the ceiling.

"Are you all right?" Gabriel asked. "I just wanted to eat something. Can't go anywhere looking like this."

With a furrowed brow, Tennant looked at him. "Understandable. Although—I had hoped you'd be gone by now," he said coolly. "Forgot about the runes. They'll last another few days, given how very visible they still are. Inconvenient. Very...." He hesitated. "Very unlucky for you that you are still here, Gabriel. I think I should apologize right away. As long as I am still able to hold up a conversation, that is."

Gabriel clenched his teeth. Admittedly, he hadn't expected such harsh words, but then, he'd spilled the news of his secret longing pretty rashly and without giving a damn about Tennant's feelings in the matter.

"I'll hide in my room until my skin's free of them," he snapped. "Mind if I grab some toast?"

Tennant didn't answer. Instead, he stared at him like a snake might stare at a mouse seconds before devouring it.

Something was different. "What did you mean, hold up a conversation?" Gabriel asked. "You okay?"

Tennant shook his head. "Definitely not."

Gabriel took a step in the doctor's direction. "Your eyes—they're black. No. Your pupils are dilated. What did you do? Get drunk? Smoke a joint?"

Tennant snorted out a bitter little laugh that was so very unlike him that Gabriel felt a cold rush of dread run down his spine. Something was wrong here, very wrong.

"What's up?" he urged. "Are you in pain? Is it your shoulder? Listen, Doc, tell me what to do, and I'll do it!"

Tennant laughed, the sound laced with madness and sarcasm. "Sure you will," he bit out. "That's why I didn't want you here. Knew something was wrong. Didn't believe it at first. But now, with you being so close, it's too late anyway. There's no use denying it any longer." Before Gabriel could react, Tennant locked both his hands behind the younger man's neck, pulling him down, close enough for Gabriel to feel the doctor's breath on his lips.

He gulped. This was far too close for his own good, and he had no idea what had got into Tennant. "Are you drunk? What's going on?"

"You were right," Tennant rasped, digging his fingers deep into the red strands of Gabriel's hair. He slipped off the sofa so that they knelt in front of each other. "Someone is trying to kill me. Right now. Right here. Perhaps I will jump out of the window at any moment, or maybe I will cut my throat with the kitchen knife." Closing his eyes, he got a little bit closer and breathed in, his nose buried in Gabriel's hair. "I always considered the fragrance of your skin to be quite tantalizing," he whispered. "Now, it is irresistible. Please believe me, I didn't want this to happen, but as it is, I do not really have a choice."

Bewildered, Gabriel freed his hair and his head and pushed himself out of Tennant's reach. "What's wrong with you? Who's trying to kill you, and how, and why are you acting like this?"

Tennant was on all fours now, resembling a beaten dog more than anything else. His breath came in heavy gasps, and the muscles of his forearms stood out like cables.

"The wood," he rasped. "Where I was shot. Blood on the ground. My blood. Someone is using my blood to manipulate me. I ignored it at first. Tried to fight it. It began right after you went to your room. I thought it was because of what you said, that you want me. Fantasize about me. Turns out I was wrong."

The lines on Tennant's skin, usually disguised by the necklace, flared up, and he gasped. In one fluid movement, he ripped off the chain with the pendant. It was glowing an angry red, and where it landed on the wooden floor, it burned a hole into the planks.

"Damn it!" he breathed. "I can't fight it. Please, Gabriel. Help me. Just this one last time. I am perfectly aware of how unfair this is and that I shouldn't do this to you, but frankly, I don't want to cut my own throat."

Gabriel thought, *Right, this can only be a nightmare*, and got up. He stood in the far corner of the living room, where he could see books sitting on the table and hear the faucet dripping in the kitchen.

"This is a nightmare," he said aloud, but that was the moment when Tennant hissed with pain and pressed both hands to his groin.

Without hesitation, Gabriel went to him, wrapping an arm around the doctor's waist and dragging him back to the couch. With flying fingers, he opened the man's shirt, fearing the shoulder wound would be inflamed again, expecting fever at best and sepsis at worst.

Tennant's skin was hot, but not because of fever. The patterns on his skin glowed golden, the pulse in his throat beat wildly, and when Gabriel's fingers searched for the wound that had already healed nicely, he moaned and arched his back into the touch.

"More," he whispered, almost begged. "Touch me. Kiss me. Fuck me. Please."

"*What?*"

Tennant's eyes were nearly black, so widened were his pupils. "Fuck me. Can I put it any clearer? Someone's using Blood magic against me, someone wants me dead, and the magic rules my body and my mind. My hormonal balance is upside down, I am currently being pushed into heat, and therefore I need you to fuck me, or I shall have to do something very stupid in order to rid myself of the need. Like put my head into boiling water. Like bite open my veins." His hands found a way under Gabriel's shirt, pulling it out of his jeans.

Tennant's hot hands sent goose bumps up the younger man's spine and made him hard. Made his breath quicken with anticipation. Still, he caught Tennant's hands and pinned them on either side of his head, which had fallen back against the soft leather of the couch.

Tennant nearly purred with delight.

Swearing, Gabriel snatched his hands away and got off the couch. To be safe, he put the table between them. "I don't know what this is, but I can't just fuck you, Doc. I mean, I won't do it. You're drugged, or the equivalent of being drugged. Cursed, maybe. Someone is doing this to you, and we should find out who and why, and we definitely shouldn't go to bed together. Mustn't, I meant to say, we mustn't go to bed together."

Tennant grinned and got up. Faster than Gabriel thought possible, he came around the table and cornered him between the wall and the bookshelf.

"You smell like freshly baked bread," he stated matter-of-factly. "Like water in the desert, like silk on naked skin."

Crossing the small distance remaining between them, he pressed his body against Gabriel's. The doctor's hands moved down over

Gabriel's bottom; his mouth searched for the sensitive spot between Gabriel's neck and shoulder. For a man inexperienced in physical love, he did a tremendous job in arousing a stunned, if not dumbstruck, partner.

Not that Gabriel planned to be a partner in this game.

"This is madness," he shouted, pushing Tennant away. "You're not yourself. Even touching you under such circumstances would be wrong, and anything more would be rape. There must be another solution, there must—"

"No," Tennant said, unimpressed by Gabriel's objections. "Too late. Had you left before I'd reached this state of arousal, at least you'd be out of the picture. As it is, you have two choices: you let me suffer from an illegal rune someone drew with my blood to drive me to madness or death and watch me scream while I try to rip my brain out of my skull, or you do what you have wanted to do with me now for some time."

"I can't!"

"You want me. Badly. Your own words." Carelessly, Tennant ripped open his shirt, buttons happily hopping across the floor. "Take me. I do not object. On the contrary, I'm begging you to fuck me. I'd call that consensual, and is that not all that counts?"

Gabriel paled, but he stopped himself from caressing the glowing patterns with his eyes. Still, he couldn't help but look lower, searching for signs of Tennant's arousal. However, he hadn't expected those signs to be so very visible. Tennant was hard, and it showed clearly through the fabric of his trousers.

"I cannot do this," Gabriel croaked in desperation, but his own cock was already hard, and his fingers twitched in anticipation of pulling Tennant's trousers down over those narrow hips. "You don't want me to just fuck you. You want to love the one who touches you. You don't love me, and that's why you'd never willingly let me anywhere near you, which is why I need to leave!"

"You talk too much," Tennant growled. He crossed the distance between them in two large steps, took Gabriel's head between his hands, and kissed him.

It was the most inexperienced kiss Gabriel had ever received and, at the same time, the most beautiful one. Tennant's teeth scraped his lips; he tasted his own blood, and then a tongue pushed into his mouth, too fast and too demanding and yet totally irresistible. Greedily, he parted his lips, welcomed the intruder, and pulled Tennant closer, as close as possible. He liked full-body contact when kissing, so Gabriel locked one hand behind the doctor's neck and the other grabbed hold of his bottom.

Perfect.

Nevertheless, he broke the kiss before he really started to enjoy it. "Stop it," he rasped. "Just a sec."

"Why?" Tennant kissed his cheek and the side of his neck, eyes closed. Gabriel's legs became weak.

Fast and brutal, he pushed the doctor backward against the wall and grabbed hold of his wrists again. This time, he didn't let go, although Tennant's eyes instantly glazed with desire.

"I said stop it," Gabriel snapped, wiping the hair out of his face with a quick jerk of his arm. "Is it true what you said—that you are like this because of a rune someone's using to harm you?"

"Yes."

"And if I refused to go to bed with you, it would be bad for you?"

"Extremely bad. Insanity at best. I would probably kill myself trying to escape the need. I need someone else to take care of me. I need you to go to bed with me." Lasciviously, Tennant rubbed his groin along Gabriel's thigh.

There was no use denying it: his resistance wasn't dwindling anymore, it was already gone. "You really want this?" Gabriel asked hoarsely.

"More than anything right now."

"Then we'll do it my way, is that clear?"

Breathing fast, Tennant seemed to have trouble standing on his legs. "Whatever you do, however you want to do it, is fine with me— just do it!" His fists crumpled Gabriel's shirt, and in his eyes shone a mixture of madness, pain, and need.

Gabriel clenched his teeth. This was going to be a lot harder than he'd ever expected. He didn't know if he could see this through. Despite his longing to take his friend in every and any possible way, the whole situation was somewhat surreal, and he hated himself for looking forward to what was about to happen.

"I could take you fast and dirty. Maybe I should do that so the Blood rune magic is broken as quickly as possible," he forced himself to say. "I could take you right now up against the wall, fuck you without caring about you and quite possibly hurt you in the process, given that you've never had a cock up your ass before." Goodness, how dreadful it sounded when said out loud. "My own pleasure would be my first and only concern, and maybe I wouldn't even manage to make you come."

Tennant just shivered under his touch.

Gabriel couldn't help brushing his lips over the tender skin of the doctor's neck. "Somehow, I believe you'd hate me even more if I did it the dirty way, Doc," Gabriel whispered. "That's not how you want this to happen." Gradually, he tightened his grip around Tennant's wrists. A thin film of sweat covered the doctor's bare chest, and his shirt stuck to his arms and shoulders in a most intriguing way. To make it clear who was in charge right now, Gabriel moved in even closer and pushed a leg between Tennant's.

Gray eyes stared into blue ones. Slowly, Gabriel let go of one of Tennant's wrists. His palm whispered over silvery skin, found the waistband of Tennant's trousers, moved lower, and touched flesh, hot and pulsating even through the fabric. With his thumb, he rubbed along the doctor's shaft, caressed it, followed its shape from the tip down to the balls.

"I'll do this slowly," Gabriel whispered into his friend's ear. "Slowly and carefully, and you'll love every second of it."

Tennant groaned hoarsely. His hips moved; desperately, he tried to move closer to the teasing hand between his legs.

"I'll undress you; I'll massage you. I'll kiss you absolutely everywhere, and in the end, I'll take you, equally slowly, and you'll scream for me because it will be the best thing you've ever felt. It will take a while, but if I understand correctly, this is all about touch and lovemaking, not about speed. Am I right? We can do this as slowly as I want?"

"Yes." The answer was barely audible. "But… why? You are torn between your wish to sleep with me and your disgust at the circumstances." Tennant's voice was hoarse as he said the words. "I assume the 'fast and dirty' way would suit you more, and it doesn't matter if I like what you do as long as the sexual act is successfully completed." Contradicting himself, his fingertips danced across Gabriel's ribcage, across one hard nipple, and he sighed, harshly and longingly.

Not being able to resist the man and his needs any longer, Gabriel bit Tennant's throat lightly, sucking, licking off the sweat and the taste of arousal. With his right hand, he opened trouser buttons. With his left, he continued to hold Tennant's arm pinned against the wall.

"What I do today will set the tone for your future love life as well as for any relationship you might like to commit yourself to eventually," he said. Damn, he was hard enough to come right now without even being touched. He needed to calm down a bit, so he stopped his busy fingers and stopped kissing Tennant too. Taking a step back, he pulled his hair out of his face and bound it back at the base of his neck. Next, he went to the bathroom, rummaged in the cabinet until he found some massage oil, then returned to the living room, where his friend still stood pressed against the wall, heart beating wildly, eyes wide with desire, erection partly showing through his half-unbuttoned fly.

Gabriel licked his lips, not caring anymore that this was as wrong as it could possibly be. He not only wanted Tennant, he needed him. His own cock was screaming to be freed from the confines of his jeans.

Tennant was clearly too far gone to care about anything he said or did as long as it served to satisfy his need, so Gabriel pushed him toward the bedroom, where they fell onto the mattress, limbs entangled, the bottle of oil squeezed between them.

"Lie still," Gabriel ordered, standing up, his every movement followed by Tennant's gaze.

One by one, he slowly undid the buttons of his shirt, and it was simply exquisite to see Tennant's heartbeat quicken, to see him gulp with longing, to observe his impatient movements as he lay upon the mattress. The man was half crazy with desire. Pity it was because of a rune and not because of Gabriel's seduction skills.

Dropping the shirt to the floor, Gabriel bent to light half a dozen candles before he closed the curtains, thus bathing the room in a soft, golden light. Then, before he could give it any more thought, he unfastened his belt, undid his fly, and stepped out of his jeans. Only his briefs covered his erection now, and he intended to keep those on, at least for the moment. The feeling of the fabric keeping his member in check was arousing in itself, and right now, undressing Tennant was much more important. "Turn onto your stomach," he said, and his friend obeyed without hesitation.

Smooth back, ivy drawn along Tennant's spine and over his sides. Shadows underneath his shoulder blades moved with every breath he took. The hem of his trousers was a dark line against light skin—it was time to find out how the doctor's bottom looked naked. Gabriel sat on Tennant's legs, barely able to suppress a moan when his cock made contact with the trousers. Moving down a bit until he was settled near the hollow of Tennant's knees, he slipped both hands around the doctor's waist and finished what he'd begun earlier on: he opened the fly and with one swift movement pulled the trousers over Tennant's narrow hips. As the man wasn't wearing underpants, Gabriel could feel the hardness beneath his fingertips as he did so.

Tennant's pale bottom was decorated with a very few thin tendrils, barely visible in the dim light. It was muscular and well-shaped. What else could Gabriel do but press his lips to the skin and leave teeth marks in the tender flesh? What else could he do but squeeze oil into his palm and begin to massage this wonderful ass? After all, he had fantasized about this exact situation many times in the quiet hours of the night. He didn't even need to think about his next move.

Slowly, Gabriel massaged Tennant's back, his shoulders, his neck.

"Gabriel, please!" Tennant begged, his hips moving slowly in attempt to find at least a small amount of relief.

"Patience, Doc," Gabriel answered, but he allowed his hands to move lower to the small of Tennant's back, fingertips tracing along the slender stalk of a rose. "You look beautiful. I've dreamed about you lying naked beneath me. I dreamed about touching you. I hoped there would be a time when you would moan just like you are doing now because of my touch."

A kiss to one shoulder blade. Swiftly, Gabriel rasped his tongue over the pale skin, tasting sweat and oil and arousal at the same time. "Spread your legs, Doc. Just a bit, just enough for me to slip one hand in between. Just like that, yes."

His own erection hurt, longing for attention, so he pressed his groin against Tennant's thigh. His fingers, slippery from oil, wandered upward from the doctor's knees over the inside of his thigh and finally touched his balls, small and hard. Tennant wanted to spread his legs wider, wanted to turn onto his back, but Gabriel pressed him down, preventing both from happening.

"Easy. Slowly," he whispered, massaging the balls with his fingertips and deliberately ignoring the waiting cock. His body was pressed against Tennant's from ankles to upper arms now. His hair, already partly escaped from its ribbon, clung to the doctor's oily skin.

Pulling his hand back, Gabriel brushed over the small, puckered hole as if by accident. Tennant's breath hitched, and he rasped, "Gabe! Please, will you fuck me sometime today!"

It took some effort to hold Tennant down, so hard did the doctor try to turn onto his back. Soothingly, Gabriel kissed his friend's shoulders and neck, tenderly stroked along his sides, and when Tennant had calmed down a bit, Gabriel returned to the target of his desire, spreading the man's cheeks. Gently, he added pressure while placing kisses to the hot, oily skin. Carefully, he circled the hole until the man underneath him begged for more, begged to be fucked.

It was too tempting, too close to what he wanted to do, and finally it was impossible to resist any longer. Smoothly , Gabriel slipped one slender finger inside Tennant's ass.

Muscles clenched; Tennant moved his hips upward, bucking repeatedly against Gabriel's hand. Apparently, one finger wasn't enough, so Gabriel slipped in a second one, holding his friend as still as possible, pushing a bit deeper, just a little bit at a time. Then, swiftly, he swiped his fingers around, playing, searching, and finally finding his friend's—lover's—pleasure spot.

Tennant spread his legs even wider, yelled his lust out loud. Gabriel's own hips moved too, dry-humping Tennant's leg, and hell, this had never felt better. Gabriel had never experienced anything more arousing, and he knew he was in danger of coming too soon if he continued like this.

Impossible. He wanted to fuck Tennant properly, not just with his hand.

"Turn over. Let me see you," Gabriel commanded hoarsely, reluctantly removing his fingers. It hadn't lasted long enough, but then, there was nothing preventing him from repeating this later, after they were both satisfied.

Immediately, Tennant flipped his body around, reached out, and pulled Gabriel down for a kiss. This time, he was less hasty, his lips were softer, his mouth a hot, wet, welcoming cave, waiting for Gabriel's tongue to enter. This time, it was a long kiss, heated with desire and impatience. Tennant's hand on Gabriel's neck held him close while the other went exploring, tracing down his spine to his bottom, lower to his legs, over his hip bones, and finally slipping under the waistband of his briefs.

"Take them off," Tennant said when they both needed some air. "I want you to be as naked as I am."

Gabriel smiled at that—the thought was truly tantalizing. "As you wish." As quickly as possible, he wriggled out of them. The fabric was damp with pre-cum anyway, and besides, it was about time his friend saw what he was dealing with.

He'd promised this would happen slowly, so instead of taking Tennant right then and without warning, Gabriel lay back on the bed, spread his arms and legs, and showed his body as well as his erection, tightly pressed against his lower belly. His hair was a bright contrast to the white pillow, the Protection runes still covered his skin, and his nostrils flared when the fragrance of their arousal wafted toward him.

"Look at me," he said. "Look at me closely, and tell me if you really want this. Because if you kiss me again, there's no turning back. I'll just take you, Doc." The thought of another kiss made him lick his lips. His cock grew even more, twitching, wanting to be touched, wanting to fuck.

Tennant's gaze wandered over his body, more tender than a physical touch. Gabriel had to dig his hands into the sheets, or he wouldn't have been able to keep still.

The doctor propped himself up on an elbow. He was close, his groin pressed against Gabriel's thigh—physical contact seemed to be integral to Tennant's sanity. Gently, carefully, as if he feared hurting the younger man, Tennant touched Gabriel's cheek, then ran his fingertips down to his chest. Briefly, he lingered at the nipples, circling them until they were hard as cherry stones, then traveled even lower, toward his belly button, and finally to the soft, dark red pubic hair. Tennant smiled, disbelieving, wondrous. Curiously, he brushed his hand along Gabriel's cock, weighed his balls, then slipped lower and placed a kiss on the wet, velvet head.

Gabriel's turn to moan. When Tennant parted his lips and took his cock fully into his mouth, Gabriel hissed, "Yes!" through gritted teeth. One hand left the sheets and buried itself in black hair instead, holding the doctor's head in place without interfering with his task.

Several minutes passed during which nothing could be heard but moans and soft, sucking noises. Eventually, Gabriel rasped, "Slower, Doc. Slow down, if you don't want me to come in your mouth."

Tennant looked up at him. "I wouldn't mind," he replied, rubbing his oily body against Gabriel's. "Would you like to taste yourself?"

Gabriel blushed, something that never happened when he was in bed. Yet the contradiction between Tennant's innocence and the directness of his question was intriguing. Besides, no one had ever offered this particular act to him. Actually, it had been ages since anyone had given him a blow job, and as far as he could remember, it hadn't been half as good as the partial job done by Tennant.

Aleksei, his mind reminded him, and he pulled his friend close and kissed him again.

Tennant straddled Gabriel, pinned him down to the mattress, and *moved* on top of him, making his cock slick with the massage oil. "I want you," he breathed, "to fuck me." A kiss. A breath. "Please. Take me. Now." Another kiss. "Cannot wait any longer. Don't want to wait any longer. Please. Gabriel, please!"

Yet another kiss, deep and nearly brutal, and it was just too much for Gabriel. One flick, and Tennant was on his back once more; one push, and his legs were spread wide. With his right hand, Gabriel supported his weight, half leaning on his friend's chest; with his left, he grabbed his cock, and there was Tennant's entrance, slick with oil and slack with anticipation and desire. All Gabriel had to do was to push, ease his hard cock in, and that was just what he did. Slowly at first, just an inch, in and out, but when Tennant moved upward to meet him, breathing his short, excited gasps into his ear, Gabriel lost control just like that.

With one long, smooth movement, he slammed inside the tight, hot hole, pulled out, and slammed in again, even deeper this time, not caring anymore about his partner, not caring about anything but his own pleasure, just as predicted. Tennant was warm and willing; he threw one leg up over Gabriel's hip, which adjusted the angle, just a bit, just enough to fuck him even deeper.

Slower. Just a bit slower would be good, but it was impossible. It was just too good to slow down, it was too good to so much as try to regain control, and that was truly something that had never happened to Gabriel before—he always, under any circumstances, kept a cool head in bed.

Not now, though. He didn't groan, he didn't moan. Instead, he yelled out his lust with every push into Tennant's ass, pressing his forehead against Tennant's forehead, his free hand now grabbing hold of the man underneath him as if he feared he would lose him otherwise. This man, Aleksei, was his entirely now, and no, he couldn't slow down, not when Tennant arched his back into his thrusts, not when he raked his nails across Gabriel's back, not when he claimed his mouth for the deepest possible kiss. It was too good not to do it as hard and fast as he could, too good not to come in long, shuddering spasms, moaning into Tennant's mouth while his seed shot out of his cock and deep inside Tennant's wonderful body.

Gasping for air, Gabriel collapsed atop his friend. His cock went limp and slipped out, which was good, as it allowed him to adjust his position a bit and become more comfortable, resting his head on Tennant's belly.

Admiringly, he stroked one of the delicate tendrils painted on Tennant's sweaty skin. It almost seemed to grow under his touch. Then he heard Tennant's ragged breathing, observed his clenched fists, and realized that Tennant was still hard.

Shit. He'd been too fast, had come without thinking of his partner. Normally, that wouldn't have bothered him too much—after all, he preferred the chase, not the kill, so to speak. With Tennant, though, it was different. Not only did his friend need release, but Gabriel had promised he'd enjoy this too.

Quickly, before his friend could complain about the abrupt ending, Gabriel locked his fist around the hard shaft and squeezed, just enough to get Tennant's attention.

Then he began to pleasure his friend slowly and expertly, bringing him close to his climax in a matter of moments only to halt his movements a second before Tennant came.

"Gab... riel," the doctor croaked, both his hands clawing at the bedposts. "Make me come. I... beg you!"

"Soon," Gabriel assured him, and he closed his lips around the doctor's length.

Tennant's hips bucked, and he gave a low, raw gasp.

Gabriel sucked his friend's cock into his mouth. His hand circled the base of Tennant's length and rhythmically squeezed his balls. Adding a bit of teeth to the tenderness of his mouth, he caressed the head with his tongue, circled around the velvety tip, and stroked with his tongue across the thin slit at the top.

Gabriel flicked his tongue, somewhere in the back of his head realizing that this was something he'd never done before: give a blow job instead of receiving one.

"Goodness," Tennant murmured. "Good… grief!"

Gabriel smiled at this confirmation that the doctor indeed liked what he was doing, surprised at how easy it was and how good it felt. Until today, he had been the dominant partner in all his encounters, both with men and women. Until today, a blow job, in his eyes, had been something the inferior partner did.

Tennant's hands searched for and found his head and buried themselves in his hair, holding him lightly but determinedly down at the level of his groin. Gabriel found this strangely arousing, being pinned into a position so delicate and intimate, and he was intrigued by the feeling of power he had over his partner by simply satisfying him with mouth, lips, and tongue.

Gabriel's fingers, still slick from the massage oil, roamed deftly and nearly unnoticed while his tongue and lips teased Tennant's cock. They slipped between Tennant's legs, lightly stroking the area underneath his testicles, then continued onward to touch the inside of his buttocks.

The doctor was obviously enjoying himself, as his groans became deeper and he parted his legs, spreading them even wider to grant Gabriel better access. A moment later, Tennant bent one knee and moved his hips slightly so that Gabriel's hand could caress his buttocks. The hands in Gabriel's hair tightened—Tennant was close to his climax now, very close, and he clearly wanted to make sure Gabriel wouldn't stop this time. Tennant's hips rocked gently, allowing his cock to slide in and out of the dark cave of Gabriel's mouth. The muscles in his ass moved under Gabriel's hand, and when Tennant moaned again, using his bent leg to push upward into his mouth, Gabriel tightened his grip on his friend's bottom.

"Make me come, Gabe!" Tennant whispered.

As you wish, Gabriel thought. He flicked his tongue, cupped Tennant's balls, and sucked the doctor's cock as deeply into his mouth as it would go.

Gabe heard Tennant roar with lust. The sound was music to his ears, and only a second, half a heartbeat later, the doctor came, spilling his salty, sticky juice into Gabriel's mouth.

Satisfied, they collapsed, holding each other close without talking, without even thinking. Sated, they enjoyed the silence, the flicker of the candles, and each other's calming heartbeats.

When they had cooled off, Gabriel fished for a blanket and roughly pulled it over the both of them.

"You okay?" he asked, surprised that he sounded hoarse, but then, cock-sucking was throat-straining, to say the least. It was wonderful too.

"For the moment," Tennant replied, sounding sated and satisfied. "I knew something was amiss after we had breakfast. That must have been the time when whoever did this to me finished the Blood rune. From that moment on, I was helplessly under its control, and I still am."

"That rune seems to be damn dangerous," Gabriel pointed out. "Does it always have such a destructive effect?"

Tennant sighed deeply. "I am—well, I was—a virgin, Gabriel. The Blood rune is usually used to make one comply with another's wishes. It wouldn't have been able to drive me into insanity had I experienced physical love before tonight. You touching me, you being in bed with me, eases the pain and the need, but it takes approximately twelve hours before it fully wears off. Which means—"

"More sex before you will let me out of your grip again."

"Precisely."

Gabriel slipped one arm over Tennant's waist. A moment ago, he had wanted to say something else, but now all he managed was, "That's fine with me. I've got no intention of getting up anytime soon." Briefly, he lifted his head and looked into his friend's face. "Yeah, I can see it. Your eyes are still more black than blue. If I didn't know better, I'd say you were drugged up to your hairline."

Tennant sighed contently. At the moment, he was clearly in no danger of going mad because of the Blood rune. "I am, in a way. This is an illegal rune, designed to cause harm. It messes with my body as well as with my mind—if you hadn't been here, the best-case scenario would have been ending up in a psychiatric hospital, reduced to a dribbling idiot. Because my blood was needed to accomplish the rune, I tend to think I was led to follow the wrong track back in Wild Oak's world. We were meant to be caught by the centaurs, either so they would kill us or with the hope I'd get injured so whoever placed the wrong track could scoop up my blood. I am most grateful you didn't leave before I realized what was wrong, despite my earlier words. Remind me not to get shot again, will you?"

Gabriel smiled, enjoying the warmth of his friend's body more than anything else. "No problem. But right now, I say we doze a bit and then take a shower. Together. Agreed?"

"Oh, yes. Definitely agreed."

WARM water coursed over his head. It was strange—not too long ago, Gabriel had believed he'd had enough water for a while.

Hands moved on his skin, soapy hands, curious hands, all over his body. Tennant stood close to him, kissing him. His kisses were hot, deep, and irresistible; Gabriel loved those kisses, all of them, no matter if they were on his mouth, his throat, trailed down to his belly, or were targeted at his cock.

Actually, seeing Tennant on his knees with his lips around his length was nearly too much to bear. "Slowly, Doc," he whispered, eyes closed, face raised to the spray.

Tennant's hands moved upward. His palms found Gabriel's buttocks, squeezing, kneading. Gabriel searched for the metal bar behind him, the one the showerhead was attached to, and held fast. The water's heat relaxed his muscles; the soap, smelling of herbs and honey, cleaned his skin and even seemed to wash off the runes. A bit of shampoo left in his hair reminded him that only a moment ago, he'd been the one on his knees with Tennant massaging his scalp.

Truly, Gabriel loved to shower in pairs.

His cock hardened fast under Tennant's attention, and he tried to remember when he'd last bottomed. It had been years ago; he had no clear memory of it. Quite possibly, he'd been too drunk to object, as before today, he'd never much liked it. He had always topped, and he always got out of bed as quickly as possible.

Not today, though. Tennant was hard, too, he was in a most investigative mood, and his hands on his ass felt good.

More than just good, Gabriel decided. It felt like more. "Come up here, Doc," he said through the water's rush. "Kiss me, and then tell me what you want to do to me."

Tennant's tongue rasped over his skin. His lips closed around the younger man's nipples, and he sucked, nipped, and licked over them until Gabriel whimpered with desire. Simultaneously, the doctor stroked Gabriel's cock, maddeningly slow, until Gabriel thought he couldn't stand it any longer.

"I wonder," Tennant said, slipping one hand between his buttocks, "I wonder how it would feel."

"How what would feel?" Impossible not to press his bottom against Tennant's hand. Impossible not to try to get closer to those exploring fingers.

"I wonder how it would feel to come inside you." Tentatively, the doctor brushed over Gabriel's entrance.

Gabriel moaned. "You already came in my mouth. Wasn't that enough?" he mocked, the thought of Tennant moving inside him making him even harder.

Tennant locked one hand with Gabriel's, pulled it off the metal bar, and turned him around. "Not quite enough." A kiss to his shoulders. "I want more. I want all of you." A cock between his legs, large, hard, and hot. "Allow me to take you, Gabe. Unless... my attention is unwelcome?"

Thinking became difficult with that wonderful cock so close to his entrance, sliding along the sensitive hole, making Gabriel's legs weak, his knees wobbly, and his head hazy with desire. "Take me. Let me feel you." He reached for Tennant's bottom, found it, and pulled him closer so he could feel his heated skin.

Tennant's hand was still entwined with his high up on the bar. With the other, the doctor grabbed his own cock, guiding it, finding Gabriel's hole, adding more pressure, and finally, with a smooth push, slipping inside him.

The delicate intrusion was accompanied by an exquisite sense of being stretched, filled, to his boundaries. Tennant's cock felt like a flagpole, larger and wider than it had looked a minute ago.

Tennant slowly began to move his hips; Gabriel cautiously met his thrusts.

They breathed in unison, their heartbeats in sync. Gabriel felt kisses on his neck through the wet strands of his hair. Fingertips touched his length, making him shudder. It felt like he was being drilled in half.

Water on his face. Water on his skin. The smell of his own arousal was prominent despite the spray of water. Tennant's groans were loud in his ear, and his own—had he ever groaned like that before? Had he ever enjoyed sex like he was now? Once, there had been a reason why he hadn't liked to bottom—once, when he'd been a lot younger and hadn't trusted the men who had taken him, hadn't even known their names, hadn't liked them, hadn't loved them.

Gabriel's balls tightened in anticipation of his orgasm. Dreamlike, he locked his hand over Tennant's, guiding his strokes, clenching both their fists around his cock until the tension was quite close to pain.

"Harder," he rasped, throwing his head back, knowing that Tennant's shoulder would be there to catch it.

Tennant's grip around his cock tightened, and his thrusts became deeper, longer. For a split second, Gabriel believed it was too much to bear, too much to endure, only to realize that it was exactly what he wanted, needed, had dreamed of, had longed for. With a hoarse cry, he came, his seed spilling over both their hands, then washing away down the drain. Tennant came shortly after him, his arm slipping upward to Gabriel's waist and nearly breaking his ribs in his climax.

AFTER they'd made it out of the shower, they had collapsed on the bed, naked and damp, with empty minds and smiling lips. Without saying a word, Gabriel had pulled Tennant into a tight embrace; back to front, they had fallen asleep, content and sated and so far not regretting what had happened.

Gabriel dreamed of his friend, his lover of one night, and when he woke, he continued where his dream had led him, not caring if Tennant was awake or not, nor bothering about the fact that the Blood rune had lost its power by then.

His friend wasn't really awake, but he responded sleepily to Gabriel's attention, murmuring unintelligible words. It was clear that he enjoyed what Gabriel was doing, so there was no reason to stop.

It would be the last time, anyway. As soon as this was over, as soon as he'd enjoyed this one final fuck, he would leave and never return. There was no other way, he was certain of it. The fact that they had shared one night didn't mean that Tennant would suddenly and miraculously fall in love with him, and the thought of rejection was far too much to bear.

Pushing the necessity of leaving to the back of his mind, Gabriel caressed the sleep-warm skin of his lover and added some kisses to the faintly silvery skin before he carefully entered him. He'd never been this tender; he'd never considered sex to be more than mere physical release. Until tonight.

Holding his lover tightly, Gabriel moved slowly, wanting to make Tennant feel that this last time was more than a fuck, that he gave all he had to give, that this unbelievable tenderness was all he'd ever wanted, ever dreamed of. He didn't lose control this time. On the contrary, for the first time ever, he was wholly concentrated on his partner's pleasure.

Moving inside his friend, holding him, feeling his erection thrusting into his fist with every push of his hips, was torment as well as relief—torment because of the knowledge that there was no next time for them, relief because now he knew that he was actually able to love, able to give as well as receive. He was not the cold bastard his flings would have described him as; all that had been missing was the right person to touch his heart.

The tension built slowly as the moon shone on the bed, leaving shards of light on floor and blanket and naked skin. The side of the doctor's face, rough as sandpaper from the stubble that had grown, scratched along Gabriel's shoulder.

Perfect. Sweet. Wonderful.

Unbearable. He would miss this man, would miss him badly, so he had better make this last time remarkable so he could remember it during lonely nights under lonely bridges.

Shit. He was already feeling sorry for himself, which was not only unlike him, but bad timing as well.

A kiss. A thrust.

Two moans.

And again.

"Gabriel," Tennant breathed, his voice slurred with sleep or maybe with passion.

"Aleksei!" Gabriel replied with a smile, and this time, they came in unison.

CHAPTER THIRTEEN

AS IF nothing had changed, the moon still shone into the room. As if nothing had changed, Tennant was asleep again. Soft snores filled the otherwise quiet darkness.

Really, he would have liked to stay in bed, fall asleep, and wake up in the morning next to the man he loved.

A tiny voice told him to do just that. Instead, Gabriel went to the bathroom and took another shower, ridding himself of Tennant's fragrance on his skin, on his hands, on his cock, and in his mouth. Viciously, he scrubbed himself down, knowing that if he tried to leave with Tennant's scent in his nostrils, he wouldn't make it out of the door.

A tiny voice inside his head suggested he go back to Tennant's bed and embrace the sleeping man. He ignored it and got dressed in the old rags that waited, neatly folded, in the drawer next to his bed. He'd never thrown them away, although any sensible person would have— they contained more holes than fabric, and although clean, they were so old and ugly that anyone looking at them would be disgusted.

Well, he couldn't wear the clothes Tennant had given him. Too much temptation: by now, too many memories were woven into the fabric.

The tiny, insistent voice told him he would regret his decision once he was out of the door and asked why he was going, why he considered it necessary to leave.

"Because in the morning, he will hate me for what I have done," he told the sofa. "He will wake up, he will remember, and he will hate not only the one who drew the Blood rune but me as well. And if I tried to kiss him, to touch him, if I so much as looked at him with longing in my eyes, he'd throw me out anyway. Because he just doesn't love me."

The sofa didn't answer him. Gabriel made sure there wasn't a Tracking rune anywhere on his belongings, then shouldered his knapsack. In a pile on the counter, he left all of his money, apart from his initial thirty-four cents, and the keys to the house. Then he slipped out into the night.

GABRIEL walked several miles before the moon went down and early morning light spread over the sky. With cold feet and sneakers that were falling apart with each step, it took him longer than it usually would have, but then, he wasn't in a hurry. He watched the city wake up, heard motors starting and saw the first few cars driving down the streets. One by one, the lamps switched off. Soon, the sun would be rising.

Tired and unhappy, Gabriel looked up for the first time in more than an hour and frowned. He shouldn't be here—he didn't want to be here! The mission would have been a good place to go, the next bridge, even, but not this place. Not the little park where Pepino had died.

Clenching his fists, Gabriel stopped and took a look around. The trees had grown some tiny leaves, a few daisies were blooming, and around the bench, a police marker flapped in the wind.

Tennant had told him that a man and his dog had found Pepino's body and that he was buried by now. The cops had been here, had taken any evidence they had found, and had left again, not knowing that both killer and victim had secrets concerning their race.

Even if they bothered to seriously look into the death of an unimportant little pro, it was highly unlikely they would find the man who had killed him.

"So Pepino was half fae, then," Gabriel mused, sitting down on the bench. There was nowhere else to go, nothing else to do. He might as well stay for a while and watch the sunrise. "Would be nice to know what the killer really looks like under his disguise. Or why he was so pissed off at his son. Maybe it was just because Pepino was a pro, or maybe there's more to it. What if I find out? Run back to Tennant, waggle my tail, and beg to be let inside again?"

Disgusted with himself, he spat on the ground. It was useless to deny it—this whole falling-in-love thing was damn painful. Best to get over it quickly.

How perfectly wonderful the night with Tennant had been. How perfectly heartbreaking it was knowing that there was no way back.

Gabriel scowled. His brain insisted on turning to thoughts of Tennant, the night they had shared, the details of naked skin under his fingers, and the sound of moans in his ears. It was over, once and for all! Tennant hadn't found his way into his arms voluntarily, but because some insane bastard had forced him, and when he woke up—which would be soon—he'd be glad Gabriel was gone. That way, neither of them would have to look into the other's eyes. No embarrassment, no accusations, no useless attempts to fix a friendship that had been fragile at best before and most certainly would be broken for good after last night. He couldn't help his feelings for the doctor. It would be impossible for Gabriel not to show how much he wanted him, and even an established friendship couldn't survive one-sided love.

Still, for someone who had been forced, Tennant had obviously enjoyed their encounter. And he had been aroused before the Blood rune had been at work. Maybe, if he went back, they could find a way around this mess and start anew....

"Dream on, boy. There's no way back, and you know it. Get used to the thought of sleeping under bridges again."

The bench was wet from dew. Coldness seeped into his body; despite the clear signs of spring, it was far from being warm outside. Shoving his hands into the pockets of his jeans didn't help much. He would need to seek shelter soon, either under one of the town's many bridges or in the mission.

Absently, he pulled out the pocketknife his fingertips had found and opened it with a practiced flick. He'd done this so often, lately, using the knife to train his juggling skills. It was old, rusty, and barely held an edge, which made it perfect for its task. Otherwise, he would have cut his fingers off more than once by now.

The knife performed a perfect arc when he threw it into the air and landed safely back in his hands, no doubt because Tennant wasn't there to distract him. "Mission or bridge?" he asked the blade, now letting the knife wander from hand to hand. In so doing, he noticed for the first time that the runes were nearly gone from his skin. Only pale shadows bore witness that he had ever met the doctor, had been in his house and had learned about the strange patterns.

Damn, fucking shit.

That still left the question of where to go: seek shelter under a bridge, or meet his friends at the mission?

The bridge would be cold, uncomfortable, and silent.

The mission would be warm; he would get something to eat too. He'd drown in the smell, Billy would ask questions, Marita would ask more questions, and there would be too many memories of Pepino.

How the boy had sparkled with life, with sex appeal, with happiness the last time he'd seen him!

Gabriel's thoughts went in circles from Tennant, to the murderer, back to Tennant, once more to the murderer, and so on. It was annoying. On the other hand, both subjects had ruled his mind for weeks or even months, and all of a sudden, he was no longer involved with either of them. On top of it, he needed a new job, and he needed to decide where to sleep tonight.

Bit by bit, the sun came up, its light warming his face a little. Just sitting there and watching the sunrise soothed his mind. Very soon, the days would get longer and the nights shorter, people would be out on the streets again, and he would find a new target for his hunt.

The thought of holding someone he didn't love in his arms was revolting.

Well, he would have to get used to it, or he would need to learn to live as a monk, denying the needs of his body.

Right now, the latter option was quite appealing.

Hunching his shoulders, Gabriel was just about to get up and find something to eat when an elderly woman entered the park through the rusty gate. She was small, and her back was bent badly enough for her to need a walking stick. Slowly, she shuffled down the pebbled path, mumbling, her coat flapping against her twig-like, stockinged legs. A hat sat on her gray hair, a small handbag hung over her arm, and only when she stood right in front of Gabriel did she finally look up and see him.

"Uh," she grumbled, "that's my bench. Move your bottom, young man. If I don't sit down right now, I'll fall over, and then you'll have to help me up again. Surely, you don't want that." She lowered herself until she plopped onto the bench like a wet bag filled with old bones.

Gabriel was too surprised to even say hello.

"What?" she snapped. "Never seen an old woman sit down before? One day you might be as old as me, and then you will be glad if you can move at all, never mind going out on your own. Say, are you one of those boys who hang around on the streets all day? Not that I'm curious. But usually they don't come in here. Not many people know about this park. What's your name, anyway?" Suspiciously, she looked at him with unblinking, bird-like eyes.

"Gabriel." He didn't know why he told her his name. It just seemed polite.

"Gabriel. Aha. I see. And why are you sitting on my bench, Gabriel?"

"Nowhere else to go."

The old woman smiled, but for some reason, the sight made Gabriel uneasy. "How pathetic," she said. "You are young. There are endless places to go. Beautiful places, wonderful places. Why sit on a bench in a park no one knows about on such a fine morning?"

She was curious, and her questions had a piercing quality that made them go right through Gabriel's defenses. He had to answer; there was no way to escape her questions or her strange amber eyes. Where had he seen those eyes before?

"Answer me," she whispered.

Her claw-like hands were resting on her knees. Hadn't she done something with them just a moment ago? Moved them, painted a pattern into the air? Shouldn't he get up and leave?

"I had to leave home," he said instead, although he'd had no intention of obeying her. "Couldn't stay. Don't know why I ended up here." Talking was hard; his tongue was heavy. Had he been drinking?

"Why did you have to leave? Where is home?" Her voice had changed; it was more mellow now than raspy.

"Home is where Aleksei is." He hadn't wanted to tell her that. "I had to leave. He hates me, or he will when he wakes up."

His head hurt. But then, it tended to do so when he was tired or unhappy or hungry. Or when runes were at work, come to think of it. Surely, this old lady didn't know anything about runes? No, that was nonsense. She was just a friendly old woman with too many curious questions.

"Is he dead?"

Gabriel's heart sped up a beat. That was a question she shouldn't be able to ask. She didn't know Tennant. She didn't know what had happened last night.

He wanted to get up but found he couldn't. He wanted to speak and found it was impossible.

"Don't fight it," the old lady said. "My runes are strong. You cannot break their power over you. Answer me. Is he dead?"

"No."

"I feared as much. You screwed him?"

Gabriel bit his lips to keep in the words. Then he dug his hands into his upper arms and drilled his heels into the pebbled ground. He managed not to answer, but just barely. So she had used a rune, a Truth rune, and he had no way of getting away from her until her curiosity was satisfied.

Shit.

"You fight my rune?" There was genuine surprise in the old woman's voice. "Look at me."

Against his will, Gabriel's head turned.

Those eyes. He'd seen those eyes before. "Ronai," he said, not as surprised as he should have been. How appropriate that the killer return to his latest crime scene.

The old woman raised an eyebrow. "Fascinating. You recognize me. You are alive, although you should have died the moment you followed me through my portal. Instead, you track my steps and come back here. You escaped from my world into another one, and somehow, you even managed to obscure your route. I couldn't follow you, though I did hope you hadn't survived the journey. Apparently, my hopes were mislaid."

"Sorry to disappoint you," Gabriel croaked, shaking his head to clear his thoughts. No use. The rune Ronai was using was too strong. "You look different. Didn't know you could change your gender."

A thin smile curved the woman's crinkly lips. "I created a rune for this special occasion. It requires a lot of strength, but then, I considered it worth the risk. You are ordinary—how did you manage to follow me?

Gabriel cast the woman a thin smile. "I'm not as ordinary as I appear," was all he said.

Ronai took Gabriel's face between his hands. "And yet, you are quite interesting. I hoped you would come back here, so I placed an alarm. The moment you set foot in the park, I was notified so I could come and see for myself what sort of human was able to hunt me down."

"You killed Pepino." Hate bubbled up inside him—cold, controlled hate. Gabriel ripped his head free from Ronai's hands. "He liked you. Fucking hell, you were his father, and you broke his neck just like that!"

"He was filth." The old woman got up, walked a few steps away from the bench, and drew a rune onto the sparse grass. Light flamed up; she had opened a portal.

"I'm not coming with you," Gabriel stated. His feet and hands tingled—just a little while longer, and he would have complete control over his body again.

Ronai laughed. "But of course you will come with me. Don't you understand? You are under my control. You will do what I want, and you will tell me what I want to know. This world is too cold, and even though this park is scarcely visited, I prefer to question you elsewhere. So get up, come to me, and step through the portal."

"Say please," Gabriel bit out through gritted teeth. His feet twitched. He wanted to get up. Part of him thought it was the best idea ever to obey Ronai's orders, yet he fought hard against it. His nails broke as he dug his fingers into the wood of the bench, and he was thankful for the sharp pain when he managed to remain seated.

The little old lady's eyes became small with anger and hate. "If I didn't want to learn a bit more about you, I'd kill you on the spot," she hissed. "You are a worthless little bastard. You had me worried all week that I'd been found out, causing me to double and triple check every step I made, costing me time and strength. For that alone I should break your neck, but in addition, you saved my brother's life when you dragged him away from the centaurs, you dared to keep him sane as well, although I meant for him to die from the Blood rune. I wish to know who you are. I wish to learn about your powers. Now step through the portal!"

"No!" Gabriel shouted, still fighting the rune.

Wait, his *what*? Aleksei was Ronai's brother? The pieces fell into place, and some things that hadn't made sense at all before seemed suddenly clear.

Unfortunately, Ronai didn't give him any time to think. "You fucking little prick," the old lady hissed. She picked up a dead branch and whacked Gabriel right over the head with surprising strength.

Admittedly, Gabriel hadn't expected that to happen, so he didn't dodge it completely. The branch glanced off his head, and the blow, while not perfect, was still strong enough to knock him off the bench.

Gabriel landed on his knees, dozens of stars dancing in front of his eyes.

Before he could think about getting up or even lift his hands to defend himself, Ronai swung the branch again, this time bringing it down between his shoulder blades. With a cry, Gabriel landed flat in the dust, knowing that a third blow would knock him out—perhaps even break his skull.

Time slowed down. When he tried to move, he felt as if he were surrounded by jelly. Out of the corner of his eye, he saw Ronai, branch raised in his hand, ready to strike. Clumsily, he kicked at Ronai's ankles. He missed, but he managed to get up on his hands and knees.

"Bastard," he murmured, wiping blood out of his eyes.

Ronai threw the branch away and dug his hands into Gabriel's long hair. Jerking his head upward, he hissed, "Get. Through. The. Portal!" and pulled him along.

Gabriel didn't stand a chance. He tried to get in another kick, but he could already feel the power of the portal making him dizzy and pulling him closer. Weakly, he reached for a branch but couldn't grab hold of it, and then Ronai dragged him up to his feet and pushed him through the portal, one hand locked above his elbow.

Gabriel screamed as he fell through. Every fiber in his body screamed with him, but luckily it wasn't as bad as last time—Ronai was obviously shielding him from the portal's powers. Gabriel didn't lose consciousness, nor did his head explode. Only the wounds on his arms ripped open. The ones on his chest remained sealed, which was a relief, as he had no desire to bleed to death the moment he arrived at the other side.

Gabriel landed hard on soft grass, stumbled, and fell. Right behind him, Ronai let go of his arm and kicked his head, dragging him toward a tree to bind him. "You should have listened to me," he said, cold satisfaction in his borrowed voice. "Of course, you won't live long enough to make the same mistake again."

That said, Ronai walked off to the nearby pond. Gabriel could hear clothes rustling, but apart from that, he was too busy keeping his legs from buckling to keep an eye on Ronai.

Sunlight fell through a roof of green. The air smelled sweetly of wind and freshly fallen rain, the grass was much greener than at home, and he could hear the whisper of a brook as it bubbled busily over rocks and roots. It would have been a beautiful scene if only he weren't tied to this damn tree. And if his head weren't hurting. Or his arms. The fresh wounds on his wrists burned like hell, and the prospect of surviving the day was small.

Something was seriously wrong in his life.

Not caring about the pain streaking up his arms—after all, he was almost used to it by now—he tried to get his hands free. Naturally, it didn't work. Upon further examination, he noticed that Ronai had used specific ropes to tie him to the tree—shiny, fiercely glowing ropes covered by runes.

Asshole.

"Hey!" Gabriel called out. "Ronai! What are you doing? If you aren't too busy, I would like to smash in your head."

With every word, every shout, he ripped at his bonds until his wrists were slick with blood and his head buzzed with exhaustion. It was probably a bad idea to provoke a murderer, but then, it really wasn't in his nature to beg for mercy.

No old lady in sight. No dark blond, average-looking guy either.

Behind him, small waves lapped against the bank of the pond. Feet slapped in the mud. A short while later, a body dove into the water. Straining his neck, Gabriel tried to see the killer but only caught a glimpse of feet and half a calf.

"So you are fae, then?" Gabriel asked, trying to sound casual. Despite being bound to a tree, despite the fact that Ronai would surely kill him sooner or later, he wanted to know the truth. "Pepino was half fae; Aleksei is fae. You claim to be related to both of them. Why the hell have you killed your own people? Why did you kill the others?"

He could hear Ronai getting out of the water behind him and the small sounds of someone getting dressed. "You're clean now?" Gabriel asked, trying to wipe the hair out of his face with his shoulder. "Shouldn't have bothered. Once I get free, I'm going to drag you into the mud and then strangle you."

"Empty promises," Ronai answered from somewhere behind his left shoulder. "You cannot get free. And I like to be clean. Your world is filthy and ugly. Coming back here and not having a bath immediately would mean bringing the filth and dirt into my home. I cannot let that happen, of course."

Gabriel seriously considered shaving off his hair once he got back home. The long strands currently clinging to his face were most annoying. He couldn't catch as much as a glimpse of the murderer with it in his face.

He needn't have bothered worrying. As soon as Ronai had pulled on his soft leather trousers, he stepped in front of Gabriel, a calculating frown on his face. He wasn't an old woman anymore, nor was he disguised as the pudgy blond guy. Without the rune-necklace around his neck, Gabriel saw for the first time how the man really looked.

Gabriel's jaw dropped open. "Shit!" he said calmly, though the sight made his heart clench with longing. Ronai resembled his brother in quite a cruel way. "That's what Pepino called you: beautiful. When I saw you the first time, I didn't know what he was talking about, but now—wow, man. It's obvious you are really Aleksei's brother and Pepino's father. I can see why Sweet Rain commented on your eyes— blue like Aleksei's, only that his eyes are friendly and yours are cold. Pity that such a beautiful body hides such a rotten soul."

Ronai—or whatever his real name was—was truly a spectacular sight, as long as one didn't look at his eyes. Long legs, narrow hips, creamy, golden skin. He was muscular without being bulky and slender without giving the appearance of weakness. His dark blond hair surrounded his face like a halo. He wasn't wearing a shirt, just the trousers, and he was barefoot. Only a few patterns decorated his skin, a few lines around his ankles and wrists, that was about it. Despite the missing skin-patterns, he was very clearly fae. And if it was true what Aleksei had said about the lack of skin-patterns, Ronai was truly mad, as well.

Ronai's eyes, cruelly cold and full of hatred, narrowed. He was obviously well aware of the mockery in his captive's voice and disliked it.

"How could you be the doc's brother? I mean, he's such a nice guy, and you're such a jerk." Inwardly, Gabriel cringed. One of these days, he really should learn when to keep his big mouth shut.

Ronai didn't even bother to bare his teeth at the insult. "We were born on the same day by the same mother, only minutes apart."

"Twins. Great. I knew he was trouble, but this is absurd. How about you let me go, and I'll try to talk Tennant into handing you over to the police instead of breaking your neck? I'm sure he won't be happy to find out that his brother is walking around slaughtering people." Gabriel leaned forward as far as the bonds would let him. "Why did you do it? Didn't like their faces? Were you jealous? Or could it be that you're just a stark raving madman?"

Ronai's nostrils flared, and his teeth made a grinding noise. Clearly, it was getting hard for him to keep control. "They had no right to live any longer," he hissed. "They spread their seed. They produced offspring, children with tainted blood, and I had to stop that. Our races mustn't mix with humans. Simple, really. I do not expect you to understand."

Ronai took a step back, and Gabriel had the impression that the other man wanted to get away from him not because he considered his captive dangerous, but because he didn't even want to share the same air with him.

"Tainted blood, eh? And so you just decided to kill everyone who lives in my world?" He had no idea why he was keeping the man talking. Right now, with the prospect of having his head smashed in at any moment, it just seemed like a good idea.

"I just ended the lives of the ones who didn't belong there. Each of us must live in his own world." Ronai sounded arrogant and satisfied at the same time.

His voice made Gabriel's stomach turn with disgust. "Pepino said you were out for company yourself, so accusing others of spreading their genes is pretty much the worst form of hypocrisy I've ever heard of," he pointed out. "You killed Lorelei and Mallfrick. According to Aleksei, you killed one shapeshifter, one riverghost, and two elves. You killed Lorelei's friend, *and* you killed a fae—one of your own kind! Oh, and Pepino. That makes what… nine, all in all?"

"Eleven," Ronai corrected him, and Gabriel secretly doubled his attempts to free himself at that easy, self-confident confession. "One more vampire and one more fae. It matters not if the traitors are my own people. All that counts is that they pay for their wrong-doings."

Gabriel snorted. "What about Sweet Rain? Didn't you know that tree nymphs can't be killed that easily? Or did Wild Oak interrupt you?

Ronai began pacing in front of him, his bare feet leaving barely any visible tracks in the soft grass. "The girl was a trap," he explained. "I knew my brother wouldn't be able to resist her call—they knew each other. Once her human body had perished, I made him follow the wrong track, leading him into the centaurs' part of the woods, hoping they would kill him. That you would save his life, I didn't foresee."

Gabriel frowned. "Why kill him at all? He's your damn brother!" Secretly, he was relieved—they had been right, it had been a trap. All that was left to do now was to stop the killer from committing more murders. He'd think of how to accomplish that goal once he'd figured out how to free his hands.

Ronai was becoming more and more angry—a terrifying sight, as he practically radiated hate and was in a dangerously short-tempered mood. "He was looking into the murders, and I knew he would find out about me eventually. Anyway, this—all those murders—are his fault. He pushed me in this direction. He deserves to die, and of course, he cannot be allowed to have children with one of the whores of your world."

There was the madness. It had taken a while to rear its ugly head, but now that Ronai had warmed to his subject, it was obvious he wasn't sane. Not in the least.

Gabriel swallowed dryly. *Keep him talking*, he thought. "Apart from the fact that Aleksei seems to prefer men, a knife in his back would have done the trick easily. Why such a complicated plan?"

Ronai frowned. His hands clenched and unclenched constantly, and Gabriel could practically feel those hands strangling him already. "I cannot kill my own brother," the fae said. "Not directly. I can only arrange his death. At first, I only tried to get him out of the way. I had someone phone him so he would come to the vampire's office, hoping the police would arrest him as a suspect. I would have made sure they found out about his true nature—they would have kept him in prison until he died. My plan failed because of you. Then the centaurs failed to kill him, again, because of you. I eventually used the Blood rune, knowing that he'd never lain with anyone and that the power of the rune would therefore drive him insane."

"Well, Aleksei's neither dead nor mad, so I guess that plan has failed too," Gabriel replied flippantly.

"If you hadn't been there to save him, I would be rid of him by now," Ronai spat.

"Hate him pretty badly, don't you?" Gabriel said mildly. He was able to move his right wrist a bit more than he could a few minutes ago, so he needed to keep Ronai talking. "What did he do to you—pinch your arm when you were both kids? Or something equally nasty?"

Ronai closed the distance between them with a few long strides and locked his fingers around Gabriel's throat, adding sudden, brutal pressure. "He betrayed me," he hissed, spit flying out of his mouth with each word. "Anyway—who are you? I barely recognized you in the park. Had my rune not proven it was you who watched me kill the abomination that was my son, I would have just walked away!"

The bark of the tree dug into Gabriel's back, and breathing became harder by the second. Next to his feet, a small pool of blood was growing from the wounds on his arms. His wrists were slick with blood, making it easier to turn them. It wouldn't be long before he'd be able to slip out of the bonds.

"Pepino," he croaked, and Ronai loosened his grip a bit. "You were his dad. You fathered tainted blood. You are one fucking hypocritical bastard, you know that?"

Ronai's hands trembled, but he didn't tighten his grip again. "I walked past him sometime last year. He was lying in the gutter, stinking, high, out of his head. Filth." He gulped, lost in his memory. "He called after me. Stumbled to his feet. Touched me." Ronai blanched. "Asked for my name. Wanted to know who I was. Said I was the most beautiful man he'd ever seen." His eyes focused again. "I wore a rune. The boy shouldn't have been able to see through my disguise, but he did. Relatives aren't fooled by the rune, so I realized that he must be my own flesh and blood. His mother"—he seemed close to vomiting at the word—"had tricked me into her bed. She lived amongst us, she wore a rune my brother had made, and although I didn't know her parents, I believed her to be fully fae. She wasn't, and it was my brother's fault that I couldn't see it."

"Ah," Gabriel whispered. "Eventually, she wanted to leave your world, and you too. Did she tell you that she was pregnant?"

Ronai looked right through him, seeing something else, seeing another time. "She left, but I managed to find her. She told me she'd had a baby. She was so happy about it, and she didn't realize how wrong his birth was. I killed her. Couldn't find the boy, though. I forgot about him until the day I nearly tread on him."

"That day you learned that your son was a pro and a drug addict," Gabriel said. "Your offspring, blood from your blood, had landed in the gutter, selling his ass to everyone who was willing to pay. Half fae, but unable to keep himself off the drugs. When you saw him, you knew who and what he was: living proof that the races mustn't mix. Pepino triggered all those murders simply by having been born."

Ronai's eyes were flaming with hate and madness. "He insisted on seeing me again, and I could see how he changed," he said slowly. "Each time, he looked more fae. He quit the drugs. He kept himself clean. His genes, the fae part, became stronger with every breath he took. He was gorgeous."

"Tell me about it," Gabriel said, remembering the kiss he'd shared with the boy.

"I had to kill him. But you saw me, and you followed me. I do not know how this was possible, but I will find out."

Gabriel grinned, a wide, sunny smile. "Take a blood sample," he said. "The doc did that already, and he hasn't got a clue what I am or who I am. All he could tell you—and all you would find out if you checked my blood under a microscope—is that one of my ancestors was a shapeshifter. I'm tainted blood, as you so nicely phrased it. My mother used to say so as well. You didn't know her, by any chance?"

Ronai slammed his fist into Gabriel's face, causing his head to connect hard with the tree behind him. "You talk too much," he hissed, and Gabriel laughed as blood ran down his chin.

"Heard that one before," he rasped, thinking of Aleksei's sleeping face. He needed a little more time to free his hand, to get unbound from the tree, and to figure out a way to crush Ronai. "What are you gonna do about it? Kill me now or later?"

"I will kill you, but not now. First I'll find out what you are," Ronai replied, stepping closer. Although he'd had a bath in the pond, Gabriel could smell sour sweat and foul breath. Up close, he wasn't as beautiful—his skin was pale and unhealthy underneath the golden glow, his hair seemed greasy, and the sparse patterns on his skin looked as if they'd been drawn by an unskilled child.

Ronai fished for something in his trouser pockets, finally pulling out a stone.

"Illegal rune?" Gabriel guessed, and from the twitch in Ronai's eye, he assumed he was right. "What does it do? Make me talk like I did on the bench?"

Ronai grinned, baring yellow teeth. "It allows me to read your mind, your past, your memories, all the experiences you've ever had," he whispered. "I will walk through your mind like a man walks through the rooms of his own house. No door will stay locked, no emotion hidden, no wish or hope unseen. All your secrets will lay open to me, although I'm afraid you won't enjoy the feeling very much. In fact, the strength of the rune will destroy your mind, which is, of course, the reason it is illegal. However, I will find out what and who you truly are. Sort of like killing two birds with one stone."

Gabriel held his breath, waiting for Ronai to come close enough so he could slam his knee into the bastard's balls or headbutt him, whatever he could do to keep the murderer at a distance. He wasn't bothering anymore to hide his attempts to free his hands, either—just a little while longer, and he would be free.

Ronai stretched out one long arm, holding the stone with the illegal rune in his hand. He pressed the stone to Gabriel's cheek, his head too far away for butting and his legs too close together for a good kick.

Light filled Gabriel's head, and when he tried to jerk away from Ronai's hand, the man's grip tightened, each fingertip seeming to drill into his flesh. Flat on his cheek, the rune burned. And Ronai's eyes, cruel and cold, cut through his brain like a hot knife through butter.

"YOU know, I'd rather you did not do this."

Ronai spun around and nearly tripped in his shock at the sudden interruption, and Gabriel found his knees could in fact wobble more than he'd ever believed possible. The newly arrived man looked at both of them with mild curiosity.

There, wearing only an old pair of jeans, a lose sweater, and his running shoes, was Tennant.

"You should be in bed," Gabriel croaked, shaking all over from nearly having his brain turned into mush.

Tennant cast him an indifferent smile. "You are not easy to find, Gabriel. Luckily, you are crap at erasing Tracking runes from your clothes. Brother, pray tell me what is going on here."

With a smooth, controlled gesture, Ronai put the stone back into his pocket, brushed back his hair, and wiped a hand over his face, erasing all signs of anger, hatred, or murder from his features.

"Aleksei. I did not expect you, but it is good you came, nevertheless. You know this man?" Nodding in Gabriel's direction, Ronai made it clear with one small gesture that he considered him to be worth less than the dirt on the soles of his feet.

Tennant nodded. "I do. He was a guest in my house until he decided to sneak out in the middle of the night, taking half of my belongings, all of my money, and my necklace too. A thief, and a liar on top of it. I'm glad you caught him."

Gabriel's throat tightened with dread—he hadn't he expected anything like this. He hadn't taken any money. He surely hadn't taken Aleksei's necklace. What was this all about?

Turning his wrist once more, he suddenly felt it slip free.

Ronai's hand—the one that had held the rune-stone—was still in his pocket, and he was no more than a step away from his brother. All he had to do was to reach out and slam his hand to Aleksei's face, and he would destroy his mind and finally be rid of him. Gabriel knew that was what he was planning, so he moved his free hand slowly, inch by inch, and reached into the back pocket of his trousers, where his pocketknife waited for just such an occasion.

His fingertips tingled when he touched the metal; the knife was slippery in his hand due to the blood that was still oozing from his wounds, but he still managed to get it out and open it.

Smiling, Ronai opened his arms to welcome his brother with a hug. His hand, the one with the rune-stone, was already dangerously close to his brother's face.

Gabriel threw the knife, aiming as best he could. In the past weeks and months, he had practiced his skills until he could hold three knives in the air and catch them safely without even looking. Now, he threw the small pocketknife and watched it spin through the air, the metal glittering in the sun. It would have hit its target perfectly, would have drilled into Ronai's left eye and killed the murderer on the spot, if Aleksei hadn't seen the movement. Casually, he pushed his brother out of harm's way, as well as a few steps away from himself. Ronai stumbled backward, the knife missing him by no more than a few inches.

"Did you really think I'd allow you to kill my brother?" Aleksei asked, raising one of his eyebrows in the precise way that made Gabriel's stomach clench with hope. "Petresh, tie him up again, will you? And then you can explain to me why you are here, where you have been these past few years, and why you have captured someone I would have called a friend until yesterday."

Until you begged me to fuck you and I was stupid enough to comply, Gabriel thought but didn't dare say aloud. Passively, he let Ronai—or Petresh, as he was called—fasten the ropes around his wrists once more, this time even tighter. He wouldn't manage to wriggle out of them again.

Petresh wiped the back of his wrist over his mouth. "A friend?" he said disbelievingly. "Him? But he's the one you've been looking for. He's the killer!"

"What?" Dumbstruck, Gabriel stared from one brother to the other, hoping he'd misheard.

He hadn't.

"It's so obvious," Petresh continued. "That he just tried to kill me is further proof." Swiftly, he knelt down and picked up the pocketknife that was now stuck in the soft ground. "His hatred for our kind, for people from the hidden worlds, must be enormous. I do not know his reasons, but I know he killed the vampire and the mermaid. He confessed shortly before you arrived."

"I didn't confess anything, and I didn't fucking kill anyone!" Gabriel shouted—or rather tried to shout, as his throat was still sore from the earlier strangling. "He is the killer. He killed them, all of them. Why the hell should I mean any of your kind harm? Tell me that, Doc!"

Aleksei frowned at that. Gabriel, who thought it was because of the way he'd addressed him, added with a snarl, "What—don't you like your title anymore, *Doc*? Let me guess, it's just another lie. Like it or not, it doesn't change the facts. I don't kill, and you know that. I threw up at the sight of Mallfrick, for crying out loud!"

Petresh held the knife out to his brother. "He tricked you from the moment you met. Made you believe he liked you, made you consider him a friend. But he isn't. He's a murderer. He even used a Blood rune to get you into his bed!"

That accusation was so horrifically close to Gabriel's discarded notion of using a glass of wine and a joint to get Aleksei to kiss him that he gasped with shock.

Petresh put on a most solemn face. Aleksei looked at Gabriel thoughtfully, and then took the knife from his brother's hand. He turned it in his hands, stroked the metal, closed and opened it again.

"This is a toy," he mused. "Harmless, if not thrown, of course. I didn't know you carried a knife, Gabriel."

Just hearing Aleksei use his name calmed Gabriel's nerves—he hadn't done it so far. He hadn't looked at him either.

Now he did.

His eyes were as blue as ever, as blue as his mad brother's eyes, ice-blue, but they lacked the coldness of Petresh's eyes. Slowly, Tennant raised an eyebrow, and Gabriel thought, hoped, *believed* that there was a message in this, a sign that all of this was nothing but a farce, a trick, a way to free him from Petresh's grip. Maybe his hideous accusations—that he had stolen, that he hadn't managed to erase a Tracking rune—were also small signs that Aleksei was just playing a game in order to get him to safety.

Aleksei flipped the knife and caught it again, turning his back to Gabriel. "Are you certain, brother? Are you certain that he is the killer, that he committed the murders?" Absently, he traced a fingertip along the scar on his cheek. "Remember the last time we met?"

Petresh bared his teeth. "We fought. You lost. It is wrong to hand out runes to anyone who wants them, runes that can hide one's true identity. It is dangerous, it is stupid, and you know it. You underestimated me back then. You thought I could forgive you for betraying me. I advise you not to make the same mistake again. *He* is the killer. Believe me. You have pursued him for months now, so it is up to you to judge him."

Slowly, Aleksei shook his head. "I have known him since Christmas," he mused. "He seemed harmless to me. No knowledge of runes. Ignorant concerning personal hygiene, decent food, and manners. Why should he kill riverghosts and mermaids? Why kill his employer?"

"I can think of a reason or two for killing Mallfrick," Gabriel said bitterly, but not loud enough to be heard.

Petresh shrugged his shoulders. "Obviously, he is not who he seems to be. When I followed him to the park where the boy was killed—"

"Pepino," Gabriel cast in helpfully. This was surreal—the fact that he was bound, that he was being accused of murdering several people, and that Aleksei was so obviously tempted to believe his mad brother over him. "Or Justin. He was your son, remember? And you killed him because he was only half fae. Come to think of it—maybe there are more children with your face running through my world?"

Petresh lashed out and slammed his fist into Gabriel's mouth, cracking his lip and loosening some teeth. "You worthless little bastard!" he shouted.

Gabriel just grinned, blood trickling down his chin. Petresh nearly jumped on him.

"Easy, brother," Aleksei said, putting a soothing hand on Petresh's arm. "As you have correctly stated, I am to judge him, and I will do so. Gabriel," he said, "you must admit he has a point. Pepino knew you, and the way he was killed indicates he was not scared of his murderer."

Gabriel just stared at him and refused to answer.

"Besides," Petresh cast in, "he can use portals. He can even open them—I've seen it myself. He hides his true heritage, brother! Whatever his reasons for killing innocent people, you must stop him from continuing!"

Aleksei held the pocketknife up to a sunbeam. It was not a particularly clean knife, and the blade was rusty. "It will serve its purpose," the doctor said. His hand still locked on his brother's arm, he pulled his twin a few steps away from where Gabriel was restrained. "I am bound to believe you. I have known you all my life; I have known him only a few short months. If you swear to me that he is the murderer, I will judge him, no matter that I liked him once."

Visibly relieved, Petresh smiled. "I swear he killed all the victims, every single one. I took him because I feared there were more victims. I hoped that if I could retrieve their names, the families of the victims could be informed about their loved ones' fates."

Gabriel couldn't help it: he laughed. He knew he was as good as dead with Aleksei falling for his mad brother's lies, but this was too sick not to laugh at.

"You know, I knew you'd be my downfall eventually, Doc," he managed, his sides hurting from suppressed amusement. "I expected you to kill me the first night I slept under your roof but, well, can't have everything. It's just as well you kill me now while I'm bound to a damn tree."

Aleksei flinched ever so slightly at his words, but instead of answering, he swiftly pulled the knife over his open palm. A thin line of blood appeared. "Swear on my blood, brother," he said, his voice hoarse. "Swear, and I will kill him."

Petresh hesitated for the first time. He looked at Gabriel, taking in his bleeding wrists, his tangled hair, and the strong ropes. Then he openly measured his brother from head to toe and made a decision. "I swear," he said, placing his hand in his brother's.

A brief shake. A small nod.

"Now kill him," Petresh demanded.

To Gabriel, time became soft and yielding. Each passing second drowned him, smothered him, choked him, and each heartbeat took hours to pump his blood through his veins. *He's going to kill me*, he thought, his legs and arms now completely numb. *Just like that, without hesitation. He's going to plunge that knife into my heart, knowing I cannot fight him.*

Somehow, though, he still couldn't really believe it, even though Aleksei now stood right in front of him, looking grim, the knife—his own damn pocket knife—in his right hand.

"You should have done this before last night," Gabriel said quietly. "Would have spared you some unwanted memories."

Aleksei cast a glance over his shoulder toward his brother. Petresh was leaning against a tree several feet away. His posture was relaxed, excited, and anticipatory all at the same time. "Do it," he called. "It is the right thing, and you know it."

Aleksei narrowed his eyes and looked back at Gabriel. "Do you trust me?" he whispered as he dug one hand into his victim's hair, ripping his head up. The blade of the knife scratched along tender skin.

"Lousy time to ask me that," Gabriel replied, tantalized by those blue eyes so very close to him. "Just cut my throat and get it over with."

The knife cut deeper. "Do you trust me?" Aleksei repeated through his teeth. "Answer me, and be honest. You must be honest!"

Gabriel closed his eyes. The cold blade on his throat spoke of his death, Petresh's smile spoke of triumph, and Aleksei's hand was as steady as it could possibly be. It would be madness to answer honestly, but then, he had nothing to lose.

"Always," he breathed.

He felt Aleksei's breath on his cheek when he answered, "That's good. Wouldn't work otherwise." He felt the grip tighten in his hair as his friend steadied himself, took aim, and plunged the knife right into his chest.

CHAPTER FOURTEEN

THE blade, thin, small, and blunt as it was, cut easily through flesh and muscle. A harsh, high, disbelieving cry cut through the sunny air. The metal damaged nerves and severed veins; gore gushed out of the wound, and a bubble of blood formed, then erupted, on pale lips. The knife had pierced a lung. Aleksei had drilled it in underneath the ribcage and up toward the heart.

Legs buckled, suddenly too weak to carry the body's weight.

Fingers cramped, clutching at the wound.

"You... bastard," Petresh stammered. The fae first swayed, then crashed to the ground. His naked chest was covered in blood. It seeped out of a deep wound and into his leather trousers and dyed the green grass red.

Gabriel stared at the knife stuck beneath his heart. It was stuck in his flesh so deeply that he couldn't see the blade anymore. However, he didn't feel any pain at all, and he wondered if he were having a particularly nasty nightmare.

"You killed me," he said to Aleksei, once more trying to free his hands so he could touch the knife, his own knife, which was protruding from his chest. "I'm dead. Am... am I dead?"

Carefully, Aleksei retrieved the knife. Neither wound nor blood was to be seen, but still, Gabriel felt a rush of dizziness wash through him. His already weak legs trembled, and when Aleksei cut the bonds, the fae had to catch him, or Gabriel would have fallen face down in the grass.

Dropping the knife, Tennant said, "You are not dead. Your body is covered with Protection runes, remember? I cannot hurt you as long as you believe I won't. If you had lied a moment ago, if you hadn't trusted me, you would be dead."

"But... the runes... they're all gone!" Gabriel's voice trembled, too, but the fact that Aleksei had his arms wrapped around him helped to keep him calm.

"You might not be able to see them," Tennant said, briefly brushing his fingertips across Gabriel's still-bleeding wrists, "but the runes are there. I told you the Protection rune would be wasted on a camera, did I not?"

Tennant turned around and looked down at his brother, who lay in the grass and seemed much more dead than alive. After a moment of consideration, the fae dropped to his knees, crouching down next to him. Blood was streaming out of a wound made by a knife that hadn't even touched Petresh's skin. The mad fae choked, his lungs pierced. He was deathly pale. Helplessly, his hands clutched at his chest and throat, eyes wide with fear and hate.

"Kill you!" he wheezed. "I'll... kill you! Betrayed me again!"

Aleksei painted a rune on his brother's chest, then a second one on each wrist. The first seemed to slow the bleeding; the other two immobilized his hands.

"No, Petresh," he said. "You had your chance, and now it is over. You should not have sworn a false oath, brother, especially not where Gabriel is involved. As you have witnessed yourself, he trusts me beyond reason, beyond fear and even death. Did you really think I would make the same mistake twice? You nearly killed me the last time we argued. You swore a false oath before. Back then, I believed you. Today, I did not."

Petresh bared his teeth. "Protection runes... for him? But he isn't worth it. His blood is *tainted*! And you saved him. You even allowed him to fuck you—he said so. You're disgusting. Traitor. Worthless bastard!"

Soothingly, Aleksei wiped the sweat from his brother's brow. "He is dear to me, Petresh. Why else do you think I came looking for him?"

Petresh tried in vain to break the runes that kept him bound to the ground. "You knew he didn't do it." There was a clear accusation in his words.

"Of course. I know the things he is capable of, and murder is not amongst them. Besides, I used a Truth rune right after we found the vampire's body."

"What was left of him," Petresh sniggered, a most unpleasant sound. "He'd had seven children, Aleksei. Seven! More tainted blood! More filth threatening us!" He coughed blood.

Aleksei drew another rune, and the injured man relaxed slightly. "You are such an idiot, Petresh," he said, bitterness and sadness lacing his words. "We all have tainted blood. The portals have existed since the first word was spoken, and there has always been contact between the races. If I looked closely enough, I would find human traces in my blood, and in yours too. Centaur traces, maybe even dragon traces. You killed for no reason. You killed simply because you wanted to."

Silently, Gabriel stepped behind his friend. He still didn't completely understand why he wasn't dead, why the fae lay bleeding, maybe even dying, instead, but that mystery could wait.

"His son triggered everything," he offered. "Ronai—Petresh—couldn't accept that his child was a drug-addicted hustler. He decided that no one who could produce more disgusting offspring had the right to live in the human world and began his spree. In the end, he killed his own son as well."

The thought of the boy's dead body made his throat tight. Wiping his eyes dry, he continued, "Pepino told me he'd met his father, and that he had quit the drugs for him. He was happy. For the first time in his life, the boy was happy, and this bastard here just breaks his neck."

Kneeling next to Aleksei, he looked at the bleeding man. "What now, Doc?" he asked. "Will you let him die? Will he go to prison, or what?"

Both brothers looked at him, and Gabriel was momentarily stunned at the similarity of their features. They were not identical twins, but they were very much alike in the shape of their eyes, their jaw lines, and maybe even how their lips twitched when they were amused.

Aleksei, though, was neither cruel nor brutal. He lied if he had to, he kept his secrets, but he was an honest man.

Petresh, on the other hand, was not only a killer but a man without principles, morals, or scruples. The brothers couldn't have been more different, and Gabriel was glad about it.

"Prison," Petresh rasped. "Never. I'll walk freely on this earth, and I will finish what I have started." He struggled, and the hatred he harbored for his brother as well as for Gabriel showed in his eyes.

Aleksei became very still. "Promise me this will end here and now," he urged. "Hand yourself over to the fae council, and let them judge you." There was a tremble in his voice, but Gabriel doubted Petresh noticed it.

In fact, the man on the ground just laughed. Knowing what this laugh meant—that Petresh considered himself in charge, that he thought he was right, that he would continue killing as soon as he was able—it was a horrible sound.

"Coward," Petresh hissed, gasping for air. "You should join me. Kill him first, and then let me go!"

Aleksei focused his gaze on Gabriel for a long moment. "I don't think so," he finally stated. "He is special. I wouldn't kill him if it meant saving my own life. Because of your Blood rune, I had to force him into my bed. That alone would be enough to stop you from ever using runes again."

Petresh's eyes widened, his fingers clawing helplessly at the soft grass, yet he was unable to free his hands. "You wouldn't dare!"

"You just confirmed that you will continue killing, little brother, and I cannot let that happen. I will take the knowledge of the runes away from you. You will be locked in this world, unable to leave it even if someone opens a portal for you. It would tear you apart, and you know that."

Grimly, Aleksei took a twig, broke it apart, and drew complicated, powerful runes on his brother's still-bleeding chest. "I do not want to kill you," he added. "And there is no other way except to keep you in this world. I truly hope you find some peace. Of course, I will still have to report you to the council."

Petresh began to fight against his bonds, yelling hoarsely and trying to hinder his brother from completing his task.

Gabriel didn't need to be asked: he pressed both hands to Petresh's shoulders and held him down, ignoring the shouts and the eyes blazing with hatred.

"Hurry," he said brusquely to Aleksei. "I'd like to leave this world and go back to my own—the sooner the better."

Aleksei gave him an odd look, but as he had to concentrate, it was very brief. Focusing on his brother, Aleksei finished his task and finally leaned back, looking exhausted and sad.

Petresh shouted, crying his hatred into his brother's face, calling him everything from "worthless traitor" to "dirty bastard."

"I take it that means you will try to find a way around the restrictions that bind you to this world?" Aleksei asked when Petresh stopped to take a breath.

The mad fae lay motionless in the blood-soiled grass, gasping for air and clearly in pain. "I'll come after you and kill you slowly, and your fucktoy too!" he snarled. "I'll cut him to pieces, and I'll make you watch. If he's so precious to you, I want to see how you react when I carve out his eyes!"

Aleksei blanched. "You don't leave me a choice," he whispered, and he picked up the knife that lay a few feet away in the grass. "I would never have thought I would have to do this one day, and especially not to you. We are brothers, Petresh!" Disbelievingly, he stared at the blade in his hand, then at the man on the ground. "We played together as children, we made fun of our sister, we slept under the same roof. We were both loved by our parents. What happened to you? Why do you force me to do this?"

"Don't you *dare* do it!" Petresh screamed, but before he could begin to swear again, Gabriel ripped off the sleeve of his shirt and stuffed it into the man's mouth. "It works," he said, shrugging, when Aleksei flashed him a quick, thin smile.

Aleksei pulled the blade across his palm. Blood welled, not much, but enough for the doctor to let a few drops fall to his brother's chest.

Quickly and determinedly, he placed his hand above Petresh's heart, then touched his brother's eyes, mouth, and forehead. Petresh fought with all his might, tried to spit out the gag, tried to kick and get free, but to no avail. Gabriel's grip on his shoulders was strong, and the Binding runes did the rest—he was immobilized, and he couldn't even plead for mercy.

"You will not remember your name. You will forget your past," Aleksei whispered into his brother's ear, clearly troubled by what he was doing but not willing to stop. "You won't recognize your own people. You will not know about the portals, the other worlds, or the other races any longer." With each word, he drew a small rune on his brother's skin. The color of the blood blended with the golden glow of Petresh's skin; the runes looked fierce and cruel in the late morning light.

"You will fall asleep, and when you wake up, you will be like a blank page, all that you were wiped from your mind and your soul. You will have to learn to talk again, to walk, even to eat." A tear ran down Aleksei's cheek. His brother's eyes, a moment ago blazing with fury, dropped closed.

"You won't know my name, or our parents' names, or your son's name. You will forget that you have killed. When you wake, you will be like a newborn child. All I can do is promise that someone will take care of you. Not I. You will not see me again as long as I live, and that is something else I promise to you."

Crying bitter tears, Aleksei placed a kiss on his brother's brow. The last rune he carved into Petresh's flesh underneath the left collarbone, using Gabriel's knife.

The body of the man whose name had once been Petresh and who had called himself Ronai reared up one more time. Then his muscles went slack, and he dropped back onto the grass, not fighting anymore and barely breathing. The wound to his chest was partly healed, his skin was splattered with blood and covered in runes, his mouth was slightly parted, as if he were sleeping peacefully. Only his eyes moved under his closed lids, tormented by unseen dreams, perhaps watching memories fleeing into the everlasting darkness of oblivion.

Clearly unaware that tears were still streaming from his eyes, Aleksei slipped his arms under the limp body and lifted his twin up.

"Wait for me," he told Gabriel, who now sat leaning against one of the trees, thoroughly exhausted. "I have to take him to the council. They will look after him and make sure that he never remembers who he was. I'll be back, but I don't know how long it will take me."

Numb with shock, grief, and anger, Gabriel just nodded. He was cold and tired. He would have preferred going with them, and he feared Aleksei's return, because they would have a few issues to iron out. He'd never been good at solving issues, neither his own nor anyone else's.

"Take your time. I'll wait. Can't go anywhere without you anyway." He sounded bitter, but he didn't care anymore. All he wanted to do was lean against the warm bark of the tree, listen to the birds, and try to forget the past few hours. Or months, even. Working for Mallfrick and living mostly on the streets had been less challenging than being with Tennant, and much less heartbreaking.

He felt a soft tingle when Aleksei opened a portal, and he felt his heart clench when the fae stepped through it without as much as looking back. He'd get used to it.

GABRIEL plucked at the ropes, gently peeling them off the wounds around his wrists. It was a relief, getting rid of them—the magic in them hurt, and once they were gone, the numbness quickly faded into nothingness. After about ten minutes, when his heart had stopped racing and his breathing had calmed down, he got up on staggering feet and washed in the little pond Petresh had bathed in not too long ago. It was awkward, but he wanted to get rid of the blood and the sweat and the faint fragrance of fear that was still in his nose.

It didn't really work, though. The blood was gone, and so was the sweat and dirt, but the fear remained, and with it the memories lingering in the back of his head like a dangerous animal ready to strike. Vaguely, Gabriel wondered whether he would be able to sleep tonight. And where he would sleep, of course. Somehow, the guest room in Aleksei's house seemed out of the question.

"Damn," he murmured, fighting with his trousers. The fabric stuck to his wet skin. They were nowhere near clean, but of course, he couldn't sit around naked.

Actually, he couldn't sit at all. Restless, nervous, he listened for footsteps, seeing danger behind every shadow, especially when the sun went lower and the shadows grew to monstrous sizes.

He paced, listening for Aleksei to come back. Wondering, worrying, hoping—what if they could solve this mess? What if they talked once they were back in their own world?

Eventually, Gabriel became too tired to walk around, so he chose a tree with a good view of the entire clearing and forced himself to sit down and remain seated. He waited for Aleksei until evening, watching birds building nests and catching worms. Once, a deer came by, eyed him trustingly, and hopped on without being concerned by his presence.

Gabriel, however, didn't feel peaceful at all, and when Aleksei finally came back shortly before the sun disappeared, Gabriel was clenching his teeth and balling his fists so badly he wanted to jump up and run away from this place as well as from the impending confrontation with Aleksei. For he was sure that there would be a confrontation, and a nasty one, at that.

Aleksei looked beaten and haggard in the dwindling light, much older than he had the night before, when Gabriel had seen his face lit with ecstasy. His gait was slow, halting even, as if it had cost him a lot to come back to this world.

A few muttered words, and a portal opened. "Let's go," the fae said. He sounded as tired as Gabriel felt, but in his voice was a steely undertone Gabriel had never heard before.

Hesitantly, Gabriel got up. He swayed, suddenly feeling too lightheaded to remember how to walk. Surely, going through yet another portal wasn't a good idea?

"You don't need to be afraid," Aleksei remarked coolly. "Nothing will happen to you as long as you stay in physical contact with me. I'll take you"—just the slightest pause—"back to my place. There are some things I'd like to explain."

Gabriel nodded.

He found it most disturbing that Aleksei hadn't said, "I'll take you home."

THE kitchen in Aleksei's house seemed too small for the both of them. Gabriel sat at the table, his chair pushed back against the wall so he would be out of the way. Aleksei, though, was busy looking for vegetables, spices, and a pan. Obviously, he was in a cooking mood.

"I don't think I'm that hungry," Gabriel finally bit out, wanting to get up and get on with it.

"You will eat." With precise movements, Aleksei chopped the garlic in too-small slices.

"Look, I'm fine, and the wounds are already nearly healed. No need to bother with dinner—I'll just leave you in peace and be on my way now that this is over, Doc."

Aleksei slammed the knife onto the counter and whipped around. "Don't call me that," he hissed. "I adopted the name from a television series a few years back. It's a lie, like so many others I've told. You know my name. Use it. And you are *not* fine!"

"But—"

"No discussion. You shouldn't have gone through a portal for another two months, but what did you do—you bumped into the killer who dragged you into his world and bound you with runed ropes on top of it. They were designed to weaken a captive even further, and I can see in your face how much it has weakened you. Plus, I had to bring you back here again so you wouldn't starve out there, and now *you will eat*!" He took a plate and put it onto the table, where it promptly broke in half.

Silence rang as loud as church bells.

After several long moments, Gabriel carefully changed the subject, not daring to move an inch away from the table. "I guess I should stay away from portals for a while."

"You should be glad going through didn't rip you apart. It cost me a lot of strength to bring you back here unharmed."

Gabriel stared at Aleksei's back, hoping he would turn around, but he didn't. "Thanks," he finally bit out. What else could he have said?

"Any idea why Petresh didn't kill you on the spot?" Aleksei asked without turning his head.

"He was curious," Gabriel replied slowly. "Wanted to know why I could follow him after he'd killed Pepino, and how I managed to get away from him later. Told him you weren't able to find out, either, but he didn't believe me. He was about to turn my brain into mashed potatoes with a rune-stone when you arrived."

"I know," Aleksei snapped. "I was listening to your conversation with him for several minutes before I intervened. The rune-stone would have revealed that you are under my protection. I couldn't let that happen."

Gabriel had to close his eyes for a moment, remembering the first night under Aleksei's roof. "Protection runes. I painted one on my camera, remember? You looked at me as if I were an imbecile. Which I am, I guess."

Aleksei's hands stilled, his head bowed. Apparently, something was more interesting than the chopped garlic. "A Protection rune is powerful, and it does what it says: it protects, in your case from your portal-induced injuries. It also protected you from bleeding to death when Petresh used rune-ropes to bind you. And it protected you from my attack, of course." He picked up a cloth and wiped his hands clean. Sighing deeply, he continued, "A Protection rune is permanent. Once used, it cannot be undone. When you came back from the rock in the ocean, you were dying. I decided to save your life, and for that, I needed the rune. In a way, it binds me to you—that is how I found you, not through a Tracking rune. There were none of those on your belongings."

Gabriel nodded. "Knew it. That and the crap you talked about me having stolen from you. I knew it was your way of telling me you were playing a role. I knew I could trust you."

Why the hell did it hurt so much to say those words? They were true, after all. The problem was, he felt a lot more than just trust, but

Gabriel couldn't see how he could ever tell Aleksei without sounding pathetic, or worse, desperate.

"Had you not trusted me, you'd be dead by now. I admit stabbing you was a harsh way out of the mess you had gotten yourself into, but then, I couldn't figure out another way in the short amount of time I had. Petresh had always underestimated me. In a way, I am glad of it, because otherwise, my plan might not have worked."

"That's why he swore a false oath, then." Gabriel had decided that talking was better than silence. When he talked, he didn't need to think of leaving.

"Precisely. He simply didn't consider the possibility I might not believe him." Aleksei still hadn't turned around, talking instead to the garlic and the fish he was about to prepare. "Some years back, he was accused of having killed a girl—Pepino's mother, as I know now. He denied any involvement with her. He swore an oath as he did today. He even attacked me when I had doubts about his version of events." Absently, he rubbed the thin scar on his cheek. "In the end, I believed him. He was always excellent at proving his point."

"Today, you were prepared for his lies." Watching Aleksei's shoulders tense, seeing him struggle with the events that had happened, Gabriel wished he could get up and embrace him, hold him close, give him some reassurance that what he'd done had been right. But he didn't dare. *After all, I'm still a coward, not even brave enough to say what I really want to say instead of discussing Petresh's fate,* he thought, and disgust washed through him.

Aleksei sighed deeply. "He was arrogant enough to believe I'd fall for the same trick twice. He underestimated me, and he massively underestimated you, Gabriel, and that is why I judged him. His false oath backfired on him. Your trust in me was unbroken, and therefore, it was him instead of you I injured and nearly killed, although I stabbed the knife into your chest." With slow movements, he began washing the salad, his shoulders hunched as if he were cold.

Gabriel sat at the kitchen table in a house that wasn't home anymore and didn't know how to comfort him. "You didn't want to do it, did you?" he finally asked, knowing it was a lame way to stay for a little while longer. "Erase your brother's memory and carry him away so someone else could take care of him, that is."

Washing the salad seemed to take more time than usual. "No. Petresh was very proud of his heritage. He considered it a privilege to be fae, and I know that what I have done to him would be worse than death in his eyes. Maybe I should have let your knife hit him, but then, I couldn't allow you to take on the responsibility for my brother. That is why I pushed him aside. He is my flesh and blood. It was my job to find him and my job to judge over him."

Water was still running down the drain, but Aleksei seemed unaware that his hands were no longer moving. The remaining lettuce leaves lay forgotten on the counter. Silently, Gabriel got up and shut off the tap.

Aleksei stepped back. That there was distance now between them instead of closeness, awkwardness instead of the easy friendship they'd developed, nearly choked Gabriel. "You did what you had to do. And life is always better than death."

"Without knowing who he is and what he is, unable to use runes or to cross into other worlds, Petresh wouldn't have called it life. He won't be able to cause harm ever again. It is the best and fairest thing I could do, and still, I will need a while to come to terms with it."

Gabriel took a bottle of wine and poured Aleksei a glass. "I will leave after dinner," he said quietly, cursing himself that he wasn't able to say, "Please, let me stay."

Aleksei nodded. "I assumed you would say that. I cannot blame you, although I would have liked you to—" His voice broke off, and instead of continuing, he took a generous sip from his glass.

"You would like me to what?" Gabriel asked after several moments had passed in silence and it became clear that Aleksei had no intention of saying more.

Aleksei took another sip. "It does not matter anymore."

"It matters to *me*!" Gabriel snapped, suddenly angry. "We were friends, Aleksei. I know it's not really my fault, but eventually, I managed to mess things up by... by taking you to bed instead of looking for another solution. Maybe knock you unconscious or something. Anything but taking you when you were so badly affected by that rune. And still… isn't there a way around it? Can't we at least be friends?"

He knew he sounded desperate, but it didn't matter. He'd always been desperate, all his life, so there wasn't a reason why it should be different now that the subject really mattered to him.

"Friends." Aleksei looked at him fully for the first time in hours. "You want to be friends with me? Then how come I woke up alone this morning? How come you ran from me as soon as your desire was satiated? A friend would have stayed, Gabriel. So don't talk about friendship when it is so very obvious that there is no deeper connection between us anymore. Maybe there never was." Barely concealed anger showed in his words, and his knuckles were white from clutching the fragile glass. It was a miracle he didn't break it.

"I left because I wanted to spare you the sight of me in the morning, okay? I practically raped you—you were in no condition to make coherent decisions, and if you truly think you weren't more than a one-night stand for me, you are one stupid idiot."

Aleksei threw the glass against the opposite wall. Wine sprayed throughout the kitchen.

Seeing him so very angry, so unlike his usual calm self, was a shock for Gabriel—even when Aleksei had dealt with his brother, he had been cool and controlled.

"Bullshit," Aleksei said, and suddenly, the patterns on his skin darkened to a shade that was nearly black. It made him look dangerous. "Had there been another way, I would have told you—I didn't want to force you into my bed. I never wanted to be touched by anyone who didn't want to do it out of his free will. But you told me you wanted me beforehand. I knew there was something between us. When you were gone this morning, it occurred to me that sex was all you were interested in. I admit, I wasn't happy about it. And to put you at ease, knocking me unconscious would have only resulted in a slower, but by no means less painful way into madness."

"But—"

Aleksei didn't give him a chance to say anything. "I woke up *alone*," he said. "I was cold, and I was lonely. You leaving hurt much more than I thought possible. I would not have come after you had the runes not told me you were in danger. So feel free to leave. I won't try to hold you back again."

Even his eyes are dark, Gabriel thought. His throat was dry, and the smell of food that wafted through the kitchen was revolting— Aleksei had put the fish into the pan as if there was no doubt they would have dinner together.

"You were gone when I woke up," Aleksei repeated, his voice soft and surprised now. "You seemed to have enjoyed the night in my bed as much as I did. Still, you preferred to leave me behind. I concluded your willingness to stay under my roof had ended because of what had happened. You tell me where I am wrong, Gabriel, if I am wrong at all."

There was so much to say that Gabriel didn't even know where to start. "I took advantage of you!" he finally managed. "You weren't yourself, you were in no condition to make coherent decisions— definitely not about sleeping with me. Although I knew that, I didn't have enough self-control to find another way to solve the problem. I didn't even think about another way, and that alone is unforgivable. You said the Blood rune was the equivalent of being drugged up. If you had told me to hurt you or to kill you, I wouldn't have done it. I landed in bed with you because I wanted you so very much—and still want you, in case you were curious. I knew you didn't want me. The rune forced you to kiss me. When the power was broken, I had no reason to believe you'd look at me with anything but disgust and hatred. Couldn't stand the thought. So I walked out of here, leaving you behind, even though all I wanted was get back into bed with you."

Shit. He hadn't meant to sound so desperate. He really hadn't planned to shout, either, and it made him blush. Really, he needed to get the blushing under control.

Gabriel turned away and crossed his arms over his chest. He felt like he was breaking apart, and this damn talking-things-over thing was much more painful than he'd thought. "I should hit the road now," he added weakly, because he truly didn't know what else to say.

He didn't hear Aleksei come close—occasionally, the fae's ability to move without the smallest sound still stunned him—and when Aleksei put a hand on his shoulder, he jumped.

"I don't want you to go," the fae said. His eyes were still nowhere near their usual ice-blue, and the patterns on his face were shockingly stark against his pale skin, but there was curiosity in his face instead of anger. "I never did. From the moment I saw you, I was fascinated. From the day I took you in, I wondered what drew me toward you. It took a Blood rune and my mad, cruel brother to make me understand that what I feel for you is beyond friendship, and I'll be damned if I let you walk out on me before we sort this out."

Gabriel swallowed. There were many things he wanted to say. Most of all, he wanted to say… but no, he couldn't. He'd never said those words in his life to anyone, simply because he'd never loved anyone before.

And now Aleksei was too close, and his gaze was too intent, and the hand on his shoulder was too warm, and then there was that faint fragrance, barely perceptible but impossible to ignore, and Gabriel's knees went weak with relief and fear and desire and a dozen other emotions he couldn't even name.

"I—" he croaked, placing his hand over Aleksei's.

"Did it never occur to you that I am a person best to be avoided?" Aleksei asked quietly. "My brother nearly killed you twice, Gabriel. Because of me, you saw death and murder. I took you with me to Wild Oak's world because I couldn't bear the thought of going there without you. It was highly irresponsible of me to take you, and I apologize. And for forcing you into my bed without telling you how much I wanted you in my bed beforehand as well."

Gabriel blinked. Then he relaxed ever so slightly. His back was pressed against the kitchen door, and Aleksei stood only an inch away. He wondered whether the fae knew how badly he wanted him to come a little bit closer and how badly he wanted to say those three ridiculous words.

Instead, he squeezed Aleksei's hand, felt the warmth and tension the fae radiated. "I wanted you so very badly," Gabriel said hoarsely.

"For weeks and months. I told you when I came back from that ocean and you were cutting my clothes off."

"I didn't think you knew what you were talking about," Aleksei replied. His hand moved until it was locked behind Gabriel's neck. "You were badly injured, delirious even."

"All I knew was that you were finally touching me, and I wanted you to keep going." Gabriel had gotten his voice under control; his hand, though, still had a will of its own. It moved toward Aleksei's cheek, and he touched the stubble growing there with his fingertips. "I even thought about getting you drunk, seducing you with the help of a joint or two. When Ronai used that Blood rune… when I couldn't resist touching you…." Briefly, he closed his eyes, then forced himself to look at Aleksei again. "Being with you was what I'd dreamed of for a long time. Knowing you'd been forced to accept my touch, knowing you'd never let me kiss you under any other circumstances."

Suddenly, unexpectedly, Aleksei's features softened. "It seems I should not make assumptions where you are concerned. Assumptions lead to wrong conclusions. Like concluding that you didn't care about me." Calmly, he took Gabriel's hand, turned it, and pressed his lips onto the palm. Then he stepped back. "You cannot compare the workings of a Blood rune with the workings of a drug," he continued, and Gabriel felt a rush of hope wash through him at those words. Had Aleksei just kissed him?

"Drugs dull the mind, alter reality, and cause one to make poor decisions. I have tried some of them, so I know what I am talking about. The Blood rune ruled my body but allowed me to tell you exactly what I wanted to happen. I didn't fight against the rune because I wanted you to be in my bed and in my arms. I *wanted* you to sleep with me, Gabriel. I wanted you to sleep with me very much."

"What?" Gabriel asked, briefly glancing over his shoulder in case Aleksei was talking to someone else. "You… what? You wanted me? But you said you… you require emotions for someone before you so much as let someone kiss you, so…."

Aleksei raised an eyebrow, and Gabriel's stomach flipped at the sight. "What makes you think I haven't developed emotions for you?"

Aleksei asked. "Do you think I let just anyone stay in my house? Do you really believe I would have allowed you to read my books, or taught you about runes, if I hadn't liked you from the first time I saw you and, well, wanted more quite soon afterwards?"

The chair creaked in protest when Gabriel slumped into it. "I can't believe it," he croaked, searching for signs of inebriation, or maybe madness, in his friend's face. "I was lusting after you, believing—convinced, even—that you weren't interested. Damn, Aleksei, couldn't you have said something?"

Aleksei frowned, but all anger was gone now. "I am not particularly experienced in showing my feelings," he said. "I wasn't even certain what I felt for you other than deep fondness and a vague wish for something more without being able to define it. Therefore, I waited for you to make a move. Naturally, I didn't expect to be the target of my brother's wrath, nor that he would force me to obey the call of my needs." He picked up the second glass, poured in some wine, and held it out to Gabriel. "Take a sip," he suggested. "You look as pale as a ghost."

Shaken to the bones, Gabriel took the glass, eyed the wine, and shook his head. "I don't think I should drink right now. You'll only argue I'm drunk, and I really should tell you that I, well…."

"Tell me what?"

"That I…. Damn, Aleksei. I've never said this to anyone, see, and I'm sure I'm messing everything up and all, but I think you should know…." His voice trailed off. He was scared of three little words. How pathetic was that?

"Tell me, Gabriel," Aleksei urged. He reached out, capturing Gabriel's face between his hands. "Tell me, or leave."

Gabriel swallowed. "I… I…" he stammered, not daring to look into Aleksei's eyes. "I want to be with you. For good, I mean. It's more than sex, although I want that too—and lots of it. Not being near you is unbearable, not hearing your voice, not knowing where you are… I can't stand it. Your house has become my home, the first one I ever had. And you, *you* are the one I want. That's why I couldn't resist you. That's why I left."

"Tell me!"

"I love you," Gabriel croaked. "There. I said it. And I'm sorry if it's not what you want to hear. Actually it's all I've wanted to say for a long time."

A small smile tugged at Aleksei's lips, the first one since the night before. "That answers the question of which one of us is a stupid idiot. I always thought that if you love someone, you don't run away from them. If you love someone, you stay, you talk, and you try to fix any problems that come up."

Now Gabriel felt his lips twitch too. "So far, I've always run away from trouble. Guess there's no sense in running away from you again, though. Seems you always find me." Hesitantly, he pulled Aleksei down so they were at eye level. "I don't know if this is the right way to correct the mess I've caused," he whispered. "Problem is, if I don't kiss you soon, I might be too frightened to try at all."

"That would be quite the tragedy," Aleksei replied dryly, and then they were laughing together and, a moment later, kissing. When they realized the kitchen had begun to smell of burnt fish, it was too late to save their dinner.

Neither of them was very hungry, anyway.

Epilogue

~~~~~~

As FAR as weather was concerned, it was not a pleasant evening—too humid, too windy, with the promise of a thunderstorm. The sun had gone down long ago, which was bad, as the darkness made it even more obvious that Gabriel was late. He should have met Aleksei an hour earlier.

He rushed along the streets, his long hair whipping behind him as he ran. He could have taken a cab, but the thought of sitting still for even a short while had been unbearable. He was bursting with energy. The walk from his office to La Laterna Magica had been welcome exercise after the day he'd had. And not only today, to be honest. The past few weeks had been incredibly busy, filled with research, failures, more research, and more trips to the hidden worlds than he considered reasonable. At least he knew by now how to use the portals without help and without getting slashed into meat pie—Aleksei had done a thorough job of teaching him how to protect himself.

Gabriel slowed down a bit. He had no intention of reaching the restaurant dripping with sweat. Tonight, he'd even taken special care with his clothing, not wearing jeans and a pullover for a change but more costly garments. After all, he could afford them now, only eighteen months after he'd first met Aleksei. He very much hoped Aleksei would appreciate the gesture. They hadn't seen each other in a while, and Gabriel wanted to impress his friend, so he'd asked Monique to get something that would suit him and suit the event too.

Monique. For a moment, Gabriel thought of his secretary, the dragon-like lady who had looked after Mallfrick for several years. After her employer had been killed, she'd been officially without a job, but instead of staying at home, she'd gone to the office and continued doing her job by informing each of Mallfrick's former clients that the private investigator was dead and that no one was left to finish their cases. She'd sent a bill to everyone who owed Mallfrick money. She'd informed anyone who demanded an appointment that he wasn't available anymore. And when Gabriel walked in, she'd hugged him as tightly as possible and told him that if he wanted a job, he could have Mallfrick's, along with his office and her service.

Gabriel hadn't even thought about it. He had agreed immediately and promised to pay her once he changed the firm's reputation and began to earn some money.

"No more dirty pictures of cheating husbands," he had told Monique. "No spying jobs anymore, at least not on innocent people."

"Fine with me," Monique had said through pursed lips. "I didn't like that part anyway. Pray tell me how we are going to pay the bills, though."

"There must be other possibilities," Gabriel had answered.

And there were—lots of possibilities. About a month after Gabriel had taken over, he changed the name from "Mallfrick, Private Investigator" to "Lost and Found." He placed advertisements in the local newspapers stating that from now on, anyone who wanted to know about the whereabouts of children with mixed blood could come to him and he would find them. He didn't expect much to come of the ad—after all, children with mixed blood were not well liked in the human world—but he'd been proven wrong in less than a week.

Actually, people were beating a path to his door. Often, grandparents wanted to know about their grandchildren, the same ones they'd forced their daughters to give up right after birth. Equally as often, people wanted to know about their heritage, if an aunt was still alive, if it was true that grandfather's sister had married a merman, or if a beloved child was truly still alive and happy with a partner of nonhuman blood.

Gabriel and Monique were stunned at the response to the ad, and in less than six months, their office was where one was pointed when in need of help with matters of the hidden worlds.

Eventually the police turned up, but Gabriel, having foreseen that, had arranged for himself a passport, a license, and a lawyer. The license allowed him to do his job, the lawyer proved it was legal to search for relatives, and there was no law that could force either Gabriel or his clients to reveal their identities once they'd been found. After all, it wasn't illegal to have mixed blood, no matter what the general opinion might be.

"I'll rot in my grave before I hand anyone over to the cops," Gabriel had told Monique, which had earned him one of her rare smiles.

"Mr. Mallfrick would have been proud of you," she answered, and that compliment, surprisingly, meant a lot to him.

GABRIEL was nearly at the restaurant now, and he couldn't wait to see Aleksei, especially after Monique had insisted on fine-tuning his outfit as well as his appearance, which had cost him another few minutes. Most of the time, she stuck to her role as secretary, and when a client was present, she always called him "sir" or "Mr. Jordan,"—strange ways of addressing him, in Gabriel's eyes. Occasionally, though, she effortlessly slipped into the role of a slightly grumpy older sister, making sure he didn't make a total fool out of himself.

Like tonight.

He'd closed the file he was working on, locked Senator Dubaku's check in the safe, then dressed in the small bathroom next to his office. The clothes, purchased by Monique, fit perfectly—he had never owned such expensive shoes, so soft and silent, or such trousers, which outlined the shape of his legs in such a lascivious yet subtle way. The trousers were midnight black, the shirt a pale gray that matched his eyes.

The vest, though—he really hadn't worn a vest before in his life, and he felt slightly ridiculous putting it on. But Monique had bought it, and he knew he'd better wear it or she would scold him like a naughty child.

He had brushed his hair quickly, pocketed his wallet, and was about to go and meet Aleksei when Monique called him back.

"You cannot go like that," she stated categorically. "Your hair needs some attention, the vest needs to be closed, and your eyes... I'll have to do something with your eyes. Sit and be quiet while I take care of you."

"Monique—"

"Be quiet," she had repeated, "and close your eyes. After all, this is not a business meeting."

Gabriel grinned. "Of course it's not a business meeting. You think I'd wear anything like this for a client?"

He could hear Monique rummage in her drawer, and a moment later, her cool, dry hands were touching his face as she did something to his eyes. Her breath smelled of peppermint, and he could just catch the fragrance of her perfume. As far as he knew, she was living a quiet life when she wasn't in the office. He made a mental note to invite her to dinner sometime—he'd be lost without her.

"Would you please go to the bank first thing on Monday?" he'd asked, trying not to move. "A third of Dubaku's check for the mission. Tell Billy that he needs to persuade Father Barley to invest some of it and that I will come and see him on Wednesday."

"Certainly," Monique had said.

When she finished with whatever she'd done to his eyes, she had braided a few strands of his hair into thin plaits at each side of his face. Her fingers had moved swiftly, and when Gabriel tried to see what she was doing, she just tugged sharply at the strands and told him to sit still again.

"You don't want hair in your food, do you?" she asked, and at that, Gabriel had to grin.

"I am capable of eating, you know. Done it all my life without any help."

Monique, finished with his hair, had ignored him and began buttoning the black vest. It was tight; he could feel the fabric press against his rib cage, and he was slightly uncomfortable with the close contact. "Look—"

"Get up, let's have a look at you," his secretary had interrupted him. "Yes. That's much better. Perfect, actually. Take a look in the mirror, please," she'd said, and she'd boldly pushed him toward the entrance, where a full-length mirror hung on the wall next to the coat rack.

Gabriel's eyes had threatened to pop out of their sockets when he saw his image. Not that he hadn't checked in his bathroom to see if there were stains on his shirt or stubble left on his chin—but he hadn't expected to look that *different*. The buttoned-up vest emphasized his narrow hips and seemed to broaden his shoulders. Thin braids, two or three on each side of his cheeks, kept the hair out of his face. His eyes, surrounded with kohl, appeared bigger, more prominent, and promising.

"I cannot go out like this!" he'd exclaimed, slightly shocked. "I look like, like—"

"You look absolutely irresistible," she had interrupted him. She opened the first few buttons of his shirt and brushed a bit of lint off his sleeve. "And isn't that the sole intention when someone is meeting his lover after two months' absence? If Dr. Tennant isn't rendered completely speechless at the sight of you, I will eat my keyboard. Now go and have a nice evening. I assume you will come in late on Monday?"

Gabriel blushed. "I do hope so," he had murmured, snatching up his jacket and practically fleeing the office.

THE entrance of La Laterna Magica was dimly lit, the door closed, and the surrounding buildings gave the impression that the area was abandoned. All in all, it was not an appealing sight, and someone who didn't know about the exquisite restaurant behind the plain door would have turned around immediately, seeking a friendlier atmosphere.

Gabriel's heart beat wildly when he knocked at the door, and it wasn't because he'd run half the distance from his office or because he was massively late.

Igor opened the door for him and waited politely for Gabriel to hand him his jacket.

"Is he here?"

"Yes, sir. Dr. Tennant arrived approximately one hour ago. However, he has not yet ordered dinner," the waiter replied.

Igor was about to lead the way into the restaurant, but Gabriel held him back. Since he'd begun dining here on a more or less regular basis, he'd come to terms with the haggard waiter despite the man's impolite manners and the sneer he managed to put into his voice whenever he opened his mouth.

"Igor, is he mad at me for being late?" Gabriel asked in a hushed voice. "I couldn't make it sooner, but I would like to know... well, I haven't seen him in a while, you know."

The ghost of a smile appeared on the waiter's thin lips. "Dr. Tennant has not chosen to share his opinion with me concerning your delay," he murmured. "Although it seems to me that he is more worried than angry, sir." The waiter opened the door that separated the entrance hall from the restaurant, holding it to allow his guest to enter. "At the usual table," he said.

It was less scary to walk through the candle-lit room, feeling all eyes on him, than it had been a year ago, but it was still not something Gabriel enjoyed doing, especially not when he was so clearly dressed for seduction, as he was tonight. Out of the corner of his eye, he saw Ryan and Laura as well as Tony and Jack, both couples regular customers. They smiled "hello" at him, whereas others openly stared at him—when he was making such an obvious entry as he was now, even the rune that usually hid him didn't work.

Tonight, he didn't mind. His eyes were focused on Aleksei, who sat reading at his favorite table, his nose buried in the book, not yet aware of Gabriel's presence.

Silence spread throughout the small room—altogether, there weren't more than ten tables at La Laterna Magica—and Aleksei looked up. His eyes widened, his jaw dropped, and a heartbeat later, he put the book down and stood up.

Gabriel felt a grin spread over his face, wide and happy, and it washed through his body, too, making him feel as if he could fly, as if he could embrace the world, all worlds, simply because his lover was clearly so very glad to see him.

Monique had been right—her additional attention to his appearance had been worth the extra few minutes he'd been late.

"Aleksei," he said, wrapping his arms around his lover's waist, and he kissed him.

Their tongues touched, and Aleksei deepened the kiss. Gabriel could taste the wine he'd been drinking and the bread he'd eaten while waiting for him. His muscles tensed when he pulled his lover closer, one hand on the small of Aleksei's back, the other slipping lower to his thigh. How he loved kissing this man! How he loved feeling his body respond to his touch, knowing Aleksei had longed for this moment as much as he had. Gabriel couldn't end the kiss right now, he didn't want to end it—he could kiss his lover forever, and he didn't give a damn that every customer was watching. Aleksei tasted too good, looked too damn good, kissed far too well to stop now.

"Gabe," Aleksei breathed, pulling away and tightening his grip on Gabriel's hair at the same time. "Gabriel, we need to stop, or I'll have to take you right here, on the table, between the bread and the wine with everyone, including Igor, watching us make love."

Gabriel rested his forehead against Aleksei's and chuckled. "Interesting fantasies you've got!" he murmured, quickly brushing his palm over his lover's bottom as he took a step back, delighted at the gasp the movement caused. "Unfortunately, lovemaking will have to wait until we are home. I'm too hungry, and besides, I prefer to enjoy your attentions without an audience." Gabriel reluctantly took a seat. "Hi," he said belatedly. "Sorry I'm so late. I needed to write the final report, or I wouldn't have gotten the check." With deep gulps, he emptied the glass of water a waiter had poured for him.

"So you found her?" Aleksei asked. "The girl?"

Gabriel nodded. "Oh, yes. I found her. Senator Dubaku's one and only daughter, disappeared at the age of sixteen, considered dead for the past twelve years. The general opinion was that she had been kidnapped and killed. When Dubaku heard of *Lost and Found*, he contacted me and begged me to find his child. Which I did."

"Where was she?" Having scanned the menu, Aleksei placed their order and asked Igor if it was possible to be served as quickly as possible. "We are both quite hungry," he said with a smile. Igor answered by nodding briefly.

Gabriel couldn't stop devouring Aleksei with his eyes. It had taken him two long months of searching for the girl once he'd found proof that she wasn't dead—she had decided to visit the elves' world, and he had followed her. He hadn't been home during all that time; he hadn't even spoken to Aleksei, only dropping a line every now and then whenever he'd found the time and someone willing to deliver the letter. He'd slept under the stars, in trees, on various beaches. More often than not, he hadn't slept at all. Senator Dubaku's daughter had been hard to find and even harder to convince to meet her father to talk things out.

"She's married to an elf," Gabriel said. "She has two children with him and erased her tracks quite well. If Wild Oak hadn't helped me, I wouldn't have found her, and if your sister hadn't intervened, she wouldn't have agreed to meet her father. Apparently, Senator Dubaku was a hard man when he was younger, believing that hitting his children was an appropriate way to teach them respect. She fled and found love. Last night, they met in a neutral place, and she even allowed him to talk to his grandchildren. He was grateful for my efforts, to put it mildly, although she won't be returning to this world."

Aleksei reached across the table and touched one of Gabriel's braids, running it through his spread fingers. "I'm glad you found her," he said. "Of course, I never had any doubts. Did I tell you how adorable you look?"

A crooked smile curved Gabriel's lips. "This was mostly Monique's doing. She chose the clothes, and she did the fine-tuning. The kohl, the braids, the vest—believe me, not my idea."

"Irresistible. Unnecessary, but wonderful nevertheless. You wouldn't have a chance of escaping me tonight even if you were wearing rags, beloved." The gleam in Aleksei's eyes spoke unmistakably of sheer lust.

Gabriel's trousers were becoming tighter by the second. "We should have met at home," he replied hoarsely.

"Ah, no. Anticipation is part of the pleasure, is it not?" Aleksei teased. "And besides, I cannot cook half as well as the chef here."

"Who cares about food when you are on the menu?"

They looked at each other and laughed. When dinner arrived, they ate and spoke about this and that, erotic tension building up with every word, every gesture, every moment of silence. Gabriel told Aleksei everything about his search, forwarded greetings from his sister, and ensured his lover that he had no intention of taking on such a strenuous job again too soon. Aleksei reported on a rapist he'd been ordered to find and capture, of the hearing before the fae council concerning Petresh and the murders he'd committed, and the fact that a stray cat was now living in their garage.

"Oh, and I've got something for you," Aleksei said after they'd eaten their dessert. "I adapted it for your needs. Here." With that, he placed a long, slim parcel wrapped in black paper and decorated with a plain silver ribbon on the table.

Slowly, Gabriel pushed his empty dish away and picked up the parcel. It was light, and he took his time opening the paper without destroying it. Finally, he lifted the lid.

Inside the box was a knife with a black hilt and a long, thin blade. It looked sharp—it was sharp, as Gabriel found out when he ran his thumb over the strangely opalescent metal.

"It's beautiful!" he managed after a few seconds, flipping and catching the knife. "Perfectly balanced, ideal for cutting as well as throwing. Did the centaurs make it?"

"Of course. No one can work with metal like they do. The blade won't get dull, nor will it break unless you attempt to kill a dragon with it. I considered it time you got a proper knife, especially after your old one fell apart a few weeks ago."

Gabriel turned the knife in his hands, admiring its lightness as well as its beauty. "My pocketknife," he mused. "I asked Monique to get me a new one, but she didn't."

"I might have mentioned that I would like to take care of it," Aleksei answered. "It is not a pocketknife, but you can carry it openly on your belt or in your boot, whichever you prefer. It cannot be seen, nor can it be stolen or lost. You could hold it to someone's neck, and he would only feel the coldness of the blade, unable to touch it or even catch a glimpse of it."

No wonder none of the guests screamed when I took it out of the box, Gabriel thought. "Let's go home," he said aloud, fastening the sheath on his belt and slipping the knife in. Nearly weightless, it felt as if it belonged there. "I need another kiss, and I need it fast, before I do something hasty."

"As you wish," his lover replied with a smile.

THEY took a cab home, unable to keep their hands off each other. Gabriel had a firm grip on Aleksei's cock, kneading it through the fabric of his trousers and drinking in each moan the action produced. His lover, leaning against his shoulder, had one arm slung around his waist and kissed his neck, the corner of his mouth, and his temple, knowing only too well how very arousing Gabriel found the tenderness of each kiss. The driver seemed glad to see them go.

The path up to the house stretched endlessly, but finally, they made it inside, the door closing with a loud bang behind them. Aleksei had the younger man pressed against the wall in no time, pushing willing legs apart with his knees. "You've been gone for too long," he rasped, his fingers undoing vest buttons. "I love you too much not to see you for such a long time. The bed is too big without you, the house too quiet—I'm afraid I will have to take you right now."

Clothes were shed all over the floor of the entrance hall until they were skin to skin. Gabriel heard the soft clink of the knife when it hit the tiles. Aleksei's breath caressed his neck as his strong hands spread his cheeks. An endless, highly anticipated moment later, he felt his lover's cock enter. Perfect intrusion; ecstatic fulfillment. He'd dreamed of this during dark nights and in broad daylight. He'd imagined his lover moving inside him while touching himself in those lonely hours.

Each thrust threatened to split him in half; each retreat made him worry Aleksei would stop. He was hard himself but refused to wrap his fingers around his length—if he did, it would all be over too soon.

His groans sounded loud in his ears. Aleksei's hands were so tight on his hips that they would surely leave bruises. Occasionally, the fae liked their lovemaking to be rough. Like now. His thrusts were short and nearly brutal; he'd come soon.

"Fuck me deep," Gabriel rasped, spreading his legs wider, pushing himself back against his lover's groin. Biting his lips and balling his hands into fists, he tried to keep his balance, tried to stand firm under his lover's attack.

One last push, right along his prostate, made him groan and clutch Aleksei's thigh, urging him on, letting him know that it wasn't deep enough yet, not hard enough, that he wanted more, needed more. And suddenly, Aleksei's grip tightened around his waist, and he came, face buried in Gabriel's hair.

COCK painfully erect and pressed against the wall, Gabriel needed some time to catch his breath before he managed to turn around in his lover's embrace. Seed trickled down his legs, and all he wanted was to make Aleksei hard again, to have his turn, to make Aleksei scream with lust and pleasure.

Swiftly, he bent and rummaged in the pockets of the jacket lying at his feet.

Metal clinked. It wasn't the knife, though. The handcuffs closed around Aleksei's wrist with a dry click that was full of promise.

"You didn't think this would be over so soon, did you?" Gabriel whispered into his lover's ear, rubbing his erection against his partner's silvery skin. "Because from my point of view, the night has just begun."

The second cuff went around Aleksei's other wrist, and he moaned with delight. "Bedroom," he demanded, his pale skin glowing with desire. "Tie me to the bedposts, Gabriel. Please?" His cock was already stirring again.

"I love it when you beg," Gabriel answered with a malicious smile.

RHYTHMICALLY creaking wood, accompanied by sharp, harsh groans.

Metal, gripped by sweaty hands.

Candlelight, just bright enough to see the ecstasy on Aleksei's face and in his half-open eyes.

At first, and only for a short while, a warm, wet mouth and the tantalizing sight of Aleksei's lips enveloping his length. Afterward, a hot, welcoming ass, swallowing his cock up to his balls.

His hands on either side of Aleksei's head, his full weight pinning his lover down, restraining his movements in addition to the cuffs. Both of his lover's legs were wrapped around his waist, and with each thrust, Gabriel considered it possible that he would die any moment now simply because of the perfection of their dance.

"Love you," he breathed into Aleksei's ear, and when the fae managed to gasp, "You too," Gabriel could feel the smile that came with the words.

Raw, hot lust rushed through him and made him blind to his surroundings—it always happened eventually whenever he made love to Aleksei. The fact that his lover was bound to the bedposts only heated his desire, if that were possible, and when he felt the fae's muscles tense, when he heard the low scream and smelled the sweaty, musky, salty fragrance of his lover's come, he came himself, biting Aleksei's neck, marking him as his and wishing with all his might that this moment would never end.

CAREFULLY, Aleksei rubbed his wrists. Around both joints were angry red lines, visible signs of how hard he'd pulled at his bonds.

"Handcuffs really turn you on," Gabriel teased, tracing a vine from belly button up to collarbone. "If I had known, I would have procured some a lot sooner."

"Hmmm." Aleksei rested in Gabriel's arms, warm, sated, and relaxed.

Gabriel kissed the spot where he'd bitten the fae. "I need to stop doing this. It looks painful." Quickly, he pressed his tongue to the bite marks and was surprised to see Aleksei suck in a luxurious breath.

"An exquisitely strong erotic stimulant," the fae stated. "Don't you dare quit doing it. Actually, don't you dare stop doing whatever you want to do with me." He stretched his muscles and arched his back like an overgrown cat.

Not yet willing to let go of the subject, Gabriel touched the marks the handcuffs had left on Aleksei's skin. "You can't walk around like that. Without help, these will turn into nasty bruises, especially if we decide to do this again in the morning."

Aleksei just laughed. "I don't care about a few bruises." Oncoming sleep and the pleasure of lovemaking slurred his voice.

"I do," Gabriel objected, fishing for the second object he'd taken out of his jacket earlier. "Here. Open it, put it on, and let's see if it works as intended."

Aleksei turned in his arms. "A present?"

Goodness, how he loved those raised eyebrows. "A present. For you. Did you really believe I'd forget to bring you a present after being gone for so long?"

And how he loved his lover's blush, as it was such a rare thing to see.

Eagerly, Aleksei opened the small parcel. It was barely longer than his palm, thin, weighing next to nothing. Still, it had taken Gabriel many long hours to create what was inside, and without Marita, he wouldn't have been able to do it at all.

When Aleksei took out the silver bracelet embedded with moonstones, Gabriel held his breath. It was a very personal gift, and he had no idea if it would be welcome. Aleksei didn't wear jewelry apart from his necklace, which was a necessity. "If you don't like it," he began, but his lover shut him up with a passionate kiss.

"It's marvelous!" the fae exclaimed after he'd broken the kiss. "Most beautiful—where did you get it from?"

Relieved, Gabriel smiled. "I didn't get it, I made it for you. With Marita's help," he explained. "It should fit you perfectly. Marita is a silversmith, as I found out a few months ago. She turned my crude sketch and the measurements I gave into something real, but that was not what made my head ache—it's the runes I engraved in the silver. Put it on. You should see the effect immediately, I hope." Taking the bracelet out of Aleksei's hand, he put it around the fae's wrist. The catch closed with a soft sound.

Immediately, the red lines from the cuffs, as well as the very visible love-bite on Aleksei's neck, paled. Less than two minutes later, they were gone.

The fae sat up in bed, not sleepy anymore. He took the bracelet off again, but his skin remained spotless. With narrowed eyes, he examined the piece of jewelry, touched the runes engraved inside as well as outside, and finally looked at Gabriel. "You managed to recreate the rune on your neck!"

Resolutely, Gabriel put the bracelet back on Aleksei's arm. "The part that speeds up the healing process, yes. Wear it at least until morning," he insisted. "Just in case the cuffs caused some deeper damage to muscles or nerves. I haven't got a clue if you want to wear it on a permanent basis. You don't have to—no offense taken if you only use it when you need its healing powers. I just thought I couldn't come back home without a present, and—"

"Beloved," Aleksei interrupted him, taking his face in his hands. His ice-blue eyes were sparkling with joy. "Shut up, will you? I have never before received anything this beautiful. I will wear it, and I won't take it off willingly. Do not apologize for loving me enough to gift me with something you made with your own hands."

"Actually," Gabriel replied, "I will not apologize for loving you at all," and leaned in for another kiss.

AT THE far end of a different world, high up in cold mountains, a creature sat on the bare rocks. At its scaly feet, a circle was drawn in a patch of snow.

Eyes wide and unblinking, the creature watched a couple talking to each other, embracing each other, kissing each other. Soon, the two would be making love again, as they had done repeatedly in the past few hours.

The creature, neither male nor female, nodded approvingly. "Little one," it breathed into the circle at its feet. The words were no louder than the coo of a dying dove. "You are exactly where we want you to be. That's good. That's very, very good."

One long arm erased the circle from the ground. With it, the picture of the two men vanished.

"Our child; our weapon," the Banshee murmured into the wind that caressed its gray hair, stony skin, and the area around the hole that served as a mouth. "In the end, you will do as ordered. That was what you were raised for. That was why you were born."

Silent snowflakes drifted from the sky. The Banshee rose and sniffed the wind for prey, as it was weak with hunger. The time was not yet ripe. The little one would be allowed to enjoy his lover's embrace for a while longer before duty called him to show where his true loyalties lay: with the ones who had made him, created him, and shaped him into the person he now was to serve their purpose, and their purpose alone.

SAM C. LEONHARD is a journalist by profession who lives in southern Germany. Writing has been part of her life since age twenty, but somehow it was never enough to report the latest news about small-town politics. She wrote short stories for friends and family until a few years back she discovered the world of fandom. The Petulant Poetess is where she feels at home; slash became an addiction as soon as she stumbled over the first story.

If not writing—which isn't half as often as she'd like—Sam takes care of her son, her dog, a few cats, the madness at work, and life in general. She likes to believe she's got some humor left after years of dealing with people who usually don't understand what she's talking about when she says she's writing fantasy and gay porn on top of it.

You can contact Sam at sc.leonhard@googlemail.com.

Supernatural Romance from DREAMSPINNER PRESS

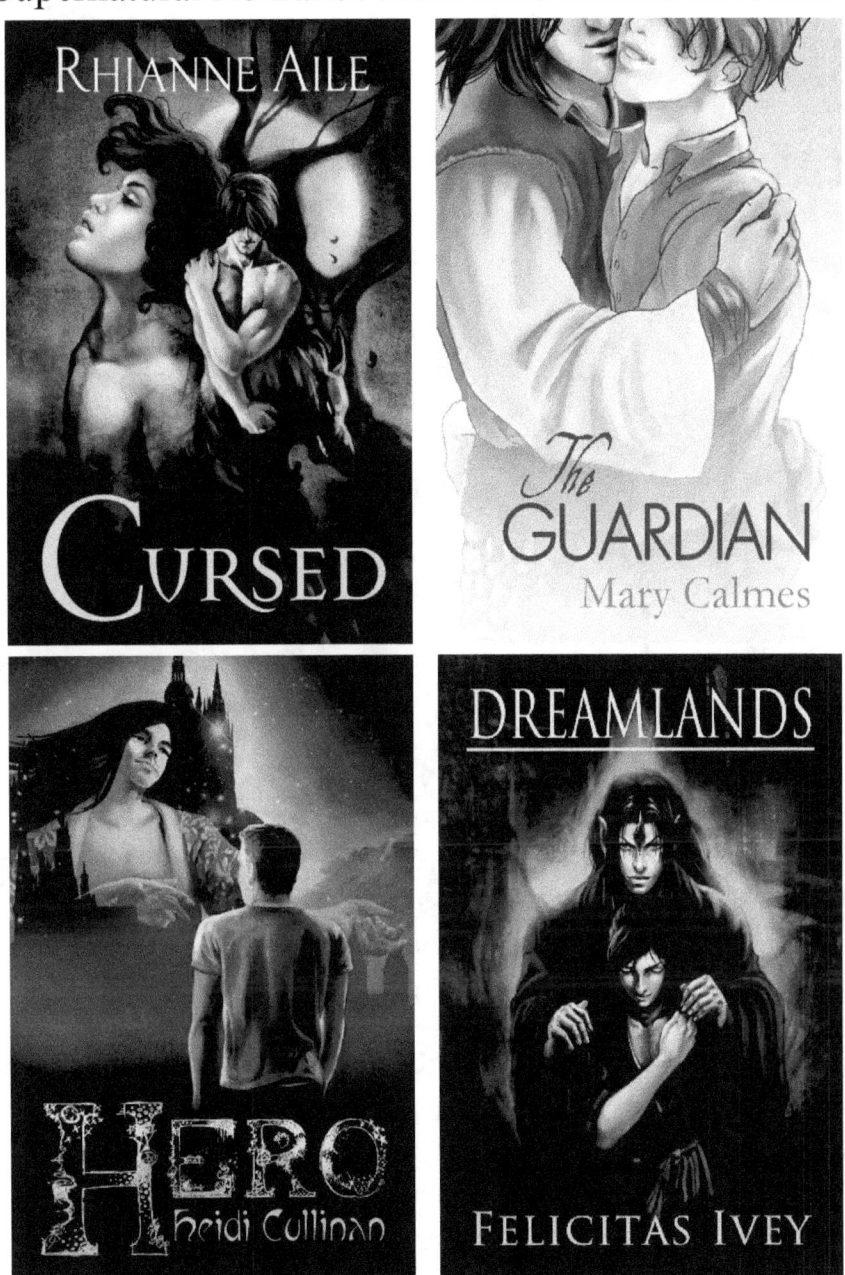

http://www.dreamspinnerpress.com